The American Heiress

A NOVEL

DAISY GOODWIN

St. Martin's Griffin
New York

For my father Richard Goodwin – my ideal reader

THE AMERICAN HEIRESS. Copyright © 2010 by Daisy Goodwin Productions. All rights reserved. Printed in the United States of America. For information, address St. Martin's Press, 175 Fifth Avenue, New York, N.Y. 10010.

www.stmartins.com

The Library of Congress has cataloged the hardcover edition as follows:

Goodwin, Daisy.
  [My last duchess]
  The American heiress : a novel / Daisy Goodwin.—1st U.S. ed.
     p. cm.
  Originally published as: My last duchess. London : Headline Review, 2010.
  ISBN 978-0-312-65865-6 (hardback)
  1. Americans—England—Fiction. 2. Aristocracy (Social class)—England—Fiction.
  3. England—Social life and customs—19th century—Fiction. I. Title.
  PR6107.O6625M9 2011
  823'.92—dc22

                                                              2010048539

ISBN 978-0-312-65866-3 (trade paperback)

St. Martin's Griffin books may be purchased for educational, business, or promotional use. For information on bulk purchases, please contact Macmillan Corporate and Premium Sales Department at 1-800-221-7945, extension 5442, or write specialmarkets@macmillan.com.

First published in Great Britain by HEADLINE REVIEW, an imprint of HEADLINE PUBLISHING GROUP, an Hachette UK Company

First St. Martin's Griffin Edition: April 2012

10 9 8 7 6 5 4 3 2 1

Acclaim for Daisy Goodwin's dazzling debut novel,
The American Heiress

"Deliciously classy. A story that gallops along, full of exquisite period detail."   —Kate Mosse

"[An] exceptionally thoughtful and stunning historical novel that will leave you reeling and astonished . . . and give you the urge to reread it the instant the last page is turned."   —*Bookreporter.com*

"Top-notch writing brings to life the world of wealth on both sides of the Atlantic. This debut's strong character development and sense of place will please fans of historical romance, including book club members."
—*Library Journal* (starred review)

"I was seduced by this book, rather as Cora was seduced by her duke: with great skill and confidence. Intriguing, atmospheric, and extremely stylish, I was still thinking about it long after I had reached the end."
—Penny Vincenzi

"Smart, emotional, entertaining writing proves Goodwin is adept at creating the perfect atmosphere and backdrop for the turn of the century and a world where money can buy a title, but not happiness or acceptance. Like Henry James and Edith Wharton, Goodwin delves into this seemingly gracious world of opulence to uncover its harsh side, and brings a cast of fascinating characters into a delicious tale that captivates."
—*RT Book Reviews* (4 ½ stars)

"A propulsive story of love, manners, culture clash, and store-bought class from a time long past that proves altogether fresh."   —*Publishers Weekly*

By Daisy Goodwin

Silver River

Edited by Daisy Goodwin

101 Poems That Could Save Your Life

That's my last Duchess painted on the wall

'My Last Duchess', Robert Browning

The American girl has the advantage of her
English sister in that she possesses all that
the other lacks

Titled Americans, 1890

Part One

LADY FERMOR-HESKETH.

MISS FLORENCE EMILY SHARON, daughter of the late Senator William Sharon, of Nevada.

Born 186—.

Married, in 1880, to

SIR THOMAS GEORGE FERMOR FERMOR-HESKETH, seventh Baronet; born May 9, 1849; is Major of Fourth Battalion, King's Regiment; has been Sheriff of Northamptonshire; and is a Deputy Lieutenant and Justice of the Peace of the County.

Issue:

Thomas, born November 17, 1881.

Frederick, born 1883.

Seats: Rufford Hall, Omskirk, and Easton Neston, Towcester.

Creation of title, 1761.

The family has been settled in Lancashire for seven hundred years.

Titled Americans, A List of American Ladies Who Have Married Foreigners of Rank, 1890

CHAPTER 1

The Hummingbird Man

Newport, Rhode Island, August 1893

THE VISITING HOUR WAS ALMOST OVER, SO the hummingbird man encountered only the occasional carriage as he pushed his cart along the narrow strip of road between the mansions of Newport and the Atlantic Ocean. The ladies of Newport had left their cards early that afternoon, some to prepare for the last and most important ball of the season, others so they could at least appear to do so. The usual clatter and bustle of Bellevue Avenue had faded away as the Four Hundred rested in anticipation of the evening ahead, leaving behind only the steady beat of the waves breaking on the rocks below. The light was beginning to go, but the heat of the day still shimmered from the white limestone façades of the great houses that clustered along the cliffs like a collection of wedding cakes, each one vying with its neighbour to be the most gorgeous confection. But the hummingbird man, who wore a dusty tailcoat and a battered grey bowler in some shabby approximation of evening dress, did not stop to admire the verandah at the Breakers, or the turrets of Beaulieu, or the Rhinelander fountains that could be glimpsed through the yew hedges and gilded gates. He continued along the road, whistling and clicking to his charges in their black shrouded cages, so that they should hear a familiar noise on their last journey. His destination was the French chateau just before the point, the largest and most elaborate creation on a street of superlatives, Sans Souci, the summer cottage of the Cash family. The Union flag was flying from one tower, the Cash family emblem from the other.

He stopped at the gatehouse and the porter pointed him to the stable entrance half a mile away. As he walked to the other side of the grounds, orange lights were beginning to puncture the twilight; footmen were walking through the house and the grounds lighting Chinese lanterns in amber silk shades. Just as he turned past the terrace, he was dazzled by a low shaft of light from the dying sun refracted by the long windows of the ballroom.

In the Hall of Mirrors, which visitors who had been to Versailles pronounced even more spectacular than the original, Mrs Cash, who had sent out eight hundred invitations for the ball that night, was looking at herself reflected into infinity. She tapped her foot, waiting impatiently for the sun to disappear so that she could see the full effect of her costume. Mr Rhinehart stood by, sweat dripping from his brow, perhaps more sweat than the heat warranted.

'So I just press this rubber valve and the whole thing will illuminate?'

'Yes indeed, Mrs Cash, you just grasp the bulb firmly and all the lights will sparkle with a truly celestial effect. If I could just remind you that the moment must be short-lived. The batteries are cumbersome and I have only put as many on the gown as is compatible with fluid movement.'

'How long have I got, Mr Rhinehart?'

'Very hard to say, but probably no more than five minutes. Any longer and I cannot guarantee your safety.'

But Mrs Cash was not listening. Limits were of no interest to her. The pink evening glow was fading into darkness. It was time. She gripped the rubber bulb with her left hand and heard a slight crackle as light tripped through the one hundred and twenty light bulbs on her dress and the fifty in her diadem. It was as if a firework had been set off in the mirrored ballroom.

As she turned round slowly she was reminded of the yachts in Newport harbour illuminated for the recent visit of the German Emperor. The back view was quite as splendid as the front; the train that fell from her shoulders looked like a swathe of the night sky. She gave a glittering nod of satisfaction and released the bulb. The room went dark until a footman came forward to light the chandeliers.

'It is exactly the effect I had hoped for. You may send in your account.'

The electrician wiped his brow with a handkerchief that was less than clean, jerked his head in an approximation of a bow and turned to leave.

'Mr Rhinehart!' The man froze on the glossy parquet. 'I trust you have been as discreet as I instructed.' It was not a question.

'Oh yes, Mrs Cash. I did it all myself, that's why I couldn't deliver it till today. Worked on it every evening in the workshop when all the apprentices had gone home.'

'Good.' A dismissal. Mrs Cash turned and walked to the other end of the Hall of Mirrors where two footmen waited to open the door. Mr Rhinehart walked down the marble staircase, his hand leaving a damp smear on the cold balustrade.

In the Blue Room, Cora Cash was trying to concentrate on her book. Cora found most novels hard to sympathise with – all those plain governesses – but this one had much to recommend it. The heroine was 'handsome, clever and rich', rather like Cora herself. Cora knew she was handsome – wasn't she always referred to in the papers as 'the divine Miss Cash'? She was clever – she could speak three languages and could handle calculus. And as to rich, well, she was undoubtedly that. Emma Woodhouse was not rich in the way that she, Cora Cash, was rich. Emma Woodhouse did not lie on a *lit à la polonaise* once owned by Madame du Barry in a room which was, but for the lingering smell of paint, an exact replica of Marie Antoinette's bedchamber at le petit Trianon. Emma Woodhouse went to dances at the Assembly Rooms, not fancy dress spectaculars in specially built ballrooms. But Emma Woodhouse was motherless which meant, thought Cora, that she was handsome, clever, rich and free. That could not be said of Cora, who at that moment was holding the book straight out in front of her because there was a steel rod strapped to her spine. Cora's arms ached and she longed to lie down on Madame du Barry's bed but her mother believed that spending two hours a day strapped to the spine improver would give Cora the posture and carriage of a princess, albeit an American one, and for now at least Cora had no choice but to read her book in extreme discomfort.

At this moment her mother, Cora knew, would be checking the placement for the dinner she was holding before the ball, tweaking it so that her forty odd guests knew exactly how brightly they sparkled in Mrs Cash's social firmament. To be invited to Mrs Cash's fancy dress ball was an honour, to be invited to the dinner beforehand a privilege, but to be seated within touching distance of Mrs Cash herself was a true mark of distinction, and was not to be bestowed lightly. Mrs Cash liked to sit opposite her husband at dinner ever since she had discovered that the Prince and Princess of Wales always faced each other across the width not the length of the table. Cora knew that she would be placed at one end sandwiched between two suitable bachelors with whom she would be expected to flirt just enough to confirm her reputation as the belle of the season but not so much that she compromised her mother's stratagems for her future. Mrs Cash was throwing this ball to display Cora like a costly gem to be admired but not touched. This diamond was destined for a coronet, at least.

Directly after the ball the Cashes were leaving for Europe on their yacht the SS *Aspen*. Mrs Cash had done nothing so vulgar as to suggest that they were going there to find Cora a title; she did not, like some other ladies in Newport, subscribe to *Titled Americans*, a quarterly periodical which gave details of blue-blooded but impecunious young men from Europe who were looking for a rich American bride, but Cora knew that her mother's ambitions were limitless.

Cora put the novel down and shifted uncomfortably in the spine harness. Surely it was time for Bertha to come and unbuckle her. The strap across her forehead was digging in; she would look ridiculous at the ball tonight with a great red welt on her brow. She wouldn't mind in the least discomfiting her mother but she had her own reasons for wanting to look her best. Tonight was her last chance with Teddy before she had to leave for Europe. Yesterday at the picnic they had come so close, she was sure that

Teddy had been about to kiss her, but her mother had found them before anything could happen. Cora smiled a little at the thought of her mother sweating as she pedalled to catch up with them. Mrs Cash had dismissed bicycles as hoydenish, until she realised that her daughter could use them to evade her, and then she had learnt to ride one in an afternoon. She might be the richest girl in America but surely she was also the most persecuted. Tonight was her coming-out party and here she was strapped into this instrument of torture. It was time she was released. In one stiff movement she rose and rang the bell.

Bertha was in the kitchen with the hummingbird man. He came from the same part of South Carolina as she did, and every year when he came up to supply the Newport hostesses with their favourite party trick, he would bring Bertha a message from what was left of her family. She had not seen any of them since the day ten years ago when she had been picked by the Reverend to go North, but sometimes when she walked through the kitchens on baking day and smelt the hot sweet smell, she thought she saw the swish of her mother's blue and white striped skirt. These days she could barely remember her mother's face but that smell would knock her back into the old cabin so fast it would bring tears to her eyes. She had sent letters at first with the presents and the money, figuring that her mother would find someone to read them to her, but now she had stopped, she didn't want some stranger reading aloud to her momma the secrets of her heart.

'Your momma said to say that your Uncle Ezra passed,' said the hummingbird man, removing his bowler hat, perhaps as a sign of respect, perhaps to impress Bertha with the noble planes of his skull. Bertha bowed her head; she had a dim memory of being carried into church on Uncle Ezra's shoulders and wondering if it was safe to hold on to the hair coming out of his ears.

'It was a fine burial, even Mrs Calhoun came to pay her respects.'

'And Momma, how's she doing? Is she wearing the shawl I sent her? Tell her that the mistress brought it back from Europe.'

'I'll be sure to let her know . . .' The hummingbird man paused and looked down at the shrouded cage on the floor where the hummingbirds slept. Bertha knew there was something wrong; the man had something to say that he didn't quite have the words for. She should help him, ask him the question that would let him reveal what was troubling him, but a strange reluctance came over her. She wanted her mother to stay in her blue and white striped dress, warm and sweet and whole.

There was a crash from the kitchen behind and the humming-birds stirred, their short futile flights disturbing the air like sighs.

'What colour are they this time?' asked Bertha, welcoming the distraction.

'I was told to make 'em all gold. Wasn't easy. Hummingbirds don't like to be painted; some of 'em just give up, just lay them-selves down and don't fly no more.'

Bertha knelt down and lifted up the cloth. She could see flickers of brightness moving in the darkness. When all the guests sat down for supper at midnight they would be released into the winter garden like a shower of gold. They would be the talking point of the room for maybe a whole ten minutes; the young men would try and catch them as favours for the girls they were flirting with. The other hostesses would think a touch grimly that Nancy Cash would stop at nothing to impress, and in the morning the maids would sweep the tiny golden bodies into a surrendered heap.

'Did Momma give you any message for me, Samuel? Is there something wrong?' Bertha asked quietly.

The hummingbird man was speaking to his birds, making small popping noises with his mouth. He clucked his tongue and looked at Bertha sadly.

'She told me to tell you that everything was fine, but she ain't fine, Bertha. She's so skinny now she looks like she might blow away in the hurricane season. She's wasting away, I don't give her another winter. If you want to see her again, you should make it quick.'

Bertha looked down at the birds fizzing like Roman candles in their cage. She put her hands to her hair, which was smooth. Her mother's hair was frizzy – it had constantly to be suppressed under headscarves. She knew that the hummingbird man was expecting emotion from her, tears at least. But Bertha had not cried for years, ten years in fact, since she had come North. What would be the point? After all, there was nothing she could do. Bertha knew how lucky she was, she knew of no other coloured girls who had become lady's maids. From the moment she had been made Miss Cora's maid, she had tried to speak, dress and behave like her as far as she was able. She remembered her mother's calloused hands and found she could not look at the hummingbird man.

The Blue Room bell rang again. One of the maids came out of the kitchen and shouted, 'That's the second time Miss Cora's bell's gone, you had better get up there, Bertha.'

Bertha jumped. 'I have to go now. I'll come and find you later, once the ball gets going. Don't go until I see you.' She tried to conceal her relief at the interruption with the vehemence of her tone.

'I'll be waiting for you, Bertha,' the hummingbird man said.

The bell jangled again. Bertha walked as fast as she dared up the servants' staircase. Running was forbidden. One of the house-maids had been dismissed for going down the marble staircase two at a time. Disrespectful, Mr Simmons the butler had called it.

She knocked on the Blue Room door and went in.

Cora was almost crying with frustration. 'Where have you been, Bertha? I must have rung three times. Get me out of this infernal thing.'

She was tugging at the leather bands encircling her body. The spine straightener, which had been made to Mrs Cash's special design, had all the buckles at the back and so was impossible to remove without help.

Bertha tried to appease her. 'I'm sorry, Miss Cora, the man with the hummingbirds had news from home, I guess I didn't hear the bell.'

Cora snorted. 'It's hardly an excuse that you were listening to gossip while I was trussed up here like a chicken.'

Bertha said nothing but fumbled at the buckles. She could feel her mistress twitching with impatience. As soon as she was free of the harness, Cora shook herself like a dog trying to get dry, then she spun round and grabbed Bertha by the shoulders. Bertha braced herself for a telling off, but to her surprise Cora smiled.

'I need you to tell me how to kiss a man. I know you know how, I saw you with the Vandemeyers' groom after their ball.' Cora's eyes were glittering with urgency. Bertha drew back from her mistress.

'I don't think kissing is something you can tell,' she said slowly, playing for time. Was Miss Cora going to let Mrs Cash know about her and Amos?

'Show me then. I have to get this right,' Cora said fiercely and leant towards Bertha. As she did so, a low shaft of light from the setting sun hit her conker-coloured hair, setting it ablaze.

Bertha tried not to shrink away. 'You really want me to kiss you the way I would a man?' Surely Miss Cora was not serious.

'Yes, yes, yes.' Cora tossed her head. The red mark from the harness was still visible on her forehead.

'But Miss Cora, it ain't natural two women kissing. If anyone were to see us I'd lose my place.'

'Oh, don't be so squeamish, Bertha. What if I were to give you fifty dollars?' Cora smiled enticingly as if offering a child a sweet.

Bertha considered this. Fifty dollars was two months' salary. But kissing another woman was still not right.

'I don't think you should be asking me this, Miss Cora, it just ain't fitting.' Bertha tried to sound as much like the Madam as she could; she knew that Mrs Cash was the only person in the world that Cora was frightened of. But Cora was not to be put off.

'Do you imagine that I actually want to kiss *you*? But I must practise. There is someone I need to kiss tonight and I have to do it right.' Cora shook with determination.

'Well . . .' Still Bertha hesitated.

'Seventy-five dollars.' Cora was wheedling now; Bertha knew she wouldn't be able to hold out for very long when her mistress wanted something that badly. Cora would just persist until she got her own way. Only Mrs Cash could say no to her daughter. Bertha decided to make the best of the situation.

'All right, Miss Cora, I will show you how to kiss a man, but I would like the seventy-five dollars now if you don't mind.'

Bertha knew quite well that Mrs Cash did not give Cora an allowance, so she had every reason to ask to see the money. Miss Cora was a great one for making promises she couldn't keep. But to Bertha's surprise, Cora produced a purse from under her pillow and counted out the dollars.

'Can you set aside your scruples now?' she said, holding out the bills.

The maid hesitated for a second and then took the money and tucked it away in her bodice. Seventy-five dollars should stop the hummingbird man looking at her like that. Taking a deep breath, she took Cora's flushed cheeks gingerly in her hands and bent her head towards her mistress. She pressed her lips against hers with a modest pressure and drew back as quickly as she could.

Cora broke away impatiently. 'No, I want you to do it properly. I saw you with that man. You looked as if, well,' she paused, trying to find the right phrase, 'as if you were eating each other.'

This time she put her hands on the maid's shoulders and pulled Bertha's face towards hers and pushed her lips to Bertha's, pressing as hard as she could.

Reluctantly Bertha pushed her mistress's lips open with her tongue and ran it lightly around the other woman's mouth. She felt her go stiff for a moment with shock and then Cora began to kiss her back, pushing her tongue between her teeth.

Bertha was the first to pull away. It was not unpleasant kissing Cora, it was certainly the most sweet-tasting kiss she had ever had. Better than Amos, who stank of chewing tobacco.

'You taste quite . . . piquant,' said Cora, wiping her mouth with a lace handkerchief. 'Is that all you have to do? You haven't left anything out? I have to do this correctly.' She looked earnestly at Bertha.

Not for the first time, Bertha wondered how anyone could be as educated as Cora and yet so ignorant. It was all Mrs Cash's fault of course. She had raised Cora like a beautiful doll. She wouldn't mind having Miss Cora's money or her face, but she sure as hell wouldn't want to have Miss Cora's mother.

'If it's just kissing you're having in mind, Miss Cora, then I reckon that's all you will require,' Bertha said firmly.

'Aren't you going to ask me who it is?' Cora said.

'Begging your pardon, Miss Cora, but I don't want to know. If the Madam was to find out what you're about . . .'

'She won't, or rather, she will but by the time she does it will be too late. Everything will be different after tonight.' She looked at the maid sideways as if challenging Bertha to ask her more. But Bertha was not to be drawn. So long as she didn't ask questions, she couldn't be made to answer them. She made her face go slack.

Cora, however, had lost interest in her. She was looking at herself in the long gilt cheval glass. Once they had kissed, she was sure that everything else would fall into place. They would announce their engagement and she would be a married woman by Christmas.

'You'd better get my costume ready, Bertha. Mother will be here in a minute, checking that I have followed her instructions *à la lettre*. I can't believe I have to wear something so perfectly hideous. Still, Martha Van Der Leyden told me that her mother is making her dress like a Puritan maid so I suppose it could be worse.'

Cora's dress had been copied from a Velázquez painting of a

Spanish infanta that Mrs Cash had bought because she had heard Mrs Astor admire it.

As Bertha took the elaborate hooped skirt from the closet, she wondered if the Madam had chosen her daughter's costume as much for the way it restricted the wearer's movement as for any artistic considerations. No gentleman would be able to get within three feet of Miss Cora. The kissing lesson would have been in vain.

She helped Cora out of her tea gown and into the farthingale. Cora had to step into it and Bertha had to fasten the harness like shutting a gate. The silk brocade of the skirt and bodice had been specially woven in Lyons; the fabric was heavy and dense. Cora swayed slightly as the weight of it settled on the frame. It would only take the slightest pressure to make her lose her balance entirely. The dress was three feet wide so Cora would have to go through all doorways sideways. Waltzing in such a dress would be impossible.

Bertha knelt and helped Cora into the brocade shoes with Louis heels and upturned toes. Cora began to wobble.

'I can't wear these, Bertha, I will fall over. Get the bronze slippers instead.'

'If you're sure, Miss Cora . . .' Bertha said cautiously.

'My mother is expecting eight hundred people tonight,' Cora said. 'I doubt she will have time to inspect my feet. Get the slippers.'

But Cora's words were braver than she felt; both girls knew that the Madam never missed anything.

Mrs Cash was making one last survey of her costume. Her neck and ears were still bare, not through austerity on her part but because she knew that any minute her husband would come in with a 'little something' which would have to be put on and admired. Winthrop had been spending a lot of time in the city lately, which meant that a 'little something' was due. Some of her contemporaries had used their husband's infidelities as a way of purchasing their freedom, but Mrs Cash, having spent the last five years shaking Cash's Finest Flour from her skirts, had no desire to tarnish her hard-won reputation as the most elegant hostess in Newport and Fifth Avenue by something as shabby as divorce. So long as Winthrop was discreet, she was prepared to pretend that she knew nothing of his passion for the opera.

There had been a time once, though, when she had not been so sanguine. In the early days of their marriage she could not bear to let him out of her sight, for fear that he would bestow that same confiding smile on someone else. In those days she would have thought jewels no substitute for Winthrop's unclouded gaze. But now she had her daughter, her houses and she was *the* Mrs Cash. She hoped that Winthrop would bring her diamonds this time. They would go well with her costume.

There was a tap at the door and Winthrop Rutherford II came in wearing the satin breeches, brocade waistcoat and powdered wig of Louis XV; the father might have started life as a stable boy but the son was a convincing Bourbon king. Mrs Cash thought with satisfaction that he looked quite distinguished in his costume, not many men could carry off silk stockings; they would be a handsome couple.

Her husband cleared his throat a little nervously. 'You look quite magnificent tonight, my dear, no one would think this was the last ball of the season. May I be permitted to add a little something to perfection?'

Mrs Cash moved her head forward as if readying herself for the axe. Winthrop pulled the diamond collar from his pocket and fastened it round her neck.

'You anticipate me, as always. It is indeed a necklace,' he said.

'Thank you, Winthrop. Always such taste. I shall wear the earrings you gave me last summer; I think they will make a perfect match.' She reached without a moment's hesitation for one of the morocco leather boxes on the dressing table, leaving Winthrop to wonder, not for the first time, if his wife could read his mind.

The opening bars of the Radetsky March floated up from the terrace. Mrs Cash stood and took her husband's proffered arm.

'You know, Winthrop, I would like this evening to be remembered.'

Cash knew better than to ask what she wanted the evening to be remembered for. She was only interested in one thing: perfection.

CHAPTER 2

A Spirit of Electricity

HERE WAS A MOMENT AS THE VAN DER LEYDEN family stood at the top of Sans Souci's famous double staircase, waiting to be announced, when Teddy Van Der Leyden thought his mother might have regretted her choice of costume. To be wearing plain dimity and fustian in a room full of satin, velvet and diamonds took an effort of will. But Mrs Van Der Leyden had wished to make a point and it was a point worthy of sacrifice. The family's sober dress was a silent reminder to the assembled guests and particularly their hosts that the Van Der Leydens could trace their lineage all the way back to the *Mayflower*. Their lineage did not peter out in a floury dead end. The sombre black and white was a sign that even here in Newport, some things could not be bought.

Teddy Van Der Leyden knew his mother's purpose and was amused by it. He was quite happy to wear a starched white neck-band and black cloak, although he would have preferred to be one of the founding fathers, Jefferson perhaps. He understood her need to distinguish herself from all this unvariegated opulence. Every corner of the mirrored ballroom glittered, each jewel reflected into infinity.

He had been coming to the resort every summer for as long as he could remember and had been happy enough, but this year was different. Now that he had decided to go to Paris, he felt impatient with the observances of the Newport day. Every hour was accounted for – tennis at the club in the morning, carriage drives in the afternoon, and every night there were balls that started at midnight and did not end till dawn. Day after day he met the same hundred or so people. Only the costumes changed.

There was Eli Montagu and his wife dressed as Christopher Columbus and what Teddy took to be Madame de Pompadour. He had already met them that morning at the Casino, and yesterday on the bicycle excursion which had ended so precipitously. He would meet them again tomorrow at the breakfast given at the Belmonts and then at the Schooner picnic. He didn't wince as his mother did when he heard Eli's vowels or shudder at the brassy tint of Mrs Montagu's hair; he rather liked the fact that when she smiled she showed her teeth. But he didn't want to talk to them nor did he want to make a point by not talking to them. He looked around for Cora. She was the only person he wanted to see. She was always surprising. He remembered the way she had blown the hair out of her eyes when she was cycling yesterday, the way the offending tendril had fluttered and then rested on her cheek.

He moved out of the receiving line and over to one of the champagne fountains. A footman in full Bourbon livery offered him a glass. He drank it quickly, watching the arrivals flooding in through the great double doors. Most of the guests had chosen to come as *ancien régime* French aristocrats – he had seen three Marie Antoinettes and innumerable Louis already. Perhaps it was a compliment to the Versailles-inspired surroundings; perhaps it was the only period of history that matched the opulence of the present. Now he felt glad of his Puritan clothes. There was something uneasy about railway barons and steel magnates dressing up in the silk hose and embroidered tailcoats of another gilded age.

And then he saw Cora and his discontents were forgotten. Her dress was ridiculous; her skirts stuck out so far on either side of her that she would clear a path through the ballroom like an oar through water when she danced, but even in the absurd costume she was radiant. Her red-brown hair hung in ringlets against her white neck and shoulders. He thought of the small beauty spot he had noticed yesterday at the hollow of her throat.

She was standing just below her parents who were installed on a velvet-draped dais. She was surrounded by young men and Teddy realised that he must ask Cora for a dance or he would never get a chance to talk to her. He walked towards her, passing a Cardinal Richelieu and a Marquise de Montespan. He waited for an opening among the young men and then he caught her eye. She squinted a little to make sure it was really him and then went back to her dance card, but Teddy knew she was waiting for him to approach. He walked round the scaffolding of her skirt and stood behind her.

'Am I too late?' he asked her softly.

She turned her head in his direction and smiled.

'Much too late for a dance. They all went ages ago. But I guess I might need to catch my breath after a while. Maybe around here?' She pointed to a waltz on her dance card with her little ivory pencil. 'We could meet on the terrace.' Her eyes flickered towards where her mother was standing in majesty. Teddy understood the look – Cora did not want her mother to see them together.

Did Mrs Cash think he was a fortune-hunter then? He shuddered to think how horrified *his* mother would be if she imagined that he was making advances to Cora Cash. Mrs Van Der Leyden might attend a ball given by Mrs Cash but that did not mean she saw Cora as a suitable wife for her son, no matter how rich she was. They had never spoken about it but Teddy sensed that his mother thought that his desire to go to Europe and paint was the lesser of two evils.

In the winter garden, Simmons the butler was inspecting the supper tables. Down the length of each one ran a stream contained in a silver channel, agitated by tiny pumps so that it sparkled with an effervescent current. At the bottom of the stream was pure white sand and Bertha was pushing stones into the sand to look like submerged boulders. Each of these boulders was in fact an uncut gem – diamonds, rubies, emeralds and topazes. Beside each place setting was a miniature silver shovel so that the guests could 'prospect' for these treasures. Bertha had been told by the butler to make sure that the 'boulders' were distributed evenly. Despite the enormous wealth of many of the guests, there would be fierce competition among the 'prospectors' to amass the most rocks. There had been an unseemly scramble for the Fabergé bonbons at the Astor ball the week before.

Bertha pushed sand artfully around a 'boulder' so that a crystalline spar just punctured the surface. Simmons had told her not to make them too easy to find. He was meant to do this task himself but Bertha knew he felt it beneath him. He hadn't told her what the rocks were but Bertha well understood their value. She would wait until they got to the end of the last table before taking one. Supper was to start at midnight when Mrs Cash would go on to the terrace to light up her costume and lead her guests into the winter garden like a star. At the same time the humming-birds would be released to create the illusion that the guests were entering the tropics. Bertha reckoned that Simmons would be so involved in ministering to this procession that he would hardly notice a missing gem.

Teddy waited for Cora on the terrace. It was a hot, still night. He could hear a cicada somewhere near his feet. An orange moon lit up the pale stone surrounding him. The slabs of marble covering the terrace were not smooth but had been worn into grooves by generations of feet. The entire terrace must have been brought over from some Tuscan villa, reflected Teddy, so that the Nine Muses who stood on the balustrade would not look their age. He could only admire Mrs Cash's thoroughness. Nothing, in her world, was left to chance. And yet here was Cora, screwing up her eyes to find him on the terrace, unchaperoned and uncaring. He knew from the way that Mrs Cash had pedalled after them yesterday when they had pulled ahead of the cycling party, her marble complexion turning quite pink, that she would not approve of her daughter being here. He knew, too, that he should not be alone with Cora, she was not part of the future he had decided on, yet here he was.

As she walked towards him through the apricot-hued pools of light cast by the Chinese silk lanterns hanging in the trees, he could see a red filigree dappling her collarbone and throat. She stopped before him, the panniers of her skirt making it impossible for her to stand anywhere but straight in front of him. He could see a faint prickling of flesh on her forearms that made the soft golden hairs stand up like fur. There was, he knew, a tiny scar on the underside of her wrist. He would have liked to take her hand to reassure himself it was still there.

'It is the most beautiful night,' he said. 'I was worried this morning that there would be a storm.'

Cora laughed. 'As if my mother would allow bad weather on the night of her party. Only inferior hostesses get rained off.'

'She has a remarkable eye for detail; she has set the standard very high in Newport.' Teddy spoke lightly. They both knew that the old guard like Teddy's mother thought that the parties thrown by incomers like the Cashes were over the top and vulgar.

Cora looked directly at him, her eyes scanning his face. 'Tell me something, Teddy. Yesterday, if Mother hadn't caught up with us, what would you have done?'

'Continued our charming conversation about your chances of winning the archery and then cycled home to dress for dinner.' His tone was deliberately light, he didn't want to think about the colour in Cora's cheeks yesterday or the gold flecks in the iris of her right eye.

But Cora was not to be deflected.

'I think that you are being . . .' she frowned, searching for the right word, 'disingenuous. I think that you were going to do this.' She put her hands on his shoulders and leant towards him, swaying unsteadily against the counterweight of the dress. He felt the warm dry touch of her lips on his. He knew that he should stop this now, draw back and pretend that nothing had happened and yet he wanted to kiss her so much. He felt her toppling in her ridiculous costume and he put his hands on her waist to steady her, and then he found he was kissing her back.

When, at last, they drew back from each other, neither smiled. Cora said, 'I was right then.'

'You were right about the intention. Of course I want to kiss you, what man wouldn't? There are fifty men out there who would give anything to take my place, but I had promised myself not to.' Teddy smiled at his good intentions.

'But why, if that was what you wanted?' She sounded suddenly much younger than eighteen.

Teddy looked away from her at the horizon where he could see the moonlight playing on the sea. 'Because I am afraid.'

'Of me?' Cora sounded pleased.

He turned to face her. 'If I fall in love with you, it would change everything, all my plans.' His voice trailed away as he saw that the flush had spread down across her chest; down, he was sure, beneath the infanta's modest neckline. He picked up her hand and turned it over, pressing the scar to his lips.

Cora trembled and the shudder ran through the construction of her dress.

'Do you know I am going away to Europe?' she said in a strained voice.

'The whole of America knows you are going to Europe, to find a suitable consort for the Cash millions.' Teddy tried to bat away her emotion but Cora did not respond in kind. She leant towards him, her eyes dark and opaque. When she spoke, her voice was almost a whisper.

'I don't want to go, you know. I would like to stay here – with you.'

Teddy dropped her hand and felt the heat of Cora's stare. He wanted to believe her, even though this would make his choice so much harder. She kissed him again, more fiercely this time. It was hard to resist the foxy smell of her hair and the downy smoothness of her cheeks. He could hardly feel her body through the architecture of her costume but he could feel the pulse beating in her neck. Who was he to resist Cora Cash, the girl that every woman in Newport envied and every man desired? He kissed her harder, grazing her lip with his teeth. He wanted to pull the combs and jewels out of her hair and take her out of her prison of a costume. He could hear her breathing quicken.

The music stopped. Then came the crash of the supper gong rippling out into the still night air.

For the first time Cora looked nervous. 'Mother will notice I have gone.' She made a gesture as if to go back inside, but then she turned back and spoke to him in a torrent of urgency. 'We could go now to the city and get married. Then she can't touch me. I have my own money, Grandfather left a trust for me which is mine when I am twenty-five or when I marry. And I'm sure Father would give us something. I don't want to go away.' She was pleading now.

Teddy saw that it had not occurred to her that he might refuse to accept her proposal.

'You are the one who is being disingenuous now. Do you really think that I can elope with you? Not only would it break your mother's heart, it would surely break my mother's too. The Van Der Leydens are not as rich as the Cashes but they are honourable. People would say I was a fortune-hunter.' He tried to take his hands from her waist but she held them there.

'But they would say that about anyone. It's not my fault I'm richer than everyone else. Please, Teddy, don't be all . . . scrupulous about this. Why can't we just be happy? You like kissing me, don't you? Didn't I get it right?' She reached up to stroke his cheek. And then a thought hit her, amazing her with its audacity. 'There isn't someone else, is there? Someone you like more than me?'

'Not someone, something. I want to be a painter. I'm going to Paris to study. I think I have a talent but I have to be sure.' Even as he said it, Teddy realised how weak he sounded against Cora's passionate intensity.

'But why can't you paint here? Or if you have to go to Paris, I could come with you.' She made it all sound so easy.

'No, Cora,' he said almost roughly, afraid she might persuade him. 'I don't want to be that kind of painter, a Newport character who sails in the morning and paints in the afternoon. I don't want to paint pictures of ladies and their lapdogs. I want to do something serious and I can't do that here and I can't do that with a wife.'

He thought for a moment that she would cry. She was waving her hands in front of her face as if trying to push away his words, swaying clumsily in her galleon of a dress.

'Honestly, there is no one I would rather marry than you, Cora, even if you are too rich for me. But I can't now; there is something I want more. And what I need can't be bought.'

She looked back at him crossly. He saw with relief tinged with regret that she was not so much heartbroken as thwarted. He said firmly, 'Admit it, Cora, you don't really want to marry me as much as you want to get away from your mother. A sentiment

I can fully appreciate, but if you go to Europe you will no doubt find yourself a princeling and then you can send her back to America.'

Cora gave him an angry little shove. 'And what, give her the satisfaction of being the matchmaker? The mother who married her daughter to the most eligible bachelor in Europe? She pretends she is above such things but I know she thinks of nothing else. Ever since I was born my mother has chosen everything for me, my clothes, my food, the books I can read, the friends I can have. She has thought of everything except me.' She shook her head sharply as if trying to shake her mother out of her life. 'Oh Teddy, won't you change your mind? I can help you; it wouldn't be so very terrible, would it? It's only money. We don't have to have it. I don't mind living in a garret.'

Perhaps, he thought, if she really cared for him . . . but he knew that what he principally represented to her was escape. He would like to paint her, though, angry and direct – the spirit of the New World dressed in the trappings of the Old. He couldn't resist taking her face in his hands and kissing her one last time.

But just as he felt his resolve weaken, as he felt Cora's shudder, the Spirit of Electricity exploded into the darkness and they were illuminated. Mrs Cash stood like a shining general at the head of her legion of guests.

There was a ripple in the air as a sigh of surprise was expelled across the terrace.

The radiant bulbs cast harsh shadows across the contours of Mrs Cash's face. 'Cora, what are you doing?' Her voice was soft but penetrating.

'Kissing Teddy, Mother,' her daughter replied. 'Surely with all that candle power, you can see that?'

The Spirit of Electricity brushed her daughter's insolence aside. She turned her glittering head to Teddy.

'Mr Van Der Leyden, for all your family's pride in your lineage, you appear to have no more morals than a stable hand. How dare you take advantage of my daughter?'

But it was Cora who answered. 'Oh, he wasn't taking advantage of me, Mother. I kissed him. But then my grandfather *was* a stable hand so you wouldn't expect any better, would you?'

Mrs Cash stood in shining silence, the echo of Cora's defiance ringing in the air around her. And then, just as Mrs Cash was about to deliver her counter blow, a tongue of flame snaked round the diamond star in her hair, turning her headdress into a fiery halo. Mrs Cash was all at once ablaze, her expression as fierce as the flames that were about to engulf her.

For a moment no one moved. It was as if the guests had all gathered together to watch a firework display, and indeed the sparks springing from Mrs Cash's head shone prettily against the night sky. And then the flames began to lick her face and Mrs Cash screamed – the high keening noise of an animal in pain. Teddy rushed towards her, throwing his cloak over the flaming head, and pushed her to the ground, pummelling her body with his hands. The stench of burnt hair and flesh was overwhelming, a gruesome echo of that hint of feral musk he had smelt on Cora moments before. But Teddy was hardly aware of this; later, all he remembered was the band striking the opening bars of the 'Blue Danube' as Cora knelt beside him and together they turned her mother over to face the stars above. The left side of her face was a mess of charred and blistered flesh.

Teddy heard Cora whisper, 'Is she dead?'

Teddy said nothing but pointed to Mrs Cash's right eye, her

good eye. It was bright with moisture and they watched as a tear made its way down the smooth stretch of her undamaged cheek.

In the conservatory the hummingbird man took the cloth from his cage. The gong had sounded, that was his signal. Carefully he opened the door and then stood aside as his birds scattered like sequins over the dark velvet of the night air.

A minute later Bertha found him standing in front of the empty cage.

'Samuel, I have something I want you to take to my mother. This should take care of her while I am in Europe.' She held out a little purse with the seventy-five dollars. She had decided to keep the 'boulder', it was not the sort of thing her mother would be able to sell easily.

The hummingbird man said, 'There was nobody to see them fly out. They looked so fine too.'

Bertha stood there with her hand still outstretched. Slowly, Samuel turned to face her and without haste he took the purse. He said nothing, but then he did not need to. Bertha filled the silence.

'If I could leave now I would, but we sail at the end of the week. This is a good position. Mrs Cash, she's looked after me.' Bertha's voice rose, as if asking a question.

The hummingbird man's stare did not waver. 'Goodbye, Bertha. I don't reckon I'll be coming up here again.' He picked up his cage and walked into the darkness.

CHAPTER 3

The Hunt

Dorset, England, January 1894

'BE CAREFUL WITH THAT NEEDLE, BERTHA. I DON'T want to be blooded before the hunt has even begun.'

'I'm sorry, Miss Cora, but this wash leather is tough to work and you keep moving so. If you don't want to get stuck, I reckon you'll have to keep still.'

Cora tried to stand motionless in front of the oval cheval glass as her maid stitched the chamois leather bodice together so that it was perfectly moulded to the contours of her body. Mrs Wyndham had insisted that the only riding habits worth having were from Busvine, 'He shows the form to perfection, my dear, almost indecently so. There's something quite naked about his tailoring. With a figure like yours, it would be a crime to go anywhere else.' Cora remembered the gleam in Mrs Wyndham's eyes as she said this and the way the widow's bejewelled hands had speculatively spanned her waist. 'Nineteen inches, I would say. Very nice indeed. Made for a Busvine.'

In order to ensure that the habit had the requisite smooth line, Cora could not wear her usual corset and stays. She wore a specially cut undergarment of chamois leather which she had to be sewn into so that no hooks or bumps would disfigure the unforgiving tailoring. Cora almost thanked her mother for the hours spent in the spine straightener when she saw how fine and upright she looked in her habit. Her chestnut hair had been pulled back into a high chignon, exposing the tender nape of her neck. As she adjusted the brim of her hat so that it tilted at just the right angle over her left eye, she felt quite equal to the day ahead. It was only when she pulled the veil down over her face to see whether she should stain her lips red as Mrs Wyndham had advised, 'Just a spot of colour, dear, for snap,' that she thought of her mother and the way the left half of her face was now shrouded in a gauzy white veil to conceal the devastation beneath. Cora knew that her mother would expect her to go in and submit herself for approval, but she hated the sight of her mother's naked, maimed face before she had put on her veil. Of course her mother's accident had not been her fault precisely, but she felt responsible nonetheless.

Cora reached for the cochineal stain and dabbed a little on her lips. That woman was right again, the splash of colour made all the difference. Cora had not liked the way that Mrs Wyndham had looked her over as if pricing horseflesh. She had felt ashamed when her mother had brought her in, 'to introduce us to the right people'. She was almost sure that her mother had paid Mrs Wyndham for her services. Still, Mrs Wyndham had been right about the Busvine. The leather felt warm and soft against her skin. She bent forward, intoxicated with the freedom the habit gave her to touch her toes. As she straightened up, she found the loop on the left side of her habit, which allowed her to lift it up out of the way as she walked. The left side of the skirt was about three feet longer than the right so that her legs would be covered at all times as she rode side-saddle. The trick was to hold the excess fabric across the body with the right hand so that it looked like Grecian drapery. Cora fiddled with the material until she had achieved the desired effect.

Bertha looked on with impatience; she wanted Miss Cora out of here so that she could have some breakfast. Her stomach was rumbling and breakfast for the upper servants was served promptly at seven thirty at Sutton Veney.

There was a knock at the door and one of the housemaids walked in shyly.

'If you please, miss, the master says that your horse is being brought round from the stables.'

'Tell Lord Bridport I will be down directly.' Cora turned to Bertha. 'Can you tell Mother that Lord Bridport insisted that we leave promptly, which means I didn't have time to visit her this morning.'

'She won't be happy, Miss Cora. You know how she likes to make sure you look the part.'

'I know, I know, but I don't have time to stand there while she picks over me. It is bad enough being sneered at by all those English ladies with their red hands and their small blue eyes looking at me as if I was a savage. I don't need Mother telling me how her whole happiness depends on seeing me splendidly married.' Cora picked up her ivory-handled crop and brandished it at her maid. Bertha looked at her wearily.

'I'll pass on the message to the Madam. What do you want to wear tonight?'

'The pink mousseline from Madame Fromont, I think. It will make all those English hags green with envy. Shame I can't wear the bill around my neck. I would like to see their faces when they realise that I can spend more on one dress than they spend on their clothes in a year. They're all so dowdy, and yet they dare to look down their long dripping noses at me, even though they're all desperate for me to marry one of their namby-pamby sons.' Cora brought the crop down on the bed with a thwack.

She smiled when she saw Lincoln waiting for her in the stable yard, twitching his head impatiently. A sixteen-hand grey stallion, Lincoln was the finest product of her father's stables. Cora was not ready to admit that she might find a British horse to suit her, so she had brought her favourite hunters with her, walking them every day on the deck of the SS *Aspen*, her father's steam yacht. Lincoln's breath condensed in a white cloud in the chill January morning. There had been a frost and the ground was white and hazy with mist. But the sun was beginning to break through and for the first time since she had come to England, miserable and guilty about her mother's accident, Cora felt excited at the thought of the day to come. To ride as hard as she could, with no conversation to make or customs to observe, was an irresistible prospect. She felt as if she had taken off more than her corset. She felt unbound.

The Myddleton considered itself the finest hunt in the south-west. Lord Bridport, the Master, was stingy when it came to his house and children but stinted nothing on his beloved hounds. His mother had been one of the first society ladies to ride to hounds and the Myddleton was now as famous for its 'Dianas' as for the quality of the sport. Mrs Wyndham had looked Cora over in her drawing room in Mayfair and had declared, 'The Myddleton for you, my dear. I think you will keep up.'

At the time Cora had not been quite sure of the older lady's meaning, but now, as she rode up after Lord Bridport, she understood that the competition had already begun. So far her exposure to smart British womanhood had been restricted; Cora and her mother had arrived in London at the end of the season when all the people of fashion had left for the country, or else were lying low so as not to draw attention to the fact that they had no estates to go to. Lord Bridport's wife and daughter were not in Cora's view 'smart' even if they could trace their lineage back to the Conqueror. But here were women whose Busvine habits fitted as closely as her own. Her appearance did not cause the ripple of anticipation that always heralded her arrival anywhere in her native country. Not a single shining head turned in her direction as she followed Lord Bridport into the throng. Cora was not sure how she felt about this, to be anonymous was an unfamiliar sensation.

'Ah Charlotte, may I introduce you to Miss Cash. Miss Cash, my niece by marriage, Lady Beauchamp.'

A blond head turned fractionally in her direction and gave her the faintest of nods.

'And here is my nephew Odo. Miss Cora Cash – Sir Odo Beauchamp.'

Odo Beauchamp put even his wife's elegant habit to shame. His pink coat and white breeches were immaculately tailored. His hair was as blond as his wife's but her chignon was tight, while a suggestion of a curl had been allowed to escape over his collar.

He turned his wide face with its limpid blue eyes and flushed cheeks to Cora. 'How do you do, Miss Cash. Is this your first time riding to hounds? I suspect you have wilder sport in your country.'

His voice was surprisingly high and light for such a big man, but it had an unmistakable edge. Cora replied in her most American drawl.

'Oh, we hunt foxes at home right enough, but we find them pretty tame after the bears and the rattlesnakes.'

Odo Beauchamp lifted an eyebrow. 'You American girls are so spirited, let's hope you feel as plucky after a day with the Myddleton. That's a very large animal you have there, I hope you can remount without help.'

'Where I come from, Sir Odo, a lady would be ashamed of herself if she rode out on a horse she couldn't manage herself.' Cora smiled.

'An Amazon, no less. Charlotte my angel, you must come and admire Miss Cash. She is quite the thing.' Odo waved a gloved hand at his wife. The blond head turned; Cora got the impression of wide-set blue eyes and a certain hardness to the mouth. Her voice was unexpectedly deep for a woman.

'Come, Odo, you mustn't tease Miss Cash. You don't want to spoil her first impressions of the Myddleton. It must be quite unlike anything you are used to, Miss Cash, although I know that American girls like nothing better than to give chase.'

Cora heard the sneer and narrowed her eyes. 'Only when there is something worth pursuing,' she replied.

Further hostilities were halted by the yelping of the hounds picking up the scent.

The huntsman blew his horn and the riders followed Lord Bridport as he cantered up after the hounds. Cora dug her heels into Lincoln's side. He took off at a smooth pace, pushing his way to the front. He cleared the first hedgerow without hesitation, and Lord Bridport gave her an encouraging wave.

The hunting country of Virginia where Cora had learnt to ride was flat and open, but here the landscape was thicketed with fences and coverts. The pace was hard and Cora was soon breathless. But Lincoln was enjoying himself, he took fence after fence without even breaking his stride. He, at least, had no reservations about this unfamiliar terrain. The field began to thin out. Cora found herself alone at the front, until a substantial young man in a pink coat came alongside her.

'Pleasure to watch you taking those fences. Lovely, quite lovely.'

Cora smiled but spurred her horse on. It wasn't altogether clear from the young man's tone whether his pleasure was directed at her or Lincoln and she didn't care to find out. But her admirer kept his horse abreast of hers.

'I've been hunting with the Myddleton since I was a nipper. Best pack in the country.'

Cora nodded in her most dismissive manner. The man in the pink coat was not be rebuffed, though.

'Saw you from the off. There's a girl with spirit, I thought. A girl who could appreciate a sportsman like myself. A girl who would like nothing better than to see what I have to offer.' He caught Lincoln by the bridle and slowed the animals down to a walk. Cora began to protest but he shushed her and, holding her bridle tightly, took off one glove and began to roll back his sleeve. To her astonishment she saw that his hand and arm were covered by a detailed tattoo of the huntsmen, the riders and hounds of the Myddleton. The portly figure of Lord Bridport was unmistakably cantering up the man's forearm. Cora could not help but laugh.

'Fine piece of work, eh? Took three days and a quart of brandy. The work is remarkably detailed. Can't see all of it myself of course, covers my whole back. Take a closer look if you like. Don't be shy.'

'I can appreciate the detail quite well from here, Mr . . .?'

'Cannadine's the name. Won't you at least have a look at the fox? People tell me it is remarkably true to life.'

Mr Cannadine put the reins in his other hand and started to pull off the other glove. Cora could see the red nose of the fox peering out from the man's sleeve.

'I'm sure it is, Mr Cannadine, but perhaps some other time, I don't want to lose the scent.'

Cannadine looked downcast. 'Giving me the brush-off, eh? People say the fox is worthy of Landseer. Don't show it to everyone, of course. But don't often see a gel who can ride like you.' He let go of Lincoln's reins to put his glove back on and Cora took the opportunity to pick them up and pull the horse's head up.

'So nice to have met you, Mr Cannadine.' And she dug her heels into Lincoln's side so that the horse went straight into a canter. Cora heard Mr Cannadine shouting as he set off after her.

The hunt was approaching a spinney. Mr Cannadine veered left after the rest of the pack, so Cora took her chance and turned right. She had no desire to see any more of Mr Cannadine's fox. If she went round the wood from the other side she would lose him.

It was a handsome beech wood, the trees were mostly bare but the lower branches were hung with mistletoe and ivy. A pheasant suddenly shot up in front of Lincoln. He stumbled and slowed. Cora let him walk for a while to check that no harm was done. She steered the horse into the wood itself, thinking she would catch up with the others faster. The air was quiet apart from Lincoln's heavy snorting and the strange rattle of the leaves still clinging to the branches. And then she heard it: a low exclamation, somewhere between pain and pleasure. Was it animal or human? she wondered. Cora rode on a few paces and then she heard it again, louder this time and somehow thrilling. It was coming from a dense piece of undergrowth towards the centre of the wood. She could see green fronds of bracken and the handsome smooth trunk of a great beech tree. Without quite understanding why, Cora turned her horse towards the sound. It was more urgent now, then there was a sharp cry that made her start. It was a sound she recognised even if she had never heard it before. She should not be here, this was a private place. She tugged Lincoln's reins, pulling his head sharply to the right and dug her heels into his flanks, desperate now to get away. The horse responded to her urgency and took off so swiftly that Cora had no time to avoid the low-lying branches coming towards her. The first knocked her hat off and the second struck her on the forehead and she knew no more.

The first thing she saw were the branches arching over her like a ribcage. Stunned by her fall, she sensed every detail sharply but she could not put them together. Bones and the smell of leaves and a hot wind blowing in her ear.

Wind? Cora turned her head. She realised she was lying on the ground. The breath tickling her cheek was from a horse, her horse, she fancied, who was pawing the ground impatiently, and snorting. The sound reminded Cora of something else, another noise she had heard but she could not place it. Her head felt muzzy, why was she lying on the ground? She saw a dark shape lying next to her. A bucket, or a chimney pot – no, it was a hat. Cora tried to raise her head but the effort was too much. She lay back and closed her eyes but at once opened them again. She must not sleep, there was something she had to remember. The horse whinnied. Something about a play, how did she enjoy the play, Mrs Lincoln. Lincoln was the name of the horse, her horse. But why was she lying on the ground? What was the sound that was pushing against her consciousness? She couldn't grasp it, it kept slipping out of reach. Other things were crowding in now – a crown of flames, a face she couldn't see behind a veil, a kiss that was not a kiss, a half-glimpsed fox. And then a voice.

'Can you hear me?'

Was is it a real voice, or just part of the jangle in her head?

'Are you hurt? Can I be of assistance?'

Cora tried to find the voice, and there was something leaning over her – a face, she thought, not the fox man, someone different. His eyes were looking at her, looking for something, she thought suddenly, but then he spoke again.

'Can you hear me? You have fallen from your horse. Can you move your limbs?'

My limbs, thought Cora, in limbo. I am in limbo, always in limbo. She smiled and the man, who she saw now was a young man, smiled back. It was not an easy smile, but a hard-won smile of pure relief.

'Oh, thank God, you are alive. I thought for one minute when I saw you that you were . . . Here, let me help you.' He put his arm under Cora's back and helped her to sit.

'But this,' she said, 'is not my country. I shouldn't be here. I am an American girl.' She didn't know why exactly but for some reason it was very important to say that now. There was something she knew that she did not want to be taken for. The young man nodded his head in acknowledgement.

'No indeed, this is my country. This is my wood, my land. My family have lived here for seven hundred years. But you are most welcome, Miss. . .?'

'Cash. I am Cora Cash. I am very rich. I have a flour fortune, not flower you can smell but flour you make bread with. Bread, you know, is the staff of life. Would you like to kiss me? Most men want to, but I am just too rich.' And then she felt the darkness coming again, and before the young man could answer, she fainted into his arms.

CHAPTER 4

Hot Water

THIS TIME WHEN CORA OPENED HER EYES SHE
saw a wooden angel looking at her with vacant eyes. She
was in a bed, a bed with a roof and curtains. But she awoke clear-
if sore-headed. She was Cora Cash, she had fallen off her horse
and now she was where? And wearing what? She gave a little
scream of dismay and suddenly there was a flurry of movement
and heads male and female bending over her.

'Miss Cash – you are Miss Cash, I think,' said a voice she recognised. It was the man in the wood. Something had happened
there. But what? There were things there she could almost feel,
sounds she could almost hear, shapes she could almost distinguish
but they lay behind a veil she couldn't penetrate. This was irritating, there was something important there, if only she could
remember. Like her mother, Cora had no patience for obstacles.

'Miss Cash from America I believe,' said the voice again with
a suggestion of meaning that Cora found vaguely troubling. This
man with dark hair and clear brown eyes seemed very well-
informed, and why was he smiling?

'I found you lying on the ground in Paradise Wood. I carried
you back here. I've called the doctor.'

'But how do you know my name?' Cora said.

'Don't you remember our conversation?' The man was teasing her, but why?

'No, I don't remember anything since riding out this morning – well, nothing that makes sense anyway. I remember your face but that's all. How did I fall? Is Lincoln all right?'

'You mean the fine American horse? He is in the stables where his Republican opinions are causing my groom much anguish,' the man said.

'And how long have I been here? What about Mother, does she know where I am? She will be furious. I must go back.' Cora tried to sit up, but the movement made her feel nauseous, she could feel hot bile flooding into her mouth. To vomit in front of this strange Englishman would be unbearable. She bit her lip.

'My dear Miss Cash, I'm afraid you must stay here until the doctor arrives. Head injuries can be treacherous. Perhaps you would like to write to your mother.' The man turned to the woman beside him; Cora guessed that she was some kind of servant.

'Perhaps you could get some writing paper for Miss Cash, Mrs Softley.'

The housekeeper left in a rustle of bombazine.

'You know my name, but I don't know yours.'

The man smiled. 'My friends call me Ivo.'

Cora sensed that he was holding something back. She felt annoyed. Why was nothing in this country straightforward? She felt as if she was being forced to play a game where everybody knew the rules but her. She decided to attack.

'Why do all you Englishmen have names that sound like patent medicines? Ivo and Odo and Hugo. Bromides and bath salts, every one of them.' She waved her hand dismissively.

The man made her a little bow. 'I can only apologise, Miss Cash, on behalf of my compatriots. Men in my family have been called Ivo for many hundreds of years, but perhaps the moment has come to move with the times. Would you like to call me Maltravers? It hasn't been my name for very long, but I suppose I must get used to it, and I don't think it has any medicinal properties.'

Cora looked at him in bewilderment. How many names did the man have?

His voice was not the strangulated roar that she had begun to think was handed out to all upper-class Englishmen at birth. It was very low and he spoke quietly so that the listener had to lean forward to catch every word. Cora realised that this man must be important, not many men could mutter and be completely confident that every word would be listened for and understood. She felt awkward. Did this man know who she was, that she was not just any American girl? She came back at him with as much dignity as she could muster.

'You are laughing at me for daring to question perfectly ridiculous things about your country that you take as quite normal. You do what you do not because it is the best way but because that is the way you have always done it. Why, in the house where I am staying, there are ten housemaids whose job it is to carry hot water up long staircases and endless corridors every morning so that a guest can take a bath in front of the fire. When I asked Lord Bridport why he didn't have bathrooms like we do in the United States, he said they were vulgar. Vulgar! To wash. No wonder all the women here look so grey and dingy. I have seen girls, quite pretty girls, with dirty necks. At least where I come from we keep ourselves clean.' She looked at her host defiantly.

She might be confined to bed in a strange house but she would speak as she found.

Her host did not look offended by her outburst; in fact he was smiling.

'I will have to take your word for that, Miss Cash. You were not at all clean when I found you in the forest and I regret that I have never visited your country. I am afraid you will be equally disappointed with the washing arrangements here. I have no moral objections to bathrooms, quite the contrary, I only object to their cost. But I can assure you that I wash very thoroughly. Perhaps you would care to inspect my neck?' He leant forward and proffered his neck to Cora as if to the scaffold. It was indeed clean and though the dark curls were longer than would have been acceptable in America, Maltravers did not smell, as so many Englishmen seemed to, of wet dog. No, he had another scent entirely. Cora couldn't quite describe it. She felt an urge to push her fingers through his hair. Again she bit her lip.

'Your neck is immaculate. I congratulate you.' Cora tried to hang on to her indignation. She was definitely not going to be charmed.

'But tell me, how many housemaids do you need to bring the hot water for the hip baths? How many steps do they have to climb? How long are the corridors they have to struggle down? Surely piped water would be more economical in the long run, not to mention kinder to the servants?' She tried to sit up so that she could hear his answer clearly and in an instant he was behind her with another pillow.

'Is that better? Excellent.' He paused. 'If we had running water, we wouldn't need so many housemaids and that might upset them mightily, not to mention their families who rely on them to send them money.'

'There are plenty of things for girls to do these days besides carry hot water and lay fires. They could teach or make hats or learn to use typewriting machines.' Cora knew that her mother was always losing her maids to shops and offices. The wages were better and they could have all the admirers they liked.

'Indeed they could, Miss Cash. But I suspect that most of them just want to earn a wage until they get married, and a big house like this is a very good place to find a husband.'

'Yes, I've heard about the marriage market in the servants' hall from Bertha.'

'Bertha is your maid?' The man's tone was amused.

'Yes, she came over with me from the States.'

'And as an American girl, she has no objections to being in service?'

Cora almost laughed. Hadn't she given Bertha three of her old dresses last month? How could Bertha be anything but happy.

She said in her most dignified tone, 'Bertha, I assure you, is very grateful for the opportunity to work for me. I wonder if you can say that about any of your maids?'

Maltravers' reply was lost as the housekeeper came in with a writing desk which she arranged on the bed in front of Cora. She had brought a quantity of thick cream paper. Cora picked up a sheet with a crest at the top and the single word Lulworth underneath. She had been in England long enough to understand that understatement was all. Lulworth was clearly an 'important' house and its owner must have some kind of title. But then why hadn't he told her when he gave his name? The English were infuriating. Everything was designed to put an outsider at a disadvantage. If you had to ask, you didn't belong.

The man walked to the end of the bed and looked down at

her. 'I shall leave you to write to your mother in peace. But before I go, satisfy my curiosity on one point. Why, if you find the English system so distasteful, are you here? I thought you Americans rather liked our quaint customs and antiquated ways, yet you don't seem to find us charming at all.'

Cora looked at him. His tone was light and yet there was an edge to his voice. She was pleased that she had nettled him. He had the advantage, but still she had piqued him.

'Oh, I would have thought that should be obvious. As an American heiress I have come here to buy the one thing I can't get at home, a title. My mother would like a prince of the blood, but I think she would settle for a duke. Does that satisfy your curiosity?'

'Perfectly, Miss Cash. I hope you will invite your mother to spend a few days here at Lulworth. I won't hear of you leaving until the doctor has given you a clean bill of health. And I rather think your mother will like it here, despite our lack of bathrooms. You see, while I may not be a prince, I am the Ninth Duke of Wareham.'

Cora felt the bile rushing into her mouth again. She waved her hands in front of her face.

The Duke was all concern. 'Mrs Softley, I think Miss Cash is feeling unwell.'

Cora managed to contain her nausea until the Duke had left the room.

CHAPTER 5

The Black Pearl

MRS CASH WAS ARRANGING FOLDS OF TULLE around her neck. By candlelight, in the foxed silver of the pier glass, the effects of the accident were almost unnoticeable; only the shiny tautness where the flesh had been burnt showed up in this forgiving light. For anyone sitting on Mrs Cash's right side there would have been no reason to suspect there was anything wrong; it was only when she turned her head that the ravages of the fire were revealed. At least, thought Mrs Cash, her right profile had always been generally the more admired. She had been lucky, the flames had not actually reached her left eye, although the area around it had been singed. The scars as they formed had pulled the skin tight, so that in this half-light the damaged side of Mrs Cash's face was a grotesque facsimile of youthfulness. She half closed her eyes and through the blur she could see the spectre of the girl she had been. She pulled at the hairpiece of curls she wore so that the tendrils covered the misshapen lump of flesh that had been her left ear. As she felt the waxy smoothness of the scarring, she flinched. The doctors had told her that she had been fortunate that her skin had healed so quickly, but she hated touching its smooth deadness, which she minded even more than the shooting pains she still felt. She straightened up and began to dust her face with powder.

There was a knock at the door and the butler came in with a letter on a silver salver.

'This has just arrived for you, ma'am. From Lulworth.'

Mrs Cash had not heard of Lulworth but judging from the little pause the butler made before he pronounced the name, she guessed that it was a place of some significance. She took up the letter and recognised, to her surprise, her daughter's loopy scrawl.

'But this is from Cora. Why is she writing to me? I thought she was hunting?'

The butler bowed his head. Mrs Cash's question was rhetorical, although as the letter was unsealed, every servant in the house could have given her an answer.

To the butler's surprise Mrs Cash did not gasp or reach for the sal volatile when reading her daughter's letter. Indeed, if the butler had been on Mrs Cash's right, he might have seen the beginnings of a smile.

In the servants' hall, Bertha was mending a lace nightgown that Cora had torn because she was too impatient to undo the buttons before pulling it over her head. It had been one of those nights when Cora had come upstairs from dinner noisy and truculent after an evening spent listening docilely to Lord Bridport's views on crop rotation. Bertha hadn't unlaced her fast enough and Cora, snatching the nightgown from her, had pulled it over her head, ripping the two-hundred-year-old Brussels lace that covered the bodice as she did so. Cora hadn't even noticed the tear but Bertha, who looked forward to the day when the nightgown and the lace would be passed on to her, had felt the ripping cloth as a laceration. The lace had been made by nuns, the work so fine and exquisite that it was almost an act of worship. It was taking all her concentration to sew the jagged cobweb edges together seamlessly. She had been so absorbed in joining one filigree flower to its mate, marvelling at the intricacy of the net showing white against her brown fingers, that she had missed the entrance of the groom from Lulworth with the letter for Mrs Cash, but now she caught Cora's name in the conversation between the housekeeper and the cook and she looked up from her sewing.

'Miss Cash was lucky that she didn't break her neck like the poor Duke that was. It was the new Duke that found her. Lucky he was in the woods, otherwise she might have been out there all night,' the housekeeper said.

'I don't think it was luck that put the Duke in that wood. Remember what day it is.' The cook looked at Mrs Lawrence the housekeeper with meaning. The housekeeper gave a gasp of remembrance and bowed her head.

'Is it the anniversary today? I'd almost forgotten. That poor young man and so soon after the old Duke's death too.' She closed her eyes for a moment and when she opened them she saw Bertha looking at her.

'Looks like you'll be going over to Lulworth, Miss Cash.' Bertha started at the name. Mrs Lawrence had told her when she arrived that all the visiting servants were known by the name of their employer, but still it felt strange.

The housekeeper continued, 'Your lady had a fall out hunting and she's been put to bed over at Lulworth. The groom came over with a letter for your young lady's mother. Mr Druitt is up there now waiting for a reply.' At the sight of Bertha's face, the house-keeper softened her tone. 'She'll be all right. If there was anything wrong, the Duke would have come himself.'

The cook chuckled. 'I expect he didn't want to leave Miss Cash's side. There's an awful lot of holes in the roof.'

'The Duke's not married then, Mrs Lawrence?' Bertha felt that the cook's hint had given her licence to ask. But she knew she had to be careful, the line between an innocent question and a liberty was a fine one. Soon after she arrived she had asked Lady Beauchamp's maid what her wages were and had been made to realise her mistake. As Miss Cash's lady's maid she was accorded a certain seniority in the servants' hall – she took precedence over the parlourmaids going into dinner, for instance – but her status did not allow her to ask questions. Mr Druitt had taken her aside and told her that while such things as wages and so forth might be the subject of much talk where she came from, here in England some things were kept private. Bertha had bowed her head and learnt her lesson.

Despite her lecture from the butler, Bertha was enjoying her stay at Sutton Veney. At home she ate at the bottom of the servants' table with the other coloured girls. Here she went into dinner every night on the arm of Sir Odo's valet. The first night she had retreated to her room, but Mrs Lawrence had sent one of the housemaids up to tell her that her presence was required in the servants' hall. Jim the valet had blushed when Mr Druitt had told him to take Miss Cash's maid into dinner. Their conversation was limited as Druitt liked to hold forth, but every time Bertha glanced his way, Jim would be looking at her. He was handsome enough; at least he looked as if he had been raised in the fresh air, unlike so many of the servants whose pasty complexions suggested they had spent all their life underground. Since that first night, Jim had been waiting for her every evening to take her into dinner and she found herself bumping into him on the servants' staircase two or three times a day.

Bertha looked at the two women, waiting for them to rebuff her. But the cook did not draw back at Bertha's question; in fact she looked rather pleased at the opportunity to show off in front of her rival, the housekeeper.

'No, the new Duke's a bachelor. I used to work in the kitchen over at Lulworth before I came here. Slave labour that was. They still cook over an open range in the kitchen there and forty people sitting down for dinner. Things are better here even if Lord Bridport is always asking after yesterday's joint. I was there when Miss Charlotte came to Lulworth. They were always together, Lord Ivo and Miss Charlotte, playin' with their bows and arrows. They used to come down to the kitchen begging for food to take out on their archery expeditions. Shame she had no money, Miss Charlotte would have made a handsome duchess.'

'Some more tea, Mrs James?' interrupted the housekeeper, clearly nettled at this exhibition of superior knowledge of the Duke.

Bertha picked up her work basket and went up the back stairs to Cora's room. The room was in the right-hand wing of the house and looked over the park at the front and the stable block at the side. The light was beginning to fade and Bertha could see the footman walking round the stable yard with a torch, lighting the lanterns. The yellow balls of light hung in the grey dusk like jack o'lanterns. The lamplighter had reached the lamp nearest the entrance to the arch when a rider came in. As he put his torch up, Bertha could see a gleam of blond hair under a riding hat.

Bertha pressed her forehead against the cold glass. She wanted a glimpse of the blonde woman's face but the hat was tilted too far down for her to see anything but the curve of a smooth cheek. The rider flung her reins to the groom and swung down from her horse, revealing a glimpse of white beneath her blue habit. As she turned, the lower half of the woman's face became visible and Bertha saw that her mouth was curved upwards in what might have been a smile. Bertha shivered. The room suddenly seemed empty without Cora.

For the first time since she had arrived in England, Bertha felt homesick – not for the half-remembered smell of her mother, she had long ago learned the futility of that – but rather for the well-lit certainties of her American life, where she had one hundred and fifty dollars in her sewing box and she knew the price of everything.

She went to the wardrobe and began to take out Miss Cora's most elaborate costumes. Whatever happened next, she knew that her mistress would want to look her expensive best.

Mrs Cash had wanted to leave Sutton Veney as soon as she had received her daughter's note, but Lord Bridport had persuaded her that it would be better to go in the morning. As she sat down to dinner, Mrs Cash was grateful for the opportunity to find out something more about the man she now thought of as Cora's duke.

'You must be beside yourself with worry about your daughter,

Mrs Cash,' said Odo Beauchamp, who had been seated tactfully on her good side. 'What an unfortunate accident, and your daughter such a fine horsewoman too. Charlotte and I saw her riding out this morning looking splendid. Quite a number of people said they would have thought she was English.'

Mrs Cash sighed. 'Cora assures me that she is unhurt, merely a little shaken. So kind of the Duke to insist on her staying at Lulworth till she is recovered and to invite me to stay with her. I shall go over there tomorrow,' she smiled. 'I am quite intrigued to meet an English duke. We were lucky enough to entertain the Duc de Clermont Tonnere when he was in Newport last summer, and he could not have been more gracious, so much more so than the Grand Duke Michael of Russia. He travelled with his own plate as if he didn't think there would be anything sufficiently magnificent in America. But I fancy he saw the error of his ways by the end of his visit.'

Mrs Cash's ducal reminiscences were interrupted by the footman serving the soup. Lord Bridport insisted on dinner taking no more than an hour, so each of the seven courses remained for only a short time in front of the diner. Mrs Cash, who found that the prospect of Lulworth had awakened her appetite, realised that she must focus on the lobster bisque. As she concentrated on conveying the soup to the undamaged side of her mouth, Odo took his chance. As the sole heir to a considerable fortune and due to inherit even more from his maternal grandfather, Odo was not abashed by Mrs Cash's wealth, nor was he in the least interested in her catalogue of foreign titles.

'I quite envy you going to Lulworth, if it weren't under such dramatic circumstances. It's a lovely house, one of the few really fine houses around here. It's not a great big dukery like the ones up north, it's more subtle than that. Lulworth has charm,' Odo tittered, 'if a building can be said to have charm. And you must see the chapel, it's exquisite, a little rococo gem.' He made a circle in the air with a finger to indicate the curves of the chapel. 'Of course I haven't been there since the old Duke's funeral, but I gather things have gone downhill since then. Wretched death duties I suppose.' Odo looked down the table to where his wife was sitting and raised his voice a little.

'I almost feel sorry for Ivo. He was such a perfect younger son, excellent shot, popular with the ladies, clever. There was some talk of the Diplomatic after he came out of the Guards, but then Maltravers, his elder brother, broke his neck eighteen months after the old Duke died, and it all came to Ivo. That was about a year ago, and since then he has become such a bore. He's shut himself up at Lulworth and won't come out to play. Didn't come to town for the season, nobody's seen him for months. Even Charlotte can't tempt him out and they used to be *such* friends.'

At the mention of her name, his wife began to talk with uncharacteristic animation to the Rural Dean on her left. If Mrs Cash had not been in the habit of only observing what was directly connected to her own interests, she might have noticed the flush spreading across Charlotte Beauchamp's cheeks. But Mrs Cash's attention was all with Odo.

'So there is no Duchess at Lulworth?' she said as nonchalantly as she was able. She didn't remember seeing Wareham's name in the list of noble bachelors in *Titled Americans*, a magazine she would never admit to buying, though she was exhaustively acquainted with its contents. She was certain she would not have missed an eligible duke.

'Not even a dowager,' said Odo, looking at Mrs Cash directly, his exophthalmic blue eyes glistening. He had noticed his wife's animation and the sudden colour in her cheeks. His tongue darted over his lips involuntarily. He paused to drink some claret. He knew he had Mrs Cash's full attention, and he was aware, too, that she was not the only listener; his wife was still chattering to the clergyman but she would hear every word.

'No, the moment the old Duke died, Duchess Fanny was off. Barely out of mourning before she married Buckingham. Of course everyone knew what special friends they were, but still . . . She was probably worried that someone else would snaffle him up, although who else would want poor old Buckingham, God knows. But the Double Duchess couldn't be happier.'

'The Double Duchess?' It was the closest Mrs Cash had come to a squeak since childhood.

'First Duchess of Wareham and now Duchess of Buckingham, first woman I know to have done the double.' Beauchamp smiled. 'Some people think that poor old Wareham died just in time. Duchess Fanny had spent a fortune on Lulworth. She even had a branch line built so the Prince of Wales could get there faster. But now she entertains him at Conyers – Buckingham's place. The shooting is better at Lulworth, but dear old Buckers has the wherewithal.'

Mrs Cash pulled at the tulle covering her damaged left cheek and wondered why her neighbour was being so forthcoming. At home she knew to a cent how much her friends and enemies were worth and whether they figured in the Social Register or were on Ward McAlister's list for the Patriarchs' Ball. But things were different here. Mrs Cash had taken great pains to learn the order of precedence among the English nobility – she liked nothing better than a set of rules. But she had been astonished, not to say shocked, to discover on her arrival in London that she was as likely to encounter an actress like Mrs Patrick Campbell as a countess at the smartest society events. In Newport or even New York you might engage such a person to perform at a party but it would be quite unthinkable to entertain them on equal terms socially. When she made this point to Mrs Wyndham, whom she had persuaded, at some cost, to introduce Cora and herself into society, Mrs Wyndham had reacted in such a way that Mrs Cash had felt the unfamiliar and unwelcome sensation of being laughed at. 'Oh, you can go pretty much anywhere now if you are amusing enough,' said Mrs Wyndham. 'Or rich enough,' she added, narrowing her gaze at Mrs Cash.

Mrs Cash had resented the implication very much and had considered breaking off her relationship with her sponsor. But, as Mrs Wyndham knew very well, Mrs Cash needed her help. Cora was rich enough and beautiful enough to be sought after, but only Mrs Wyndham was prepared to tell her that Lord Henry Fitzroy had syphilis or that Patrick Castlerosse had been named as the co-respondent in the Abagavenny divorce. So Mrs Cash was surprised and delighted to find Lord Bridport's nephew so willing and indeed eager to satisfy her curiosity about the Duke of Wareham.

'But when you say that the Duke has shut himself away, is there any reason why he should? Is he ill?' Mrs Cash was wondering whether the Duke of Wareham's health was another of those topics that was common knowledge only among those who belong.

'Nothing wrong with him at all physically. Mentally, well, I really couldn't say. He's a Catholic of course, like all the Maltravers, so Lord alone knows what twisted Papist fancies are at work. Oh, don't worry, Mrs Cash,' said Odo, seeing the expression on her face. 'It's a very old Catholic family, they're not converts. No, I think the Duke is having money troubles. Lulworth is a huge estate but rents are down. Duchess Fanny spent every penny and more on entertaining Tum Tum, and then old Wareham and poor Guy died so close together, which meant paying death duties twice.' Mrs Cash assumed that Tum Tum was the Prince of Wales, and that this was a nickname that, as a foreigner, she would not be safe in using.

Odo was still speaking. 'No wonder Ivo is lying low. Shame really, because what he needs is a nice rich wife. Who knows, Mrs Cash, perhaps you will spirit him back to Newport and find him a lovely young heiress? She'll have to be beautiful, though. Ivo is very particular.'

Mrs Cash was deciding how to reply when a small hubbub erupted at the other end of the table. Charlotte Beauchamp, who had been fingering the choker of black pearls around her throat, had inadvertently touched upon a weak link in the stringing, and the necklace snapped, the pearls exploding across the table, rattling across plates and ricocheting off the crystal glasses. Charlotte, making a sound somewhere between a shriek and a laugh, was trying to recover the pearls as nonchalantly as she could. The Rural Dean found one in his claret and embarked on a long-winded allusion to Cleopatra's dinner with Antony.

'She said she would give him a priceless dinner, so he was very surprised to be given indifferent food and then Cleopatra took off one of her pearl earrings, dropped it into her glass of wine where it dissolved and she offered him the glass to drink. What a magnificent gesture. I can't claim to be Antony of course but, my dear Lady Beauchamp, you are surely a modern Cleopatra.'

The Dean stopped, rather amazed at where his unexpected eloquence had taken him.

Charlotte was busy trying to retrieve the pearl with a teaspoon when her husband called out, 'I hope, Dean, that you are not suggesting that my wife should have herself delivered to you in a carpet, the better to seduce you. You really mustn't put such fancies in her head.'

The Dean looked rather pleased with himself. 'Age cannot wither, nor custom stale her infinite variety.'

'Eighteen, nineteen, twenty,' said Charlotte as she counted the pearls rolling about on her dinner plate. 'Only one missing. Is it in your waistcoat pocket, Dean, I wonder?'

'I will ask Druitt to have a thorough search afterwards,' said Lady Bridport hastily, alarmed equally by the thought of Charlotte going through the Dean's pockets as by the Dean's willingness to quote Shakespeare at a civilised dinner party. She rose and gave the signal for the ladies to withdraw.

When Odo went to visit his wife's bedroom later that evening, he found her in her peignoir at the dressing table. He noted the blue veins that threaded her slender arms as she pulled the silver hairbrush through her long fair hair. Cleopatra was altogether too coarse an image for Charlotte, he thought. She had the head of an Italian Renaissance beauty. When he had last been in London, Snoad the dealer had shown him a painting by the Sienese painter Martini of Bianca Saracini. She had long fair hair and a high forehead like Charlotte's, in her hand she held a snowball to signify her purity. He must have Charlotte painted, although he could think of no one who could do her justice. Meanwhile, he would buy the Martini and give it to Charlotte for her birthday. She liked presents.

'I'm sorry about your necklace, Charlotte. Such an exotic colour. Have I seen it before?'

Charlotte's hair flickered in a sudden storm of static. Odo took the brush from her and began to brush it himself. He liked to pacify it into a shining sheet. Charlotte flinched and avoided his eyes in the mirror as she said, 'It belonged to my great-aunt Georgina – you know, the one who was in India. I never thought to wear it before but, faced with all those American sparklers, I didn't want to appear dowdy.'

'Pearls before swine, eh?' He put the brush down, and pulled back her hair so he could kiss her neck. 'Such a pity I lost you today at the meet. Where did you get to?' Odo began to pull the fastenings of her peignoir.

'Oh, I don't know, my stirrup kept twisting and by the time I had fixed it, you had gone. Had to spend hours dodging that buffoon Cannadine.'

Odo squeezed her nipple hard. 'Cannadine indeed. Poor Charlotte. But you know I don't like it when you disappear. I shall have to punish you.'

He picked up the hairbrush.

In the servants' hall, Bertha was finishing her supper. She was eating some kind of pudding laced with currants. It was a dish that everyone else seemed to relish, but she found it hard going. She longed suddenly for an ice-cream sundae. That had been her treat on her afternoons off at home, ice cream from the drug-store in Newport. She would go there dressed up to the nines in one of Miss Cora's fanciest cast-offs, with a parasol and a bonnet with a veil. Bertha could just pass for white, and in her second-hand Paris finery the man behind the counter was not about to question her colour. It was the combination of cold ice cream and hot chocolate sauce that made her gasp with pleasure. She couldn't understand why Miss Cora, who could have all the sundaes she wanted, didn't eat them night and day. That was luxury all right.

There was a tap on her shoulder. She looked up and saw Jim. 'Think you dropped this, Miss Cash.' He put something in her lap. It was a handkerchief, not one of hers, inside which was a tiny screw of paper. She hid it up her sleeve as she knew that Druitt and Mrs Lawrence were watching her.

As she walked out of the hall, she unfolded the note and read it by the light of her candle. In careful rounded script she read:

Meet me by the stables. I have something for you.
Yours ever,
Jim Harman

He was waiting there by Lincoln's stall, stamping his feet in the cold. When he saw her, his face relaxed into a smile.

'You came then. Good girl. You won't be sorry.'

'I should hope not, I could lose my place for this.'

'Look.' Jim held out a clenched fist to her. Bertha hesitated. 'Go on, open it'.

Bertha pulled back his fingers one by one. There, on his outstretched palm, was a black pearl. Under the lamplight she could see its faint iridescent sheen like a slick of oil on a puddle. It was as big as a marble and almost perfectly spherical. Bertha took it and rubbed it against her cheek.

'It's so smooth. Where did you find it? You did find it, didn't you?' She looked at his face, hoping he would meet her eyes. He didn't flinch.

'I was waiting at table tonight, on account of it being such a big party, and just as I was coming round with the savoury, one of the ladies went and broke her necklace by fidgeting with it at the table. She thought she picked 'em all up but this one rolled under my foot and I stood on it tight until all the ladies went upstairs. I wanted to give it to you. You're a black pearl, Bertha, that's what you are and it's only right that you should have it.'

Bertha looked at him, astonished. No one had ever talked to her this way before. Honey talk, that's what her mother would call it. 'Honey talk is fine and dandy but make sure you get the ring first.' Bertha's mother had never had a ring though. The man who had seduced her had been white, so there was no question of marriage. Mrs Calhoun had kept her on in the laundry after Bertha was born. The Reverend called it an act of Christian charity, but Bertha's mother never looked grateful. But Bertha did not pull away as Jim leant down to kiss her. It was different from all the other kisses she had had, softer, more tentative. His hands were holding her head as if it was made of glass.

When he drew back she said, 'Don't you mind?'

'Mind what?' he whispered.

'My skin. Don't you mind kissing a coloured girl?'

He didn't answer but kissed her again, this time with more urgency.

Finally he said, 'Mind? I told you, you're my black pearl. When

I first set eyes on you in the servants' hall I thought you were the most beautiful thing I had ever seen in my life. When old Druitt told me to take you into dinner I thought I'd died and gone to heaven.'

There was no mistaking the sincerity of his tone. Bertha was touched. She felt for his hand and squeezed it. She saw Jim's blue eyes go round with concern.

'You're not cross, are you, that I kissed you? You just looked so fine standing there, I couldn't help myself. It wasn't that I thought I could, I don't think you're fast or anything.' He looked so worried that Bertha laughed and swung his hand.

'No, I'm not cross. Not at all.' She leant towards him, the better to show him how far from cross she was, but they heard foot-steps and Jim drew away.

'I must go. Save this for me.' And he touched his finger to her lips and was gone.

Bertha turned back towards the house, rolling the pearl between her fingers. It grew warm in her hand. She slipped it into the bodice of her dress and as she walked into the house she could feel the glow somewhere just above her heart.

CHAPTER 6

A Link in the Chain

IF MRS CASH HAD BEEN EDUCATED AS ELEGANTLY as her daughter, if she had read Byron, or had pored over Doré's engravings of Dante, she would have recognised Lulworth with its turrets and its twisted chimneys silhouetted against the shining sea as a glorious example of the Picturesque. But Mrs Cash was the daughter of a colonel of the Confederate Army, and when she had been growing up, there had been no call for poetry. Mrs Cash was a crack shot and could command an army of servants but she had not had a sentimental education.

After the Confederate surrender at Appomatox, Nancy Lovett, as she then was, had been sent North to stay with her aunt in New York. She was a handsome girl with dark hair and a delicate but firm jaw. Her mother had sent her into enemy territory with misgivings, but Nancy had not looked back. She liked the rich colours of her aunt's house, the wide skirts, the elaborate pelmets. She enjoyed the plentiful food and rosy prosperous company. When Winthrop the Golden Miller's son had proposed, she had accepted gladly. Her mother had sighed and thought about what might have been, but her father was by then in the institution where he would die three months later. Later, as Nancy the bride solidified into Mrs Cash the society matron, she had felt some of the lacunae in her education; she could not speak a word of French, for example. But for a woman with such a natural talent to command, her inability to talk to the French Ambassador in his native tongue was the faintest of setbacks. Colonel Lovett had been a keen disciplinarian before his 'indisposition' and he would have appreciated his daughter's ability to impose order.

So Mrs Cash did not gasp, as so many visitors had before her, at the romantic charms of Lulworth. The house with its four turrets flanked by lacy Jacobean wings studded with mullioned windows was imposing but delicate, like a queen whose coronation robes cannot disguise the slenderness of her waist or the fragile tilt of her head.

No, like the commander she was, Mrs Cash sized up the strengths and the weaknesses of her new billet. She could tell from the irregular façade with its towers and battlements that the food would be at best tepid by the time it reached the dining room. Driving in through the park gates, Mrs Cash looked up only briefly at the bronze stag over the cast-iron gates; she was far more interested in the dilapidated state of the gatehouse windows. By the time she was halfway up the drive of two-hundred-year-old elm trees she had made a realistic assessment of Lulworth's plumbing.

But even Mrs Cash could not fault the magnificent matching pair of footmen who handed her out of her carriage. The Lulworth livery of green and gold was certainly elegant, she had never seen shoulder tassels of such splendour. She would have smiled with appreciation, if it hadn't been so painful. She had to husband her smiles for more important occasions. Perhaps the Duke might give her the name of his livery maker.

A voice murmured in her ear, 'Welcome to Lulworth, Madam. His Grace has asked me to take you to see Miss Cash and then he hopes you will join him for lunch.' She followed the butler up the stone steps through the great arched door into a vaulted hall with a carved stone chimney piece at one end. The blackened oak of the roof timbers was not to Mrs Cash's taste, she preferred her wood gilded, but she felt its weight.

'If you would like to come this way, Madam.'

Mrs Cash followed the servant up a wide wooden staircase lit by a glass lantern roof. There were fantastical beasts on the newel posts: gryphons, salamanders and lions. Mrs Cash admired the carvings but noticed that they had not been carefully dusted. At length they reached a wide gallery and the servant turned left and proceeded until he reached a door about halfway down.

Cora was lying in an immense wooden bed hung with green damask with carved angels at each corner. She looked pale and, to Mrs Cash's irritation, rather plain. Much of Cora's charm lay in the vividness of her colouring: the bright chestnut curls, mossy green eyes and rosy skin. Lying there with dark circles under her eyes and with her hair limp and unkempt against the snowy mounds of linen, she did not look at all like the belle of Newport. Mrs Cash, for the first time since her daughter's accident, began to worry about the extent of her injuries. She hoped that her daughter had not been, in some way, damaged.

'Hello, Mother.' Cora smiled.

'Cora, I am so relieved to see you.' Mrs Cash bent over to kiss her daughter's cheek and stayed there for a moment before sitting down on the bed, making sure that her daughter had her right side and saying, 'What an unbecoming nightgown, it makes you look quite sallow.'

Cora's smile vanished. 'It belongs to the Duke's mother.' She started to play with one of her limp ringlets. 'Mother, did you bring Bertha with you?'

'You would think that a duchess, a duchess twice over, would be ashamed to wear something so shabby. The cheapest kind of cotton and not a scrap of lace. I wouldn't even give this to my maid.' Mrs Cash pinched the cuff of fabric round her daughter's wrist. Cora pulled her hand away.

'Mother, did you bring Bertha?'

Mrs Cash was looking at the canopy above the bed. She lowered her head slowly and met her daughter's gaze. 'Bertha is following in the Bridport governess cart. You surely didn't expect her to travel with me.'

Cora sighed, and lay back against her pillows. She had found it difficult to sleep last night in this strange house that creaked and shivered in the dark, prey to fears she could not give shape or name to. The doctor had said she might feel some light-headedness for a few days, but had said nothing about hallucinations. But the irritation and annoyance that pecked at her the moment her mother began to talk was reassuring. Her mother was real enough. This part of her mind, at least, was unharmed.

Mrs Cash was wandering through the room on a tour of inspection. She turned to Cora. 'These English houses are so haphazard. There is no planning, nothing matches. I could do so much with this house.' Mrs Cash paused and narrowed her eyes a little as if mentally remodelling their surroundings. Those casement windows with leaded frames – so antiquated and dismal. The English had lived in their houses so long that they no longer noticed them. It took a New World eye like hers to see them as they really were. The situation here was really quite good, if a little isolated. How long, she wondered, would it take to build a new house worthy of an American duchess?

Cora read her mother's thoughts. 'Mother, you know that my being here is nothing more than an accident.'

Mrs Cash chose to misunderstand her. 'My poor girl, how frightened you must have been. Still, it was really most fortunate that you should have been rescued so promptly. And by such a Samaritan.'

Cora realised that nothing would prevent her mother from believing that her accident and subsequent rescue was a sign that Providence was supporting her ambitions for her daughter. Cora might think she was a free agent but Mrs Cash and the Almighty knew better. Indeed, Mrs Cash was prepared to concede that Fate's method of bringing her daughter within proposing distance of a duke was more ingenious than anything that she might have engineered. The only blemish in the divine plan was that Cora's injury was not so serious that she would be obliged to stay at Lulworth indefinitely. A broken ankle would have been so much more definite. Really, there was nothing more appealing than a pretty girl confined to a sofa. Still, it couldn't be helped. The important thing was to get Cora out of that hideous nightdress into something more becoming. She began to regret leaving Bertha behind, perhaps it wouldn't have been so bad to have brought her in her coach. But she didn't want the Duke to think that she was the kind of woman who travelled with the help. A pointless scruple it turned out, as the Duke had not been there to greet her in person. Was that intended as a slight, or was there something in the impenetrable English rule book which meant that hosts above a certain rank never waited at the door to welcome their guests? It was one of the many things she would ask Mrs Wyndham.

She turned to Cora. 'I must leave you now, Cora, the Duke is expecting me at lunch.'

'I don't think you'll be disappointed, Mother. Maltravers is everything a duke should be. But I wouldn't make your dissatisfaction with the décor too plain. I have the feeling that he is very attached to this house.'

'As if I would do anything so ill-bred! Really, Cora, sometimes I think you forget that I am mistress of a house quite the match of this one.'

'I am not sure the Duke would agree. I don't think he is in the habit of comparing himself with others.'

Mother and daughter glared at each other. Cora closed her eyes in feigned weariness. But Mrs Cash was not to be silenced so easily.

'Even dukes can count, Cora,' she said, sweeping from the room.

Cora lay back, imagining her mother's impatient progress through the house. Unconscious when the Duke had brought her to Lulworth the day before, she had so far only seen the inside of the bedroom and a glimpse of the dark corridor beyond. If only Bertha were here. She needed to see the house for herself, but she couldn't very well wander the corridors in the Duchess's second-best nightgown. Not for the first time, Cora cursed her mother's notions of propriety.

Mrs Cash found a footman waiting outside her daughter's room, ready to escort her to the dining room. The wide oak boards creaked as she walked carefully down the polished steps.

The footman opened the library door.

'Mrs Cash, Your Grace.'

Mrs Cash wondered if she should curtsy, but thought on the whole not. She had been expecting one of those milky Englishmen whose youthful slimness was almost a reproach to the corpulence to come, but the Duke was darker almost than any Englishman had a right to be, his hair was black and his slightly hooded eyes were a golden brown. She couldn't make out his age. She knew he couldn't be more than thirty but there was nothing youthful in the grave way he took her hand. Deep grooves ran from his nose to his mouth and there were flecks of grey at his temples.

'Mrs Cash, welcome to Lulworth. I hope your stay will be a pleasant one even if the reason for your visit is not.' His words were cordial enough but he did not smile or meet her eyes. For the first time in many years, Mrs Cash felt awkward. She had come here expecting to assess the Duke's suitability as a match for her daughter, but the man before her was not acting like a suitor. Perhaps he was not aware of the prize that was within his grasp. But from what she had seen of Lulworth, he could not afford to be indifferent.

She replied in her most gracious tones. 'Your Grace has been most kind in taking in my unfortunate daughter. Who knows what would have happened if you hadn't found her. A young girl, alone and hurt and so far from home.'

The Duke replied, 'Oh, I don't think she would have come to much harm in an English beech wood, and from what little I have seen of your daughter, she seems more than able to take care of herself. American girls have so much spirit.'

Mrs Cash was not encouraged by this speech. It sounded as if the Duke had judged her daughter and found her wanting. She felt at a disadvantage, an entirely unfamiliar and unwelcome sensation.

The Duke led the way into the dining room where they were joined, rather to Mrs Cash's surprise, by a priest.

'Mrs Cash, may I present Father Oliver. He is writing a history of Lulworth and the Maltravers.'

The priest, whose face was as perfectly round and smooth as a balloon, advanced towards her beaming. 'Delighted to make your acquaintance, Mrs Cash. I am so fond of your country. I was in New York only last year staying with Mrs Astor. What a peerless woman. Such manners! And taste!'

Mrs Cash smiled weakly. She wondered if Father Oliver knew that her acquaintance with the fabled Mrs Astor was not as intimate as she would like. Was everyone here determined to wrongfoot her? She might throw the most talked-about parties in Newport but so far Mrs Astor had never accepted one of her invitations. It was one of the reasons that she was so anxious for Cora to marry splendidly. Even Mrs Astor could not look down on a duchess, or the mother of a duchess.

But despite the Duke's apparent indifference to her, she noticed that he beckoned her to sit at his left so that the undamaged side of her face would be turned towards him, even though as the only woman present she should have been on his right. Mrs Cash was surprised and grateful at this tactful gesture. Father Oliver sat on the other side of the table. Father Oliver said grace, to which the Duke said Amen very loudly. The food was, as she had predicted, barely lukewarm.

They ate their soup in silence and then the Duke said, 'I'm afraid you will find us very quiet here, Mrs Cash. My mother used to entertain on a grand scale, but now that she has moved to Conyers the parties have gone with her. My mother is so wonder-fully energetic.' He said the word 'mother' with a peculiar emphasis, almost as if he was calling their relationship into doubt.

'Why, the quiet couldn't be more delightful,' Mrs Cash assured him. 'Cora and I came to Europe after a hectic summer in Newport. We had nearly a thousand guests for Cora's coming-out ball. People were kind enough to say that it was the event of the season. But after my accident,' Mrs Cash fluttered her hand towards her cheek, 'the doctors said I must rest and recover my strength.' She watched the Duke's face carefully but he did not react to the mention of the thousand guests.

'Did you have a pleasant crossing, Mrs Cash?' asked Father Oliver solicitously. 'No storms in the Atlantic, I trust. My last journey was so rough that some of the passengers were asking me to hear their confessions! I became quite the parish priest for the upper deck.' Father Oliver was talking too much and too fast, but he had been at Lulworth for six weeks now, and too many meals had been eaten in silence. There had been few visitors and none like Mrs Cash. He had been asked to write the history by the Duke's brother. It had been a handsome commission but he sensed that the current Duke was not as eager as his brother had been to commemorate his family's past.

He leant towards the American woman. 'Which boat did you come over in, Mrs Cash? I believe there is a new vessel on the White Star line that has its own tennis court.'

Mrs Cash's smile of triumph spread over the good side of her face. Here was a chance to make her place in the world quite clear.

'We have our own steam yacht, the *Aspen*. My husband Winthrop had it built five years ago, after a bad crossing on a steamer. He has a dread of being cooped up with strangers.'

Father Oliver was silenced, but the Duke looked up, interested.

'Oh, that explains it. I was wondering how your daughter had brought her horse over.'

'Horses you mean, Duke,' Mrs Cash said with a little trill of satisfaction. She decided that it was time to use the more familiar form of address – 'Your Grace' felt altogether too subservient. 'She brought three hunters with her and insisted on walking them on deck morning and evening whatever the weather. There were days when I thought all four of them would be washed overboard. But Cora is so headstrong. She takes after my father the Colonel. He had more decorations for gallantry than any soldier in the Confederate Army.'

'You are from the South then, Mrs Cash?' enquired Father Oliver.

'My family, the Lovetts, is one of the oldest in Virginia. The original Delmore Lovett came over from England two hundred years ago. Not many families can go that far back. Our family place L'Hirondelle was one of the finest plantations on the Chesapeake River.'

'Two hundred years? I had no idea you Americans had so much history,' said the Duke, but before Mrs Cash could answer, the priest broke in.

'"Was", Mrs Cash?'

'It was razed to the ground by Sherman. I don't think my father was ever in his right mind after that.'

'How savage,' murmured the Duke.

'It is only through God's grace that Lulworth did not suffer a similar fate in the seventeenth century, Your Grace,' said Father Oliver. 'Think of what Cromwell's armies did to Corfe Castle just twenty miles away from here. They could so easily have marched to the coast. Indeed, it is very surprising they did not, given that the Second Duke was such a close friend of the King. But like so many families, they had a foot in both camps. Your namesake, Lord Ivo, the Duke's younger son, was in the Protector's army. He must have been the reason that Cromwell didn't head south. So fortunate.'

'Fortunate indeed,' said the Duke without enthusiasm. Mrs Cash looked at him in surprise.

'But without ever relinquishing the true faith, Your Grace,' said Father Oliver unctuously. 'The Maltravers are one of the very few aristocratic families that can claim an unbroken allegiance to Holy Mother Church since the Norman Conquest. To a convert like myself it is an extraordinary achievement. You are, if I may say so, Your Grace, a living link to a simpler time when the whole country was united in one faith.' The priest folded his hands at this last remark as if giving a blessing.

The Duke pushed his plate away with a hint of impatience and turned to Mrs Cash.

'You must forgive Father Oliver's enthusiasm, Mrs Cash. He is very attached to his subject.'

'Oh, I understand. We have a great respect for family history where I come from, even if our stories don't go back as far as yours.' She lifted her chin a little as she said this and for the first time she met the Duke's eyes. She stared at him coldly. He might feel ambivalent about his ancestry but she did not. She had not liked the way he had dismissed her proud family history as colonial pretension.

The Duke saw the annoyance in her face and smiled at her, a charming smile that made him look much younger.

'My father used to call himself a link in the chain. I suppose we all have our chains, Mrs Cash.'

Mrs Cash gave a dignified little nod. 'Yes indeed, Duke. And now if you will excuse me, I must go and see Cora.' She rose and the men got to their feet. The Duke walked over to the door and held it open for her.

'I hope Miss Cash will soon be able to join us downstairs. I am looking forward to meeting her properly.' He sounded sincere and Mrs Cash gave him another nod. Perhaps he was, after all, interested in her daughter.

'Cora is not the kind of girl to stay in bed for a moment longer than she has to. But I will decide when she is ready to get up.' Having asserted her maternal rights, she swept past the Duke towards the great staircase.

On her way up to Cora's room, Mrs Cash walked through a gallery lined with pictures of the Maltravers family. She stopped in front of the Second Duke, resplendent in blue satin with long dark curls falling over his lace collar. He was framed by a great damask curtain and behind that the ramparts of Lulworth. At his feet were two brown dogs lying on silk cushions with gold tassels. His face had a melancholy cast, his eyes were a little too moist and the lips a little too full for Mrs Cash's taste, but the man in the picture had a look she knew well: the complete indifference of inherited position. It was something she saw rarely in New York but she recognised it instantly; it was the quality she herself most aspired to. She knew that unlike her hall of mirrors or the cedar-lined yacht, this was not something that could be acquired or even reproduced. It had to develop over time, like the patina on bronze. It was a coating that meant you had no doubts at all about your place in the world or concern about the world's perception of you. Mrs Cash knew that she gave a good imitation of this indifference, but as she looked at the Second Duke she was aware that her celebrated composure did not have the authenticity of this long-dead aristocrat standing quietly but splendidly in the centre of his world. She wondered if Cora's children would ever gaze at the world with such serene lack of interest.

She put out a finger and ran it over the gilded moulding of the picture frame, caressing its baroque curlicues.

It came up black with dust.

CHAPTER 7

Bows and Arrows

CORA STAYED IN HER ROOM FOR THREE DAYS. ON THE fourth the doctor said she was well enough to get up. The Duke hadn't been to see her since that first day, and she had been forced to listen to her mother's interminable accounts of his attentiveness as a host. But he had not been attentive to her. For an instant, Cora wondered if the Duke might actually prefer her mother's company, but this thought was dispelled when she looked at herself in the cheval glass. She was wearing her prettiest evening gown, pale green silk with silver embroidery on the bodice. She had made Bertha lace her even more tightly than usual, so that her waist appeared to vanish beneath the confection of lace and silk above. The diamond drops in her ears sparkled against the warm brown of her hair. She pinched her cheeks and bit her lips to give her face some colour. The Duke, of course, had not seen her looking like this, at her best. It was possible that he had not quite taken in the extent to which she, Cora Cash, was as beautiful as she was rich.

'What do you think, Bertha? Do I look well enough to go downstairs?'

Bertha did not even look up from the petticoat she was folding.

'I think you know the answer to that question already, Miss Cora, judging by the way you've been gazing at yourself in that mirror.'

'Yes, but sometimes I look at myself and all I see is the bump in my nose and the mole on my neck. I admit that tonight I can see other things as well but if I can see things so differently, then maybe other people do too.'

'I think the other people will think you look just fine, Miss Cora. No one is going to be looking at your bump.' Bertha straightened the folds of the petticoat with a snap.

'So you can see it? The bump? You know, if it wasn't there, I would have a perfect classical profile. I wish I could just shave it off. Mother has a friend who had paraffin wax injected into the bridge of her nose to make it perfectly straight. Perhaps I should do that. It's awful to think that I could be really beautiful if it weren't for that one little thing.'

'Don't forget the mole on your neck, Miss Cora, and that scar on your knee you got falling off your bicycle.'

'Oh, but no one can see the scar on my knee!'

Bertha was now threading a satin ribbon through the eyelet edging of a cambric chemise. She looked up at Cora for a moment with a gaze so steady that Cora was forced to laugh, even if it was a little uncertainly. They both knew how she had come by that scar. Teddy Van Der Leyden had been teaching her to ride a bicycle. He had been running along beside her, steadying the saddle, and then he had let go. She hadn't noticed at first and had sailed along freely, but then she had looked around, expecting to find him. Realising that she was cycling unaided, she had promptly fallen off, skinning her knee. She had cried then, more from the humiliation than the pain. Teddy had laughed at her tears, which had made them come even faster. Finally he had taken pity on her and had whispered into her ear, 'Get back on the bike now, Cora. You can do it. Don't you want to be free?' And he had given her his handkerchief to bind up her knee and had helped her up as, still trembling, she got back on her machine and slowly wobbled off. She had been scared at first but then suddenly it all came together and she pedalled faster, feeling the breeze lifting her hair and drying her tears. Teddy had been right, she did feel free. When she rode out she had to be accompanied by a groom but there were no rules about bicycles – now she could simply pedal away. She realised that Teddy had seen and understood this and she had liked the feeling of being noticed.

Cora shivered impatiently. 'I know you think I am being ridiculous but it would be awful to think I was beautiful if I really wasn't. I would be no better than those dreadful English girls who think they are so fetching when really they look like simpering carthorses with their flaring nostrils and their bulging eyes.'

'And they ain't as rich as you neither, Miss Cora,' Bertha said.

'Then why hasn't the Duke been to see me for three whole days? He must know that I have been bored to tears up here. Even Mother has hardly been to see me. Out of sight, out of mind.'

'I'm thinking that the Madam seems a lot like her old self since we've been here. She ain't bored to tears. She was wearing that diamond necklace with the sapphire drops the master gave her. I ain't seen her wearing that since—'

Cora held up her hand. She hated to have that night mentioned. Especially now. That evening in Newport had started so well, she and Teddy had come so close to an understanding – and then it had all changed from hope to disaster in a second. Even now when Bertha accidentally singed her fringe with the curling tongs, she would feel bile rising up into her throat as she remembered the terrible stench of her mother's burning hair. If it hadn't been for Teddy, she thought, her mother could have died.

She remembered how when the bandages were removed, Mrs Cash had asked for a mirror. Cora had brought her the tortoise-shell-backed hand mirror that had once belonged to Marie Antoinette. Her hand had trembled as she handed it over, she didn't want to see her mother's reaction to her ravaged face, but Mrs Cash had not flinched when she saw what the flames had done. Mrs Cash had looked at this unfamiliar countenance with the same glacial indifference as she might regard one of her husband's operatic 'enthusiasms'. Apart from the careful dressing of tulle and net she employed to disguise the livid side of her face, Mrs Cash made no concessions to her misfortune and such was the control she had over herself and others that when strangers met Mrs Cash, it was her eyes that held them, not the mystery behind the veil. Later they might wonder and make discreet inquiries, to which they received whispered replies: 'Some kind of accident at her daughter's coming-out ball, her head a ball of flame, Cash's comet, the New York wags are calling it. Teddy Van Der Leyden is the only reason she wasn't fried to a crisp.' A sad story but no one who had encountered the adamantine surface of Mrs Cash's composure would have had the temerity to feel for her anything resembling pity.

Her mother had never mentioned the scene she had witnessed on the terrace before her dress had caught fire, and Cora saw no reason to bring it up. It was possible that the shock of the conflagration had affected Mrs Cash's recall of the minutes preceding the accident, possible but not likely; Cora suspected that her mother remembered every detail but had chosen to put her memories aside as long as it suited her to do so. It was wrong that Teddy's part in saving her life had also been put to one side, but Cora could only feel relief that her mother had decided not to blame her. It was hard enough to face the possibility that it had been her fault. She could not help feeling that her kissing Teddy had been the spark that had started her mother's blaze.

The dinner gong sounded and Cora allowed herself one more glance in the mirror. Perhaps the bump wasn't so very prominent on her left side if she pulled the curls of her fringe down a little. Was the green silk really appropriate, or was it just a little too frivolous? Perhaps she should change into something more interesting. Something that suggested that she could be fascinating as well as decorative. The blue velvet with the square neckline that Teddy had once said made her look like a Renaissance duchess, Isabella Gonzaga. But did she want to look like a duchess?

The blue or the green? The Old World or the New? Cora didn't know. A week ago she could have made the decision without a qualm but now ... She turned to Bertha in appeal, but the maid was standing by the door.

'All right, I'm coming. Don't look so cross, I'm the one who is going to be late, not you.'

'And when do you think I get my dinner, Miss Cora? You may not have worked up an appetite lying in that bed, but I'm famished. The sooner you're downstairs sparkling at the Duke, the sooner I can eat.'

Cora suspected that English servants would not talk to their mistresses so frankly; indeed, Mrs Cash would have been horrified if she had heard the exchange, but that was precisely why Cora put up with her maid's tartness.

As she walked down the wide steps, the train of green silk and lace carefully looped over her left hand, she found the house both grander and more intimate than she had imagined. She passed any number of ducal portraits on the stairs but she stopped when she saw an arrangement of small detailed oils of grey lurcher-like dogs, clearly beloved pets. Beneath each canvas was the name, date and motto of the animal. 'Campion' in the lower left-hand corner had died only three months previously. She wondered if the animal described as '*semper fidelis*' had belonged to the Duke. She hoped her mother had not seen them; Cora could imagine only too well how much she would enjoy the notion of dynastic pets.

At the end of the staircase lay two double-height intricately carved oak doors flanked by a pair of perfectly matched footmen who flung them open as Cora approached. As an American heiress, Cora had grown up under high ceilings but even so she could not help but be impressed by the scale of the vaulted gallery, running the whole length of the south front. Cora could see the Duke and other guests standing by the carved chimney piece in the middle of the room at least forty feet away. The Duke was in the middle of a story when Cora walked into the room and as all the listeners were straining to catch every word that he delivered in his low voice, no one looked round. Cora paused. Normally she would feel no qualms about joining a group in a strange house. Normally she would stride into the throng, her hand outstretched, her bright American charm at full tilt. But something about the way the Duke commanded the attention of his half-dozen listeners, including Cora's mother, made her hesitate. Cora could not hear what he was saying but she could tell that this was not just polite attention on the part of the listeners, the Duke held his little audience in thrall. A moment later, he reached a hiatus in his story, looked up and caught sight of Cora. He raised an eyebrow, and then resumed his tale. She saw him lift his arm and swing it down suddenly, and she heard the word 'chukka' – he was talking about polo apparently. But why was he ignoring her?

Cora stood like a pistachio ice melting in her mint frills and Brussels lace. She had spent the last three days imagining the moment when she would reveal herself in her full splendour to the Duke. She was expecting that look in his eyes that she had seen so many times before in other people, the look that meant they were not seeing her but all that she represented, the marble palaces, the yachts, the gilded hummingbirds. She could not blame them for this, for she was all these things. Would she be Cora Cash if she wasn't dressed by Worth, and surrounded by luxury? Of course she was as pretty and amusing as any of her contemporaries, but Cora knew that it was her money that produced that little pocket of hush which preceded her whenever she walked into a strange room. It was her money that triggered all those sideways covert glances, the conversations that faltered when she approached. No one was unaffected by the money – even Teddy who did not want it had let it push him away.

So she had come fully prepared for the brief moment of disappointment when she would see the Duke shaping himself around the bulk of her inheritance. She was almost looking forward to seeing him moulded by its weight. It had not occurred to her that he could be indifferent.

She could feel a cold rivulet of sweat running down the inside of her corset and the heat of a flush burning its way across her chest. Could she steal away back to her room? She did feel rather faint. But the Duke had seen her, he would know that she was retreating. Stiffly and without any of her usual jauntiness, Cora advanced into the room, her steps making the wide oak floorboards creak as if in pain. She forced herself to smile as if she had noticed nothing amiss.

And then she heard her name being announced by the butler. 'Miss Cash, Your Grace.'

And all at once Maltravers broke off from his story and advanced towards her as if seeing her for the first time.

'Miss Cash! How delightful to see that you have recovered so ... fully.' The Duke's gaze took in the green silk, the Brussels lace, the artfully curled fringe, the perfectly matched string of pinky pearls, the faint flush beneath them. Had he really ignored her just now? thought Cora. Did she really have to be announced by a flunkey before he could acknowledge her in his own house? This was a degree of formality at which Cora, despite growing up in the codified atmosphere of New York and Newport, could only marvel.

She did her best to give Maltravers her most charming smile. She did not want him to see her confusion. Whether his hesitation was deliberate or not, she would not give him the satisfaction of watching her falter. He was being perfectly attentive now but she could see nothing, not a dent in his manner, that suggested he knew that she could buy him and everything he possessed and hardly notice it.

He was leading her into the circle around the fire, introducing her to the assembled company as the miraculously restored, the indomitable Miss Cash. His tone was light and if there was a touch of irony, it was lost on Mrs Cash, who accepted this praise of her daughter's powers of endurance as a fitting tribute to her talents as a parent. Cora realised that Bertha had been correct in her assessment of her mother's return to form. Mrs Cash was looking particularly regal in a gown of purple brocade with gold passementerie. A diamond and sapphire parure sparkled at her neck, her wrists, and her undamaged ear lobe. Cora did not need to look at the other women in the room to know that none of them could match her mother's display. In this world of hidden meanings and unspoken rules, there was no mistaking Mrs Cash's value. Her mother's queenly mien was emphasised by the priest at her side, who listened to her every word with all the attentiveness of a cardinal.

Cora found herself talking to the Hon. Reggie Greatorex, the younger son of Lord Hallam, a young man in his late twenties who had been at Cambridge with the Duke.

'Maltravers tells me you brought over your own horse from America and that it puts all our domestic animals to shame. It really is most unfair of you Americans, Miss Cash, to outclass us so effortlessly. You come over here so magnificently equipped that I fear we have nothing to offer you, except of course our undying devotion.'

Cora laughed, she had had years of practice at dealing with the Reggies of this world. Polished, blond and, she suspected, idle, Reggie probably knew more about the exact magnitude of her inheritance than she did.

'Oh, come, come, Mr Greatorex, are you telling me that your

family can't trace their lineage all the way back to William the Conqueror? Something that you know full well we newly minted Americans can never match.'

Reggie replied in kind. 'Oh, I would trade all the Ethelreds and Athelstans in the Greatorex lineage – Saxons being, you know, so much smarter than mere Normans – if I could belong to a nation of such magnificent creatures!'

'Yes, but you look down on us all the same. I have read your Mr Wilde. What is it he says? American girls are as good at concealing their parents as English women are at concealing their past.'

Reggie threw up his hands in mock horror. 'Not my Mr Wilde, I can assure you, my dear Miss Cash. Not only is he Irish, but he is an Oxford man. Moreover, he is quite wrong. Who would want to conceal your mother, for instance? She is quite magnificent. She would give any of our duchesses a run for their money.'

Cora looked at him, suddenly curious.

'Do you think so? I've never met an English duchess. Are they very formidable?'

'The old guard perhaps, but it is quite fashionable these days to be charming rather than regal. There are duchesses about who can be positively kittenish. Ivo's mama, for instance, has quite the girlish laugh.'

Cora stopped short. 'The Duke's mother? Is she here?' She wondered if she had made some terrible faux pas by not recognising her.

Reggie laughed at her confusion, 'Don't worry, if Duchess Fanny were present, you would know it. Although I'm surprised she isn't here. Maybe she doesn't know that Ivo has stumbled across an American heiress. You are an heiress, Miss Cash, aren't you? I just assume that all Americans are rich these days, though I suppose that can't be true. Judging by the jewels your mama is sporting, it must be in your case.' He opened his blue eyes so wide to show how dazzled he was by the Cash fortune that Cora laughed.

'But where is the Duchess? Doesn't she live with her son?'

'Oh no. Duchess Fanny married again as soon as she could after Wareham died. Not ready for the dower house.' Reggie looked around to make sure the Duke was out of earshot and then said in a lower voice, 'Ivo didn't like it one bit but then he's a moody cove, I don't blame the Double Duchess for taking off.'

Cora looked at him curiously. 'You are very indiscreet, Mr Greatorex.' Her tone was light but she was testing him.

Reggie simply smiled. 'Do you really think so? It must be you drawing all these secrets out of me. Normally I am the soul of discretion, but I feel the urge to confide in you.'

'I am flattered. I wish I had something interesting to tell you in return.'

'Well . . .' He narrowed his eyes a little. 'You could tell me how you got here. Ivo hasn't had company at Lulworth since he got the title, and then this morning I got a telegram summoning me to a house party.'

'That's no secret. I was hunting with the Myddleton and I got lost.' Cora was not about to tell her new friend about Mr Cannadine and his tattoos. 'I was in a wood and something startled my horse, I must have hit my head on a branch. The Duke found me unconscious. When I woke up I was here in the house.'

'A damsel in distress, eh. Well, lucky old Ivo.'

'Oh, but surely I was the lucky one. If the Duke hadn't found me, who knows what might have happened,' Cora protested, but Reggie looked at her assessingly.

'No, I still say he's the lucky one,' and then he smiled and Cora smiled back, showing her small white teeth. After the strange encounter with the Duke, it was reassuring to find herself in familiar territory. She was used to being admired by charming young men. Reggie clearly understood her value even if the Duke did not.

Mrs Cash could sense a flirtation at a hundred paces. She beckoned to her daughter with a hand glittering with sapphires.

'Excuse me, Mr Greatorex, I am being summoned.'

'You must go. I believe your mother is about to give me a look and I will certainly crumple.'

Cora moved over to the chimney piece supported by carved caryatids whose proportions echoed those of Mrs Cash.

'Cora, I want you to meet Father Oliver. He is writing a history of the Maltravers family. Such a fascinating subject, so much tradition, so much self-sacrifice. I think it is just the sort of thing that you like.' She raised her voice slightly so that the Duke, who was standing close by, could not fail to hear her. 'My daughter is a great reader. She has had every kind of tutor and has outdistanced them all. You must ask the Duke to show you his library, Cora.'

This had the desired effect of making it impossible for the Duke not to be drawn into the conversation.

'As to the library, I am afraid that Father Oliver is a guide far more suited to a lady of Miss Cash's intellectual gifts than myself. My brother was the scholar in the family. He was fascinated by the vicissitudes of the Maltravers – it was Guy who asked Father Oliver here. Guy was very proud of our recusant status. He felt that the Maltravers family's refusal to accept the tenor of the times and leave the Church of Rome was proof that we were somehow of a finer moral weave than others.' He smiled wryly.

'I think if Guy had not been the eldest son, he would have followed his true vocation and become a priest. When we were children we were always playing Crusades. He was the Knight Templar and I was always the Saracen. Guy would fire his infernal toy arrows at me through the arrow slits until I surrendered. I always did surrender, of course.' The Duke halted. Cora was about to make some droll comment but realised with a sudden hot gust of embarrassment that Guy the older brother must be dead. She looked at the Duke, but he had recovered himself and addressed her with exaggerated gallantry.

'So, Miss Cash, you must let Father Oliver show you the library, but I will show you the best places to play Crusaders!'

'Do you still have the bow and arrows?' Cora responded in the same tone.

'Of course, you never know when you might have to repel marauders.' The Duke smiled at Cora when he said this but she heard the warning there. She felt his words like a slap. She was there by pure accident, after all; how could he imply that he was under siege? She wondered if she could persuade her mother to leave in the morning.

The butler appeared to announce that dinner was served and Reggie, smiling and uncomplicated, took her into dinner.

Cora found herself seated between Reggie and Father Oliver. The Duke had her mother on one side and Lady Briscoe, a stout lady with an ear trumpet who was evidently a neighbour, on the other. Reggie flirted with Cora over the fish; Father Oliver told her about the Reformation over the entrée. The food was neither plentiful nor particularly appetising. As one of the footmen bent over her to serve her, a large white globule fell from his powdered hair on to her plate. She looked at it astonished. The footman gasped in horror and snatched the plate away. Reggie, who had seen the whole thing, winked at her.

'That's the problem of staying in a house without a mistress. The servants can get awfully slack. Things were a good deal sprucer when Duchess Fanny was here.'

'I can't say I envy the future Duchess if her duties consist of making sure the footmen powder their hair properly. I think it is a ridiculous habit anyway. Why make the servants adopt a fashion that their masters gave up a century ago at least. I think there is something of the tumbrils about it.' Cora's tone was rather strident. She had conveniently forgotten that her mother's own footmen had equally antediluvian hairstyles.

'Oh, Miss Cash, what a modern girl you are. But I think you underestimate how much we English enjoy our traditions. I'm sure that the footman takes great pride in his snowy white hair and knee breeches. The whole point of being a footman is to look magnificently *ancien régime*. They have enormous cachet in the servants' hall and get paid according to their height. Do you really want to bring these glorious creatures down to earth by forcing them to go unpowdered in drab broadcloth?'

'I just think they might prefer it.'

The footman in question was handing Cora some gravy. She turned to him and said, 'What is your name?'

The footman blushed and said, 'Thomas, miss.'

'Can I ask you a question, Thomas?'

'Certainly, miss,' he said with obvious reluctance.

'Do you enjoy powdering your hair every day? How would you like it if you could wear your hair naturally?'

The footman looked at the floor and muttered, 'Very much, miss.' Cora looked at Reggie triumphantly, but then the servant continued, 'It would mean I had been made up to butler. Now if you'll excuse me, miss, I need to finish serving.'

Cora nodded, feeling not a little foolish. But Reggie was too tactful to press home his advantage and changed the subject deftly.

As the meal drew to a close, the Duke looked at Mrs Cash and said, 'In the absence of a hostess, Mrs Cash, I wonder if you would be so kind as to lead the ladies to the drawing room. I apologise for the imposition but it will only be for one more day. My mother will be arriving the day after tomorrow with my step-sister Sybil.'

'Oh, how delightful, Duke, I would so much like to meet them, but I fear that Cora and I cannot impose upon your hospitality any longer. As you can see, she is quite recovered and we really should return to Sutton Veney.' Mrs Cash's words were more emphatic than her tone.

The Duke took up the challenge.

'But my dear Mrs Cash, my mother is hoping so much to meet you and your daughter. She will be quite disappointed not to find you here after she has made the journey from Conyers. And to be honest, Mrs Cash, my mother's disappointment is not an easy thing to endure. Unless you have some very pressing engagement, perhaps I can prevail on you to stay for another week or so. I would so much like to show Miss Cash more of Lulworth than the wood where she met her accident.'

Although there had been no doubt in Mrs Cash's mind about her intention to stay, the Duke's last remark was reassuring. She took it as a declaration of interest and looked over at Cora to see whether she had registered this too. But Cora was talking to the young man on her left, altogether too animatedly in Mrs Cash's view, and had not heard. Mrs Cash cleared her throat and rose to her feet.

'In that case, Duke, you leave me no choice but to accept your very kind invitation; I would hate to be the cause of a duchess's disappointment. I shall write to Lord Bridport tonight. Ladies, shall we?'

The Duke rose to his feet to open the door. As Cora passed him, he looked at her and smiled, this time without reservation.

'You must allow me to show you over Lulworth, when you feel well enough, Miss Cash.'

'I would like that very much, but I insist on having the bows and arrows.' Cora picked up her train and followed her mother up the stairs.

As the footmen cleared the rest of the dishes from the table and brought in the port, Father Oliver stood up and bowed to the other two men.

'If Your Grace will excuse me, I would like to get back to the Fourth Duke. Such a devout man, quite an inspiration. Goodnight, gentlemen.'

The Duke rolled his eyes as the well-fed figure of the priest left the room. 'He has the zeal of the convert. Takes it all very seriously. Guy and he were very thick.' He paused and Reggie moved up to sit next to him. Silently, the Duke passed him the decanter. The room was empty now apart from the two men.

The only noises were the crackle of the fire in the stone fireplace and the tapping of the Duke's fingers as he inflicted an invisible rhythm on the polished surface of the table. Finally he spoke.

'Thank you for coming down at such short notice. I promise the sport will be tolerable, if nothing else.'

'It's been too long, Ivo. I haven't seen you since . . .' Reggie stopped. The last time he had been at Lulworth was for Guy's funeral.

Ivo looked at him, reading his thoughts. 'It was a year ago this week. Feels longer.'

'Is that why the Duchess is coming?'

'She would like me to think so, but she only sent the telegram yesterday.' The Duke did an imitation of his mother's breathy tones. 'I felt such an urge to be with you.'

Reggie nodded towards the door. 'The Americans?'

'Of course.'

'But how did she know?'

'At first I suspected Father Oliver of writing to her, but actually it was Charlotte. She was at Sutton Veney when the accident happened and felt that Mother ought to know.'

'And how is Charlotte? I have hardly seen her since she married Beauchamp. Never cared for him much at school. Used to keep a diary full of his ghastly "observations". Still can't understand why Charlotte accepted him.'

'Isn't it obvious?'

'But Beauchamp, of all people. I mean, he collects *china*.'

'He loves beautiful things and Charlotte has always liked to be admired.'

'But we all admired her, Ivo.'

'But none of us had the means to display her properly.' The Duke's fingers, which had not stopped moving to their invisible rhythm, suddenly hit a fortissimo chord and the glasses rattled.

There was another silence. Both men drained and refilled their glasses.

'Quite a thing, finding Miss Cash like that,' Reggie said, looking at his friend speculatively. 'Something of a windfall, you might say.'

Another rattle from the glasses. Finally Ivo said, 'Well, I couldn't very well leave her there. I had no idea that she came with all this . . . this stuff.' Ivo picked up a silver coaster and sent it flying down the table. Both men watched it as it circled and slowly grew still.

'Do you think she knew who the wood belonged to?'

'I did wonder, especially after I met the mother, but I don't think the daughter is a schemer. No, I think Miss Cash's arrival at Lulworth was entirely accidental.'

'And?' Reggie let the monosyllable hang between them.

'Oh, don't be absurd. You're as bad as my mother. Miss Cash is American . . .' Ivo's voice trailed away in disdain.

'And spectacularly rich.'

'As Mrs Cash never stops reminding me.' Ivo filled his glass again and turned on his friend. 'Have you taken a fancy to Miss Cash then, Reggie? I saw you whispering to her at dinner. Poor Sybil will be heartbroken.'

Reggie laughed. 'I'm afraid that Miss Cash has no interest in me. But I like her, Ivo. As windfalls go, you could do a lot worse.'

But Ivo was looking up at the portrait of his mother that had been painted at the time of her first marriage. Blonde and creamy, she gazed serenely down at her son. He raised his glass to the portrait and said with sardonic clarity, 'To the Double Duchess.'

Reggie realised that his friend was drunk. He wasn't sure that he wanted to hear Ivo talk about the Duchess. Ivo had always been his mother's favourite and their relationship had been relaxed and mutually admiring. Mother and son were never more aware of their own beauty and charm than when in each other's company. But that was before his mother's remarriage. She had been barely out of mourning when the marriage took place. There were those who would have enjoyed a spell of disapproval, but that would have been a luxury when the Duchess was so charming, so hospitable and so close to Marlborough House. But if society was prepared to overlook the Duchess's haste, her son, it seemed, was not.

Reggie repeated his friend's toast but without the ironical inflection.

Ivo caught the reproof and got to his feet. 'Time to join the ladies, I think, before Mrs Cash starts rehanging the pictures.'

In the servants' hall, Bertha accepted a glass of madeira from Mrs Softley the housekeeper. She was grateful for the warm length of it spreading through her chest. Lulworth was a good deal colder than Sutton Veney. There she had had the occasional sight of Jim to keep her warm. Here there was nothing to heat the chilly corridors.

The green baize door swung open with a clatter as the footmen came in carrying trays loaded with plates and cutlery.

As soon he got through the door, Thomas the footman burst out, 'Did you hear what the American girl said to me when I was serving her? Said did I like having my hair powdered, like I was some kind of performing monkey. It's not correct.'

Thomas's handsome face was red with emotion. The other footman laughed.

'You should be careful what you say, Thomas, she might be your new Duchess. His Grace is taking her round the house tomorrow. Do you think he's going to show her the holes in the roof?'

The housekeeper frowned and got to her feet. 'Thomas, Walter, that's quite enough from you. Are the ladies still in the drawing room?'

'Finishing up, Mrs Softley'.

She turned to Bertha. 'In that case, Miss Cash, you will be wanting to go upstairs to your mistress.' She paused and gave the keys on her belt a little shake. 'Thomas and Walter are foolish boys. They mean no disrespect.'

Bertha thanked the housekeeper and began the long climb to Cora's room. The stone flags were cold and unforgiving under her feet.

She wondered what kind of mood Cora would be in. She wouldn't tell her what the footmen had said. Miss Cora would be quite put out to think that in the servants' hall her destiny had already been decided. She liked to make up her own mind. But as Bertha climbed the carpetless back staircase, feeling the chill draughts from the uncurtained windows, she wondered if this was to be her new home.

The next morning a thick sea fog drifted in over Lulworth, muffling its towers and crenellations and concealing the shining view that gave even the dingiest rooms a splendid point. Cora felt the damp chill as she opened her window. She had hoped to take Lincoln out, to ride away some of the uncertainties that hung around her like cobwebs. But this was not weather to be riding in unknown country. She told Bertha to put away her habit and put on a morning dress of dove-grey wool with black frogging. It was as modest an outfit as she possessed. She remembered Reggie's eyes flicking over her mother's jewelled magnificence the night before.

There was no one about apart from the odd housemaid. At Sutton Veney the ladies of the house had gone to the morning room after breakfast to write letters and gossip but in this house there were no ladies to join. Cora knew she should look for her mother but she did not feel ready for the conversation that she guessed would follow.

Retracing her steps from the night before, she found herself again in the long gallery where the Duke had seen her and not seen her the night before. The stone walls reflected the light from the sea, bathing the room in a pearly haze. There was no fire lit and Cora could smell the chalky sweat of the limestone. She sat down in one of the mullioned embrasures and looked out at the grey sky. The fog had suppressed everything, even the sound of the sea was muffled.

Cora was looking up at the carved vault of the arch, trying to make out the carved motif at the apex, when she heard music. Someone was playing the piano. She walked to the end of the gallery in the direction of the sound. Cora stood for a moment and listened. It was dark choppy music, full of false starts and minor chords, lacy pianissimo passages and startling crescendos. Cora could play the piano well enough, she had the young lady's repertory of Strauss waltzes and Chopin nocturnes, but she knew that whoever was playing was in a different class. It was not just the technical difficulty of the piece, she had the feeling that the player was completely submerged in the music.

A set of chords faded away into silence. Cora pushed open the door a fraction. The room was another stone chamber – like the gallery it seemed older and more austere than the rest of the house. In the centre of the room under a narrow arched window was a grand piano and at the keyboard sat the Duke. He was frowning down at the keyboard as if he was trying to remember something. Then he started to play. Cora recognised the piece, it was a Beethoven sonata – but she had never heard it played like this. The opening was allegro con brio, but in the Duke's hands it was not just fast, it was dangerous. The Duke had taken off his jacket and had rolled up his shirtsleeves. From where she was standing, Cora could see his bare forearms, the tendons stretching and tensing as he reached up and down the keyboard. She stood motionless, not sure whether she wanted him to look up and discover her. Was she listening or intruding? This was private music and yet she could not bear to look away. She was fascinated by the way he swayed towards the keyboard as if he was embracing the instrument, and his complete absorption. He was, she felt sure, in another place entirely. The long glissando passage at the end of the first movement finished and he looked up for a moment. At first he looked straight through her and then she saw him register her presence with a wary smile.

She said nothing, she did not know whether she should apologise or praise his playing.

In the end he spoke first. 'Do you know the piece?'

'It's Beethoven, isn't it? My music master used to play it for me, but never like that.' Cora was being quite truthful. She was amazed that the same piece of music could sound so different.

'The "Waldstein". Beethoven was in love with Countess Waldstein, but there was no question of her marrying a musician. He wrote this for her but dedicated it publicly to her brother. He was almost completely deaf when he composed it.' He looked down at the keyboard and played a passage where the music seemed to grope for a resolution. 'Can you hear how he seems to be looking for something? Some satisfaction?'

Cora was about to say how sad it was that Beethoven never heard his own piece but in the end stayed silent. She realised that this was the obvious thing to say and she did not want to appear obvious. She knew that she was here on sufferance. What she had taken at first for the music room was clearly the Duke's personal sanctum. There were piles of books on the window ledges and a desk at the far end covered with papers. There were no chairs or sofas apart from an uncomfortable-looking metal campaign bed.

'You play very well,' she said.

He shrugged. 'You're too kind. I play adequately, that's all. But I play very well for a man, certainly.'

Cora smiled. He was right, she had been surprised at the Duke's playing at all. In her experience, the drawing-room piano as opposed to the concert hall instrument was an exclusively female instrument.

'My mother taught me to play when I was very young. She had no daughter and she needed someone to play duets with. She would summon me after dinner and we would perform for her guests. The house was always full then, I got a lot of practice.' He started playing a Brahms lullaby with exaggerated sweetness. 'This was my finale. I played my own lullaby and then I was despatched upstairs to bed.'

'Do you still play duets?'

'No. As I grew up, we could never keep the same time. My mother always wants everything to be charming. She is all about effect, while I simply like to play.' He pulled his finger down the keyboard in a soft glissando. He looked up at her. 'And you, Miss Cash, do you like to play?' The question ended in a minor arpeggio.

'Yes,' she said firmly, 'I do.' If there was challenge in his question, Cora would meet it.

'Well then, what about a little Schubert?' He stood up and rummaged among the piles of music on the floor until he found the piece he was looking for. He set it up on the piano and gestured to her to sit beside him on the stool. She walked towards him slowly, conscious that she had not played properly since leaving Newport, hoping that the piece he had chosen would not be too difficult.

The Duke gestured towards the music and said, 'Which part would you like?'

Cora looked at the music, and felt her heart pounding in panic. The semiquavers exploded across the page. He certainly hadn't chosen something easy. The lower part looked marginally calmer so she pointed towards it.

As he sat down next to her on the seat, she felt herself tense. But he was careful not to touch her. He spread his fingers out across the keys and she did the same.

'When you're ready, Miss Cash.'

Cora nodded and began. The piece started cantabile sostenuto in her part for a few bars and then the treble part came in with the melody. She played softly at first, hoping to muffle her mistakes, but as she grew more confident, her side of the piece met the melody in the upper register and suddenly they were playing together – their hands weaving round each other in the elaborate dance of the music. At one point the Duke's left hand passed over her right and she felt the heat from his palm cross hers like a flame. But she could not afford to be distracted; to play the piece 'adequately' needed all Cora's reserves of concentration and skill. The Schubert was just outside her level of competence but her desire not to fail meant that she was playing as well as she had ever done in her life. As the music reached the finale, there was a sequence of chords that were played in unison and to her surprise they played them in perfect synchronicity. Without thinking, she reached for the sostenuto pedal to hold down the final chord, only to find the Duke's foot already there. She pulled her foot away but he had felt the pressure and as they finished, he turned to her with a smile.

'I'm sorry I forgot to negotiate the pedals with you. It's been a long time since I played a duet.'

'And me. I've never played with anyone as good as you before.'

'Duets are not about individual skill but about the relationship between the two players. The whole must be more than the sum of the individual parts.'

'And were we?' Cora could not stop herself asking.

'It's perhaps too early to say entirely, but on the whole I think we will do very well. Shall we have a go at the second movement?'

But Cora knew she must retreat now. She did not want to play again and be found wanting.

'I think I have been lucky so far. I would like to practise before we play again.'

The Duke smiled. 'As you wish, Miss Cash. But as I say, I think we will do very well.'

As Cora left the room, she heard him start the 'Waldstein' sonata again. It was clearly a favourite piece. As she listened to him play, she remembered his remark about Beethoven looking for satisfaction.

CHAPTER 8

We Have a Rubens

*A*S AN UNDER-HOUSEMAID AT LULWORTH, Mabel Roe started her working day at five in the morning. It was still dark so she had to dress and wash herself by the light of last night's candle. Her hands were red and chapped, her knuckles swollen from years of scrubbing. It was not so cold this morning that she had to break the ice on the handbasin, but Mabel could see her breath issuing in frosty plumes across the unforgiving air of the attic bedroom.

Usually Mabel would linger in bed for a precious five minutes before getting up. But Iris had gone home for her mother's funeral, so there was no extra warmth in the bed to ward off the chill, no one to grumble with about the rigours of the day ahead. Still, Iris's absence meant that Mabel could spend more time than usual in front of the tiny square of mirror above the chest of drawers, adjusting her cap to sit becomingly on her thin brown hair. On the chair lay the thick brown holland apron that she wore in the morning while she was doing the fires, but Mabel picked up the light cotton apron that she wore in the afternoons and tied that round her waist. She wanted to look her best.

Mabel had been startled the first time she found the Duke in his dressing gown, sitting on the window seat, looking out to sea. When he had been Lord Ivo he had never been an early riser, except when he was hunting, but things were different now. Her job was to get the fires lit in the bedrooms without waking the occupants. Under-housemaids like Mabel were not meant to have anything to do with the 'family'. The housekeeper had told her that she must turn and face the wall if she met any of them in the corridor. To reveal that the Duke now woke with the lark would have given Mabel some status among her fellow house-maids, who discussed the family endlessly, but she had said nothing. This silent audience with the Duke was Mabel's talisman, the antidote to her aching knees and stinging hands. It had made her nervous at first to go through the lengthy ritual of cleaning out the ashes of the night before, polishing the grate and laying the new fire with His Grace sitting there so still. Once she had dropped the poker on to the marble hearth; the noise had been calam-itous, it felt like the loudest sound she had ever heard, but the Duke had hardly stirred.

He was there on the window seat this morning as usual. She wondered what he looked at so hard. There was nothing to see out there but the green hills leading down to the sea.

Mabel finished laying the fire, building a neat little pyramid of kindling that burst into obedient flame the moment she put a match to it. She gathered together all her tools – the stiff hearth brush, the tin of blacking, the matches – and put them back in her work box; she wiped her hands on her apron and stood up slowly, her knees cracking as she did.

The Duke said softly, 'Thank you, Mabel.'

Mabel very nearly dropped the ash bucket. She scraped her knees together in something like a curtsy and mumbled, 'Yer Grace.'

He had never spoken to her before, and yet he knew her name. She felt herself going scarlet and backed out of the room as speedily as she could. She stood in the corridor, her heart pounding and the palms of her hands clammy with sweat. She leant against the wall and closed her eyes. The Duke knew her name. She felt like a character in a *Peg's Paper* story. He had noticed her; surely this was the start of something.

Her reverie was interrupted by Betty who was coming from the Cash girl's bedroom.

'What you doing, Mabel?' she said in a fierce whisper. 'Don't you know the old Duchess is coming today and we've got to turn out those rooms this morning? If you don't get on you'll miss breakfast. This isn't the time to be daydreaming, and how come you're wearing your best apron and it's covered all over with smuts?'

Mabel looked down at the black smears on the white cotton. They were, she knew, impossible to remove.

Cora decided that she would go down to breakfast that morning before meeting the Duke for her tour of the house. As she walked along the corridor that led from her bedroom to the staircase, she saw a maid with a crumpled and soiled apron running in the other direction. Cora was enough of her mother's daughter to notice the dirty apron.

As she walked through Lulworth she was torn between her admiration of the pictures, the walnut furniture, the faded brocade curtains, objects which looked as if they had been always been there, and her awareness of a rank, musty smell that lingered here in the less frequented parts. Cora had grown up in a dust-free world that smelt of fresh flowers, furniture polish and wet varnish. Only rarely in her native country did she enter a building that was older than she was. But here she was surrounded by an unfamiliar odour, one she was too young and too American to recognise as a mixture of damp, decay and disappointment. She did notice the chill, though, and wondered that the Duke could bear to live in such a cold house.

He was not at breakfast. Cora ate alone and then decided that she would not wait on his whim; she would go to the stables and see Lincoln. She was walking down the immense flight of stone steps at the entrance of the house when she heard the Duke calling her name.

'Miss Cash, don't tell me you have forgotten our arrangement?'

The Duke had evidently been riding already, he was hatless and his cheeks were flushed from the cold.

'Not at all. I thought you must have found other business to attend to when I didn't see you at breakfast.'

'I went for a ride. Early morning is the best time for it. It clears my head for the rest of the day.'

'I envy you your freedom. I wish riding were such a carefree business for my sex. You can just jump on your horse and go. I, on the other hand, have to spend at least quarter of an hour being laced into my habit and then I have to find a groom to ride out with me, and in my experience no groom has ever wanted to ride at my pace.'

The Duke made her a bow. 'Miss Cash, I accept the challenge. I will ride out with you and I promise not to baulk at your pace, however reckless. If we break our necks, at least we shall do so together.'

Cora bridled at the implied criticism, she knew she was an excellent horsewoman. 'I assure you, Duke, I am not in the habit of falling off my horse. What happened the other day was completely out of character. Unfortunately the fall has destroyed my memory of the moments leading up to it, but I am sure that something quite untoward must have happened for me to lose control like that.'

'Perhaps you saw a ghost. Lulworth is full of them: headless cavaliers, wailing monks, medieval chatelaines rattling their ghostly keys. You won't find a housemaid who will go into the gallery after dark in case she bumps into the Grey Lady.'

'The Grey Lady?'

'One of my ancestors, Lady Eleanor Maltravers. It was in the Civil War. Our Civil War, we had one too ... The Maltravers were Royalists of course, but Eleanor fell in love with a neighbour's son who went to fight for Cromwell. When she was told that he had been killed at the battle of Marsden, she fell into such despair that she threw herself off the cliffs. Turned out that the boy she loved wasn't dead after all so she can't leave the house till she finds him.'

'And why is she grey?'

'Oh, because she started wearing grim Puritan clothes – to please her lover or to annoy her family, who's to say?' The Duke gave Cora a knowing smile that suggested she might know something about the latter situation.

Cora was wondering whether to smile back when two rangy grey dogs raced between them, yapping shrilly and jumping up on to Cora's skirts, leaving a pattern of dirty brown paw marks.

'Aloysius, Jerome, stop it at once.' The Duke spoke with an authority completely unlike his usual quiet tone. The dogs subsided instantly. 'I'm sorry about your skirt, Miss Cash. Would you like me to get a maid to sponge it down?'

Cora shook her head. 'No indeed. I want my tour. But I am curious about your dogs' names. Back home we call our dogs things like Spot or Fido. These must be very special animals to warrant such fancy names.'

The Duke leant down to one of the dogs and pulled its ears. 'The Maltravers have been breeding Lulworth lurchers for God knows how many generations but I think I am the first duke to name them after medieval popes.' He stood up and the dog ran lightly to the bottom of the steps. 'And now, Miss Cash, you shall have your tour.' He bowed to her and raised his hand in a mock flourish.

'Lulworth was originally built as a hunting lodge for Edward the Third. The long gallery, the dining room and the music room where you found me yesterday,' he gave her a half smile of recognition, 'were part of this original building. In 1315 he gave it to my ancestor Guy Maltravers as a reward for his services in the Hundred Years War. The front of the house and the great hall were built by my namesake Ivo, the First Duke. He was a favourite of James the First, who made him a duke and gave him the monopoly on sealing wax so he was able to build all this. Ivo had very good taste, he got Inigo Jones to do the designs. They ran out of money – the Civil War was very bad for the Maltravers – but with the Restoration things improved, except for poor Eleanor, and they were able to finish it. After that things went downhill rather. The Maltravers stayed Catholic when the rest of the country went Protestant so they spent a lot of time down here, praying. The family has only become smart again since my mother married into it. She had no intention of being a dowdy duchess. She spent a fortune on the place, put in the new servants' wing and built the station so that her smart friends could get here easily from London. Very energetic woman, my mother, she did more to Lulworth in the last twenty years than had been done in the last two hundred.' The Duke's voice trailed off. They were walking along a paved path that led up a small hill to the right of the house. At the top was an elegant white stone building. The Duke paused on the steps flanked by two weathered stone pillars.

'And this is the chapel, which as Father Oliver will have no doubt told you is the oldest consecrated Catholic site in continuous use in England. This chapel was built by the Fifth Duke who had a French wife who was very devout. She didn't like saying her prayers in the draughty medieval chapel, so she ordered her husband to build her something modern, and this is the result.' Ivo held open the grey painted door for Cora. As she walked past him, her hand brushed against his. It was the tiniest contact, as fleeting as a moth's wing brushing her cheek, but it sent a tremor through her arm. She gave a gasp and Ivo looked at her.

'It's beautiful, isn't it? A French bonbon in deepest Dorset.'

Cora nodded. The chapel was perfectly proportioned. The main body was circular. A gallery ran round the top beneath a domed ceiling painted with voluptuous saints and attendant cherubs. The walls were white, and the woodwork a pale greyish-green picked out in gold. The pews were upholstered in the same shade of velvet. There were two padded armchairs in the front row, with coronets and the ducal W embroidered on the backs. The altar was covered with a green velvet cloth decorated with elaborate gold embroideries. An ivory prie-dieu hung between two gold candlesticks. The overall effect was rich but graceful – rather, thought Cora, like the Duke himself.

Cora had never been in a Catholic church before. Catholicism was something she associated with the Irish maids at home. On Sunday mornings they would be taken in a shiny-faced, giggling bevy to Mass at the local Catholic church. The Irish girls always looked so excited, as if they were going to a ball rather than to a place of worship. Cora, who found attending the Episcopal church on Sunday mornings an ordeal only mitigated by the knowledge that of all the exquisite examples of the milliner's art on display, hers was undoubtedly the finest, had envied the maids their gleeful high spirits.

She tried not to stare as the Duke dipped his fingers into the stoup at the entrance of the church and knelt down and crossed himself. This automatic act of devotion surprised her. She wondered if he expected her to do likewise. But he got to his feet and walked towards her without constraint.

The Duke gestured towards the ducal chairs. 'Embroidered by Duchess Mathilde herself. Must have been rather reassuring to sew your own coronet when all your friends were losing their titles and even their heads. Her mother was one of Marie Antoinette's ladies-in-waiting. Her brother lost his head to La Guillotine.' The Duke gave a theatrical shiver.

Cora noticed that in the alcove behind the altar there was a rectangular patch that glowed whitely against the faded paint that surrounded it. She guessed that a picture, quite a large one, had hung there until quite recently

The Duke noticed the direction of her gaze. 'Yes, there should be a picture there. Rather a fine one actually, my father always said it was the finest Rubens in the country even if St Cecilia was a touch on the fleshy side.' He voice trailed into silence as if he had forgotten his reason for being there. His hands absentmindedly picked at the gold tassel hanging from the ducal cushion.

'We have a Rubens,' said Cora brightly. 'Mother bought it last year from Prince Pamphilij. She is very proud of it but I find it a little overpowering. But where is yours? I know Mother would love to compare them, although of course hers will be the superior.' She smiled but the Duke did not smile back.

'Not possible, I'm afraid. The Rubens was sold, along with a very pretty set of Fragonard panels that were part of Duchess Mathilde's dowry. My mother had some royal guests to entertain and the house needed to be brought up to scratch. My father was quite cut up.' He wrenched the tassel so hard that it broke off. 'But now, fortunately, she has married into another Rubens. I'm sure she will be only too happy to tell Mrs Cash about it.'

Cora felt her face burn. She thought of the picture gallery in Sans Souci and the faded outlines of past glory that its magnificence represented. She tried to imagine what it must be like to have to give up something because you needed the money. She saw that the Duke, too, was flushed and instinctively she put her hand on his arm in mute apology – for her lack of tact, for her Rubens, for underestimating him.

'You have every right now, Duke, to think of me as the worst kind of vulgar American, but I can tell you that while there is much – so much I don't know, I am a quick study. I never make the same mistake twice.'

Ivo said nothing. For a moment Cora thought he was about to shake her hand away but then he took it in his own, turning her palm upwards.

'What a crisp line of destiny you have.' He traced the line that tapered round the mound of her thumb with his finger. Cora felt as if her whole being was concentrated under his fingertip. 'You are going into an unblemished future, Cora. A bright, confident, American destiny. You will have no faded patches on your walls, no missing pictures. There is nothing you need to learn from me, unless of course you want to.' He hesitated and then slowly raised his eyes to look at her. Cora felt she could not meet his gaze; she stared hard at the ducal W embroidered by a dead French duchess, but she could not ignore his hand on hers and the warmth she felt in the cold morning.

At last she turned to him and then quickly before she lost heart she said, 'I would like to learn how to make you happy. I think I could, you know.' Cora could feel her heart beating, her face scarlet. She had spoken before she had a chance to think and yet she knew this was what she wanted.

Ivo raised her hand to his lips and kissed the soft white skin of her wrist. 'Is that really what you want, Cora? All this?'

This time she did not look away. 'If this is what makes you happy, then yes.'

She spoke more loudly than she had realised, and the bright ring of her voice hit the clear chill air of the chapel. Ivo looked at her so intently that she felt transparent, that he could see through her, but she had nothing to hide. And when she thought she could bear it no longer, he put his hand behind her head and put his mouth on hers. His lips tasted of honey and tobacco. It was not a tentative kiss.

Cora smelt the musky scent of his neck and ran her fingers through his springy curls. She felt the length of his body pressing against her through her clothes. His arm was round her waist, his mouth moved down to kiss the inch of neck that escaped from the high collar of her morning dress. And then he pulled away from her abruptly.

'But I am making an unwarranted assumption here.'

He stepped back, his eyes searching her face. Cora stood motionless. She saw the corner of his mouth twitch; was he going to laugh? Then he dropped on to his knees.

Ivo cleared his throat. 'Cora, will you do me the honour of accepting my hand in marriage?'

Cora looked down at him. She saw that the tips of his ears were red. This had come before she was ready, everything he did seemed to take her by surprise. Surely there should be more of a courtship, a period of mutual discovery and delicious anticipation. She remembered the long summer in Newport when Teddy had seemed to hover about her consciousness. She remembered the words he had whispered in her ear the day she had fallen off her bicycle. He had seemed to understand her, but he had not made her free. At least Ivo was offering that. She wondered if she was giving in too quickly And yet, and yet . . . that kiss had been too urgent to be contained for long. She wanted the sequel as much as she regretted the lost dance of courtship. And by marrying the Duke, she would at once dispatch her mother and the lingering burden of guilt that she had carried since that evening in Newport.

Not that Cora's thoughts were quite so cogent in the minute that she made the Duke wait, kneeling before her on the stone floor of the chapel; but those were the strands which swirled around in her head before resolving into the force that made her slowly but definitely reach out her hand to pull him to her.

'Yes,' she whispered into his coat. There were tears in her eyes. Tears for the speed of her surrender, tears for all the other futures there might have been. But then he kissed her again.

They only drew apart when the chapel bell started striking

eleven. The noise was so loud and unexpected that they both laughed, as if guilty at having been caught out.

'I suppose we should go back and speak to Mother.' Cora dragged out the last word.

'And will your mother approve?'

Cora smiled. 'I think it will be the first time that she and I will agree about my future. But what about your mother? How will she feel about your marrying an American girl?'

'Well that, my dear Cora, you are about to find out. She is coming here expressly to take charge of the situation. But we have forestalled her.' Ivo took Cora's arm formally and walked down the aisle with her out of the chapel. It was an oddly solemn moment until the lurchers, who had been waiting patiently on the steps, sensed the change of situation and began to bark and lick their hands.

CHAPTER 9

The Double Duchess

HE STATIONMASTER'S STIFF COLLAR WAS DIGGING into the back of his neck. It was new and so full of starch that he could only move his head by turning his whole body. He tried to put his finger between the hard fabric and his skin but the extra pressure only made the collar even more like a garrotte. He gave up and tried to stand as still as possible. He could only look straight ahead but he could hear the distant whistle of the train. He lowered his eyes to the red carpet that lay across the platform – a little threadbare in parts but he knew that the Duchess would be pleased with the attention. The red carpet had last been taken out when the Prince of Wales had come for the old Duke's funeral. The stationmaster wondered if the Duchess would remember; perhaps the red carpet had not been such a good idea after all. Was it too late to remove it? Yes, the train was seconds away from pulling in. The stationmaster turned ninety degrees so that he could face his former mistress.

Duchess Fanny looked out of the compartment window as the familiar gingerbread-house fretwork of Lulworth Halt slid into view. She had thought it might be amusing to make the station a little more *orné*, perhaps an Oriental pavilion or something with shells, but the Directors of the South Dorset Railway had been firm: stations were of a standard design and not subject to the whims even of duchesses. She had been quite put out, even mentioning it to the Prince. This had been a mistake. Bertie had looked bored, his heavy eyelids drooping and the corners of his mouth beginning to sag. Fanny had changed the subject swiftly; she could not afford to be tiresome.

Duchess Fanny had always known, even as a little girl, the importance of not being tiresome. She was the second oldest of four sisters, daughters of a bad-tempered Somerset squire whose moods were as terrifying as they were unpredictable. Fanny was her father's favourite. She, alone of her sisters, had noticed that when her father was growing irritable, he would start to twist the buttons of his waistcoat. As soon as she saw his fat red fingers pulling at the straining mother-of-pearl discs, she would shoo her sisters away and make a point of asking her father if she could bring him something from the kitchen – a hot toddy perhaps, with cinnamon, just the way he liked it. Her father had appreciated her tact, and so when his rich widowed sister had offered to bring out one of his girls in London, he had sent Fanny.

Before she left, Fanny had considered telling Amelia, the third sister, the secret of the buttons, but decided against it. If, heaven forbid, her debut was not the success she hoped for and she was forced to return, unmarried, then it would be as well to keep this precious lever to herself. Indeed, it was only after her wedding to Lord Maltravers, the heir to the Duke of Wareham, a match that had astonished everyone that season (everyone, that is, except Fanny herself), that she felt she could afford to impart this precious piece of information to her sister. Amelia had been helping Fanny to change into her going-away outfit. Amelia's transparent envy at Fanny's good fortune, the titled husband, the beautiful clothes and jewels, the great house and position that would all be hers, had been most gratifying to Fanny. She had whispered to her sister that she wanted to give her a present. Amelia leant in eagerly, hoping for some jewelled cast-off from her sister's new magnificence and when she received her 'gift', she had laughed a little bitterly. Fanny had tried to explain to her sister the importance of being able to manage their father, but Amelia was too glassy-eyed with covetousness to understand the significance of the buttons.

Amelia never had learnt to manage men, thought Fanny. It was inevitable, perhaps, that her husband Sholto would take a mistress, but Amelia should never have allowed him to be so publicly besotted. If Amelia had ignored Sholto's infatuation with Lady Eskdale, it would have passed – no one could stand Pamela Eskdale for more than a season – but to allow herself to look wounded and reproachful had only prolonged the affair. Amelia had been tiresome; it was lucky for her that the Eskdale was even more tiresome and even Sholto had grown tired of her. She really must invite Amelia and Sholto to Conyers. To one of the larger parties, of course.

The carriage jolted and came to a stop. The Duchess smiled when she saw Weld, the stationmaster. Such a handsome man, he had been quite her favourite footman – his calves had been spectacular. She rarely took lovers outside her class – the risk of blackmail was too great – but Weld had proved as discreet as he was muscular. When he had announced he was marrying one of the housemaids, it seemed entirely appropriate that he should be nominated to the South Dorset Railway as a stationmaster. It was necessary, of course, that the stationmaster should understand the needs of the house. Weld had been quite satisfactory. The brass buttons on his tunic were always shiny and he even looked handsome in that cap (such a shame that the uniform was, like the station, standard issue).

The Duchess smiled when she saw the red carpet laid out on the platform. She guessed that this had been the stationmaster's idea, rather than her son's. This was her first visit to Lulworth since her marriage to Buckingham, it was only fitting that it should be marked out as a special occasion. The Lulworth staff had always worshipped her. She beckoned to Sybil, her step-daughter, to follow her.

'Weld, how splendid everything looks.'

'Welcome back, Your Grace.' Weld attempted his best footman bow but the collar defeated him. The Duchess was smiling, she was gliding across the red carpet, the fur trim of her pelisse brown and rich against the faded pile.

'Is the train early, Weld? I can't see the Duke.'

'No, the train is on time, Your Grace. I believe that is the Lulworth carriage drawing up now.'

The Duchess knew that the late arrival of the carriage was a declaration. She was not entirely surprised to see that the man getting out was not her son but his friend Reggie Greatorex. She turned to her stepdaughter.

'Sybil darling, look how popular you are.'

She was rewarded by the sight of Sybil blushing. There was nothing artful about Sybil. If the girl had been the Duchess's own daughter she would, by now, have learnt to blush entirely at her own volition; but by the time Sybil had come into her care it was too late to teach her even the most basic strategies. There had been moments when the Duchess had thought that Sybil might do for Ivo, but as Ivo had quite refused to come to Conyers or to Belgrave Square, there had never been the chance to put them together. She really must give the girl some powder, that blush against the red hair was so unbecoming.

'But where is Ivo, Mama? I thought he would be here to meet us.'

Fortunately Reggie had reached them before the Duchess was forced to answer Sybil's tactless question.

'Duchess, Lady Sybil, what a magnificent sight on such a grey morning. You must forgive me for taking Ivo's place but I begged him to let me come. Life at Lulworth is positively dull without you. Ivo has not inherited your genius for entertaining. I just couldn't wait to bask in some feminine company.' Reggie's beam embraced both women.

The Duchess looked at him, her pale blue eyes open wide with disbelief. 'But Reggie, from what I hear, there is no shortage of female companionship at Lulworth.'

'Oh, you mean the Americans. Well, the mother is unspeakably dignified and the daughter is pretty enough but such a modern girl. Not restful, either of them. I want to sink into female company, I want to be soothed and indulged, not buffeted about by opinions.'

For a moment Reggie thought he might have gone too far, but then the Duchess smiled and allowed him to help her into the carriage. As he helped Sybil up, he squeezed her hand and was rewarded by an almost imperceptible wink.

The Duchess settled her furs around her and nodded to Weld, who still stood to attention by the red carpet. Then she leant forward to Reggie and asked him in her most intimate tone, 'Do we *know* anything about the Americans? Charlotte wrote to tell me that the girl had fallen off her horse and that Ivo discovered her unconscious in Paradise Wood. Can she really have had such a convenient accident?'

Reggie understood now why Ivo had begged him to go to the station in his place. The Duchess was quite relentless in the pursuit of information. Nothing would infuriate her more than her son entertaining two Americans whom she couldn't quite place.

'From what I hear, she is quite the heiress. They came over to Britain on their own yacht. I don't think she is the sort of girl who would throw herself in anyone's way. I would imagine her approach to be a good deal more direct. My impression is that Miss Cash usually gets what she wants.'

'She sounds quite . . . terrifying,' said the Duchess, mollified by the mention of the steam yacht. 'How lucky for Ivo that Sybil and I were able to come to his aid. Direct Americans! My poor boy.' She rolled her beautiful eyes in mock sympathy.

'Is Miss Cash very elegant?' asked Sybil anxiously. 'My dressmaker says that she never gets any work from the American ladies as they go straight to Paris for their clothes.

'Such an affectation,' said the Duchess. 'Paris does not have the monopoly on fashion. London is full of beautifully dressed women.' She smoothed the grey broadcloth of her travelling dress with one white beringed hand.

Reggie searched for the right answer. 'She certainly looks very smart. But how would I know, since until you came I had no one to compare her to.' He smiled at Sybil. The Duchess was looking out of the window and tutting at the state of the lodge as they turned through the gates to Lulworth. Reggie hoped that Ivo would be there to welcome his mother.

The staff of Lulworth were lined up on the grey stone steps as the carriage drew up, the male servants on the left, the female servants on the right, from the butler and housekeeper right down to the scullery maid and knife boy. Reggie looked for Ivo in vain, but fortunately the Duchess was too busy composing herself for her triumphal return to notice her son's absence.

As she got out of the carriage, there was a rustle like wind blowing autumn leaves as the female servants sank into their deepest curtsy. Bertha, who was observing the scene from Cora's bedroom on the second floor, wondered if the servants here knew automatically which step they were meant to stand on to form a perfectly symmetrical inverted V, or whether they had had to be told. Did the scullery maid assume that her place was at the bottommost right-hand step, or had she settled herself a few steps higher and then been sent down to her correct station? In America there would have been all kinds of jostling for position; as a lady's maid her own position was at the top, just below the housekeeper, but that wouldn't stop the Irish housemaids from pushing themselves to the front. In England everyone knew their place.

She heard the door open and Cora's voice, high with excitement, calling her.

'Bertha, I need you now! The Duchess is here and I must be ready!'

Bertha turned from the spectacle at the window to see that her mistress had succeeded in getting out of her bodice and was tugging at the strings at her waist.

'I want the blue costume, the one with the high neck. Please hurry, I don't want to be late for lunch. Damn, these petticoats are muddy. I will have to change completely.'

Bertha went to the armoire and took out the blue costume. She had to use both arms to lift it as the skirt was a heavy broadcloth with an elaborate frogged border. Bertha looked at the row of tiny mother-of-pearl buttons on the back of the blouse and sighed. This was not a dress that could be hurried.

Her mistress was standing in a foamy sea of cotton and lace, pouting at herself in the cheval mirror. She wriggled into the petticoats that Bertha held out. At least the blue dress was in the very latest style and did not have a full bustle; there was only a small horsehair pad to hold the skirt out at the back. Arranging a bustle, Bertha knew from experience, could take half an hour. This dress had the new sleeves that ballooned out from the shoulder to be caught into a tight sleeve at the forearm. The skirt was gored, flowing out to a wide hem. The proportions were designed to narrow the waist, but Cora was tugging at the belt unsatisfied.

'Bertha, can you lace me a little tighter? I think I could go down an inch.'

'Not if you want to be ready in time for lunch, let alone eat anything.'

'Oh, I don't want to eat. . . Oh Bertha, can't you guess what's happened?'

The maid looked at Cora steadily. The girl's colour was up and there was a certain bruised quality to her mouth as if she had been eating raspberries.

'Can't you guess? The Duke, Ivo, has proposed! We were in the chapel and all of a sudden it happened.'

'And how did you answer?' Bertha fastened the nineteenth button.

'What do you think I said? Yes, of course.'

Bertha found her knees buckling beneath her and fell to the floor rather heavily. She had not fainted, rather the ground beneath her feet had simply seemed to give way.

'What are you doing, Bertha? Are you all right? Shall I fetch my smelling salts?' Cora was genuinely anxious, Bertha was her confidante and, moreover, the only person capable of confecting the hairstyle she had determined to wear that night at dinner.

Bertha looked about her blankly and then pulled herself up on to Cora's bed where she sat down heavily.

'I'm fine, Miss Cora, it was just a turn, that's all. I guess if you're going to be a duchess and all, you'll be needing a fancy French mamselle not a Carolina foundling.'

'Oh, don't be so dramatic. When I am Duchess I shall have whoever I like. I'm not going to change just because I'm getting married, except that Mother won't be able to nag me all the time. Are you feeling better now? I really must go downstairs and meet my future mother-in-law.'

Bertha rose slowly to her feet and with clumsy, unresponsive fingers fastened the last buttons at the back of Cora's high-necked blue silk blouse. She freed a couple of chestnut tendrils from the stiff boned collar. She knew why Cora had chosen this costume, she could feel the red flush of her skin under the thin silk. As she finished, Cora squirmed away from her and rushed to the cheval glass to inspect herself. No need to bite her lips or pinch her cheeks, she looked vivid enough. Bertha watched as she leant forward and kissed her reflection in the speckled mirror. Cora saw Bertha looking at her in the mirror and she laughed a little foolishly.

'Wish me luck, Bertha. It's all beginning now, everything,' and Cora swept out of the room to her future. Bertha watched her go and then moved to the window where she pressed her face against the cold glass. A mist was rolling in from the sea, shrouding the view. She watched her warm breath turn the glass cloudy and without thinking she pressed the black pearl lying close to her heart.

Cora stood at the top of the stairs; she caught sight of her reflection in a gilt mirrored sconce. Almost perfect, but . . . she looked to see if anyone was about and then adjusted her bosom under the blue silk blouse. She was squaring her shoulders for the descent when she heard a voice that sliced through the dusty calm of the house so confidently that Cora knew that it could only belong to the Double Duchess.

'Darling Ivo, it is so lovely to be back at Lulworth. I had almost forgotten how thrilling that view of the sea is when you first come over the hill from the station. But you look pale, darling. I hope you aren't taking your responsibilities *too* seriously. You've been buried away down here for so long.'

'Well, now I have you to entertain me, Mother.' Ivo's voice was flat.

'And your Americans, of course,' the Duchess cooed. 'I can't wait to meet them. Charlotte says that Miss Cash is quite the thing.' She paused for a second and then said in a lower tone, 'Dear boy, I realise how lonely you must have been. I wish you had come to see me at Conyers. I could have made things more comfortable for you.'

'And how is your husband?' Ivo replied.

'Oh darling, there's no need to be like that. Buckingham was saying only the other day how much he looked forward to your maiden speech in the House. He is a great admirer of yours, you know.'

Ivo said nothing.

The Duchess tried again. 'I think you might have told me that Reggie was here. I should hardly have brought Sybil with me if I'd known.'

'I don't remember asking you to come, Mother,' Ivo said without emphasis.

There was a pause and Cora wondered what would happen next. Was Ivo going to tell his mother about their engagement? They had only come back an hour ago and yet that scene in the chapel already seemed unreal. Had Ivo really proposed or had she somehow imagined it? Was there some kind of secret English code that she had missed? It was all so unlikely – that sudden connection, as if from nowhere. She heard footsteps coming down the gallery; she must go or be discovered eavesdropping.

'I came because I thought you might need me, darling.' The Duchess's voice was soft but Ivo did not yield.

'I'm touched by your concern, Mother, especially when I know how busy you are with all your new duties. I'm surprised Buckingham can spare you.' He looked up and saw Cora coming down the stairs. 'But here comes Miss Cash now. Miss Cash, please come and meet my mother, she wants to inspect you.'

Cora saw a blonde woman, younger and more chic than she had expected. This was not the dowager in dirty diamonds that she had vaguely imagined but a beauty who hardly looked old enough to be Ivo's mother. Only as she got closer did she see the web of lines around the eyes and the faint weathering of the skin that betrayed the Duchess's real age.

'My dear Miss Cash, Ivo is so uncouth.' The Duchess's voice had dropped into a thrilling coo like a seductive wood pigeon. 'I want to assure myself that you have been looked after. Such an unfortunate accident . . . All alone in a strange country. I dread to think what might have happened if Ivo had not happened to be riding through Paradise Wood that morning. And now forced to put up in my son's bachelor establishment. I feel for you. Ivo really has no idea of comfort. His tastes are positively Spartan.'

Cora found that she had the advantage of at least two inches over the Duchess. Normally her height was a cause for self-consciousness but here she was glad of it.

'Oh, Your Grace, I could not have been better looked after. Your son has been the most attentive host.' Cora gave her best American smile and her eyes flickered over to Ivo.

The Duchess looked at her carefully. The girl was certainly presentable. Tall, with chestnut hair and greenish eyes, she had the carriage and the neck to carry off the fashionable silhouette of the season. Some women looked puny and cowed in those enormous sleeves. Reggie had been right, she was used to getting her own way; this was not a girl whose future had depended on the close observation of waistcoat buttons. She saw her glance at Ivo. They smiled at each other. The Duchess wondered if her son realised what sort of girl she was. All the prospective brides Ivo had encountered, that she had placed in his way, had known the rules, had been inducted from birth in the rituals of their world. But this American miss was from a different world entirely.

'And I believe your mother is here also? How fortunate that she was able to join you. But like all mothers she knew that her place was with her child at the hour of need.' The Duchess looked meaningfully at Ivo.

Cora caught the look and felt the colour rising to her face. Was the Duchess hinting that she had come to save her son from an unfortunate marriage?

But the Duchess smiled sadly and continued, 'It was three years ago that Guy, my eldest son, died.' She placed her hand on Ivo's arm briefly. He made no answering movement.

They heard voices coming down the hall

'And how did you get here, Lady Sybil? At home we always take our own train to Newport. Even with two separate establishments, there is still so much stuff to be carried back and forth. My husband had to buy the railway in the end so that there would be no difficulties with the timetable.' Mrs Cash entered the hall with Sybil at her side.

Cora noted the way the Duchess's eyes lit upon the brooch her mother wore pinned to hold down her veil; it was a huge ruby in a nest of diamonds. Perhaps for the first time in her life, Cora was grateful for her mother's sense of her own magnificence. She looked at Ivo and thought she saw his lips twitch, but before she could catch his eye properly there was a flurry of introductions and they were being ushered into the dining room.

The Duchess made a great display of hesitating before she took the seat that had once been hers at the opposite end of the table to her son. Cora saw that this uncertainty was aimed at Ivo but he refused to rise to the bait. When, in desperation, the Duchess said, with a quaver in her voice, 'How charming to find myself once more at Lulworth at my end of the table, and yet of course how poignant it is when I remember how things were,' Ivo simply nodded and without looking at his mother asked Mrs Cash whether her private train had loose boxes.

Cora was seated between Reggie and Father Oliver, with the Duchess on Reggie's other side. She could see that Reggie was to be monopolised by the Duchess so she began to ask Father Oliver about the history of the Lulworth chapel. As the priest recounted in detail the various vicissitudes of Catholicism at Lulworth, Cora was able to watch the Duchess talk intimately to Reggie and the effect this was having on her stepdaughter Lady Sybil. Cora thought that Sybil was quite good-looking for an English girl, despite her dowdy clothes and miserable hair. They must be about the same age. Cora wondered how the girl liked having the Duchess for a stepmother.

At the end of the meal Cora observed a curious ritual which had puzzled her the night before. One of the footmen was scraping all the contents of the serving dishes into a series of tins. This was quite indiscriminate: fish, eggs in aspic and trifle were all piled into the same receptacles which were then stacked on top of one another in a wicker basket. She turned to Reggie and asked him where the food was going.

'Oh, I suspect it must be for the poor and infirm of Lulworth. Is that right, Duchess?'

The Duchess turned her blond head. 'Yes, there is such a tradition of charity at Lulworth, the poor man at the gate and so forth. Really quite a lot of work for the servants, but it is so counted upon . . .'

Cora looked at the Duchess. 'But is there any reason why all the food is jumbled together? I just saw the remains of a raspberry soufflé being thrown into the same dish as the mutton. Surely it would be no trouble to put the food into separate dishes?'

Duchess Fanny put down the spoon she had been holding with a clatter. At the other end of the table her son looked up.

'My dear Miss Cash, the villagers at Lulworth are not gourmets. They are quite happy to have a meal even if it isn't as cooked by Escoffier.' The Duchess's tone was light and there was a hint of a laugh in her voice, but her eyes were cold.

'But it would take so little to make the food more palatable,' Cora protested. 'There is no reason why charity should be indigestible.'

Before the Duchess could reply, Ivo spoke.

'Indeed there isn't, and when you are chatelaine of this house, Cora, I suspect that we will have the most contented parishioners anywhere in the kingdom.'

The table fell silent. Mrs Cash, who was raising a glass to her lips, froze. Ivo rose to his feet.

'Mother, Mrs Cash, I apologise for the scant ceremony, but this morning I asked Cora to marry me and I am delighted to say that she accepted.'

There was a pause. Even the servants stopped weaving around the table.

Then the Duchess put her head on one side and smiled at her son. 'Ivo darling, how perfectly romantic. Dear Mrs Cash, you must forgive my impulsive son. He, of course, needs to consult with Mr Cash.' Then her blue eyes opened wide and she said in mock dismay, 'Oh, I hope there is a Mr Cash?'

Mrs Cash moved her head by a fraction. She could find no words to express her feelings; shock, pleasure, outrage mingled in equal measure. 'My husband is in New York.'

'Then, Ivo, you must telegraph at once.' With a great swish of satin, the Duchess rose to her feet. A footman scurried to pull back her chair. She ignored her son and looked at Mrs Cash. 'Ladies, shall we?' And with her blond head held high, she moved towards the door. As she walked the length of the table, the ladies got up one by one to follow her; even Cora was pulled to her feet. Only when she reached the door did the Duchess stop and look back at her son.

He stood up and opened it for her.

As she walked past him, she laid one gloved finger against his cheek. 'Dearest Ivo, I should have come sooner. I never realised how much you minded.'

It was much later before Cora realised what she meant.

Part Two

LORD BENNET.

Eldest son and heir of the sixth Earl of Tankerville.

The entailed estates amount to 31,000 acres, yielding an income of $150,000.

The Earl owns the only herd of wild cattle to be found in Great Britain.

Lord Bennet, who at present has nothing but a very small allowance, has served in the navy and the army, and is thirty-six years of age.

Family seat: Chillingham Castle, Northumberland.

Excerpt from 'A carefully composed List of Peers, who are supposed to be eager to lay their coronets, and incidentally their hearts, at the feet of the all-conquering American Girl'

Titled Americans, 1890

CHAPTER 10

Mrs Van Der Leyden Pays a Call

New York, March 1894

MRS VAN DER LEYDEN LOOKED AT THE LETTERS lying on the silver salver. She recognised her sister's handwriting, the quaver in the way she wrote the words 'Washington Square', and her heart sank. Poor Effie, her husband's 'accident' had been so unfortunate. To clean your gun with fatal consequences at the moment when there were widespread rumours about the bank was an unhappy coincidence. She knew that Effie's letter would pain her. Her sister had let herself go and she dreaded the covert appeals for money on every page. She would help, of course, it was her duty; but it would be in a time and manner of her own choosing.

Mrs Van Der Leyden put her sister's letter aside and picked up a thin envelope that bore a foreign stamp. She recognised her son's handwriting and duly picked up the silver paper knife that had been a gift to her from Ward McAlister on the occasion of her marriage. Her son's letter was affectionate but brief. He would be returning from France on the *Berengaria* which docked on the fourteenth; he vouchsafed nothing about his plans for the future or the reason why he was returning months earlier than he had originally planned. She hoped that he had finished with painting and had come back to claim his rightful position in the family law firm, but Teddy had always been such a stubborn boy and she doubted whether, having fought so hard, he would give up so easily. And then a ghastly thought came to her and she rapidly scanned the page again. No, he made no mention of a companion, nobody that he was anxious for her to meet. That, at least, was a relief. A foreign daughter-in-law from God knows where would be a drawback even for a Van Der Leyden.

Still wondering about her son's state of mind, Mrs Van Der Leyden picked up the last envelope on the salver: a heavy slab of pasteboard – an invitation of some sort. She picked up the paper knife. Mr and Mrs Winthrop Cash request the pleasure etc. at the marriage of their daughter Cora to His Grace the Duke of Wareham at Trinity Church on 16 March. So Nancy Cash had found a title for Cora after all. Personally, Mrs Van der Leyden found the desire to link American money with European aristocracy rather vulgar, but then if you were fortunate enough to bear the name Van Der Leyden, a title was superfluous. She couldn't really blame Nancy Cash for wanting a duchess for a daughter. The Cashes were rich all right and Nancy, of course, came from a fine old Southern family, but they weren't quite the thing. Cora had only been chosen to dance the quadrille at the Patriarch's Ball after one of the Schoonmaker girls had fallen ill with rheumatic fever. Isobel, of course, had been in the original eight, which was her birthright as a Van Der Leyden. It didn't hurt Nancy Cash to be reminded once in a while that money couldn't buy everything.

It could, however, secure a duke. Martha Van Der Leyden had never heard of the Duke of Wareham. But that was probably to his credit: last season there had been quite a clutch of English lords looking for heiresses. There had been the Duke of Manchester who had made quite a play for Isobel at first but had married a sewing machine heiress from Cincinnati. It was quite clear what he was after. No, she had never heard of Wareham, but no doubt he had a crumbling mansion in need of repair. Still, Cora was a handsome girl, who would make a perfectly creditable duchess. She was headstrong and perhaps a little fast (there had been that business with Teddy at the Cash ball in Newport – Teddy had never explained to her satisfaction why he had been alone on the terrace with Cora). No, Cora Cash would do very well and really the family was not an embarrassment. There was that business with Nancy Cash's father killing himself in the asylum but, after all, thought Mrs Van Der Leyden looking at poor Effie's letter, these things could happen in the very best families.

It was only when she rang the bell to have the breakfast things cleared away that it occurred to her that there might be some connection between her son's arrival and the Cash girl's impending nuptials. But surely Teddy would not be foolish enough to imagine that he could prevent Cora from marrying this duke. Mrs Cash would let nothing come in the way of that marriage and for once Mrs Van Der Leyden agreed with her. Cora Cash might make a passable duchess but she was not a suitable candidate to be Mrs Van Der Leyden Junior. Really, she hoped Teddy had not come back with romantic notions. She would turn a blind eye to his artistic ambitions; she had heard some quite shocking things about artist's models but she was prepared to ignore this, provided it was all safely in a foreign country. But to pursue an engaged girl, that would be a scandal that even a Van Der Leyden would have difficulty rising above.

She put the paper knife down on the salver and noticed, to her disappointment, a speck of tarnish in the moulding. Pursing her thin lips, she went up the stairs to her bedroom and told the maid to fetch her hat and cloak. Her visiting dress was very much in last year's style but she was of the generation that thought it was vulgar to be in fashion and she regularly packed away the new season's clothes until the moment when to wear them would not be seen as ostentatious. It was time to pay a call on Mrs Cash. For a moment she considered walking the half mile or so to the Cash mansion at 660 Fifth Avenue – really, it was barely civilised up there – but when she thought of the marble entrance hall and the footmen in their matching livery, she decided to take the carriage.

Fifteen years ago the Winthrop Cashes had been universally mocked for their audacity when they unveiled their plans for a town house in the far north of the island. But now the Cash mansion that occupied the whole block at 60th and Fifth was at the beginning of a strip of fashionable buildings that stretched as far as 70th Street. Although the Cash mansion no longer stood in isolation, it was still the most magnificent. In a city of brownstone houses, 660 Fifth was built of honey-coloured stone. It was Mrs Cash's first house and she had, in her youthful enthusiasm, asked Spencer the architect to build her a castle, and had been delighted when he showed the plans complete with turrets and gargoyles. His designs for the interiors had come complete with tiny figures wearing doublet and hose and farthingales. Mrs Cash, who had visited the Loire Valley on her honeymoon in Europe, adored the whimsicality of his design, so different from the neoclassicism of the South or the drab narrow town houses of her adopted city. Winthrop had raised a few objections to living in the 'wilderness' above 44th Street but he soon realised that his bride was not to be deflected. She had shown the plans to his father the Golden

Miller, who had goggled at the turrets and the eighty-foot dining room and had asked who was going to pay for all this. Nancy had turned to him, put one small white hand on his arm and, looking him straight in the eyes, had said, 'Why, you are, Papa.' There had been no more discussion. The house had been built and Nancy's campaign to become 'the' Mrs Cash had begun.

As the tall footman in the full Cash livery of purple and gold held the door of her carriage open for her, Mrs Van Der Leyden felt a shiver of irritation. She had grown up in a house where the door was opened by maids in stuff gowns and white aprons. This fashion for male indoor servants dressed up like peacocks was one of the many things brought over from Europe by the new rich of which Martha Van Der Leyden disapproved. To her Knickerbocker mind, men did outdoor work looking after the horses or tending the garden, they did not prance around in knee breeches doing the work of housemaids.

A moment later Mrs Van Der Leyden sat erect on one of the Louis sofas in Mrs Cash's drawing room. A lesser woman might have been intimidated by the sheer scale of the room with its original French *boiserie*, Flemish tapestries and an Aubusson carpet that was reputed to be the largest ever made. But Mrs Van Der Leyden sat secure in the knowledge that without her presence, no social gathering in this city was considered truly respectable. She had no fear of finding Mrs Cash 'not at home'.

Her hostess sailed across the Aubusson towards her. Mrs Cash did not, as a rule, receive callers so early (it took so long to arrange her veils and gauze to her satisfaction) but this was an exception. She was looking forward to seeing her new status as the mother of a future duchess acknowledged by the redoubtable Martha Van Der Leyden.

'Dear Mrs Van Der Leyden, what an unexpected pleasure. I have hardly seen a soul since we returned from Europe, we have been so busy with the preparations with the wedding. I hope you received your invitation. It is quite the wrong time of year to get married, as everyone is so busy with the season, but Cora and Wareham are so impatient, dear things, that they would not wait. I am sure that dear Isobel would not be as inconsiderate as my headstrong girl!'

Both women knew, of course, that Isobel Van Der Leyden's matrimonial prospects looked increasingly remote with each passing year.

'I must congratulate you, Mrs Cash. Tell me about the Duke, I am so ignorant of the English aristocracy. I don't recall seeing him here.' Mrs Van Der Leyden lowered her gaze.

'Oh no, Wareham has never been to America. Cora and he had a notion to be married in the chapel at Lulworth, which is the Maltravers country seat, but I was determined that Wareham should see something of his bride's country. Sometimes I believe that the English think we still live behind stockades.'

Mrs Van Der Leyden nodded gravely, not by a flicker did she betray her understanding of just how much the wedding of her daughter to a duke meant to Mrs Cash.

'It is only fitting that Cora should be married from her family home.'

Mrs Cash smiled gratefully. If Mrs Van Der Leyden thought it was fitting then all was well.

'But forgive me for all this wedding talk. How is dear Mr Van Der Leyden? Is he still bicycling in the park? Such youthful vigour. I would be quite alarmed if Winthrop took up anything so energetic.'

'Cornelius has always been the first to try things. I believe we were the first house in the square to have electric light. Personally I see nothing wrong with the way things are, but the Van Der Leyden men are all for Progress. When Teddy returns from Paris next month I shall be quite outnumbered.' Having introduced the real reason for her visit into the conversation, Mrs Van Der Leyden observed her hostess closely, but Mrs Cash did not seem perturbed.

'You must be so happy that he is coming back. Cora, I know, will be delighted. And of course I owe your son so much.' Mrs Cash gestured poignantly towards the veiled side of her face. 'I hope he will be back in time for the wedding.'

'Yes, his ship gets in on the fourteenth.'

'The *Berengaria*? Why, that is the vessel that the Duke and his party are on. The Duke is bringing his mother, who is Duchess of Buckingham now. I am so looking forward to showing her New York.'

But Mrs Van Der Leyden had no interest in duchesses, her business with Mrs Cash was finished: she had warned the other woman of her son's return. She pulled on her gloves and made to leave.

'Do give my regards to Cora. I am sorry not to see her today, but I shall look forward to seeing her as a bride.' And Mrs Van Der Leyden walked the length of the Aubusson, reassured that Mrs Cash, who surely had the most to lose, had not shown even a flicker of concern over the imminent arrival of Teddy.

As she walked down the wide marble steps, she saw Cora coming in with her maid, followed by a footman bestrewn with parcels. Even to Martha Van Der Leyden's disapproving eye, the girl looked radiant. She was wearing a brown tailor-made costume of such severe cut that on another girl it would have looked quite forbidding, but on Cora with her conker-coloured hair and shiny eyes it was simply a frame. The older woman understood why Mrs Cash had not been concerned by Teddy's arrival. For the first time in many years, Mrs Van Der Leyden, who had seen everything, was surprised: Cora Cash was clearly in love. That look was unmistakable. Mrs Van Der Leyden was so used to seeing it in unbecoming places that she was almost touched at the idea that a girl of such beauty and wealth might actually be marrying a Duke because she loved him.

Cora looked up and saw her.

'Mrs Van Der Leyden, I am so glad to see you. Now I know I am really in New York. Everyone else tries so hard to be European, I hardly know where I am, but now I have seen you, I know exactly which country I'm in. How are Isobel and Teddy?' Cora could not help but smile when she said Teddy's name and for a moment Mrs Van Der Leyden felt her misgivings return.

'They are both quite well and looking forward to seeing you married. Your mother has been telling me all about the wedding. It will be quite the spectacle.'

'Oh, you know Mother, everything has to be the best. But did you say that Teddy would be coming to the wedding? I thought he was in Europe. I was planning to look him up on our wedding trip. Why has he come back so soon? I thought he was going to study in Paris.'

Mrs Van Der Leyden smiled faintly. 'Who knows what makes young men change their plans? Perhaps he has lost his heart to a French marquise and has come back to ask for my blessing. You young people seem to find Europe so romantic.'

She was rewarded by seeing Cora flush and the wide smile falter.

'When is Teddy coming back? I would so like to see him. Ivo and I are leaving directly after the wedding. I hope I don't miss him as I really don't know when I will be back.' For a moment she looked a little forlorn as she felt the width of the Atlantic between Fifth Avenue and her destiny.

Mrs Van Der Leyden patted her on the arm. 'I received Teddy's letter this morning, I'm sure he will be here for your wedding.' She saw no reason to mention that Teddy was travelling on the same boat as Cora's fiancé. She would leave that to Mrs Cash. 'Goodbye, my dear.' Mrs Van Der Leyden pecked her on the cheek. She could feel the heat of Cora's skin against hers. The girl was burning up. It was high time she was married.

In Cora's bedroom, Bertha was unpacking one of the thirty trunks that had arrived yesterday from Maison Worth in Paris. After the engagement, Mrs Cash had not lingered in Lulworth even though Cora would have liked to stay longer. Mother and daughter had gone to Paris where they spent a month having fittings at Maison Worth and buying shoes, hats, gloves and jewels. Mrs Cash had been planning for this moment for years. A year ago she had had Worth take Cora's measurements so that he could start creating her trousseau. When Cora had found out just how far her mother had been planning in advance, she asked her how she could have been so sure that she would marry within the year. 'Because that had always been my intention,' said Mrs Cash.

Bertha picked up a tissue-wrapped parcel and opened it carefully. It was a corset. As she held it out, Cora walked in carrying a magazine.

'Bring that here, Bertha. Is that the one Mrs Redding writes about in *Vogue*? "The bridal corset is made of pink satin, embroidered with tiny white carnations and trimmed at the upper edge with a deep pointed border of Valenciennes lace. The clasps, the large hook, and the buckles on the attached stocking supporters are all made of solid gold studded with diamonds." All correct except for the diamonds of course. Why would anyone put diamonds on their corset? I am embarrassed that anyone would think me so foolish.'

Bertha said nothing. It was not her place to point out that Cora's corset even without the diamonds would pay her salary for the next twenty years. The clasps were fashioned from twenty-one-carat gold and the silk from the corset had been woven to order in Lyons. And this corset was only one of five in Cora's trousseau. The lace alone on the numerous nightgowns, peignoirs, wrappers, bedjackets, and petticoats was probably worth more than diamonds, as all of it was handmade, some of it worn by the French queen who had had her head cut off.

And then there were the dresses, all ninety of them. Each dress packed in yards of tissue paper and suspended over a tape frame so that it would not be crushed. There were plain day dresses for writing letters in the morning, riding habits in dark blue and bottle green, visiting dresses with the widest of leg-of-mutton sleeves and passementerie fringing around the hem, strict tailor-mades for yachting with no ornament but braid, tea gowns frothing with lace and with such a forgiving silhouette that they could be worn without a corset; there were theatre dresses with high necklines and long sleeves, and opera dresses with lower necklines and short sleeves, dinner dresses with half high necklines and elbow-length sleeves, and ball dresses with full décolletage and trains; and of course the wedding dress itself which had so many pearls sewn on to its train that when it swept along the floor it made a faint crunching noise like fairies walking across gravel. Not to mention the furs: Mrs Cash had ordered a sable cloak for Cora modelled on one the Grand Duchess Sophia had worn in Paris. It was so heavy that it could really only be worn sitting down. Bertha remembered the damp chill of Lulworth and thought that Cora might be grateful for the cloak, and for all the other stoles and fur-trimmed dolmans, muffs and mantles that Mrs Cash had thought necessary for a duchess.

Mrs Cash had wanted to order Cora's state robes as well, but when she wrote to the Double Duchess about this, Her Grace had replied that 'robes were never bought, but inherited'. Mrs Cash, who suspected that robes inherited at Lulworth would be as musty and damp-smelling as everything else there, had tried to protest but Mrs Wyndham had taken her aside and told her that damp and mustiness were much prized among the aristocracy as they showed that the title was of an old creation. Only new titles had freshly made robes. Mrs Cash had allowed herself to be overruled but she still could not understand why the British liked things to be shabby. It had taken weeks before she could persuade Wareham to install a proper bathroom for Cora at Lulworth. He had seemed to think there was nothing wrong with a duchess having to wash herself in a copper hip bath in front of the fire. Bertha had heard the whole story as Mrs Cash had unburdened herself to Cora. Cora had laughed at her mother for her American passion for progress but underneath Bertha knew that her mistress was secretly relieved. Cora loved the romance of Lulworth, but Bertha had seen her shiver as she went down for dinner in a low-cut evening dress and her look when she had found ice on the inside of the mullioned window of her bedroom.

Here in Cora's bedroom it was pleasantly warm. The Cash house had had the latest steam heating system installed when it was built. Even the servants' bedrooms were heated. Bertha thought of the draughty attic she had slept in at Lulworth and wondered not for the first time whether her destiny really lay in England, but then she thought of Jim and that night in the stables at Sutton Veney. He had written to her once at Lulworth. It had not been much of a letter, but it was the first letter of a sentimental nature that Bertha had ever received and she carried it with her everywhere tucked round the black pearl.

Cora was reading aloud again. She was fascinated by all the stories about her wedding in the newspapers. In public it was very bad form to admit that you had read any of the scandal rags but in private Cora devoured them.

'*Town Topics* has pages about the wedding. It says my departure for Europe broke hearts all over New York and that my marriage will deprive New York society of one of its brightest-stars. "What a pity that one of the greatest heiresses that we have ever produced should take her talents and her fortune abroad to the benefit of some dilapidated English castle, instead of bestowing her beauty and wealth on one of her fellow countrymen. *Town Topics* has heard that Newport last summer had fully expected Miss Cash to announce a more patriotic match. We can only assume that the ever ambitious Mrs Cash is responsible for her daughter's change of direction. Mrs Cash has long sought to become the pre-eminent hostess of her day, and having a duchess for a daughter can only bring that day closer." They couldn't be more wrong, of course, Mother had nothing to do with my marriage. Why don't people realise that I have a mind of my own?'

Again Bertha said nothing. Cora tossed the paper on the floor. Bertha was counting kid gloves, thirty-two, thirty-three, thirty-four, there should be fifty pairs. Cora's gloves never lasted longer than an evening. Skin-tight and so thin that the fingernails were visible through the translucent leather, they took an age to get on and off and Cora would quiver with impatience as Bertha tried to roll them off without damaging them. Most evenings Cora would push her away and rip the gloves off with her teeth. Bertha was used to it but it always pained her, as used kid gloves of this quality fetched 25c a pair at the dress exchange where Bertha went to sell Cora's cast-offs. Mrs Cash always demanded receipts for the dresses, but the gloves were beneath her notice. Bertha wondered whether there was a trade in kid gloves in London.

The door opened and Mrs Cash came in carrying a large blue leather box in both hands. Cora did not get up. Since the engagement, Bertha had noticed that Cora was far less in awe of her mother. But Mrs Cash did not appear to notice.

'I am delighted you are back, Cora. I have something to show you.'

She sat down on the sofa next to Cora and touched the clasp of the blue leather box. It sprang open with a heavy click and from the other side of the room Bertha could see thousands of points of light dance across the ceiling as a ray of light hit the contents.

Mrs Cash took the tiara out of the box and placed it on Cora's head. It was a diadem of stars that twinkled against the rich brown of Cora's hair.

'Thank God you didn't get your father's hair, dear. Diamonds are wasted on blondes.'

Cora walked over to the mirror to see what she looked like,

and faced with her reflection she couldn't help smiling.

'Oh, it's beautiful, Mother. Where did you get it?'

'I had Tiffany copy one belonging to the Empress of Austria. She has chestnut hair like you. You will need a tiara when you are married and I wanted you to have something light and graceful. I saw some really hideous jewels in London, huge gems but such dingy settings. Really, what is the point of dirty diamonds?'

Cora turned her head to the side. 'I feel quite the Duchess when I'm wearing this.' She made a stately curtsy to her reflection. Her mother reached over and tucked in a strand of hair that had escaped from the tiara. Cora looked at her mother, and was astonished to see that her mother's good eye was wet.

Forty-eight, forty-nine, fifty, fifty-one. There was a pair of gloves too many. A new pair of gloves would fetch at least a dollar and in Bertha's opinion, taking what was surplus to requirements was not the same as stealing. Bertha looked up to see if the women were watching her, but they were too absorbed in each other. She took the gloves and stuffed them in her pocket. She might want to get married herself one day.

CHAPTER 11

Euston Station

TWO WEEKS AFTER HIS MOTHER HAD MADE HER way up Fifth Avenue, Teddy Van Der Leyden found himself making the same journey. But after ten days on board ship, the young man was happy to walk in the bright cold morning. He told himself that it was the exercise he wanted but there was another reason for walking – he needed to think. When he had heard of Cora's engagement he had felt an immediate, unreasonable sense of loss. He was not surprised exactly by the engagement, such a match had only been a matter of time; what he had not expected was how much he would mind. He heard the news from an English acquaintance in Paris who had been buzzing with the serendipity of it all. Wareham is a lucky fellow, the artistically inclined baronet had said, the American girl fell into his lap, literally. Came off her horse hunting and Wareham found her. A week later they were engaged. Couldn't have come at a better time for him – Lulworth is a terrible old barn and Wareham had to pay all these death duties, first the father then the brother. But they say the girl, Miss Cash, has pots of money, so she should be able to set all that straight. What, you know her? Is she really as rich as they say? Richer? Wish I'd been in that wood when she had that tumble.

Teddy drank absinthe that night and spent the next day in a queasy fog underpinned by the feeling that something was badly wrong. It was only in the evening that he realised that it was Cora's engagement that had brought on this feeling of dread. He had sent her to this and now he didn't like it. He had gone to London to look for her, to talk to her, but she had already left for New York. He knew, even as he bought his ticket for the SS *Berengaria*, that it was a mistake – that he had made his choice that night in Newport and now Cora had made hers. But still he carried on. If Cora really loved this duke then he could do nothing, but if she was being forced into a dynastic match by her mother, he would rescue her. He must talk to Cora once before she disappeared into a world of stately homes and coronets.

He had spent a few days in London in a haze of impatience. Once he knew that the Cashes had gone back to New York, he wanted nothing but to get back to America himself. He had made his way to Euston Station to board the train for Liverpool automatically; he just wanted to be at his destination. But there was one scene that had pierced his numbness: a couple on the platform at Euston, a man and a woman looking at each other with such intensity that Teddy felt almost scorched by it. The woman, he thought, was beautiful, he could see the gorgeous curve of her cheek beneath the deep brim of her hat. The man was tall and dark and Teddy sensed there was tension in the square of his shoulders and the set of his jaw. The couple stood there motionless, an island of stillness in the frantic bustle and clamour of the boat-train traffic. They were not speaking, all communication was in their gaze. And then Teddy saw the woman take the man's hand with a small, almost feral gesture and pull it into the fur muff she was carrying. She looked up at him with challenge in her eyes. The man leant forward stiffly, he whispered something in the woman's ear. He withdrew his hand from the muff and stood tall, although his eyes never once left her face. She turned and walked down the platform, the man looking after her. Teddy wondered if she would look back at him but she kept on walking. There was a scream from the locomotive and the man started and began to move towards the train. Teddy continued to watch the woman and was rewarded by a glimpse of her veiled face looking back at last. But the man had disappeared on to the train. Teddy wanted to tell her that the man had waited as long as he could, that there had been no loss of faith.

The scene had stayed with him as he boarded the *Berengaria*. The way the woman had placed the man's hand in her muff suggested intimacy but not, Teddy thought, marriage. Married couples would embrace openly; that gesture spoke of concealment. She had wanted something from him, but had he given it? Teddy could not be sure.

The crossing had been rough and Teddy had spent most of it in his cabin as the ship lurched nauseously from one swell to the next. But on the fourth day, the weather cleared and Teddy ventured out on deck. He was walking rather unsteadily to a group of steamer chairs when he saw the man from the station talking to two women. Teddy almost greeted him as the man had been such a big part of his thoughts for the last few days, but of course the man had not seen him and had no idea who he was. The steward with Teddy saw the direction of his glance and asked him if he knew His Grace the Duke of Wareham. Teddy shook his head –

he felt a return of his earlier queasiness as he realised that this was Cora's fiancé. He tried to walk away, but the steward was determined to tell him about the Duke, his mother the Duchess and his stepsister the Lady Sybil and how they were all going over to attend the Duke's wedding to an American girl, the richest girl in the world, they said. Nice gentleman, the Duke, very civil to the crew, and as for his mother the Duchess, well, she was something else, a real lady. Teddy could bear no more and dispatched the steward for some broth. Wrapped in rugs in his steamer chair, his book covering his face, Teddy was able to observe the Duke unseen. He was dark for an Englishman and spare in build. His features were mobile but saved from weakness by a strong Roman nose. As he listened to his mother tell some story, the Duke smiled but Teddy thought that he seemed detached, as if he was thinking of something else. His mother clearly noticed this as well and tapped him on the arm with her parasol. The Duke started, collected himself and offered both ladies his arm so they could make a circuit of the deck. They made a graceful trio.

For the rest of the journey, Teddy hid in his cabin. He didn't want to see the Duke again. He dreaded an introduction that would inevitably result in a conversation about Cora. When they reached New York he lingered in his stateroom until he was sure that the ducal party had disembarked. The last thing he wanted was to encounter Cora on the quay.

Now, as Teddy approached the park, he was still no clearer in his mind. He had come back from Europe because he wanted to give Cora a choice. But did he have the right to tell her what he had seen on the platform in London? He was sure that what he had witnessed was a lovers' farewell. Would that give him an advantage, one that he did not merit? He had had his chance with Cora after all, but he had been too scared then of all her paraphernalia to take it. Did he have the right to spoil the chances of his rival? Did he really want Cora on those terms? He was on the corner of the block that was occupied by the Cash mansion. As he walked up the street he saw Mrs Cash and the Duchess get into a carriage. He rang the bell and gave his card to the footman.

Presently there was a rustle and a vision in green swept down the stairs. His first impression was that Cora had changed, in a way that he could not immediately define. She rushed towards him and took his hands.

'Teddy, I am so glad you are here. How clever of you to come when Mother is out. All she talks about is the wedding.' She took his arm. 'Let's go into the library, the drawing room is full of wedding gifts. You look very fine, very Continental and distinguished. How is the painting? Shall I come and sit for you when I am a duchess? Or are you too grand to paint society ladies? I hear Sargent regularly turns people away if they don't interest him.'

Teddy could see she was nervous, trying to fill the room with chatter so that there would be no space for awkwardness. She looked beautiful but feverish, he could see red spots of colour on her cheeks and neck.

'Paris was everything I had hoped for. It is so far ahead of New York. I was lucky enough to work with Menasche for a while. He said I had some talent.' He looked at his hands.

'That's wonderful, Teddy. I know how much you admire him.' Cora smiled.

There was a silence. The fact of her marriage lay heavily between them. At last Teddy plunged in.

'Cora, I came here because I wanted to be sure that you were happy. I have no doubt that your mother is happy and your Duke and your dressmaker but I just wanted to be sure that you were.' He paused, realising that his tone was too light, Cora would think he was teasing her. 'I came today because I realise that last summer you offered me something precious that I was too foolish to accept. No, please, let me speak.' Cora was trying to bat away his words with her hands as if they were bees about to sting her. 'Now you are engaged to be married, I have no right to say anything at all, but Cora, can you tell me that this is what you want, that you love this man and you want to be with him?'

Cora hung her head. She picked at a green bobble that hung from the fringe on her bodice. But when she looked at him at last, her face was scarlet and her eyes were fierce.

'How dare you come and offer to rescue me! Last summer you wouldn't help me when I asked, but now that I don't need your help, you have come back. It's too late, Teddy.' She pulled at the green bobble so hard that it came away in her hand. Teddy tried to speak but she rushed on. 'Do you really think I would marry a man I didn't care for to please my mother?'

'Do you love him?' Teddy forced himself to ask, even though he dreaded the answer.

'How can you ask me that?' Cora turned her head away.

'I just want you to be sure. If you answer yes then this conversation will stop and we can pretend it never happened. But if you can't say yes, then I am here.'

Cora still looked away. Without thinking, he put out his hand to touch that flushed cheek. He felt her flinch. How could he tell her now what he knew about the Duke? She wouldn't believe him. After all, what had he seen? A parting, a passionate one but a parting nonetheless. If the Duke had to put his affairs in order before his marriage, surely there was nothing so terrible in that – any more than there was in Cora saying goodbye to him now. Anything he said would seem motivated by jealousy. He tried to put things right with her.

'Cora, I know how fine you are, don't be angry with me. I only came here because I care for you.'

Cora heard the catch in his voice and her face softened. She was about to speak when the library door opened and the girl Teddy had seen with the Duke on the boat walked in.

'Oh, I am sorry, Cora. I didn't realise you had a visitor.' There was a pause.

Cora shook herself and when she spoke her voice was light.

'Sybil, this is Teddy Van Der Leyden. Teddy, this is Lady Sybil Lytchett, she is the Duke's stepsister and one of my bridesmaids.' Her voice was a little too high. Teddy felt the warning in it.

Sybil held out her hand awkwardly. 'I just came to ask you whether you could lend me something to wear tonight. I know it's a frightful imposition, but you all dress up so much here and I have worn my best evening dress three times. Your mother gave me one of her eyebrow raises last night. I could have died. It's all very well for Mama to say that breeding shines through, but honestly, Cora, I would much rather be well-dressed than well-bred.'

Cora could not help smiling, there was something very appealing about Sybil's lack of guile, 'Of course, you are more than welcome to take anything in my wardrobe. I will come and help you find something. As it happens, Mr Van Der Leyden was just leaving.' She turned to Teddy. 'I hope you will come and see us on your next trip to Europe. I don't know what I will do over there without all my old friends.'

She looked at him then and he thought he saw some trace of doubt in her eyes. He wondered again about the scene on the platform: what did Cora really know about her duke? For a moment he forgot about himself and felt apprehensive to think of this bright American girl entering Old World shadows. But she was smiling, a bright, taut, social smile for her future stepsister's benefit, and he knew he must leave.

'Certainly I will come and see you in Europe. If nothing else I must deliver your wedding gift. I thought perhaps a bicycle? I know how fond you are of cycling.' Cora caught his gaze and he knew that she, too, was thinking of that day in Newport when she had fallen off her bicycle. They were both thinking of what might have been. He walked to the door and turned.

'If you ever need an old friend, I will be there.' Teddy could not say more. He bowed to Sybil and shook Cora's outstretched hand and left.

Out in the sunshine he felt foolish. He had wanted to rescue Cora from a ducal cage but it seemed that she was entering it willingly. He had handled things so badly. What Cora wanted, he now realised, was love, and all he had offered her was protection. And now it was too late, the wedding was in less than a week. He must write to her. At least then she would know how he really felt: that he didn't want to rescue her, he wanted to tear her away.

He walked down Fifth Avenue, his hands in the pockets of his ulster, framing the letter in his head.

He was so preoccupied that he did not notice Mrs Cash's carriage as it returned to the house. She noticed him, though. She hoped she had not been too confident. Perhaps it would be as well to monitor Cora's visitors and correspondence until the girl was safely married. Cora was so impulsive and the Duke could be so prickly.

If they were to have some ridiculous tiff and Cora were to seek solace with Teddy Van Der Leyden . . . Mrs Cash shivered. If only the Duke had stayed in New York instead of going on that absurd hunting expedition. It was very strange behaviour so close to the wedding, especially after all the unpleasantness over the marriage settlement. Winthrop had not wanted to tell her all the details but apparently the Duke had been quite put out by the fact that the money had been settled directly on Cora. He said he found the presumption behind it insulting. How could there be separation of property between husband and wife? But Winthrop had been firm, Cora was his only child and he had to protect her interests. Immediately after this conversation, the Duke had announced that he was going hunting. Mrs Cash had expected Cora to object, but her daughter had made no protest. Only the Duchess had remonstrated with her son but without success. Wareham had gone off upstate with his best man Reggie, and his valet, to shoot canvasback duck. It had made the numbers at dinner quite uneven. What a good thing she had seen Teddy leaving the house, she had almost made up her mind to ask him to dinner to amuse poor Lady Sybil. Smiling as she always did at the sight of her tall footmen waiting to hand her out of her carriage – really, they were quite the finest specimens in New York – she began to review her list of amusing bachelors who could be summoned to dinner that night.

CHAPTER 12

Two Cigarettes

*I*N THE SERVANTS' HALL OF 660 FIFTH, THE
departure of the Duke and the visit of Teddy Van Der
Leyden was the subject of much speculation. The butler, who was
English, held that the Duke was a sporting gentleman who
preferred duck shooting to being put on display in Mrs Cash's
drawing room, but the housekeeper was convinced that he had
left in a huff because he wasn't getting his hands on all of Miss
Cora's money – every detail of the row between the Duke and
Mr Cash in Mr Cash's study having been overheard by the
footman. A full report of the row was even now being turned
into a spiky little column in *Town Topics* – Colonel Mann the
editor had let it be known that he was prepared to pay hand-
somely for anything to do with the Cash wedding. Indeed, Colonel
Mann was probably better informed about the disagreement
between Cora's father and her future husband than Cora herself.
Winthrop Cash had no desire to upset his daughter and the Duke
did not talk about such things with anyone. He had told her he
wanted to get away from 'all the people gawking at him' and she,
having read that morning's *Town Topics* which contained a list
of all the paintings and fine furniture that the Duke had sold in

the past year, could only agree. If she was insulted, she could only imagine how he felt.

The argument swirled on with all parties taking sides. Only Bertha said nothing. This was not unusual. As the only coloured upper servant, her position was a strange one; no one would ask her opinion directly but as Cora's maid she was privy to all the information they craved. But Bertha was not silent from loyalty to Cora, she simply did not hear the hubbub around her. She was still replaying the scene of the day before yesterday at the New York Customs. Cora had wanted to meet the Duke's party at the docks and had taken Bertha as companion. Mrs Cash had thought the whole expedition unseemly but she had been unable to deflect her daughter. It had been cold standing in the Customs Hall and Bertha wished that she had a fur stole and muff like her mistress. At last the ducal party could be seen at the far end (the *Berengaria* disembarked its passengers in order of precedence). Cora gave a cry of excitement and started towards the tall figure of the Duke. Bertha knew she should restrain her but she was frozen by the sight of another figure standing a little to the right of the party, carrying a valise. The height and the blond hair reminded her of Jim, he had that same catlike way of walking – and then the man drew closer and his face was lit by a shaft of light from a hole in the roof above. It was Jim. Somehow he was here and he was smiling at her. She wanted to run to him as Cora had done, but of course she had to stand modestly behind her mistress. All she could do was raise one gloved hand in greeting and see Jim wink in return. No one else saw this exchange as everyone was looking at Cora launching herself at the Duke. As she did so, there was a flash and the sharp, dry smell of magnesium in the damp air of the Customs Hall. The photographer for the *Herald*, who was sent to cover all boats arriving from Europe, had got the picture of his career: Miss Cora Cash, radiant in fur, arms outstretched, and the Duke of Wareham standing to attention, his arms raised as if to ward off a blow. It was a trick of the camera, of course; the Duke had raised his arms to embrace Cora by her enormously exaggerated shoulders, but the camera only saw the defensive arms and the look of surprise on the Duke's face.

To Bertha's relief, her face was masked by Cora's furs in the published photograph. Only the raised gloved hand was visible in the corner.

After the commotion in the Customs Hall subsided, Cora leant on the Duke's arm and shepherded him to her carriage, with the Double Duchess, Reggie and Sybil following in her wake. Bertha hung back to supervise the loading of the luggage on to the wagon. Cora, she knew, would not miss her for hours and there was so much she had to say to Jim. He found her and caught her by the wrist. But she moved away from him, conscious of the witnesses all around them.

'Pleased to see me?'

Bertha nodded, she could not find the words to describe her feelings. Instead she said, 'How did you get here?'

'The Duke needed a valet and when I heard, I left Sir Odious right away and asked him for the job. I told him that I had always wanted to go to America. Course he didn't know why.' He looked at Bertha and she knew he wanted to kiss her, but she kept her distance. She was overwhelmed by his presence and what it meant. Jim felt her silence and carried on.

'Turned out his old valet suffered from seasickness and didn't want to go abroad, so he took me on right away. Oh Bertha, you should have seen your face when I came through that door. Your mouth was hanging open so wide.' He smiled at her, gleeful. But Bertha could not smile yet. There was so much to understand.

'I can't really believe you're here.'

'Didn't you get my letter?'

'Why yes, I have it here.' She patted the bodice of her dress. 'And the pearl, that's where I keep precious things. But you never said you were coming over.' She was half angry with him for not warning her.

'It was all decided at the last minute. I thought of writing to you but then I knew I was going to be seeing you, so I thought I would surprise you.' Jim put his hand on hers, right over the spot where the pearl was sewn into her dress. 'Did I do right then to come?'

Bertha heard the tremor in his voice and realised then that none of this had been easy for him. When she spoke she found herself talking in Cora's voice.

'Why, Jim, I couldn't be happier.'

He looked at her for a moment and then laughed. This was safer territory.

'The Duke could hardly believe it when she flew at him like that,' he said.

'Oh, he'll have to get used to it. Miss Cora don't hang back when she wants something.'

After they had gathered together the numerous trunks, hatboxes and valises and had them loaded on to the wagon, Bertha decided to call a hansom. Normally she would have taken a tram, but Jim and she would have to sit separately. This way she would be able to explain what was what before they got back to the house. She was pretty sure that Jim did not understand the way things worked over here.

She was right. As they left the Customs Hall together, Jim's arm around her waist, there were shouts and catcalls from the porters on the docks. Jim looked puzzled and put out, he was about to respond when Bertha stopped him.

'Don't pay them any mind, Jim, they just don't see many white folks walking around with people like me. They don't know you're not American.'

Jim subsided grumbling. This was new territory.

In the hansom, Jim held her hand in his and she found it hard to concentrate on the unpleasant realities they faced. But as the cab crossed Broadway, she pulled herself up and looked at Jim strictly.

'I can't say I'm not pleased to see you because I am but things are different here. No one is going to take kindly to us being together. They don't think it's right for white and coloured folk to keep company. That's the way it is. And if the Madam gets to know, I'll lose my place. She won't stand for any goings-on in her house.'

Jim smiled at her stern manner. 'I promise to behave, Miss Bertha.'

She wondered if he really understood. In England they would face dismissal without references if their relationship was discovered. Here in New York a white man could not have a respectable relationship with a coloured woman. It wasn't illegal to marry as it was in South Carolina, but it never happened. And Bertha was determined to have a respectable relationship.

It had almost been a relief when Jim came to tell her he was leaving town. He said that the Duke had come back to the hotel in a foul temper and had thrown a brush at him when he had put out the wrong waistcoat. He had been surprised, he hadn't thought the Duke was that kind of gentleman. Then Mr Greatorex had come in and the Duke had started playing the piano, 'Angry music,' said Jim. An hour later the Duke had sent for him and told him they were going on a hunting trip, returning the day before the wedding.

Now he was gone Bertha could collect her thoughts. It had been exhausting trying not to look at Jim, even worse showing no reaction when he touched her as he passed her on the stairs or in the corridors. She didn't know how much longer she could keep it up. It was lucky that the household was all over the place trying to keep the Madam happy. Bertha's biggest worry was the maids who had come with the Duchess and Lady Sybil; they had been quite put out when Jim had stayed behind with her at the Customs Hall. On the voyage over they had waited to see which one of them he preferred, so they could not help but notice his interest in her. Now they were constantly running after her, demanding curling papers, pincushions, the best place to procure carmine, all the while trying to find out how exactly she had come to know Mr Harness, the Duke's valet.

They were looking at her now. One of them was mending a petticoat that Bertha would have discarded long ago as beyond saving. She knew they were talking about her and she felt uncomfortable under their pale stares. She decided to leave them to their gossiping and get on with sorting out Miss Cora's trousseau.

As she pushed open the door to Cora's room, she was struck by a blast of cold air. Who had left the windows open? She walked through the sitting room to the bedroom to close the window when she noticed Cora sitting in the twilight, smoking a cigarette. She didn't know what was more surprising, Cora smoking or that she was alone.

'Sorry, Miss Cora, I didn't know you were in here. Shall I close the window? It's getting pretty cold now. What do you want to wear for dinner tonight? Shall I put out the lilac silk? You haven't worn that one yet.'

But even the promise of a new dress did not rouse Cora. She inhaled on her cigarette (where had she got them from? wondered Bertha) and blew the smoke out of the window.

Bertha went to the closet to fetch the lilac dress, which smelt of lavender and cedarwood. Every Worth dress had its own pomander, which gave the dresses their own individual perfumes.

'Oh, leave it, Bertha, I don't think I will go down tonight. I have a headache.'

'The Madam won't like it.'

'I know, but I can't face them all tonight.' She tossed her cigarette out of the window where it fell in a rainbow of tiny sparks. And then she began to speak, looking out of the window, anywhere but at Bertha.

'I was so sure before . . . about Ivo. I've wanted him to be here so much but since he came to America . . . he isn't the same. He used to touch me all the time, I mean he couldn't stand next to me without putting his hand on my arm or my waist, and if we were ever alone he would kiss me – so much sometimes that I had to make him stop. But since he came he hasn't touched me once, not properly, not unless it's expected of him. I've tried to get him alone but he is always with somebody, and now he's been gone for a whole week. Oh Bertha, do you think he's coming back?'

Bertha looked at Cora's frowning face and felt a little sorry for her. She was so used to getting her own way and yet she could not control the Duke. But it was not Bertha's role to sympathise with her – she had her own reasons for wanting Cora married and back in England. 'I do, Miss Cora. And as for the rest of it, you'll be on your honeymoon soon and you can be alone all you want.'

'Yes, but that's what I'm scared of. Suppose we don't like each other? Suppose everything that happened before was a mistake? Teddy came here this morning and offered to take me away and the awful thing is that for a moment I was tempted. Teddy loves me, I can see it in his face, but when I look at Ivo I don't know what he feels.'

Bertha knew to say nothing.

'At Lulworth it was all so easy, we understood each other. But it is all so different here. Everyone thinks he is marrying me for my money, even his mother. But I know he liked me first. I know he did.'

Cora's voice was not as certain as her words. Bertha again remained silent. She wondered if Cora knew about the row over her marriage settlement.

'Don't worry, Miss Cora, every bride has doubts before the wedding. It's only natural. Why don't you let me bathe your head in eau de cologne and then you can get dressed and go down for dinner. You don't want all those English ladies to be asking where you've got to.'

'Oh Lord, Sybil came in while I was with Teddy this morning. I'd better go down and be cheerful, otherwise she might say something in front of Mother. Poor girl, I had to lend her two dinner dresses. I don't understand why the Duchess doesn't get her some nice things.'

The lamentable state of the English girl's wardrobe seemed to cheer Cora. Bertha hustled her into the lilac dress. Once she was downstairs being admired and fussed over, her mistress, she knew, would start to feel much better. To distract her while she did her hair, Bertha told Cora about the English lady's maids and their superior ways. Cora was laughing as Bertha described their attempts to conceal their amazement at the size and splendour of Cora's trousseau. They had looked down their noses and wondered aloud if there were any dresses left in Paris.

'Oh, they was actin' like it was nothin' but I saw them put out their hands to touch your furs. They ain't seen anything so fine. I made out I didn't notice but I could see 'em swallowin' their envy. I hope you don' mind me showing 'em all the clothes and stuff, Miss Cora, but it gave me no end of satisfaction.'

'I don't mind, Bertha. I'd like to do the same with the Duchess, except she would think it vulgar.'

The dinner gong rang and Cora went downstairs. Bertha sprayed cologne in Cora's bedroom to mask the smell of the cigarette. Mrs Cash often came in to say goodnight and she would make an almighty row if she thought Cora had been smoking. Bertha was just about to go to her dinner in the servants' quarters when Mrs Cash stopped her at the door of Cora's room.

'Bertha, a word.' Mrs Cash was at her most stately.

'Yes, ma'am.' Bertha curtsied, praying her legs wouldn't wobble. She could only hope that all the smoke had gone.

'You don't need me to remind you how unusual it is for a girl of your type to be working as a lady's maid. The money you send home must mean a great deal to your mother.'

Bertha looked at the floor. She had not heard from her mother since coming back from England.

'You have worked hard and I know that Cora has great confidence in you. Indeed, she confides in you in a way that is perhaps not entirely fitting but because we have given you so much, I know you will always be discreet. That is why I chose you instead of a professional lady's maid. I knew you would soon pick up your duties, but the habit of loyalty cannot be bought.'

Bertha curtsied again. What was the Madam up to?

'Tell me, did Cora seem distressed today? Does she seem unsettled in any way?'

'No, ma'am, just nervous about the wedding, as is only natural for a bride.'

'Yes indeed, her whole life is about to change. By this time on Thursday she will be a duchess.'

And by this time on Thursday you will be the mother of a duchess, thought Bertha. She realised that Mrs Cash was as nervous about the wedding as her daughter.

'It would be quite dreadful if anything were to happen to prevent that. So, Bertha, I am asking you to be especially vigilant. If any letters come for Cora, I want you to bring them straight to me so I may judge their suitability. I don't want anyone or anything to upset her at this delicate time in her life. Do you understand me?'

'Yes, ma'am.'

'Good. And Bertha, I don't need to tell you not to speak to Cora about this. I don't want her to be . . . distracted.'

Bertha nodded.

When Mrs Cash had left, Bertha went into the bedroom and looked until she found the cigarettes. She lit one, and stood as Cora had done, blowing the smoke into the street below.

Next morning, a note was brought up to Cora's bedroom by a footman. Bertha put it in her pocket and left it there.

CHAPTER 13

The Coiled Serpent

'REALLY, I DON'T UNDERSTAND ALL THIS excitement.' Duchess Fanny tapped the wooden pew for emphasis. 'I've had two weddings and never felt any need to rehearse. All you have to remember is not to gallop up the aisle, so people have time to admire your dress, and to speak your vows clearly. Hardly taxing for a girl of your intelligence, Cora. And as for your bridesmaids, Sybil has done this many times before, she can lead the way. If you really want to practise, why don't you walk up and down a few times now, to get the timing of the thing. But not too much, you don't want to appear drilled.' The Duchess smiled at the assembled company, her pale blue eyes candid with the air of someone who has found the missing key that the whole household has been searching for. Her audience, however, did not share her conviction. When Mrs Cash at last found her voice, it was tight with suppressed emotion.

'I have not had the experience of an English wedding, Duchess, perhaps they are simpler affairs. Here it is customary to rehearse with all the members of the wedding, including the groom.' Mrs Cash was trying to control her irritation but without much success. She looked up at the great stained-glass window over the altar for inspiration. She had gazed at this window at so many society weddings in the past, imagining the moment when it would be Cora at the altar, that she knew every detail. There had never been any question about which church to use. All the smartest weddings were here at Trinity. There were airier, more spacious churches further uptown, but Mrs Cash had never even considered them. Trinity was the church used by the Astors, the Rhinebackers, the Schoonmakers and the rest of Old New York. Although Mrs Cash was pleased to think that none of them had ever seen the church looking so splendid.

Built of native granite, the building could be a little gloomy but the great arches of ivy and jasmine that hung over the congregation, echoing the stone vaulting above, made the stern church feel almost boudoir-like. She was particularly pleased with the cloth-of-gold carpet that she had had laid from the altar all the way down the nave. It was embroidered here and there with the bridal couple's monograms in silver. Even the Duchess, who had deemed the church quite 'forbidding' from the outside, had gasped at that. Mrs Cash glanced over to where the Duchess was seated under an enormous floral representation of the Maltravers coat of arms on the groom's side of the church, looking completely unconcerned by her son's absence, and felt the scar tissue on the left side of her face begin to ache.

When the Duke and his party had arrived in the country, she had given them itineraries that had made it absolutely clear that the rehearsal was a formal event. It was bad enough that he had missed nearly all of the dinners she had arranged to introduce him to New York society, but for the groom and the best man to miss the rehearsal, that really was too much. The bishop was there, the bridesmaids and ushers, even the editor of *Vogue*; only the groom was missing. And the Duchess, who really should know better, was acting as if this was some tiresome piece of American nonsense. Duchess Fanny took no notice of the stiffness in Mrs Cash's reply and continued regardless. 'Ivo would be mortified to think that you were all here waiting for him.' She lingered on the word mortified, somehow implying that Ivo would be quite the opposite. 'I'm sure he had no idea that this was such an event. He probably thought it was a women's affair.'

Nobody spoke.

The Duchess looked up at her future daughter-in-law, who was standing at the altar steps next to her father. 'Don't worry, Cora. I'm sure he will remember to turn up tomorrow.' She gave her most adorable smile.

Cora tried to smile back. Her cheeks ached as she tried to match the Duchess's breeziness, even though she could feel her eyes stinging. Suppose Ivo really had changed his mind? But she forced herself to sound as if, like the Duchess, she found his absence simply amusing.

'Oh, I hope so, Duchess. It would be so tiresome to return all the wedding gifts, and to waste all these flowers would be criminal.' She gestured at the banks of orchids, the tuberose garlands and the columns of myrtle and jasmine. The air inside the church was so thick with floral scent that Cora felt as if she could fall back and be supported by the fragrant undercurrents.

The Duchess looked at her with something like approval. If only the mother would stop making such a fuss. She decided to bring the proceedings to a close.

'When I see Ivo I will scold him roundly for being so inconsiderate, but for my part I am delighted to have had the chance to admire this church and the magnificent floral arrangements at my leisure. I don't think I have ever seen such a profusion of flowers or such tasteful arrangements. Reassure me, Mrs Cash, that this is an exceptional display even by New York standards. Our poor London posies feel quite primitive by comparison.'

Mrs Cash was somewhat mollified by this overture. It was the first time that the Duchess had admitted that anything in America was superior to its British equivalent. She was about to speak when her husband forestalled her. Standing at Cora's side, he had noticed the tears in his daughter's eyes.

'Well, as we have now been here for the best part of two hours, I think the ladies should conserve their strength for tomorrow. I expect Wareham to come back with a mountain lion at the very least. Duchess, would you allow me to escort you to the carriage?'

The Duchess lowered her eyelashes at him. Really, Cora's father was quite gentlemanly for an American. She placed her kid-gloved hand on his proffered arm with a look of complicity that made Winthrop stroke the ends of his mustache.

As they walked up the aisle of the church to the entrance, Duchess Fanny could not resist saying, 'Really, this makes me feel a little emotional, Mr Cash, walking up the aisle on the arm of a man. I feel as if I were the bride myself,' and she gave him a sideways look that made it clear that she considered him quite a suitable partner.

'Well, anybody could be forgiven for mistaking you for a blushing bride, Duchess. Why, I could scarcely credit that you were old enough to have a grown son. When I first saw you I thought you must be your stepdaughter.'

'Oh Mr Cash, you are teasing me, but I shan't pretend I don't like it. I hope you will come to England soon, I think you would enjoy it. If you come to Conyers, I promise to entertain you.'

Winthrop Cash wondered if the Duchess was really flirting with him. The little squeeze she gave his arm as she invited him to England held the promise of greater intimacy. He was not used to such signals from women of his own social class; his tastes ran to rather simpler transactions. But the Duchess was a beautiful woman and it tickled his vanity to have her look up at him with such invitation in her eyes. He found the Duchess altogether more to his taste than her son. The disagreement they had had over Cora's settlement still rankled. The Duke had expected Cora's fortune to be handed over to him; he had been astonished when Cash had explained that the money he would settle on Cora would be hers to control. 'Do you mean to say that you expect me to ask Cora for money?' Ivo had said loudly and slowly, as if speaking to someone with an imperfect command of English. Winthrop had replied that in America women retained control of their fortune when they married, he saw no reason to change things because his only child was marrying an Englishman, even such a distinguished one (the last remark made with a stiff little bow to the Duke). The implication was not lost on Wareham, who went silent. The pause lasted for some minutes until the Duke managed a smile of sorts and tried to speak with some degree of warmth.

'You must excuse me, Mr Cash, I had no idea that our ways of doing things were so very different. I should probably have brought some adviser with me but I did not foresee the need. I am not a fortune-hunter, Mr Cash, I am merely an Englishman who shrinks from burdening his future wife with the cares of running an estate. I won't pretend that my affairs are unencumbered. The depression in prices has affected me greatly. I don't want to marry Cora for her money but there is no doubt that money will be needed. We English don't mind so much being shabby but Cora has been brought up to all this . . .' he gestured round the library in the Cash mansion. In its decoration and furnishings, the American library was in every way similar to its English equivalent on which it had been closely modelled; the difference was not in the furnishings but in the absence of damp and the general air of comfort that lay across the room like a cashmere stole.

Winthrop looked at the younger man with a degree of scepticism. He knew that dukes did not marry American heiresses for love alone; moreover, this union was a transaction on both sides, even if Cora would never admit it. He could protect her fortune but he wondered if by doing so he would condemn their marriage; he thought of how much he would dislike having to ask his wife for money. He decided to make a concession to the Duke's pride – his father the Golden Miller had taught him that it was bad business not to let the defeated party walk away with honour. He would make a settlement on the Duke as a wedding gift, but he would make his gesture on the day of the wedding. He had not quite forgiven the Duke for his assumption that Cora was getting the best part of the bargain.

But thoughts of the son evaporated as the mother cooed in his ear about the splendours of Conyers and how much she would like to introduce him to the Prince of Wales. As he handed her into the carriage, Winthrop noticed that on the sliver of skin visible between the Duchess's sleeve and her glove there was a blue marking. If it had been anyone else, he would have sworn it was a tattoo.

The Duchess caught his look and laughed throatily. 'I see you have found the serpent, Mr Cash.' She peeled back her glove to give him a closer look at the tattoo of a snake that coiled itself round her wrist, the tail disappearing into the serpent's mouth on the tender white skin beneath the mound of her thumb. It was delicate work, a world away from the pictures of sweethearts and mothers that adorned the biceps of Mr Cash's mill hands.

'It is very . . . particular,' he said.

'You have no idea how true that is. There are only four tattoos like it in existence. And when you come to Conyers, I will explain its significance.'

'I don't know that I can wait that long.' Winthrop felt unreasonably excited by the Duchess and her secrets, but the moment was interrupted by the arrival of his wife, daughter and a clutch of bridesmaids all complaining about the cold and in urgent need of a carriage. By the time all the women were accommodated, Winthrop had been separated from the Duchess but not from the image of the tattoo. He felt a sudden spike of desire mixed with something like alarm. Was Cora, he wondered, ready for this world of coiled serpents and secret symbols?

The rehearsal dinner was to go ahead that night, even if as yet there was no sign of the Duke and his best man.

Only the Duchess was entirely serene. As she walked into the drawing room before dinner, she surveyed the members of the wedding and drawled in her throatiest tones, 'This is like *Hamlet* without the Prince. It really is too naughty of Ivo to neglect his duties so.' But her smile suggested that she felt that her presence more than made up for the non-appearance of her son. Only Winthrop smiled back with genuine warmth.

Cora tried to concentrate on her bridesmaids who were peppering her with questions about England. When would she be presented at court? How many rooms did Lulworth have? What would people call her? Were all the English girls as tall as Lady Sybil? Cora answered them as best she could, although she knew the only thing that would satisfy them would be Ivo himself. She was not above looking forward to seeing her bridesmaids' faces when they saw that her future husband was a handsome man as well as a duke. But her smile became more and more fixed as the last of the guests arrived and there was still no sign of Ivo. At last her mother announced that they must go in to dinner. Cora did her best to sparkle as if completely unconcerned and declared that Ivo was probably confused as to the hour, as in London no one dined before eight.

'Oh, you know men and their shooting,' the Double Duchess said helpfully. 'We should be grateful really that they have something to get them out from under our feet. Really, I don't think I could endure a man I had to lunch with every day.'

Winthrop laughed, but Cora's smile was thin and her mother's non-existent.

Cora went in to dinner with Sybil, as they were both missing their partners. The width of their enormous leg-of-mutton sleeves made it difficult for them to talk easily but Sybil turned her head sideways and said, 'You are an angel for lending me the frock. One of your friends asked me where I had got it. I said from Maison Worth as if I went there all the time!' She laughed and then she saw the expression on Cora's face. 'Don't worry, Cora, he'll be here. I'm sure he's only doing this to annoy Mama.'

And then, just as they were walking into the long candle-filled dining room, each girl felt her arm being taken by the elbow. The hunting party had returned. Ivo and Reggie were there, faces ruddy from the shooting, looking delighted with themselves, and boasting about their tally.

Cora tried not to show how relieved she was to see him and how furious she was with him for having stayed away so long, but Ivo caught the flicker of emotions on her face and said in a lower voice, 'Are you angry with me for missing the rehearsal? Your mother sent a note to the hotel saying how disappointed she was.' Ivo's tone was hardly contrite. Cora tried to temper the pleasure she took in seeing him with the coolness appropriate to his behaviour. But Ivo's hand was caressing the inside of her arm, and as he pulled out the chair for her to sit down, his hand brushed the nape of her neck.

'I had to field some searching questions from my bridesmaids. The ones that credited your existence at all were most curious about your habits. A duke is excitement enough, but a missing duke is even better. So I don't know who is more put out with you, me because you missed the rehearsal or my bridesmaids because you've spoiled a promising mystery.' Her tone was as unconcerned as she could make it.

Ivo sat down next to her. He took her hand under the table and squeezed it. The gesture was enough to make her eyes fill. She smiled, desperately trying to make the tears disperse through sheer will. She took her hand away and had a sip of Ivo's champagne.

'You know, I wondered last night if you were ever coming back. I thought perhaps you might have gone home.' She said this in a very fast muttered undertone so that only he should hear.

'Gone home?' Ivo opened his eyes wide in exaggerated astonishment. She saw that he was trying not to take her comment seriously. 'But why would I do that, when I have come all this way to marry you?'

Cora felt her mother's stare, but she had to talk to Ivo about this now; tomorrow would be too late.

'Because you feel differently. Ever since you arrived you have been . . . distant. Not like you were in Lulworth.' Her words tumbled out, all her attempts at insouciance abandoned.

Ivo heard the change in her voice and said quietly, 'But that's because we're not at Lulworth. You forget, I am a foreigner here. So many things seem strange to me here. Even you.'

Cora looked at him in astonishment. 'Me? But I have not changed. I am the same girl you proposed to.' She put her hand to her chest as she said this as if to emphasise that, underneath, she was the same.

Ivo looked at her directly and she felt she was seeing a part of him she had never seen before. 'But when I see you here amidst all this, I realise that I proposed to a very small part of you. I thought I was giving you a home and a position, but here I see that I am taking you away from so much.' He looked down at his plate which was made of gold and chased with the Cash monogram, and lifted it, exaggerating its weight. She was about to tell him how little she cared for any of it when there was a chink of metal on glass and Winthrop stood up to make a toast.

All eyes were on them now. Cora looked at Ivo anxiously but to her relief and joy he took her hand and raised it to his lips. There was a little sigh of envy from the bridesmaids. Cora felt the tightness behind her eyes loosen; this, after all, was what she had wanted.

The dinner ended promptly at nine. Mrs Cash's direction had been quite clear, there was to be no lingering. Cora stood at the top of the stairs saying goodbye to Cornelia Rhinelander, her mother's favourite bridesmaid (to have a Rhinelander as a bridesmaid at the wedding of her daughter to a duke was almost at the summit of Mrs Cash's social ambitions). Cornelia, who was twenty-four, congratulated Cora with a creditable display of enthusiasm, given her unmarried status. 'You look very well together, I think it will be the wedding of the season.' She was about to go on but then she saw the Duke approaching over Cora's shoulder and made her goodbyes. Even Cornelia could see that the Duke wanted to be alone with his bride-to-be.

A touch on her shoulder. She turned to face him. He took one of her hands in his and used the other to trace the curve of her cheek. 'I am glad I came back.' He looked as serious as she had ever seen him, his dark brown eyes deep with emotion, his mouth soft.

But Cora stiffened. She was disturbed by the implication of his remark. He had spoken as if he had overcome something, that he had come back from the brink. She had been right – he had been having second thoughts. But then she thought of the way he had lifted the gold dinner plate – it was her money that was coming between them. She almost smiled in relief.

'Did you have a choice?' She looked at him with all the longing and disappointment of the last week in her eyes.

'Not any more,' and he raised her hand, opened the buttons of her long kid evening glove and kissed her exposed wrist. 'Not any more.' He looked at her fully with what Cora felt was love and she swayed towards him. But then there were footsteps and he straightened away from her.

'Oh, there's Reggie, we must go. I don't want to annoy your mother twice in one day.' He gave her back her hand like a gift. 'Sleep well, Cora.'

Cora watched him walk down the stairs to the door. Would he turn and look back at her? But here was Reggie bidding her good night before following his friend to the Astoria Hotel where they were spending the night. When she turned back, Ivo had gone.

Shaken, she tried to slip upstairs to her room before she had to talk to anyone. She wanted to be alone to think. She rubbed the wrist he had kissed against her cheek. But as she turned towards the staircase she heard the Duchess's voice. Cora had no desire to talk to her future mother-in-law. She opened the door behind her.

She turned into the dark drawing room just as a beam of moonlight struck the table in front of her. The ceiling was pierced by a hundred points of light and then as a cloud moved across the moon, the brilliance was gone. Cora walked over to the long table where the wedding presents had been laid out ready for inspection by the guests the next day. The sparkle had come from one of the antique crystal and bronze candlesticks that had been sent by Mrs Auchinschloss. Cora flicked one of the brilliants with her finger and watched the shower of light it made in the mirror opposite. She could still hear the Duchess's husky voice on the other side of the door.

The presents had been arriving since the engagement was announced. The display had been set out on three long tables, each gift with a card announcing the giver. The more magnificent the gift, the more likely it was to have come from a friend of the bride. Cora looked at a Louis boulle clock of tortoiseshell and gilt which was about two feet high – a gift from the Carnegies. There was an alabaster bowl set with gold and gems from the Mellons, a silver punchbowl – so big that it would happily accommodate a small child – from the Hammerschorns. There were no dinner services or cutlery, as it was tacitly assumed that a duke would have no need of such things.

Cora moved restlessly around the table. There was too much here, she thought; all these glittering objects shining in the moonlight made her feel slightly queasy. Hitherto she had felt bolstered by the size and splendour of this tribute, but now it seemed worrying. So many things and for what? She stopped by a pair of boxes that lay side by side on the table. They were beautiful things made from walnut with mother-of-pearl inlay and her and Ivo's monograms in silver on the lid. She opened the box marked CW and found it was a dressing case whose sides opened out like arms to reveal crystal bottles with chased silver tops and sets of ivory manicure instruments and glove stretchers, tortoiseshell-backed hairbrushes and combs, a porcelain box for rouge, a pair of tiny gold scissors shaped like a crane with its legs turning into the blades, and a golden thimble. Every item from the thimble to the hairbrush was engraved with her monogram. Even Cora, who was no stranger to such things, was struck by the luxurious preciseness of the case, the way in which every feminine need was accommodated and allowed to nestle in its red velvet hollow. Cora looked at the card which accompanied it: From Sir Odo and Lady Beauchamp. She remembered the couple at the hunt and the chilliness of their attitude towards her; perhaps they regretted their behaviour now that she was to be a duchess. Then she lifted the lid of Ivo's box – it was like hers except that the linings were in green morocco leather and velvet, not red, and the rouge pots and tweezers were replaced by ivory-handled shaving brushes. Cora thought for a moment that it was a curiously intimate present, it disturbed her to see Ivo's bodily needs anticipated so neatly by a stranger. She noticed that unlike her case, this one had a set of drawers for cufflinks. She pulled at a tiny golden handle and the drawer came out smoothly to reveal a set of black pearl dress studs and a card. Cora picked up the card. Written on it in cramped italic writing were the words '*May your marriage be as happy as mine has been*'. Cora wondered which of the couple from the hunt had placed it there, Sir Odo with his shiny face and high voice, or his handsome, sulky wife? She was about to put the note back but then, angry with everything British and mealy-mouthed, she tore the card in two.

She pushed the drawer shut. Looking about her for distraction, she saw a birdcage with a tiny gilded bird on a perch in the middle. There was a key at the base of the cage. Cora gave it a couple of sharp turns and the golden bird began to chirp its way through 'Dixie'. This was a present from one of Mother's cousins in South Carolina – who else would send something so eccentric? But the jaunty song roused Cora. At once the pressure in her head lifted and although she could still hear the Duchess's voice, she opened the door.

She waved at the assembled company and walked up the twenty-four marble steps to her bedroom. At the top she remembered the bicycle that Teddy had offered her as a wedding present and the thought of its rude practicality amongst all the gilt and glitter downstairs almost made her smile.

CHAPTER 14

Florence Dursheimer's Day Out

LORENCE DURSHEIMER'S NOSE WAS BEGINNING to run. She had been standing on the corner of Wall Street and Broadway since six o'clock that morning. She had gone early from her home in Orchard Street thinking to be the first outside the church, but to her annoyance there was already a small knot of women established there. Florence had taken up her place beside these women, who were occupying what she considered to be her rightful spot, with the barest of greetings. None of these interlopers had her connection with the bride. Florence had trimmed the hat that Cora Cash had worn in the photograph that accompanied the notice of her engagement in *Town Topics*. It was Florence's deft fingers that had pinned the gold humming-bird just below the ostrich-feather plume. It had been the bird that had caught Cora's eye when she had entered Madame Rochas's millinery establishment.

Florence had worked hard on the Coruscator, harder perhaps than was warranted as she was paid by the piece but she had felt uplifted when Miss Cash, the heiress of the season, had raised her hand on seeing her hat. She had tried it on in the shop and Florence had been allowed to place the hat at the precise angle on Miss Cash's head and had pushed the diamond-headed hat-pin into Miss Cash's warm brown hair. Miss Cash had smelt faintly of orange blossom which had made Florence only too conscious of her own unwashed state and the sharp stink of sweat that escaped as she lifted her arms to place the Coruscator on the heiress's head. But Miss Cash had not wrinkled her nose or reached for her handkerchief as other rich girls might have done, but had smiled at her reflection in the glass and said, 'What a charming hat! Did you make it?' And Florence had nodded and had followed Miss Cash from that point to this spot on the corner of Wall Street and Broadway.

Florence would have liked to dab her nose with her handker-chief but at eleven thirty the crush was now so great that she could not move her arms. She was hemmed in on all sides by women like herself, desperate for a glimpse of the Cash wedding. A number of the women were clutching newspapers with Cora's picture on the front. They talked about her while they were waiting as if she were a sister or a friend, exchanging details of shoes, her hats, even her gold-plated bridal underwear. Florence had wondered whether she should announce that she had actually met Cora but it was easier to listen to the chatter that swirled around her and content herself with merely feeling the glow of ownership. The general feeling among the crowd was that it was a shame that she was marrying an Englishman, even if he was a duke. But Florence had seen Cora twisting her engagement ring and smiling while she waited for her hat to be boxed up. She knew it was a love match, whatever the papers might say. Florence had seen enough engaged girls pass through Madame Rochas to know the differ-ence between the ones who looked forward to married life and the ones who could not see beyond the wedding.

There was a big swell from the crowd: the bridegroom's party was arriving. Florence fought her way to the front of the crowd, wedging her head under a policeman's elbow. She saw two men getting out of the carriage, one blond, one dark. Florence knew from *Town Topics* that the dark man was the Duke and the other was his best man Reggie Greatorex. She screwed up her eyes, which had been made shortsighted by years of fine sewing in bad light. Prompted by a remark from his friend, the groom turned his head and looked at the crowd. The crowd roared and the Duke smiled and waved his hand and pointed at the white gardenia in his buttonhole. Florence could not be sure of the expression on his face but she thought she saw his hand shake as he reached to touch the flower in his lapel. The Duke's acknowledgement pleased the crowd and there was a general agreement that he was a fine-looking man. Then the coach containing Mrs Cash and the bridesmaids arrived and there was a high-pitched coo as all the women in the largely feminine crowd sighed over their clothes.

Mrs Cash was in gold brocade trimmed with sable. On her head she wore a fur toque pinned with a brilliant diamond aigrette and a delicate lace veil. Florence had made the hat after a photograph that Mrs Cash had shown her of the Princess of Wales, and although she had not been specifically asked, she had reinforced the side of the veil that would lie over the damaged part of Mrs Cash's face. The six bridesmaids wore gowns of peach satin with wide hats trimmed with ostrich feathers, and each had a pearl choker round her neck that had been presented to them that morning by Winthrop Cash. There was one bridesmaid with red hair whom Florence did not recognise and she frowned, put out that her encyclopaedic knowledge of New York society women should be found wanting; but then she remembered that one of the bridesmaids was a relation of the Duke. She felt sure that she would have remembered hair of that particular hue, rather an unfortunate contrast with the peach satin. Florence felt the droplet on her nose fall and another one well up to take its place; her eyes, too, were streaming. If only she could reach her handkerchief. Then there was a loud cheer as the crowd further up Broadway caught sight of the bridal coach pulled by four matched greys.

At last the coach drew up in front of the church. Mr Cash got out and turned to help his daughter. Florence found herself being pushed forward by the surge of the crowd. She was edging closer and closer to the entrance of the church. She could smell the lilies in the great wreath that hung over the carved doors. Florence felt someone put their foot through the back of her skirt, but she dared not turn round – she would never forgive herself if she failed to see Cora. There was another sigh from the crowd as the bride was handed out of the coach. Florence craned her head to see but her view was blocked by the coach. She stood on the tips of her toes, pushing her head up until she felt her neck would break, but at just under five feet she was too small to see the bride's face. Two women behind her were talking about the dress.

'Now would you say that satin was oyster or more cream, Edith?'

'It looks cream to me. Wonderful lace on the bodice, Brussels or Valenciennes?'

'Brussels. It's a Worth dress, he only uses Brussels lace.'

Hearing this exchange, Florence felt she would burst. Cora was her property, not theirs. Did they have pictures of Cora on every wall of their bedrooms? She, Florence, had even been born in the same year as Cora nineteen years ago and on the same day, if not actually the same month. How dare these women dissect the dress that was Florence's by right? The policeman standing over her heard her snort and looked down, amused.

'All right there, miss?' He had an Irish accent and red, protuberant ears.

'I can't see the bride and she's the only reason I'm here.' Florence's eyes were wet. The policeman had left three younger sisters behind him in County Wicklow, so he knew feminine desperation when he heard it.

'Well, we can't have that now, can we?' and with a swoop he picked Florence up by her waist and lifted her on to his shoulders. She made a little scream of protest that turned into a gasp of delight as she caught sight of Cora. The bride was standing on the red-brown granite steps of the church, her train spread out behind her like a puddle of cream. The dress was in the latest fashion with wide leg-of-mutton sleeves, a tiny waist and a flowing skirt. The fabric was a heavy duchesse satin set with pearls. As custom dictated, the neckline was high and the sleeves came right down to the wrist. On each shoulder were epaulettes of white flowers – Florence thought they were gardenias – otherwise the dress had no ornament, no bows, frills or flounces, nothing that would detract from the lace veil with its intricate réseau of fruit, flowers and butterflies. That kind of lace could not be had for love or money these days, *Town Topics* had told its readers. This veil had originally belonged to the Princesse de Lamballe who, the article went on, had lost her head in the French Revolution. Florence knew nothing about the French Revolution but she knew enough about lace to know that Cora's veil was worth enough money to buy the whole of Madame Rochas several times over. But she felt no revolutionary fervour, quite the contrary – Florence would have felt cheated if Cora had settled for anything less.

Florence had seen at least ten brides stand on the steps of that church, but she couldn't recall any of them now as she looked at Cora, whose arms were raised, trying to adjust the tiara on her head, while her father stood by rather helplessly. Florence could see the frown of concentration on Cora's face and longed to rush forward and fix the tiara so that it would frame Cora's white face and not ride too low and give her a headache. Florence sometimes worked in the cloakrooms at DelMonico's and she had helped debutantes with red weals on their foreheads where their hired tiaras had cut into their flesh. The trick was to dress the hair so that no part of the metal would touch the delicate skin around the temple. Surely Cora would have had someone to fix her hair who knew that.

At last Cora was satisfied and lowered her arms and shook her head a little to test her handiwork. As she turned, the lace veil over her face fluttered and Florence saw how white her face was and how she chewed her lower lip. She looked different to the smiling girl who had played with her engagement ring in Madame Rochas: more serious but less confident, and there were purple shadows under her eyes that hadn't been there before. Florence felt disappointed, even a little irritated. She had come here to see a radiant bride – purple shadows she could see in the mirror. Florence put two fingers to her mouth and let out the most piercing whistle she could manage. The Irish policeman pulled her leg.

'Hey, do you want to get me into trouble now? I'm meant to be keeping the peace here.'

But Florence was deaf to his protests. Cora had heard the

whistle and turned in her direction. Florence waved her arms wildly, so much so that the policeman had to put his hands on her thighs to keep her steady. The milliner had never allowed a man such liberties before, but at this moment she was oblivious to the intimacy. Cora looked right at her and she started to smile, the same smile she had given Florence when she had tried on the hat. Florence felt triumphant; she had restored the situation, she alone had given the world what it wanted, a radiant bride. Proprietorially she watched as Cora was handed her bouquet by one of the bridesmaids. The flowers had come, Florence had read, all the way from Lulworth, the Duke's home in England. Florence didn't really understand why such a fragile thing as flowers had come all that way; jewels she could understand, but not flowers. But *Town Topics* had said that all the duchesses carried flowers from Lulworth and it was a tradition that the Duke was determined not to break just because he was marrying an American girl. Florence could barely remember her journey to New York from Germany – the roll of the ship and the smell. She imagined Cora's flowers on a white cushion in their own cabin and thought of her mother clutching her shoulder as they huddled on deck.

But now Cora was taking her father's arm with her free hand. The sound of the organ came out of the open doors of the church. Florence watched as the pool of satin and lace was drawn up the steps. As it disappeared and the great carved doors swung shut, Florence felt her body go limp. She slid into the arms of the policeman, who held her upright as the crowd surged around them.

Florence Dursheimer was not the only woman to faint that day. As *Town Topics* reported later, there were four faintings, one minor concussion and a woman who went into early labour. The paper commented that it was a relief to all concerned that the New York police had managed to keep the injuries among the crowd to the bare minimum.

CHAPTER 15

'That Spot of Joy'

'WOULD YOU LIKE ME TO WARM THE PEARLS for you now, Miss Cora?' Bertha had tried to get into the habit of calling her mistress Your Grace, but she did not always succeed. Cora had corrected her at first but now the first thrill of her new title had worn off, and she did not altogether mind this reminder of her girlhood.

'Yes, thank you, Bertha. The Prince will be there tonight. Ivo says that he notices what women wear. Ivo's aunt wore the same dress twice during one week and the Prince said, haven't I seen that before, and she had to go and change into something new, and when she didn't have anything new she had to pretend she was ill and have meals on a tray.'

This was not a problem that was likely to affect Cora, who had come to Conyers with no less than forty trunks. But tonight Cora was wearing a dress she had worn before: her wedding dress which had been cut down at the neckline and at the sleeves so that it was now a dinner dress. In New York it was the custom for a bride to wear her wedding dress for the first round of visits as a newly-wed. As this was the first time she would go into society proper after the honeymoon, it seemed the perfect time to wear it. It did no harm to remind people that although she was now a duchess she was also still a bride.

Putting on the dress had brought her wedding day back in all its chaos and glory. Although Cora was used to being written about in the papers, the crowds lining her progress from the Cash mansion downtown to Trinity Church had amazed her. So many people shouting her name as if they knew her. Her father had shaken his head and said, 'It's like a royal wedding.' But Cora had worried what Ivo would think. She could imagine his mother's words: 'Crowds of people waiting for a glimpse of the bride, no wonder Cora didn't want a quiet country wedding.' Yet it was exciting that all these people had come out just to see her, not because she was going to be a duchess but because she was Cora Cash, the Golden Miller's granddaughter and probably the richest girl in the world. Her father had taken her hand and said, 'This is quite something, Cora. There was nothing like this when I married your mother. Look at those women over there screaming. Don't they have families to look after? I hope Wareham realises he is marrying an American princess.'

Cora had smiled at this but all she could think of was Ivo's horrified start when she had embraced him in the Customs Hall in front of the photographers. She knew that the roar that greeted her as she got out of the coach would be heard inside the church. The thought of Ivo wincing had almost ruined the moment but then she had seen the little girl from the milliner's sitting on a policeman's shoulders whistling and waving for all she was worth and she had felt buoyed up by the girl's enthusiasm. These people were here for her, why should she feel guilty? As she walked up the aisle she could just make out the back of Ivo's head through her veil. She thought of their first meeting and how he had shown her his neck. She willed him to look round at her but he kept his eyes straight ahead. She remembered that moment in the gallery at Lulworth when he had seen her but had pretended not to. At last she drew level with him and caught a glimpse of his face. His profile was hard and set and Cora wondered for a moment if this had all been a terrible mistake Then her father took her hand and placed it in Ivo's and she felt him hold it fast. His touch, as always, reassured her. All she had to do was hold on.

The dinner gong sounded. Cora put out her hand for the pearls. Bertha took them from her bodice where she had been warming them so that they would be at their most lustrous. It was a trick she had learnt from the Double Duchess's maid, who had been amazed at Bertha's ignorance. 'Ladies are always cold in their evening things, so you need to warm the pearls so they shine – cold pearls on cold skin, spittle on a turkey gizzard.'

Bertha fastened the necklace round her mistress's long white neck. Their dark iridescent sheen made the skin glow. The Duke had given them to Cora in Venice on their honeymoon, and Cora had worn them every night since.

Cora's hands went straight to her throat. She loved the smooth weight of the pearls against her skin. She knew that white pearls would be more usual with her dress but she liked the contrast between the white and the black, it made her feel worldly, brazen even. Every time she put them on she remembered the first time she had worn them: naked but for the necklace under the sheets of their canopied bed in the Palazzo Mocenigo. It was the fourth week of their honeymoon and they had been in Venice for three days. Cora had not known what to expect of married life. She had some inkling of the physical side of things from Ivo's more fervent embraces, but she had not realised that her old self would be so completely obliterated. After their first night together, when he had got up from the bed, she had felt the parting of their flesh as pain, it was if she had lost a skin. And that feeling had only intensified with every passing day and night; she only felt at peace when he was in her arms, when his skin covered hers. Never in her life had she been so aware of all her senses; every morning she smelled the sweet dark smell of his skin and was glad. When she was with him she had to touch him, when he was apart from her she would hug herself so as not to let the flesh that had been warmed by him grow cold.

That morning in Venice he had disappeared after breakfast. It was too hot to go out and Cora had wandered about the palazzo aimlessly. She tried to read her Baedeker but she could not concentrate on anything while he was gone. He didn't come back for lunch and Cora had gone for her siesta in a frenzy of impatience. She had undressed completely, feeling that only the cool white linen sheets would dampen the heat coursing round her body. But the sheets, too, began to twist and grow hot, so she had thrown them off and had lain there with the warm air on her skin and the sounds of the Grand Canal floating in through the open window. She must have fallen asleep because the next thing she remembered was Ivo's hand on her breast. She put up her arms to draw him to her, but he had held back. 'Wait, my impatient darling, there is something I want you to wear for me.' And he had taken a worn leather box out of his pocket. 'Open it.' Cora had leant over him and had squeezed the lid of the box open. Inside were the pearls, as big as quail's eggs and all the colours of the night from bronze to midnight purple. She picked them out of the box and held them to her throat, where they had lain, as they lay now, heavy with promise. She lifted her arms to reach for the clasp, half expecting Ivo to take over, but he simply watched her as she tried to fit the golden hook into its sprung clasp.

He leant back a little from her to admire his gift.

'Black pearls are so rare that it can take a lifetime to collect enough to make a necklace. I thought they were a fitting tribute.' He reached forward and ran his fingers along the pearls and then put his mouth on hers.

Later, he had whispered in her ear, 'I wanted you to have them, only you.' And she had kissed him and put his hand to her throat.

'Feel how warm they are now. Every time I wear them I will think of this.'

Cora felt the warmth of that remembered afternoon sweep through her body. It had been hard coming back to England after the honeymoon, not just because she now had a title and a great house to run, but because she could no longer be with Ivo all day and night. Lulworth had eighty-one servants and even though they had not begun to entertain, it felt as if they were never alone. She was no longer as certain of Ivo as she had been when they had sailed around the Mediterranean on her father's yacht. Then they had both been loose and shapeless, constrained by nothing but the weather. The occasional dinner they had taken with ambassadors and minor princes had been adventures that they had dressed up for, laughing and complicit, catching each other's eye throughout the evening, longing for it to end so that they could be alone together again. But now when Cora looked up hoping to exchange a glance with Ivo, she could not be certain that his eyes would be waiting for her. Only at night could she be sure of him. It had been quite a shock to discover that here at Conyers they had been given separate bedrooms. Ivo had laughed at her evident dismay.

'Darling, you will never pass as a duchess if people think that you actually want to share a bed with your husband.'

Cora had made him promise that he would spend the nights with her.

'But I will have to leave at crack of dawn or the servants will talk.'

Cora had pouted but Ivo had laughed her out of it.

Now she was waiting for him to take her downstairs. Where was he? Maybe she should go to him, his room must be on the same corridor. But Conyers was so cavernous that she might get lost. She thought of that poem where the bride hid in a chest and was never found, until much later when a skeleton with a veil was discovered. Not that the Double Duchess would look very hard, she thought. Her mother-in-law was invariably charming to her but Cora was not deceived. She knew that Fanny was making the best of what she considered a bad job. Fanny's ideal daughter-in-law would have been a girl she had chosen, a girl of good family, pretty but not spectacularly so, wealthy but not too rich, a little bit dowdy, who would defer to her mother-in-law in all things. Instead she had Cora who was not only American, but beautifully dressed, indecently rich and only erratically deferential. Cora suspected that the Double Duchess had organised this royal party at Conyers to remind her daughter-in-law just how much she still had to learn.

She opened the door of her room and looked down the corridor. The door had a card inserted into a brass holder on which was written 'The Duchess of Wareham'. Cora looked at it stupidly. It was still hard for her to connect this edifice with herself. But if her name was on the door then surely it would not be too hard to find Ivo. She walked down the corridor, which for an English house was almost warm. She could hear muffled voices through the door that said 'Lady Beauchamp' and then a peal of laughter. Cora moved on in search of her husband. She found his room right at the very end of the corridor (really, Duchess Fanny might as well have put them in separate buildings). There was the name card, 'The Duke of Wareham' in the same spidery hand. She turned the handle.

'Ivo, are you there, darling? I want you to come and put me out of my misery. If I wait around any longer practising my curtsy I will turn into a pillar of salt. Ivo?'

But the room was empty. Ivo had evidently dressed, his collar case was empty on the dressing table. Cora saw that Ivo had brought the travelling case from the Beauchamps; she felt irrationally annoyed that Ivo should be using it. She remembered the dress studs that had also been in the drawer, they had been black pearls too. She opened the drawer where they had lain, and found it empty. She felt suddenly desolate without her husband. On the bureau lay a shirt that he must have taken off before putting on his evening clothes. She picked it up and buried her face in it, finding reassurance in that familiar scent.

'Darling, what on earth are you doing?' He was standing in the doorway, laughing at her.

'I was missing you!' said Cora defiantly. He went over to her and kissed her on the forehead. She put her face up to his.

'Why didn't you come and get me? I got so bored of waiting I came to find you.'

'Oh, I got waylaid by Colonel Ferrers the Prince's equerry, some very tedious question of protocol. Can't think why Bertie puts so much store by all that stuff. But because he's here we will all have to play by the rules. Which means that you, my little savage, are the senior duchess present and will go in to dinner with the Prince.'

'But surely your mother is more qualified. I shouldn't take precedence over her,'

'Oh, infinitely more qualified, but sadly the Buckinghams are an eighteenth-century concoction whereas the Warehams go all the way back to James the First, so you are number seven and poor old Mama is number twelve. Ferrers has looked it up in Debrett's so there is no getting around it. Everyone has their number and those are the rules. The only person who can play around with precedent is the Prince, which I suppose is what Mama was counting on.'

'Oh Lord. Well, you had better kiss me for good luck, I feel as if I am going into battle.'

'You are, Cora, you are.'

The Double Duchess was in the Chinese room. Conyers had been built in the 1760s when the fashion for chinoiserie was at its height. This octagonal room with its lacquered furniture and hand-painted silk wallpaper was so famous that it had never been modernised. Every detail – the faux bamboo window frets picked out in gilt, the dragon's head sconces, the pagodas on the octagonal silk carpet – had been perfectly realised. Even Cora, who took splendour for granted, was impressed. Each wall showed a different scene from life in the Imperial Court. The Duchess Fanny was standing in front of a wall that showed a group of exquisitely dressed courtiers grouped around an empty throne.

Buckingham, her husband, stood slightly behind her, ready and waiting to obey his wife's every whim.

'Cora, my dear, how fresh you look. Is that your wedding dress remodelled? How charming. So few of Ivo's friends were there for the wedding. I am sure they will all be delighted to see you in your bridal finery.' The Duchess's words were warm, yet it was evident to Cora that wearing the wedding dress would not 'do'. But it was too late to change.

The Double Duchess introduced her to the assembled guests. Everybody had been told to be there at seven thirty as the Prince of Wales would arrive promptly at a quarter to eight. There was no social crime more heinous than arriving after the Prince.

'Lord and Lady Bessborough, my daughter-in-law the Duchess of Wareham. Colonel Ferrers, my daughter-in-law the Duchess of Wareham, Ernest Cassel . . . Sir Odo and Lady Beauchamp, my daughter-in-law the Duchess of Wareh—'

'Oh, but we've met the Duchess before,' said Sir Odo, his face gleaming rosily over his white tie, his large pale blue eyes sparkling with malice, 'when she was still Miss Cash. We were hunting with the Myddleton, the day that Your Grace had your accident. We feel almost responsible for the match.' Odo giggled and Cora looked around for Ivo but he was on the other side of the room talking to Ferrers the equerry.

She turned to Charlotte Beauchamp, who gave her a small tight smile and dropped the very faintest of curtsies. 'Your Grace,' she said ever so slightly, inclining her smooth blond head.

Cora nodded, doing her best to smile. Unconsciously she put her hands to her throat, seeking reassurance from the glowing pearls round her neck.

Odo noticed. 'But what a magnificent necklace, Duchess Cora!

You hardly ever see pearls of that colour and size. And such a charming contrast to the dress.'

'Ivo gave it to me when we were in Venice on our wedding tour.'

'Didn't you have a necklace with pearls that colour, Charlotte, that your aunt gave you? You and Duchess Cora must be careful not to wear your black pearls at the same time or people will think that you both belong to some secret society.' Odo was almost squeaking with pleasure at his conceit. But Charlotte did not rise to his bait.

'My necklace is far inferior, Odo. Anyway it is broken, so there is no danger of duplication.'

Odo did not reply. Cora was struck by the evident tension between the couple.

There was a sudden dip in the hum of conversation and a rustling sound that spread through the room like the wind through dry leaves. Cora turned and saw the Prince of Wales standing in the doorway. He was of average height but even the immaculate tailoring of his evening clothes could not disguise his enormous girth; she understood now why his nickname was Tum Tum. He looked older than the photographs she had seen of him and they did not convey his florid complexion or the coldness of his pale blue eyes. She realised that the rustling had stopped with her, and then she caught her mother-in-law's scandalised eye and realised that the whole room was waiting for her to curtsy. But her knees refused to bend. It was only when she saw the slow smile on the face of Charlotte Beauchamp that the spell was broken; her knees obeyed and she sank into the most graceful curtsy she could manage.

'Your Highness, may I present the Duchess of Wareham.'

Duchess Fanny stopped short of a full endorsement of her daughter-in-law.

Cora was conscious of the Prince's heavy-lidded eyes looking her over with the scrutiny of experience.

'I think your son has made a very wise choice, Fanny. I've always liked Amerrricans.' The Prince had an almost French habit of rolling his 'r's.

Cora wondered whether she could safely rise from her curtsy, or was she meant to hover in obeisance while the Prince inspected her? She decided to stand up. This meant that she now stood an inch or two above the Prince. He smiled at her, revealing uneven yellow teeth.

'I have very fond memories of your country. I saw Blondin walk across the Niagarrra Falls, you know. My heart was in my mouth the whole way.' The Prince nodded at the memory.

Cora had no idea who Blondin was, but smiled back. She guessed that the Prince must be in his late fifties; if Blondin had been famous in his youth then she knew better than to remind him of his age.

'You have the advantage of this American then, Your Royal Highness. I have not yet visited the Niagara Falls.'

'But that is a shocking omission. You must make a point of going there when you return to your country.'

'Is that a royal command, sir?' Cora said as pertly as she dared.

The Prince laughed and turned to the Double Duchess. 'I hope I am sitting next to your daughter-in-law at dinner, she can amuse me.'

The Double Duchess smiled and nodded, not betraying by a flicker her dismay at this casual destruction of her carefully considered placement.

The Prince moved on and Cora felt Ivo's breath tickling her neck.

'You've made an impression on the Prince. Mother must be thrilled.'

'But where were you, Ivo? I shouldn't have to face all these people alone,' Cora said sharply. Her heart was still pounding from her encounter with the Prince.

'Nonsense, Cora, you are quite indestructible and besides, the Prince likes to have the pretty ones all to himself.' He bent down and whispered into her ear. 'But remember that I shall be watching you.'

Cora blushed and looked down in confusion. When she dared to raise her gaze, she caught a glimpse of Charlotte Beauchamp staring at them.

'Ivo, why does Charlotte Beauchamp stare at me like that?'

Ivo hesitated, then he took her hand and kissed it. 'Cora, my love, you must be used to staring by now. Poor old Charlotte is probably feeling put out that she is now no longer the reigning beauty. Don't worry about her.'

Ivo's tone was breezy but Cora felt there was something out of place that she couldn't quite identify. She noticed that he did not look over at Charlotte but kept his eyes on her.

Cora had no time to puzzle over her husband's evasions during dinner. She was fully occupied with entertaining the Prince, who had the most disconcerting habit of changing the subject the moment he grew tired of it. Cora was in the middle of describing the alterations that she was making to Lulworth when the royal eyelids flickered and he interrupted her with a question about the hunting in her native country. It was only during the serving of the fish course, when the Prince turned to talk to the Double Duchess on his other side, that Cora was able to look down the table and see that Ivo was sitting next to Charlotte Beauchamp. They were talking not to each other but to the people sitting on either side of them. Cora wanted to see how they spoke to each other but here was the ptarmigan and the Prince was turning back towards her.

'I shall look forward to seeing Lulworth again. The shooting there has always been good. As soon as you have got the house to your liking, we will visit. I know the Prrrincess would like you.'

Cora remembered what Ivo had told her about the building of the railway line and how it had almost bankrupted his father. She wondered how pleased Ivo would be to entertain the royal couple.

'I look forward to entertaining Your Royal Highnesses at Lulworth, although being an American I feel I cannot have anyone to stay until we have sufficient bathrooms.'

The Prince rumbled with laughter. 'Hear that, Fanny? Your new Duchess thinks Lulworth is unhygienic.'

The Double Duchess smiled at him lazily. 'We seemed to manage, though, didn't we, sir. Perhaps I am just set in my ways but I cannot help but think there is more to life than hot water. But Cora has grown up with every convenience, so it is only right that she should mould Lulworth to her own taste. I just hope the character of the place may be preserved. It is such an atmospheric house.' The Duchess's voice dropped to its most thrilling timbre. 'Although I love it here at Conyers, I do miss the romance of Lulworth, the mist on the trees in the morning, and the Maltravers ghosts. Poor Lady Eleanor and her broken heart. I do think there is something peculiarly English about Lulworth. It is as if a little bit of England's soul had been frozen there forever.'

The Prince leant over to Cora, and raised an eyebrow. 'The question is, can Lulworth have soul *and* hot water?'

Cora did not hesitate. She was tired of Duchess Fanny's condescension. 'Most definitely, Your Highness. In my country we have houses that have history *and* bathrooms. We even have ghosts.' She flashed her most jaunty smile at the Prince and her mother-in-law. The Prince gave her an appraising glance. The American girl had spirit.

'Well, there you have it, Fanny. The voice of the New World,' and he shot the Double Duchess a malicious glance, to show that he thought that she had been bested by her daughter-in-law. And then, as if suddenly bored of the rivalry between the two women which he had stirred up, he began to drum his fingers on the table. The Double Duchess saw this with alarm and hastily changed the subject to the composition of the bridge fours after dinner.

Cora leant forward in the hope of seeing Ivo. He was still talking to Lady Bessborough even though by rights he should be talking to Charlotte. As she turned back to her plate, she noticed that Odo Beauchamp was staring at his wife. Despite their rancorous little exchange earlier, it struck Cora that he was looking at Charlotte as if he could not bear to let her out of his sight.

The meal went on and on. The Prince tackled each one of the nine courses with relish and teased Cora, who found she had lost her appetite, for not doing the food justice.

At last the Double Duchess gave the signal for the ladies to withdraw. When the ladies had followed her into the drawing room, Cora was surprised to find that Charlotte came to sit next to her.

'So have you survived the ordeal?' Charlotte's voice was friendly. Cora smiled uncertainly. 'I think so. It was a very long dinner.'

'The Prince likes his food. Anything less than nine courses and he thinks you are trying to starve him. I simply dread the day he decides to stay with us. Everything, the guests, the menus, the seating plans, even the sleeping arrangements have to be approved before he comes. Even Aunt Fanny gets nervous.' Charlotte looked over to the Double Duchess, who was drinking coffee with Lady Bessborough.

'I didn't know she was your aunt. Does that mean you and Ivo are cousins?' Cora was curious. Ivo had never mentioned that he was related to Charlotte.

'No, aunt is just a courtesy title. My mother and Aunt Fanny were friends as girls. Then they both got married.' Charlotte gave a little shrug. 'Aunt Fanny married a duke and my mother married an army officer who died when I was a baby. But they remained friends. My mother died when I was sixteen and Aunt Fanny took me in. She had promised my mother that she would bring me out. She kept her promise.' Charlotte's smile had a slightly hard edge to it.

Cora tried to imagine what it would be like to have no family.

'I can't think what it must be like to be an orphan.' She thought of the way her mother had monitored every minute of her life until her marriage.

Charlotte gave her a half smile. 'I hope you won't be shocked if I tell you that it is liberating.'

Cora was shocked, but then she thought of the endless afternoons in Sans Souci and she nodded at Charlotte. 'I think I understand.'

Charlotte put her hand on Cora's arm. 'Good. I hope that means we can be friends.'

Cora was surprised at this but tried not to show it. She said in what she had come to think of as her Duchess voice, 'I hope so too.'

Before Charlotte could say any more, there was a flurry of activity as the men arrived. The guests were organised into bridge tables. Charlotte was summoned by the Double Duchess and with a rueful backward glance at Cora she was swallowed up into the card players.

And then to Cora's relief she saw Ivo's tall figure coming towards her.

He sat down next to her in the place just vacated by Charlotte. She was about to tell him about her conversation, when he said quietly, 'In a minute my mother is going to ask me to play the piano. When she does I want you to come with me. We'll give them the Schubert.'

Cora looked at him in dismay. 'But Ivo, I haven't been practising. I can't play in front of all these people.'

He smiled at her. 'Don't worry, no one here is going to notice if you hit a wrong note. We will do very nicely.'

Cora swallowed and tried to smile back.

As Ivo had predicted, a moment later the Double Duchess approached them.

'Dear Cora, would you mind awfully if I asked Ivo to play for us? It would be such a treat.' She turned to her son. 'I don't remember the last time I heard you play.'

'Don't you, Mother? It was a long time ago.' Ivo stared at his mother, who lowered her gaze.

Ivo stood up and kept Cora's hand in his so she had no choice but to follow him. Cora saw the flicker of incomprehension in her mother-in-law's eyes as he took her with him to the piano, and then as they sat down together in front of the keyboard, she watched the Duchess turn her face to the side suddenly, as if she had been struck.

Ivo's hands were poised over the keys. He looked at Cora gravely. 'Are you ready? One, two, three . . .'

They plunged into the Schubert. Cora played harder than she had ever done before. She could feel the Duchess watching her. As they played, the room grew silent, even the card players paused to listen. Her part supported his rippling arpeggios with a succession of minor chords; if her timing was a fraction out, the piece would sound discordant and harsh, but Ivo was with her, hovering above the foundation she was laying with his own comments and inter-polations. A few bars before the end, Cora had forgotten the other people in the room, she was completely caught up in the music. She could feel Ivo's leg pressed against hers and she found herself swaying with him as they reached the finale. As they came to the last bars, she knew they were perfectly in time and she gave her last chord every ounce of feeling she possessed. The sound faded away and she leant against him.

Ivo whispered in her ear, 'I told you we would do well together.'

And then he was up, smiling his acknowledgement of the applause that greeted the end of the piece. He turned to her and lifted her hand and kissed it. The applause grew louder still. Cora felt herself blushing.

She heard the Prince saying to Ivo, 'So you've found yourself a new parrrtner, Wareham. I rrremember you used to play with your mother. But I think your new Duchess is quite capable of keeping up with you, what.'

'You are very perceptive, sir.' Ivo made a little bow to the Prince.

Duchess Fanny approached in full throaty flight. 'My dears,

what a musical honeymoon you must have had.' She turned to Cora. 'I hope Ivo didn't make you practise all the time?'

Cora smiled but said nothing. She knew that her mother-in-law was furious at having been upstaged. As Fanny moved on, Cora caught a glimpse of Charlotte Beauchamp, who was sitting very still, her arms folded. As the Prince went back towards the card table, Charlotte rose to greet him and Cora saw that she had four red marks on her smooth white upper arm where the nails had dug into the skin.

That night, Cora sent Bertha away as soon as she was out of her dress. Before her marriage she would have told her maid everything about the evening, but Ivo had made it clear that he did not think that a duchess should be gossiping with the servants. He had even wondered whether Bertha was an altogether suitable maid for a Duchess, but Cora had refused to listen, Bertha was the only familiar thing in her new life. But out of loyalty to Ivo's wishes, she no longer confided in her maid as she used to. Now as she sat in front of the dressing-table mirror brushing her hair, she felt lonely. She thought of writing to her mother. Mrs Cash would want to know every detail of her encounter with the Prince. She wondered what her mother would think if she wrote what she really thought, which was that the Prince was fat and alarming and that he had pressed his foot against hers several times during dinner. She ran her hand over the smooth skirts of her wedding dress lying on the chair; she would not wear it again.

She was tired, but she was too anxious to sleep. She wanted desperately to see Ivo. If only she could go and find him. She sat on the bed, twisting her hair, waiting for the door to open. At last she heard his step outside. He looked flushed and before she could tell him anything he was kissing her bare neck and shoulders and tugging at the strings of her peignoir and she was caught up in the urgency of the moment.

When he finally reared up, giving a yelp of what was both pain and pleasure, she pushed herself towards him, willing him to continue. She wanted him to stay deep inside her forever – only by keeping him there would he be really hers. As he collapsed, spent, she still yearned for him. She lay in the dark for a while, listening to him breathe; once he stirred and pulled her to him, whispering her name. She moulded herself against him and at last she, too, fell asleep. But when she woke in the morning, he was gone.

CHAPTER 16

Madonna and Child

*I*T WAS THE FIRST REALLY COLD DAY OF THE YEAR and the track leading down to the sea was beginning to be covered by fallen leaves. This was Cora's favourite part of the ride: going down the narrow pathway through the wood where the undergrowth was so dense that she could see only a few feet ahead, and then about halfway down the rumble would begin and she began to smell the salty tang of the sea air through the rotting smell of leaf mould. The wood ended and then she was on the cliff overlooking the cove. She thought that it looked like a lady's drawstring purse, a weighted oval with an opening through a break in the cliffs into the sea. The mist that had lain over Lulworth all week had finally been blown away. Today the sea beyond the cliffs was dark blue and here in the shallower waters of the cove it was almost turquoise. The sun had turned the sandstone cliffs a warm gold. But for the bite in the air, it might have been summer. There were sheep grazing on the fields surrounding her, their white shapes echoed by the stray white clouds in the sky. Cora loved the scale of the cove, the coastline was so charming here compared to the rocky outcrops and pounding surf of Rhode Island. She looked at her pocket watch – eleven o'clock. She should turn back, Ivo might return tonight and she wanted to make sure that everything was ready.

After their week at Conyers they had come back to Lulworth, but Ivo had almost immediately been called away to his estates in Ireland. There had been a rent strike and Ivo did not trust his steward to handle it alone. She had wanted to go with him but there had been Fenian activity in the area and he had declared it too dangerous. The last seven days were the longest they had been apart since their marriage six months ago in March. Ivo had suggested, almost seriously, that she might go back to Conyers while he was away but Cora had chosen to stay at Lulworth. She had wanted to get to know the house, to make it hers. When Ivo was there she was always conscious of his relationship with the house; every inch of it, she knew, had meaning for him. On their return from their honeymoon, Cora had been shown the Duchess's rooms, a set of exquisitely panelled rooms on the south side of the house facing the sea. She had been delighted with their proportions, their lightness and the distant glimpse of a triangle of sea through the shouldered hills. She had at once decided to make these rooms her own and had ordered new furnishings, jettisoning the red velvets and beaded fringes that the Double Duchess had favoured in favour of a Liberty fabric with birds and pomegranates. The first night after the rooms were finished, Cora had got ready for bed and waited for Ivo. He had been late, it was past eleven, and when he came in, instead of embracing her, he had skirted round the room, touching the curtains and the walls like a dog getting to know unfamiliar territory. In the end she had taken his hand and led him to the bed but there he had been restless and angular and had left her in the small hours. He had even smelt different, there had been a sour undercurrent to his normally warm sweet skin. This behaviour had gone on for three nights, with Ivo behaving as normal during the day but turning into a twitchy facsimile of himself at night. Cora had tried to talk to him about it but he had been evasive, so the next night she had gone to his room, the Duke's room, and Ivo had fallen on her before she had even closed the door. Clearly no amount of new curtains could erase his mother's presence from her rooms. After that she only used the Duchess's apartments during the day when Ivo was out on the estate.

Cora tilted her face to the sun and closed her eyes. It was not warm, thanks to the south-westerly wind, but she enjoyed the light burning through her eyelids. The sun was the thing she missed most; at home she had always taken it for granted but here every sunny day felt like a blessing. She opened her eyes and looked out to sea and saw a flash of white in the waters just beyond the mouth of the cove. She kicked Lincoln's flanks and trotted along the cliff for a closer look. As she grew nearer she saw that it was a pod of dolphins lacing through the waves. There were about five of them moving in unison as they spiralled through the water. Cora had seen individual dolphins before in Newport but this was the first time she had seen a pod and she found herself smiling till her cheeks ached.

Usually, about halfway back to the house, Lincoln would prick up his ears and she would let him canter home. But today she did not let him have his head but reined him in tightly as they walked sedately back up the hill. Lincoln snorted in protest but Cora did not relent. Normally she liked to be shaken up but today she wanted to prolong her state of dreamy content. As she approached the stables a groom ran out to take Lincoln.

'Good morning, Your Grace.' The groom touched his cap and led Lincoln over to the mounting block.

'What a beautiful day! I saw some dolphins in the bay. Is that common round here?'

The groom scratched his head. 'Well, I'z bin here close on seventeen years and I ain't never seen no dolphins, Your Grace.' The groom clicked his teeth and held out his hand to Cora as she dismounted. 'They say as dolphins are lucky, and Lulworth ain't had much luck lately, though I reckon that's changin'.' And the groom smiled, showing a row of broken brown teeth, his eyes moving across her body.

Cora's understanding lagged behind as she struggled to decipher the man's thick Dorset accent, but then she felt herself flushing. What did he mean? How could he possibly know? She had only begun to suspect herself these last few days. No one else knew, except possibly Bertha, and she was unlikely to start gossiping to the grooms. She threw down her whip and gloves and stalked off towards the house. As she reached the garden entrance, the butler appeared with a telegram on a silver salver. She tore it open.

'It's from the Duke, Bugler, to say he will be here for dinner. Have they finished in the chapel?'

'Yes, Your Grace. I think the men are only waiting for you to come and approve their work.'

'Have you seen it? Do you think the Duke will be pleased?'

Bugler looked at her from under his hooded eyelids. He had worked at the house for thirty years, starting as a footman, then under-butler, and he had been in his present position for the last ten years. He had many duties: the upkeep of the family silver, the maintenance of the cellar, upholding good behaviour in the servants' hall, even the conveying of bad news (it had fallen to him to tell Duchess Fanny about her older son's death) but he was not paid to have opinions. The new American Duchess should know better than to ask.

'I really couldn't say, Your Grace.'

'But you saw the old one, do you think this one is as good?'

'They both seem to be of the same size, Your Grace.'

Cora gave up. 'Tell them I will be up there directly I've changed.'

Bugler noted with disapproval that the new Duchess ran up the stairs to her rooms, holding her habit so high that he could see her legs nearly to her knees. Cora was running because she had felt an overwhelming desire to be sick. If only she could reach her room first. But her door was a good hundred yards away. To her horror she found herself on her knees retching on the carpet in the corridor. She prayed that Bugler had not seen. Feeling clammy and shaky, she got to her room and rang for Bertha.

Before Bertha reached the Duchess, the mess on the carpet had been cleaned up by Mabel the housemaid, who had seen the whole episode. By the time that Bertha had sponged her mistress's temples with eau de cologne and had helped her into her morning dress, and the cook had sent up some dry toast and weak tea, the news of the Duchess's indisposition had spread through the servants' hall, much to the jubilation of the second footman, who had drawn May in the downstairs sweepstake on the birth of an heir.

Aloysius and Jerome, the Duke's dogs, followed Cora as she walked up the path to the chapel. It had been nearly a year since she had first seen the chapel. Every time she had entered it since then, she had felt reproached by the rectangle of light paint above the altar. In Venice she had written to Duveen Brothers, the art dealers who her mother used, and asked them if they could trace the painting of St Cecilia that had hung there. In July she had received a letter telling her that the painting had been sold to one Cyrus Guest of San Francisco, who was not minded to sell. Undaunted, Cora had asked the dealers to find another painting by Rubens that would fit in the alcove above the altar in the Lulworth chapel. Two weeks later Duveen wrote to say that there was a Madonna and Child by the same painter being offered for sale by an impoverished Irish earl. Was the Duchess interested in viewing it? Cora decided to buy the painting on the spot. A Rubens was a Rubens, after all. The price had been higher than she had expected but she had found that reassuring.

She told the dogs to stay on the steps of the chapel. They did not mind her as they minded Ivo, so she went into the chapel quickly, shutting the door behind her so they would not follow her in. At first she could not see anything, but then a shaft of light broke through the windows in the cupola and fell directly on the altar and lit up the painting. The Madonna, who was wearing an orange robe, was clutching the infant Jesus to her with one arm and looking at an illuminated book that rested in the other. They were in a bower of pale pink roses, and the book that Mary was looking at lay on an intricately patterned Persian carpet. Cora was struck by the picture's tenderness, the way that Jesus, blond and naked as a cherub, was resting his head so trustingly on his mother's breast. She could not help noticing that the Madonna had hair of the same chestnut hue as her own.

A voice behind her said, 'They say that Rubens used his wife and baby son as models for this picture. I think that gives the picture its intimacy.'

Cora turned to see a small dark man in a very white collar, smiling at her.

'Ambrose Fox, Your Grace. Mr Duveen asked me to come down with the painting to make sure you were happy with it.'

Cora held out her hand and after a moment's hesitation the man shook it.

'Tell him it is perfect. I think it looks very well here in the chapel, don't you, Mr Fox?'

'Yes indeed, Your Grace. It looks quite settled.'

'I am so relieved. You see it is a surprise for the Duke. There was another Rubens here before, but it was sold and I wanted to replace it. The other one was of St Cecilia but I think the Madonna and Child is just as good, perhaps even more appropriate. I wonder, have you seen the other picture? I never did but if you have you could tell me whether this one is as good.'

Cora knew she was talking too much to someone whose status was not clear – was he someone you invited for lunch or sent to the housekeeper? But she felt overwhelmed by the painting. She had not known when she had agreed to buy it how apt it was. She had never had much to do with children, but there was something about the way that the baby's hand was spread out so possessively on his mother's breast that made her realise, for the first time since her suspicions began, where she was heading. Would her baby lean on her like that, claiming her for his own?

'The St Cecilia is generally regarded as one of Ruben's finest works but I would have thought it a little imposing for a chapel of this size. I think that this work is of the right scale and, dare I say it, the right mood for this place.'

Cora looked at him sharply. Was he suggesting anything? But Mr Fox gazed back at her unblinkingly. His confidence impressed her, she would ask him for lunch. There were, after all, plenty of other pictures that needed replacing.

The dogs were waiting for her outside, and they began to bark when they saw the stranger with her.

'Please don't mind them, Mr Fox, they will calm down once they realise you are with me.'

'These are the famous Lulworth lurchers I suppose, I recognise them from the Van Dyck portrait of the first Duke. Splendid creatures.' But in spite of his confident words, Cora couldn't help noticing that Mr Fox looked extremely nervous. She batted the dogs away with her hand and motioned for him to follow her back to the house.

Ivo looked surprised when Cora suggested they visit the chapel after dinner.

'Of course, if you want to go, but wouldn't you rather go in daylight? There is no gaslight in the chapel.'

'Oh, but there are candles, it will look much prettier.' Cora had already asked Bugler to have the candles lit.

She rushed through dinner, twitching impatiently as Ivo cleared his plate. At last he put his napkin down and she stood up.

'Shall we go now? Up to the chapel?'

'Can't it wait until I have had a cigarette?'

'I really don't think so, Ivo. Please, darling.'

With exaggerated slowness, Ivo got up and started to move towards the door. Cora was by now in a frenzy of impatience. She took him by the arm and pulled him through the door.

'You American girls are such hoydens,' he said, laughing at her vehemence, but he took her arm and they walked up the path. He teased her all the way about being an American bully until they turned the corner and he saw that the chapel was lit up inside. Cora felt his hand tense around her arm.

'Is there something wrong?'

'No, it's just that I haven't seen the chapel lit up at night for a while. The last time was when Guy was laid out here.'

Another evening Cora would have shuddered at her thought-lessness. But tonight she was too full of the revelations to come to pay complete attention to his mood. As they reached the chapel doors she stopped.

'I have something to show you, but I want it to be a surprise, so close your eyes.'

'Do you have the Holy Father in there, or the Holy Grail? Really, Cora, we will make a Catholic of you yet.'

'Ssh, stop talking, just shut your eyes and come with me.'

At last Ivo closed his eyes and she guided him into the chapel.

The Madonna and Child glowed in the candlelight. Cora felt she would burst with her own cleverness; she was making Lulworth magnificent again.

'You can open your eyes now.' She turned away from the painting to look at Ivo's face.

He opened his eyes and looked around him puzzled, and then he saw the Rubens and went very still, gazing at the painting with an expression that Cora could not read. She waited for his set face to crack open with surprise and pleasure. When he did nothing but stare, she thought perhaps he did not know what it was.

'It's a Rubens, you know, like the one you had before.'

Still Ivo was silent. She put a hand on his arm, but he did not move. He was gazing at the painting, his face completely motion-less. The muscles of his arm were hard under her hand. Part of her knew to be silent but another piece of her wanted to scream. This was her surprise and he was not playing his part.

She willed herself to wait, watching a rivulet of wax run down the side of one of the candles. Finally when its warmth had gone and the drop had stiffened, she spoke again.

'I did try to get the other Rubens, the one that was here before, the one of St Cecilia, but the man who bought it was American—'

'And he didn't need the money.' Ivo's voice was flat, this was a statement not a question. Could it be that he was angry because she had not been able to buy the original painting?

'Of course I haven't seen the painting of St Cecilia but Mr Fox, who brought the painting down from Duveen's, has, and he thought that the Madonna was actually better suited to this position.'

'It is a fine picture.' Ivo's voice was still colourless.

'Rubens used his wife and baby as his models.' She moved closer to the painting. Every time she looked at it she saw more in it. There was a basket of fruit in the lower right-hand corner, with grapes and plums. Some of the grapes had been eaten. Behind the Virgin's right shoulder there were trees opening on to a rural landscape that looked green and cool. Underneath her orange robe the Virgin was wearing a sleeve of damask pink. She wondered if she might have a dress made up in those very colours when she had her baby.

'Look at the baby's hand, Ivo. See how tightly he is holding on to his mother.' She reached out her own hand to him, willing him to come forward.

But Ivo did not move. 'I know the painting.'

Cora was astonished. 'Really? But how? Duveen's said it had never been on the market before.'

'No, it hasn't.'

'So how did you . . .' Cora trailed off when she realised where Ivo must have seen the picture.

'It was in the Kinsale family for two hundred years. It used to hang in their chapel.' Ivo's voice was expressionless.

'I didn't realise you knew the owners.' Cora began to feel cold. She persisted. 'But does it matter, Ivo? They needed the money. I gave them a good price and now you have a Rubens over the altar again.'

Ivo raised his arms. For a moment Cora thought he was going to embrace her, but then he dropped them and was once more still.

'Ivo, what's wrong? I only did this because I thought it would make you happy. You minded about the other picture, I know you did.' Cora ground her shoe into the stone floor in frustration.

'Of course I minded! But Cora, you can't make everything better just by buying a new picture. The Lulworth Rubens had been here since the Fourth Duke. When I came into the chapel I used to think of all my ancestors who had knelt in front of the same painting saying the same words. Now St Cecilia is in California and we have a lovely new Rubens courtesy of my very rich wife.' He looked at her face and shook his head. 'You don't understand what I'm saying, do you? And why should you? My scruples must seem absurd to you.'

'Not absurd, just puzzling. I thought you wanted my money for what it could do here.' She peered at him, trying to read his face.

'No Cora, I needed it. There's a difference, but I see you don't understand.'

It was true she didn't understand. She had bought the picture to show him how she would make Lulworth great again, but instead of pleasing him she had offended him instead. How could she have misjudged him so badly? She realised that she really knew very little about the man she had married.

At last he walked over to her and looked down at her. She put her arms on his shoulders and after a pause he reciprocated by putting his arms round her waist.

'Oh Cora, can you believe that there are some things in life that can't be bought?'

She looked up at his dark face and noticed the light creases that ran between his nose and chin and the flicker in his eyelid. She was relieved that whatever had made him so sombre was passing. She had felt for a moment, there, that he was a stranger.

'Of course I know that. Would you like to hear about one of them?' She smiled, having won the conversation back on to her territory.

He looked at her closely and his glance moved down her body. 'Do you mean that you are . . .'

'Yes I do – well, I'm almost certain. I was sick this morning, and my corsets won't lace properly.' She put her hands to her still tiny waist.

He took a step away from her as if he had been pushed backwards by the force of her news, put a hand on one of the pews to steady himself, but missed it and almost lost his balance. Cora looked at him bemused, it was unlike Ivo to be clumsy, but then he straightened up and his face re-formed into a smile.

'I am glad. It was too melancholy being the last of the Maltravers. Have you seen a doctor?'

'Not yet, I wanted to tell you first, although some of the servants seem to have guessed.'

'They always know everything first. Do you have any idea when it will . . .'

'May. Well, at least I think so. I can't be sure until I have seen the doctor.'

'My clever girl.' He bent his head and kissed her on the forehead.

'So you see, I had my reasons for buying a Madonna and Child,' she said a little reproachfully.

Ivo hung his head in mock supplication. 'Of course you did. Everything you do is perfectly reasonable. I have been churlish, Cora, and you must forgive me. We do things differently, that's all.'

He put his arms round her neck and pulled her to him. She remembered the first time they had kissed, here in the chapel. He had been unexpected then, the speed of his proposal, the certainty of his embrace; and now, did she really know him better? Physically perhaps, when they kissed now it was a communication, not an exploration, but there was a part of him that was still opaque. But she dismissed this from her mind. Whatever he thought about the Rubens, there could be no doubt that he wanted an heir.

It was days later before she allowed herself to think about the scene in the chapel again. She thought of his cold, still face and the way he had not looked at her but only at the picture. Afterwards it was all right, although Cora could not help noticing that now when he entered the chapel he never looked straight ahead; he would enter, dip his fingers in the stoup of holy water and walk to the altar with his head bowed. It was only when he approached the altar to take Communion that he would raise his head and look at the picture, as if it was his own particular cross to bear.

CHAPTER 17

Bridgewater House

THE DAYS WERE BEGINNING TO DRAW IN NOW. Cora watched the lamplighter make his way down Cleveland Row to the park, adding his punctuation to the light that spilled from doorways and from behind curtains into the gathering gloom. She was tired from the journey up from Lulworth but she had felt her spirits lift when the carriage had drawn up outside the limestone pillars that flanked their London house. Bridgewater House, with its façade by Barry, had been a wedding gift from her father, although, of course, it had been chosen by her mother, who had been surprised to find that the Duke had no permanent residence in town. This house, with its enormous central hall and colonnaded gallery was, in Mrs Cash's view, on the right scale. She had thought it entirely fitting that it had been built by the same man who had remodelled Buckingham Palace.

There had been a Maltravers house once, in St James's, but the Duke's grandfather had sold it. Cora had wondered whether she should try and buy it back, but after her experience with the Rubens she was wary of offending her husband. Besides, she liked this house with its drawing room that had six long windows overlooking Green Park.

She saw a carriage draw up outside the house and a liveried footman walk up to the front door. Who would be calling now? wondered Cora. She hoped it was Sybil. At least then they could talk about clothes. With Sybil she could forget about being a duchess and return to the serious business of sleeve width. Cora thought they could not get any wider but then she had thought that six months ago, and had been proved quite wrong.

The footman brought in Lady Beauchamp's card.

Cora was surprised and pleased. The Beauchamps had left Conyers the day after Charlotte had expressed the hope that they would be friends, on account of a death in the family. Cora had been sorry not to see more of her. Cora had no female friends in England apart from Sybil, and while Sybil was charming, her awkwardness and her awful clothes meant that she was more Cora's protégée than her equal. Charlotte was in a different class. There was something intriguing about her and she was one of the few English women who Cora regarded as a worthy sartorial rival. She wondered how wide Charlotte's sleeves would be.

She was not disappointed. Although Charlotte was dressed in half mourning for one of Odo's cousins, her dress made no concessions to grief, bar the colour, and the lavender tones of her gown were a spectacular foil to her blonde sleekness. She had abandoned the full sleeve of the summer for a puffed shoulder that tapered into a tight cuff. The cuffs and hem were covered in silver braid. Around her shoulders she had a silver fox fur and she wore a hat with mauve and grey plumes. She glided towards Cora and took her hands.

'I am so pleased to find you at home, Duchess,' Charlotte's voice was warm. 'I was driving past on my way home from the

Lauderdales' and I saw that your shutters were down. Have you been in town long?' She gave Cora's hand a little squeeze.

'No, we've only just arrived. Ivo has decided to take up his seat in the Lords.' Cora felt proud at being able to say this. She gestured to Charlotte to sit on a gilt Louis Quinze sofa. The other woman sank into it gracefully.

'Well, now you are here, we must introduce you to some amusing people. If Ivo is going to take up politics you will need some distraction. You mustn't think that everything is as dull as Conyers. Of course, if the Double Duchess asks, you have to go, but the Marlborough House thing is so *vieux jeu* now. I think it all used to be tremendous fun, gambling and divorces and what have you, but now Bertie is only slightly less stuffy than his mother.'

Cora smiled. 'I wouldn't say that Conyers was dull. Americans like me can't be blasé about royalty. But it was certainly exacting. So much to remember, I was so worried about saying the wrong thing. I was sorry you had to leave, I was relying on you for guidance.'

Charlotte adjusted her sleeve. 'Oh Duchess, I don't think you need any help from me. You seemed to have everything in order. I hear the Prince is quite smitten.'

Cora couldn't disguise her pleasure. 'I wish you would call me Cora, I am still getting used to being a duchess.'

Charlotte nodded. 'Very well, Cora it is, and you must call me Charlotte. I will never get used to being Lady Beauchamp.' This last remark was thrown off with a laugh, but Cora was surprised nonetheless. Charlotte noticed Cora's expression. 'Oh dear, have I shocked you again? I keep forgetting that Americans marry for love.'

Cora looked back at her steadily. 'Well, this one did.' She smiled self-deprecatingly. 'But the title is quite hard to get used to. Sometimes I find it difficult to believe they are talking about me.'

'Whereas every English girl has been dreaming of being called Your Grace since the schoolroom. You won't get an ounce of sympathy from me on that score, Cora.'

Cora laughed. She found Charlotte dangerously good company.

'But English girls are trained for this life. So many things I should know. Ivo is quite tolerant but the servants are merciless. Every time I ask for something, they say just as you wish, Your Grace, and then I know I have sinned. I asked Bugler to light the fire for me in the library and he looked as if I had hit him. He said I will send a footman to take care of that, Your Grace. By the time it was done, I was shivering with cold.' She made a little pout of mock distress.

'You asked the butler to light the fire? But that is a serious case of lese-majesty. I am surprised Bugler didn't hand in his notice. To be a duke's butler is only a little less important than being a Duke.' Charlotte gave an accurate impression of Bugler's most stately expression.

Cora rang the bell for tea. 'Well, at least the servants here in London are new, I don't have to worry about hurting their feelings.'

Charlotte leaned towards Cora. 'I am having a small party on Thursday. You must come. Louvain will be there.' She looked at Cora through her lashes to see if the name registered.

'The painter? I thought he lived in Paris. My mother tried to get him to do her portrait but he said he was too busy to come to America. She was furious.' Cora remembered her mother's wrath vividly. Louvain had not been too 'busy' to paint the Rhinelander girls earlier in the year.

Charlotte smiled. 'He is very choosy about his subjects. I sat for him earlier this year. Fifteen sittings in his draughty studio by the river. He absolutely insisted on painting me in my riding habit – and he called me Diana all the way through the sittings. I would have given up but Odo was adamant I continue, and Louvain can be very charming when he wants to be.' Charlotte shrugged, causing the feathers on her hat to quiver. 'He has told everybody that he won't do any more portraits, but I am sure if he were to meet you,' she gestured towards Cora who was wearing a gorgeously beribboned tea gown from Madame Vionnet, 'an American duchess, how could he resist?' She stopped for breath as the footman brought in the tea things. 'Oh Lord, is that the time? I must fly. So, Thursday then.' Charlotte stood up, shaking out her mauve skirts so that the little train at the back fell perfectly on the floor behind her.

Cora thought about Louvain. His portrait of Mamie Rhinelander in her peignoir had divided New York society last year. Her mother had called it vulgar but Teddy said it was a masterpiece.

'Well, there are things I have to attend to, but as far as I know we have no other engagements that night.' It sounded rather ponderous but Cora was not minded to confide the news of her pregnancy to the other woman. Charlotte appeared not to notice the evasiveness, gathered her furs and left.

As the Double Duchess's ward, Charlotte was almost an honorary member of the Maltravers family, hence her presence at Conyers; yet Cora could not remember Ivo ever talking about her. She had tried hard to find out more from her husband but Ivo, she was learning, could turn a conversation in any way he pleased, and it did not please him to talk about the Beauchamps.

Cora rang the bell for the footman to take away the tea things and went over to the bureau. She took out a sheet of writing paper which had an embossed coronet on the top (her mother had ordered the paper to go with the house) and wrote a note to Mrs Wyndham asking her to call. She had found the older woman rather alarming when she had first arrived in London, but now she could do with some of her unrelenting worldliness. She knew it was time for her to start taking on the mantle of Duchess; she remembered with dread the Prince's threat to visit Lulworth. In New York she would have known exactly where to begin, but here she was nervous about making a mistake. Mrs Wyndham, she felt sure, would know where to start, and Cora had no qualms about asking her because she knew that her goodwill was essential to Mrs Wyndham's 'business'.

Cora had never asked her mother how much money she had paid for procuring their invitation to Sutton Veney but judging by Mrs Wyndham's carriage and her charming house in Curzon Street, it had not come cheap. Mrs Wyndham was a woman who put a price on everything, a quality which Cora was coming to appreciate. The English were so peculiar about money. There had been Ivo's reaction to the Rubens and then there was the matter of Sybil's birthday present. Cora had sent her a sable wrap. Sybil had been delighted but the Double Duchess had pulled Cora aside for a word. 'You really mustn't give such extravagant presents, Cora dear, there is a fine line between generosity and bribery.' The Duchess had even tried to make Sybil return the furs, but her stepdaughter had refused. The Duchess had been equally caustic when Cora had appeared at Conyers wearing the tiara that her mother had given her, instead of the Maltravers 'fender', a heavy edifice of diamonds which was impossible to wear without getting a headache. When Cora pointed this out and explained that her tiara had been modelled on one worn by the Empress of Austria, the Duchess had sighed and said that she had always been proud to wear the Maltravers tiara when she had been Duchess of Wareham. Cora, with Ivo's permission, had sent the 'fender' to Garrards the jewellers to be remodelled, and had been astonished when a polite note had been sent back regretfully informing her that the tiara was not worth redesigning as the stones were not real. When she had told Ivo, he had laughed bitterly and said that he supposed that his mother must have sold the gems to pay her dress bill.

Even her charitable schemes had been found wanting. At Lulworth, Cora was full of ideas to improve the estate. Her first act was to separate the food left over from the Lulworth table into different courses before it was distributed to the poor. The servants had grumbled about the extra work, and the poor had done nothing to express their gratitude. She had proposed building a school for the children of the village – a scheme which Ivo had originally encouraged; but when she had had plans drawn up and started designing uniforms, he quashed the whole idea as too expensive and troublesome. When she replied that the money was not a problem and she was quite prepared to take on the running of the school, he sighed and said that there some things about English life that she didn't yet understand. But because Ivo put his arms round her and kissed her as he said it, Cora had let it go. There would be time enough for philanthropy after the baby was born.

When the footman arrived to take away the tea things she asked him to take the note directly to Mrs Wyndham. With any luck she would come tomorrow. There was much that Cora needed to discuss.

Bertha was delighted when she found that she and Jim were to travel to London together alone. Even though they lived in the same house and saw each other every day, they were rarely able to be together for more than a moment. They had to be so careful. She felt constantly watched. Most of the Lulworth servants had been there for years so they were wary of newcomers, particularly foreign ones. Only butlers were allowed to marry and remain in service. Bertha was fairly confident that Cora would protect her, but she did not want to put Jim's future in jeopardy. If he lost his post without a reference he would find it very hard to get another job, and if they were to marry, then his experience as the Duke of Wareham's valet would be invaluable. The fashion for the new palace-type hotels meant that there was always work for experienced servants with impeccable references. If Jim could get a job at the Savoy, and she could find work at a milliner's, they might be able to afford to get married. And Bertha was clear that marriage, rather than these fumbling encounters in corridors and shrubberies, was what she wanted. She liked Jim's kisses, and the feel of his hands on her body, but she had no intention of letting things go any further without a ring.

Today was Bertha's chance to raise the idea of the Savoy with Jim. They were travelling up to London together alone, as they were the only servants that the Duke and Duchess were bringing with them from Dorset. Mrs Cash, when she bought the house, had also engaged a full household staff, including a French chef and a Swiss laundry maid. But Bertha's hopes of a conversation with Jim faded when she saw that they were the only occupants of their third-class carriage. Within minutes of the doors closing and the train leaving the station, Jim pulled down the blinds and pounced on her. Bertha tried to resist him but he was so sweetly eager that she soon lost any desire to do anything but enjoy the present moment. And later on, when other people got into the carriage at stations along the way, she was too aware of his leg pressed against hers, the hand that kept brushing her fingers and the kisses that he would steal every time the train went through a tunnel to think about anything else. So she had suggested that instead of taking a hansom they go on foot to Cleveland Row from the station. The walk would be a good time to talk uninterrupted.

But Jim was excited to be in London. He sniffed the air around him like a dog. As they walked across Waterloo Bridge, he was enchanted by the view of Parliament in one direction and St Paul's in the other. He bought her a bunch of violets from an old gypsy woman, who told him he had a lucky face but glared at Bertha. Although London was better in that respect than New York, at least no one jeered at them in the street. Bertha knew that Jim did not notice these things; it was what she loved about him – he thought she was magnificent and he expected everyone else to feel the same. They walked through Trafalgar Square and along the Strand, until they came to the Savoy Theatre and the hotel which stood next to it.

She pointed towards it. 'They pay good wages in there, you know. We stayed there our first week in London, and the head waiter told me he was getting a hundred guineas all told, together with his tips.' Bertha pointed out a magnificently dressed employee to Jim.

'It'd be hard, though, getting used to all those different people.

Everyone wanting things to be done differently. Lord knows His Grace is bad enough with his soft collars and hard collars and his bathwater just so, but fancy having a new master every week and some of them foreigners.' Jim fingered his stiff collar.

'Foreigners ain't so bad, are they, Jim?' Bertha put her arm through his. He smiled at her.

'Some of them are tolerable, I suppose.' He jerked his head back towards the hotel. 'So this is what you have in mind for me? Is that the way of it then?'

'Well if you found work there and I took a job trimming hats, we could make a living.'

Jim stopped and looked at her. Bertha realised she had gone too far and she laughed it off. Perhaps marriage wasn't on Jim's mind.

'We will both need jobs if we lose our posts for being late!' she said, pulling at his arm. A garden bus went by on the Strand. 'Come on, this will be quicker than walking.' They got on to the platform at the back and climbed up the stairs to the top deck. It was cold up there but the fug on the bottom deck was unbearable. They found seats at the front behind the driver. She looked at Jim's profile; behind him there was a hoarding advertising Pear's Soap, 'For a Pearly Complexion'.

'I'm sorry, Jim, I didn't mean to presume.' She put her hand on his arm. He squeezed it by way of reply and they sat in silence until the bus reached Pall Mall.

As they walked up Cleveland Row, Jim said slowly, 'It's not that I don't want to be with you, Bertha, but service is all I've ever known. I was the boot boy at Sutton Veney and then when I grew tall they made me a footman and now I'm valet to a duke. I never thought I'd come this far. But I'm a lucky man. I met you, didn't I?'

They were too close to the house for Bertha to be able to kiss him, but she stroked his arm and said, 'We've both been lucky.'

As they approached the house, and began to draw apart from each other, they saw a lady in furs hurry down the steps. Jim recognised her at once.

'Good thing she didn't see us. She's a mean one, Lady Beauchamp. There were two housemaids as lost their place at Sutton on account of her. Said they were rude to her, as if that were likely – they were local girls who wouldn't say boo to a goose. No, I reckon as they saw something they shouldn't, they were sent off that quickly. Still, I suppose anyone would go sour married to that Sir Odious. I'd rather go back to being a boot boy than work for him again.' Jim's handsome face was grim at the thought of his former employer.

Bertha realised that she was fortunate. Miss Cora was hard work but they'd been together for eight years now and so she was Bertha's hard work.

They walked down the area steps to the tradesmen's entrance. Bertha could see M. Pechon the French chef piping rosettes of cream round a glistening mountain of aspic in which anchovies and sprats had been suspended as if swimming in a gelatinous sea. There were many days when Bertha envied her mistress, but today was not one of them.

Cora had been right in thinking that Mrs Wyndham would respond swiftly to her summons. Madeleine Wyndham was delighted when she saw the Wareham crest on the seal. Cora had been her greatest match to date, although in all honesty she could not take credit for having introduced her to Wareham. What, Mrs Wyndham wondered, did the young Duchess want her for? Cora had been different to most of the young American girls and their parents who came her way. Most of them were quite 'au naturel', beautifully dressed hoydens who had the manners of farm girls and had nothing to recommend them apart from youthful high spirits and, of course, money. But Cora had arrived already 'finished', there was nothing to improve. Indeed, the only thing that separated Cora from a well-bred English girl was her confidence. Serene in the knowledge that she was the heiress of her generation, she had an air of assurance quite unusual in a girl of her age. She was spoilt, of course, most of the Americans were; but on the rare occasions she failed to get her own way, she looked amazed rather than petulant.

Mrs Wyndham wondered if Cora was having trouble with her mother-in-law. She had met the Double Duchess at countless gatherings over the last twenty years, but every time they encountered each other the Duchess pretended never to have seen her before. She wondered if the Duchess would keep this up now that her son had married an American. When Madeleine had first arrived in London fifteen years ago, she had quite often been asked about the Natives in her country as if she had herself only recently emerged from a wigwam. She had once, in jest, gone to a masquerade ball dressed as an Indian squaw, only to have a number of dowagers ask her if she missed wearing her native costume.

But that had been at the end of the seventies, before the heiresses had started arriving. Mrs Wyndham did not come from a very wealthy family. Her father had owned a hotel in Manhattan and there was gossip that he had met his wife when she was working there as a chambermaid. Both her parents had always denied this but the rumour was enough to place a cloud over the family's social prospects. Madeleine was well-liked at Miss Porter's Academy but her friendship with the Rhinebackers, Stuyvesants and Astors stopped at the school door. It had been Mr Lester, Madeleine's father, who had proposed going to Europe; he wanted, he said, to look at how they ran hotels over there. Within a month of arriving in London, Madeleine had met the Hon. Captain Wyndham, and within two months they were engaged to be married. Madeleine found the captain with his beautiful manners, resplendent moustaches and aristocratic family (his father was an Irish baron) far superior to any of her American beaux and accepted him gladly. She knew that when he proposed he had hoped that she was rich, but he had not flinched when he realised the modest scale of her fortune.

They had been very happy for the ten years of their marriage, which ended when the captain had taken a fence too fast and had broken his neck. He left his widow with a son and a small annuity which would hardly support them. But providentially her father had sent her a family from Philadelphia, who had stayed at his hotel in New York and who were curious to meet his aristocratic daughter. The eldest girl had been a beauty, thankfully a quiet one, and extremely rich and Mrs Wyndham had introduced her to Lord Castlerosse, an old friend of her husband's. The marriage received huge attention in the American papers and soon Mrs Wyndham found herself a necessary stopping point on an American belle's grand tour – somewhere between a visit to M. Worth and the Forum by moonlight.

At first she had not asked her charges for money, relying instead on 'presents' from the grateful milliners, jewellers, and dressmakers to whom she directed her American friends. But after a while she realised that her scruples were unnecessary. The American families that relied on her to introduce them into the best English society were happy to pay her; in fact the fathers preferred a commercial transaction to an unseen web of obligation and favours. And she soon learnt that the higher the price, the more her new friends valued her services. Mrs Wyndham had taste and tact, and she knew how to get her girls, and on not a few occasions their mamas, to look their best. There was a difference, she would tell them, between dressing smartly and overdressing. American girls were, on the whole, far more fashionable than their English contemporaries, but it did not do to rub their noses in it. Even though many of her young charges had sable cloaks and diamond tiaras, that did not mean they should wear them. Such things were best left for married ladies and even then she could not really countenance diamonds in the daytime.

When she had first come to London, Mrs Wyndham had been as bemused as her protégées, but having been punished by knowing glances and raised eyebrows every time she did something perceived to be 'American', she was now more English in her habits than the crustiest of dowagers. Growing up in a hotel, she had acquired a good memory for names and faces; after fifteen years in London she knew everybody and her command of Burke's Peerage was unmatched. No genealogical nuance of the aristocracy was lost on her; she could talk with authority about the Spencer red hair or the Percy chin or the Londonderry madness, and she had long ago learnt never to comment on a likeness in a younger child when visiting an aristocratic nursery. Mrs Wyndham knew to within a sovereign every single girl's portion and every man's income. Her network of lady's maids, French chefs and butlers, whom she was in the habit of 'recommending', kept her supplied with the kind of information that made her invaluable to her friends. She always knew the latest gossip, often before the participants themselves were aware of it. At a society ball, she was probably the only person, apart from a jeweller with a loupe, who could tell which jewels were real and which were paste.

But even Mrs Wyndham had very little to teach the Cashes. They had come to her because Mrs Cash wanted entry to the very choicest circles. Mrs Wyndham's friendship with the Prince of Wales meant that in London at least, she was received everywhere. When Mrs Cash had heard about the royal connection, she had made hints about introducing Cora to one of the younger princes but Mrs Wyndham had refused to understand her. At last, exasperated by Mrs Cash's persistence, she had told her that she could buy Cora pretty much any husband she chose within the ranks of the British aristocracy except for a royal one. If she wanted a prince she would have to go to Europe where you could find royal titles by the score.

As Mrs Wyndham drew up outside the neo-classical façade of Bridgewater House, the clock at St James's Palace chimed eleven. It was early in the day for a call but Cora had implied in her letter that she wanted a tête-à-tête. Mrs Wyndham knew the house well: she had housed many of her American protégées there, and she had received a handsome commission when she had persuaded Mrs Cash to buy it for her daughter.

Cora was standing at the top of the long marble staircase. Looking up at her Mrs Wyndham saw at once that the girl was different to the one she had met the year before. Some of those changes were physical; Mrs Wyndham assumed that the Duchess was by now pregnant, but the new softness was more than corporeal. The bright stare had gone. Something had dented that air of ownership. Mrs Wyndham was surprised, she had not put Cora down as the type to be altered by her marriage, she had seemed so self-possessed.

'Thank you so much for coming to see me, Mrs Wyndham,' said Cora.

'Oh, my dear Duchess, you can't imagine how thrilled I was to get your note. I rushed over here as soon as it was decent. I hope you are pleased with the house. Such a pleasant aspect, I always think. It would be hard to find a more elegant street in London. And how is the Duke? I hear there was some trouble in Ireland.'

'Yes, there was a rent strike and the bailiff was held up at gunpoint. Ivo came away most disheartened. I think he should sell the Irish estate and buy something in Scotland but he won't hear of it.' Cora's tone was light but there was a note of petulance.

'Well, no, Dunleary has some of the best fishing in Ireland. No sportsman would want to give that up. You know how attached gentlemen are to their sport.' Mrs Wyndham smiled wistfully, conveying in her glance the dead husband who had fallen while hunting with the Quorn. A reference that was lost on Cora.

'Ivo is attached all right. He missed the rehearsal for our wedding because he decided to go on a hunting trip. My mother was scandalised. Of course American men like their sport too but they have their occupations, they can't just take off in the middle of the week. Only today Ivo has gone all the way to Windsor to look at polo ponies.'

'Such a noble game, but I hope he will be careful. I remember what happened to his poor brother.' There was a pause as both ladies reflected on the death of the Eighth Duke.

Cora gestured to Mrs Wyndham to sit in one of the Louis

fauteuils by the fire (Mrs Cash had had them sent over from America).

'It's interesting that you should mention Ivo's brother, Mrs Wyndham. I know so little about Ivo's earlier life. And he so rarely speaks of it. Did you know the family well?'

Mrs Wyndham lowered her eyelids, she hated to admit ignorance. 'Not well exactly, but I saw the Warehams from time to time in London, and I was there for Charlotte Vane's coming-out ball, which of course was given by the Duchess. Such a beautiful girl, she did very well for herself, considering. Odo Beauchamp is independently wealthy even beyond what he will inherit from his father.' Mrs Wyndham noticed that Cora looked suddenly alert when she mentioned Charlotte's name.

'You say that Charlotte Vane did well for herself, considering. Considering what?'

'Oh, her complete lack of fortune. Her father was a gambler and lost it all at the tables. She was lucky that the Duchess took her in after her mother died, I don't know what she would have done otherwise. Far too pretty to be a governess. But the Duchess and Charlotte's mother were cousins on the Laycock side, and I suppose not having a daughter, she thought it would be nice to have a girl to dress up. She was very kind to Charlotte, I dare say she would have settled something on her if she could. Instead she did the next best thing and saw her well married. Odo is not to everyone's taste but he dotes on Charlotte and gives her everything she wants. Of course with her looks she might have done better than a baronet, but better a baronet with money than a marquess with mortgages.' Mrs Wyndham looked in her reticule for her lorgnette, so she could see clearly what effect her conversation was having on Cora.

'She looks like she enjoys spending money. She is quite the

fashion plate,' Cora was going to add, 'for an English girl', but stopped as she wasn't sure how Mrs Wyndham, who by now had almost completely lost the American twang in her speech, would take this remark. Sometimes it was hard to remember that Mrs Wyndham had grown up in Manhattan not Mayfair.

'Indeed, I believe her picture was in the *Illustrated London News*. Most regrettable. A respectable woman's name should only appear in the newspaper three times in her life: when she is born, when she is married and when she dies.'

Cora smiled faintly, thinking of the many newspapers and magazines which had printed her own picture in the last few months. *Town Topics* had doubled its circulation at the time of her wedding. She had not enjoyed the articles about her trousseau but she had found it hard to object to the photograph of her that had run in the paper with the caption: 'Is this the definitive American Beauty?' Mrs Wyndham really had become quite British. Ivo had the same disdain for the press.

'Charlotte Beauchamp was here yesterday, asking me to a musical evening. She seemed quite anxious that I should go. I wondered if I should accept.' She looked anxiously at the older woman. Mrs Wyndham realised that, for all her poise, Cora was nervous of getting it wrong. She would be delighted to advise her. It had taken her twenty years to learn how to get it right.

'Well, of course! You are the catch of the season. She, no doubt, is anxious to claim you as her own protégée. I am sure every hostess in London will feel the same. But you must be careful, my dear, to bestow your favours equally. You can't afford to make any enemies so early in your career.' Mrs Wyndham tapped the table for emphasis and continued.

'Everyone will be watching you to see what kind of Duchess

you will make. I'm sure most of them will be grateful for a new young, charming hostess, but you must remember that there are some who will be only too happy to see you fail. Your age, your wealth, your nationality make you conspicuous, not to mention your rank. Just take care you get yourself noticed for the right reasons. So by all means go to Charlotte Beauchamp's, but make sure the next time you appear in public it is with someone who is unquestionably old school like Lady Bessborough or even your mother-in-law. Keep them all guessing until you have decided where you want to be.'

Cora grimaced at the thought of her mother-in-law, but she understood Mrs Wyndham's point.

'But surely Ivo has already been identified as one thing or another?'

'When a man marries, my dear, it is for his wife to set the tone. If the Duke is thinking of going into politics – I heard he is taking his seat in the Lords – then the biggest asset he can have is a wife who knows everybody.'

Cora looked a little daunted by this, so Mrs Wyndham changed the subject. 'Now you will think me very indelicate for asking but I claim my privilege as your fellow countrywoman. Are you expecting a happy event? You have a look that suggests that you might be.'

Cora admitted that she was right.

'And when do you expect the little Marquess? I feel sure you will produce an heir. The Maltravers are so good at boys.'

'Sir Julius thinks May.'

'A spring baby. How delightful! Of course you will miss the season but there is plenty of time for that. I am so glad you are with Sercombe. Such a superior physician, and very liberal with the chloroform. Really, when I think of the agonies we women had to endure before. Why, Milly Hardcastle who had twin boys said that she hardly felt a thing. Luckily there are no twins in the Maltravers family, unless of course they run on your side.'

Cora shook her head. She felt her stomach churn and the bile rising up her gullet.

'Will you excuse me, Mrs Wyndham.' Cora rushed out of the room.

Mrs Wyndham tutted sympathetically. Poor child. Perhaps she should not have referred to the dolours of childbirth, it had clearly alarmed her. She wondered if she should wait for Cora's return. No, she had a luncheon in Portland Place. She would leave a note. She picked up a piece of monogrammed paper and wrote,

'I am very conscious that you are without a mother's care and guidance at this delicate time. Please allow me to assist you in any way that an older compatriot can. Your friend, Madeleine Wyndham.'

Perhaps, thought Mrs Wyndham as her carriage turned into Pall Mall, she should have warned Cora to be on her guard with Charlotte Beauchamp. There had been rumours earlier this year of a liaison with Louvain the painter; given that Charlotte had not yet produced an heir, this was hardly prudent behaviour. But then Mrs Wyndham's attention was distracted by an intriguing display of parasols in the window of Swan and Edgar and the moment passed.

CHAPTER 18

An Ideal Husband

THE CARPET OUTSIDE THE BEAUCHAMP HOUSE IN Prince's Gate, Cora noticed, was green instead of the usual red. It looked as if a roll of turf had been laid out between the door and the pavement. As she stepped on to the carpet in her silver slippers, Cora wished that Ivo was with her. When she had told him about Charlotte's invitation, he had grimaced. 'At home with the Beauchamps and all their artistic friends? Honestly, Cora, I can't think of anything worse.'

Cora had pleaded, but Ivo had not been persuaded to change his mind. Every time she mentioned the party, he laughed and said he was too much a philistine to go to the Beauchamps. So she had come alone, although now she was at the house, she wondered why, a feeling that intensified as she walked up the stairs to the drawing room. She heard a swell of noise and laughter as the door opened. Inside she caught a glimpse of yellow walls and black paintwork as Charlotte greeted her.

'Cora, I am so pleased you are here.' She took Cora's hand in hers and gazed into her eyes with such intentness that Cora flushed. 'Don't look so anxious, I promise you, it will be amusing, not like Conyers at all. Louvain is here, and Stebbings the poet, you know, and he's brought some men who are publishing a new magazine.'

Cora followed her hostess into the room. She could see at once that Charlotte was right, this was a very different kind of party. There were no diamonds here, even dirty ones. The lighting was quite dim, there was no chandelier, only wall lights with coloured glass shades that bathed the interior in a curious yellow light, as if the whole room were set in aspic. The men seemed paler than normal and several of them, Cora noticed, had hair that touched their shoulders. Charlotte was as smartly dressed as ever in mauve chiffon with black lace but Cora noticed that some of the other women were wearing oddly limp garments that bore no relation to any fashion that she was familiar with. She was amazed to see that some of the women were smoking in public.

Charlotte led her over to two men who were looking at a periodical with a yellow and black cover. She heard one of the men say, 'They wouldn't have him, you know. He wanted to contribute but Aubrey said no.'

'Not serious enough, I suppose. Poor Oscar.'

Charlotte clapped her hands. 'Gentlemen, may I present you to my new Duchess. Mr Louvain and Mr Stebbings.'

Cora held out her hand and smiled brightly. 'Why, I am delighted to meet you both. I never saw your picture of Mamie Rhinebacker, Mr Louvain, but I heard of nothing else in New York last year. And Mr Stebbings, you mustn't be cross that I haven't read your work yet, but I'm new to this country.'

Charlotte laughed. 'Goodness, no one here has read Stebbings' book, although we all fully intend to.' She gave the poet a proprietorial glance.

Cora saw the poet flinch and she tried to shake his hand in

such a way as to show her sympathy. He had sandy hair and his skin was so covered in freckles that she could hardly see the blush creeping over his face.

'I shall certainly read it, Mr Stebbings. I am very fond of poetry.' The poet blinked his colourless lashes and murmured something inaudible. Cora felt she had embarrassed him, so she turned to Louvain who met her eyes and gave a faint smile. As she stepped back to speak to Charlotte, she was aware of the painter's eyes still upon her.

'I have been looking forward to seeing your portrait, Charlotte,' she said.

'Well then,' Charlotte replied, 'you have only to turn your head.'

Cora turned and saw the painting on the wall behind her. Louvain had painted Charlotte wearing her riding clothes, her hat in one hand and her whip in the other. Cora realised at once why Louvain had insisted on painting Charlotte as a contemporary Diana. The dark costume was a foil to the pale intensity of Charlotte's face, whose expression was alert, defiant and, despite her gentle colouring, predatory. The hand that grasped the whip looked ready to strike, the curve of her mouth was about to declare the *coup de grâce*. She looked slightly dishevelled as if she had just dismounted. She was beautiful, but, Cora thought, alarming as well. But then she looked at Charlotte, who tonight was all smiles and softness, and wondered if she was right in sensing an edge to the portrait.

'You have done Lady Beauchamp justice, Mr Louvain. I have seen her in the field and she is fearless.'

'Thank you. A portrait is all about the exchange between the sitter and the artist. In Lady Beauchamp's case, I saw at once that I could only be her prey.' He made Charlotte an ironic bow.

Charlotte laughed and moved away.

'And did she catch you, Mr Louvain?' Cora risked asking.

'I'm not sure she wanted to, Duchess,' Louvain replied.

Cora felt again the heat of the painter's gaze. She looked up at him and saw that his eyes were a pale blue, so pale as to be almost colourless. Cora was well used to being looked at but usually, she felt, people were looking at her clothes or her money; Louvain was looking at *her*. His eyes were slightly narrowed; she saw in them neither admiration nor envy. No, he was taking her measure. She crossed her arms protectively, and forced herself to speak.

'You had a lucky escape then. The subject of your painting looks as if she would show no pity. I am surprised you did not give her a bow and arrow,' Cora said. She hardly knew what she was saying, her only thought was to keep going – she found the pale gaze unsettling.

'Do you think she needs one?' Louvain smiled.

He had, Cora noticed, quite a beautiful mouth, the upper lip finely drawn into a masculine version of a cupid's bow. He was soberly dressed in a dark suit, the only indicator that he was an artist was the yellow carnation he wore in his lapel.

'Well, perhaps not, her intention is quite clear.' Cora was about to continue when a voice spoke behind her.

'And what intention would that be, Duchess?' Sir Odo was standing next to her, his skin as shiny as ever with a red spot on either cheek. He had let his hair grow to aesthetic lengths and it lay like two spaniel ears on either side of his face.

'To carry all before her.' Cora smiled painfully. She felt on edge.

'Yes, she likes to be at the head of the pack.' Sir Odo laughed and a little spray of spittle fell in the space between them. 'Shame that Louvain here won't do any more portraits. Ivo must need some new pictures to replace all the ones that Duchess Fanny sold, eh?' To Cora's relief the baronet went off to speak to a footman.

Louvain was still looking at her. Cora felt the hairs on her arms prickle. The painter nodded. 'Actually, I do want to paint you.'

'Already? You flatter me.' Cora tried to look away from him but found she could not. 'And how would you fill the space between us, Mr Louvain? I worry that you might reveal me in all my shallowness.' She laughed nervously.

'Do you really think so? I think I might see other things that you would prefer to keep hidden, but I don't think you have anything to be afraid of. And it is not my intention to flatter you, I assure you. I am sure you are quite adequately flattered elsewhere. No, when I say I want to paint you, I say that not to appeal to your vanity, but to your interest in truth. I think you would like to be seen instead of always being looked at. Am I right?' His eyes never left hers as he spoke. She felt her heart flutter in her chest.

'It sounds very,' Cora paused, trying to find the right word, 'intimate. I hope I can withstand your scrutiny.'

'If you want absolute fidelity you can go to a photographer and get it. I won't paint you just as you are, but as I see you.' Louvain narrowed his eyes again as if trying to distil her image in his mind.

'And what do you see?' she said faintly

'I can only tell you with my brush, Duchess. I don't want to put my thoughts into words. I try to keep my impressions as colour, light and shade for as long as possible.'

'I see,' said Cora. She would have liked a more definite answer.

'When you come to the studio, wear something simple. I want

to paint you, not all the fuss that surrounds you. Shall we say next Monday morning?' Louvain spoke as if there could be no doubt that she would make herself available.

Cora knew she should not let this continue unchecked. 'I'm not sure that will be convenient, Mr Louvain. I may be returning to Lulworth next week.'

'Bury yourself in the country at this time of year? Surely not. No, you must come to my studio on Monday,' Louvain said firmly.

Cora bridled. 'Really, Mr Louvain, I can't rearrange my whole life at your whim,' she said as haughtily as she could.

Louvain opened his arms in a supplicatory gesture. 'Please, Duchess. A week is all I need to start with.'

Cora raised an eyebrow. 'You work very fast, Mr Louvain.'

Louvain pulled out his watch from his waistcoat pocket and, consulting it, he said, 'Thirty-four Old Church Street at eleven o'clock. Don't be late or I will lose the light. And remember, wear something simple. Goodbye, Duchess.' And he walked away.

Cora wanted to think about this encounter, and wondered if she could leave, but before she could move she saw Sir Odo approaching accompanied by a woman who was wearing a clinging gown of purple and green, unsupported, as far as Cora could see, by stays.

'Duchess, you must meet Beatrice Stanley, the actress. She was in *A Woman of No Importance* last year, you know. She has promised to recite for us later. Too thrilling.'

Cora held out her hand, she still had not acquired the English habit of bowing. The actress took it with a languid clasp. She had a very long white neck, on which her small head with its cloud of black hair balanced precariously. She had huge dark eyes which gazed mournfully at Cora.

'How do you do, Mrs Stanley,' Cora said. 'I came to London just too late for the play, but I hope I will see you on the stage soon.'

'Mr Wilde has two plays coming in the New Year, so you won't have to wait too long,' Mrs Stanley replied coolly.

Cora paused, at a loss. 'You know, I've never met an actress before.'

'Really? I have the advantage then, as I have met a number of duchesses, although never an American one.' Having established the upper hand, Mrs Stanley smiled at Cora. 'Do you like England, or am I asking you to betray a confidence?'

'I like very much what I know of it, but there is still so much I haven't seen,' Cora said.

'Have you been to the *Second Mrs Tanquerary* yet? Mrs Pat gives the performance of the season.' The actress waved her arm languidly.

'No, I haven't, but now you have recommended it I shall force the Duke to take me.' Cora smiled at the thought of forcing Ivo to do anything.

'Oh, I don't think you will have any trouble, Duchess. Your husband was always a great fan of the theatre.' Mrs Stanley lowered her lashes at Cora.

Cora felt the blow but knew she must not show weakness. 'The Duke has so many interests, but we shall certainly make a point of seeing you in your next play. What is the name of it?'

'It is called *An Ideal Husband*, Your Grace.' And having delivered her exit line, Mrs Stanley glided off to prepare for her recital.

Cora hoped that this exchange had not been overheard, but Sir Odo was behind her and cleared his throat.

'You mustn't mind Mrs Stanley, Duchess. She only does it to annoy because she knows it teases. I'm sure Wareham barely remembers her.' He giggled and Cora was furious with herself for being there. She guessed that the story of the ideal husband would be everywhere by the end of the evening. But she must not give Odo Beauchamp the satisfaction of appearing humiliated. She smiled in what she hoped was a worldly manner.

'I've made it a rule never to ask Ivo about his past. That way he can't ask about mine.' It was the best she could muster.

Sir Odo gave her a condescending smile. 'Some more tea, Duchess? Mrs Stanley is to give us her Ophelia. Such a treat.'

Cora smiled back, drank her tea, and sat on a conversation seat upholstered in mauve velvet as Beatrice Stanley performed the mad scene from *Hamlet*. She had a melodious voice and, when acting, a sweetness of expression that surprised Cora. When the performance was over, she clapped as loudly as her kid gloves would permit and made herself congratulate the actress warmly. Then she looked around for Charlotte to say goodbye. She was standing under the portrait, smoking a cigarette and laughing at something that Stebbings the poet had said.

'Goodbye, Charlotte, such an interesting party. Thank you so much for inviting me.'

'Oh, I hope you found it amusing.' Charlotte exhaled a long plume of smoke. 'Tell me, did Louvain ask you to sit for him? He left before I could ask him.'

Cora laughed. 'Not so much ask as command. He assumed I would have nothing better to do.'

Charlotte gave her a slow smile. 'And do you?'

Inexplicably, Cora found herself blushing, but before she could reply, Charlotte said, 'I don't think you can refuse to be Louvain's last portrait.'

Cora laughed a little nervously. 'Well, I would certainly have to find a good reason. And now if you'll excuse me,' and she made her way to the door. As she walked down the stairs to the black and white checkered hall, she heard footsteps behind her.

'Duchess!'

It was Stebbings. He smiled at her shyly. In his hands he had a book bound in yellow.

'May I give this to you, Duchess? I would like you to read my poem. You seem to be a woman of feeling.'

'Thank you, Mr Stebbings, I am flattered you think so.' Cora took the book, which had a woman wearing a masquerade mask on the cover. She appreciated the contrast between the vivid yellow of the cover and the dark green of her dress.

'No one in there has read it, they just talk about it. But I thought that you might be different.'

Cora felt sorry for this anxious young man and touched by his interest in her. 'I will certainly read it and I will write and tell you what I think.'

'You can find me at Albany. I shall wait for your letter.' And he took her hand and wrung it so fervently that Cora felt quite worried about her wrist.

'Goodbye, Mr Stebbings.'

'*Au revoir*, Duchess.'

Her encounter with Stebbings had taken the sting out of her visit to the Beauchamps and she found herself smiling as she got into her carriage. She was grateful to have at least one admirer.

She arrived at Cleveland Row just in time to change for dinner, and asked Bertha to fetch her the apricot mousseline dinner dress with the black ribbon trim as she considered it particularly fetching.

Reggie Greatorex and Father Oliver were in the drawing room with the Duke.

'Darling, how very charming you look. Did you enjoy yourself at the Beauchamps?' Ivo kissed her cheek.

'It was certainly interesting,' she said brightly.

'Did Charlotte throw you amongst the lions, Duchess?' Reggie smiled at her.

'Well, I met Louvain, and a poet called Stebbings. He gave me a copy of *The Yellow Book*. Have you seen it? It is quite beautiful.'

'Good Lord, Cora, one visit to Charlotte's salon and you have come back an aesthete. Promise me you won't start wearing rational dress and drooping everywhere.' Ivo put his arm round her waist as if to assure himself that she was still wearing a corset.

'I have seen *The Yellow Book*,' said Father Oliver. 'There is something rather febrile about it, don't you think? As if they are trying just a little too hard to be modern. I always feel that nothing palls faster than a book that is trying to shock.'

'Are you saying that this book is unsuitable, Father Oliver?' said Ivo. 'Should I confiscate it from Cora in order to preserve her moral character? I don't want her to be a decadent duchess.' He smiled and gave Cora's waist a squeeze.

Cora longed to lean into him and let it go, but she was annoyed by the way they were all talking over her as if she had no thoughts or opinions of her own. She drew herself a little apart.

'I think I am quite capable of deciding for myself whether a magazine is suitable or not. And from what I have seen of *The Yellow Book*, I think I am quite safe.'

'Of course, Duchess,' said Father Oliver soothingly. 'I didn't mean to suggest for a moment that you shouldn't read it. I think the Duke may be exaggerating for effect.' He smiled knowingly at Ivo.

Ivo laughed. 'The idea is preposterous. But Caesar's wife and all that. A duchess, especially a young and beautiful one, has to be seen to be virtuous. A woman's reputation is a fragile thing, and a duchess's is like gossamer.' His voice was light but there was an edge to it.

Seeing the look on Cora's face, Reggie broke in.

'Did you hear the story about the drawing of Mrs Pat in *The Yellow Book*. There is a picture of her done by this chap Beardsley that looks like a wraith. Ricketts, the editor of the *Morning Post*, gets a copy and says he likes the magazine but where is the portrait of Mrs Patrick Campbell? Beardsley thinks there has been a mishap and sends him another copy. Ricketts writes back and says, I still can't see anything in the book that resembles Mrs Patrick Campbell!'

Cora laughed and the tension dissipated as Ivo laughed too.

At dinner Reggie entertained them with stories about his time as a page at Windsor Castle. But Cora was tired and thankful that she had instituted the sixty-minute rule here at Cleveland Row. She had to conceal a smile as a footman whisked away Father Oliver's *oeufs en cocotte aux truffes* while he was in the middle of a long and elaborate story about intermarriages between the Maltravers and Percy families in the sixteenth century.

She went to bed early. She hoped that Ivo would not stay in the smoking room forever. Bertha helped her out of her dress and corsets, which were getting increasingly uncomfortable, and she sat at the mirror brushing out her hair, enjoying the respite from stays and hairpins. It was only when she got undressed at night that she realised just how trussed up and pinned down she had been during the day. There were red welts under her breasts where her corset had dug into her expanding flesh. Her scalp was sore from the pins that held the diamond and feather aigrette to her head. The back of her neck was red from the diamond clasp of her pearls.

But then she heard Ivo whistling a tune from *The Mikado* in the corridor and she forgot about the lacerations of the flesh.

'You see, I didn't linger. Here, let me do that for you.' Ivo picked up the hairbrush and began to pull it through Cora's thick brown hair. He did it well, applying just the right amount of pressure to smooth out the tangles without pulling on her scalp. There were times when Ivo said things that Cora did not understand but every time he touched her she felt that they were in perfect accord. She looked at him in the dressing-table mirror. His thin face was soft, it didn't have the creases and angles tonight that sometimes made him look so stern.

Ivo whistled a few more bars from *The Mikado*. Cora tried to catch his eye in the mirror.

'You know, I realised today how little I know about you,' she said.

Ivo's whistling turned into singing. 'Three little maids from school are we, full to the brim with girlish glee, three little ma-aaaaids from school.'

Cora persisted. 'I mean, I know nothing about your childhood really, or your youth or how you lived before you met me.' She caught his free hand and kissed it. Ivo carried on brushing, his dark eyes glittering.

'But Cora, I was nothing before I met you. Simply a cipher with strawberry leaves. Do you really want to hear all about Nanny Hutchins who drank, and Nanny Crawford who didn't. Or the time that I threw a stone into the hothouse at Lulworth and was chased round the pond by the head gardener. Or how Guy and I used to spend days tapping the panelling looking for the priest's hole with the secret staircase that leads down to the sea. Or the day that the under-butler got the keys to the cellar and got so drunk that he climbed into my mother's bed at two in the morning. Or my inability to master the finer points of Latin prose and being beaten for same, or my first pony, or my dear departed dog Tray, or my first Communion, or the first time I tasted ice cream . . .' As he spoke his strokes with the brush got faster and faster so that Cora's hair was beginning to flicker with electricity. She put up her hands and seized his arm, laughing in spite of herself.

'Ivo! Enough. My head is going to explode,' she said in mock exasperation.

'But I thought you wanted to know about my early life,' Ivo said reproachfully. He got free of her restraining hands and went back to the brushing, albeit rather more gently.

Cora was grateful for the mirror, somehow it was easier to talk to his reflection. She said carefully, 'I want to know everything, even the things you might not want to tell me.'

'Such as?' Ivo stopped brushing and raised an eyebrow at her.

Cora wondered if she should leave well alone, but she thought of the uncorseted actress and she went on. 'Well, your past . . .' she struggled to find the right word, 'liaisons. I mean, I am not so naive as to suppose that there were no women in your life before you met me.'

'Women, Your Grace? The very idea!' Ivo drew up his hands in mock horror.

Cora persevered. 'It's just that if I don't know about them, I look foolish. I was mortified today at the Beauchamps.'

Ivo stopped brushing for a moment and then brought the brush down hard on a particularly sensitive part of her scalp. He had stopped whistling.

'And why was that?' His voice was quiet.

Cora found that she did not dare meet his eyes in the looking glass. 'Because Odo Beauchamp introduced me to Mrs Stanley and of course everybody knew except for me that you and she were once . . . friendly.' She dared look at him now and saw to her surprise that far from looking angry, he looked relieved.

'So you met Beatrice.' He began to brush her hair again with long rhythmic strokes. 'She was very kind to me once.'

Cora looked at him sharply. She thought he might be a little more contrite. She turned round to face him. 'I'm sure she was kind to you once, but she humiliated me today.'

Ivo gave a look of genuine astonishment. 'But honestly, Cora, I don't know why you should feel humiliated. You are a duchess with youth, beauty and everything you could ever want, while Beatrice is nearly forty, with no husband to speak of and an uncertain future. I am sorry if she made you feel foolish but I think she is the one who deserves sympathy.'

Ivo's tone was unexpectedly serious, Cora could not understand why he was taking the other woman's side.

She stood up, her hair crackling with static as she turned her head. 'Well, I still think you should have told me. I don't want us to have secrets from each other. I hate walking into a room and feeling that everyone there knows more about you than I do.'

Ivo looked down at his hands. 'I'm sorry, Cora, that you felt unprepared. I have never wanted to burden you with my past, just as you,' he looked Cora in the eyes, 'have not disclosed everything to me.'

Cora took a step backwards in amazement. 'What do you mean? I have nothing to "disclose".'

Ivo shrugged. 'So the Newport swain that your wretched papers kept comparing me to unfavourably was purely a fiction then?' he said lightly.

Cora felt something close to anger. 'But that was before I met you,' she said.

'Precisely,' said Ivo, and he put the hairbrush back on the dressing table, lining it up with the hand mirror and the boxes of pins and powder.

Something about his careful movements infuriated her.

'But they were laughing at me, Ivo!' Her voice was petulant.

Ivo turned round and spoke so quietly that Cora had to lean towards him to hear every word. 'Do you really want me to feel sorry for you? You can't accept the privileges of our rank and not understand that you will also be stared at and gossiped about. You didn't mind it when there were crowds outside the church for our wedding, did you? There were pictures of you in the New York papers as well as all kinds of articles about the most intimate details of your trousseau and fortune. I bore all that without complaint even though I found it vulgar beyond belief because I knew that in your world these things were quite normal. So I'm sorry if you felt embarrassed today but perhaps now you under-stand how I felt every day in your country, being spoken of quite freely in the press as a penniless fortune-hunter.' His voice was almost a whisper but Cora felt the chill in his words. She was more alarmed by his quietness than she would have been by a more obvious display of anger. She wondered how things had come to this point.

She had pictured Ivo making a tender confession which she accepted with exquisite tact, but instead they were having a quarrel with no real purpose. Ivo was angry with her when clearly it was her prerogative to be angry with him. She looked at him and saw no softness in his face at all, and she started to cry. She tried to check herself but every time she attempted to hold back, she felt another wave of tears demolishing her self-control. She heard a violent heaving noise and realised that it was the sound of her own sobbing.

At last she felt his hand on her face, smoothing the hair away from her cheek. He gave her a big white handkerchief to dry her eyes. She blew her nose in it viciously. He laughed.

'Poor Cora, I won't let you go out alone again. I thought it might amuse you to be the toast of the town.' He led her over to the chaise longue at the end of her bed and made her sit down.

Cora knew she should leave well alone but she couldn't help herself saying, 'Did you love her?' She spoke through a curtain of hair.

Ivo paused and spoke carefully. 'I was fond of her.'

'Did you want to marry her?' Cora knew that the question was absurd but again she couldn't resist.

'Dearest Cora, you're the only woman I have asked to be my duchess.'

Cora wiped her face with the sleeve of her peignoir. She felt very tired. 'And how did it end?' she whispered.

'End?' He looked surprised. 'It wasn't like that.' Ivo picked up the black pearls on Cora's dressing table and started to feed them through his fingers like a rosary. 'No, things ended when my brother broke his neck.'

'What do you mean?'

Ivo put the pearls down with a clatter.

'Everything changed when Guy died. It was the worst day of my life. My brother was dead and I was the Duke.' Ivo stood up and went over to the bell pull. A footman appeared almost immediately. 'Get me a brandy and soda.'

When the footman returned with the decanter and soda siphon on a salver, Ivo poured himself a stiff drink and began to pace up and down the room, talking as much to himself as to Cora.

'Guy was the only thing I have ever believed in. He was a good man, almost a saint. If he hadn't been the oldest son I think he would have been a monk. He only ever did the right thing and yet he was dead and I was the Duke. It made no sense at all.'

Cora said nothing, she had never seen Ivo like this before. He moved restlessly around the room, not looking at her but talking with quiet insistence.

'I never wanted to be Duke, never. There are younger sons who think of nothing else but the health of their older brother. But I was glad that I was not going to inherit. I saw what happened to my father – he pretty much bankrupted himself trying to behave in the way he thought a duke should and all he got for it was the dubious pleasure of being cuckolded by the Prince of Wales, among others.' He drained his glass and went back to the decanter.

Cora could hardly believe what he had just said. 'You mean your mother and the Prince are . . . more than friends?' She tried not to sound shocked but she couldn't help herself. Duchess Fanny and the Prince, why hadn't she realised?

'Oh, I don't think they are now, but when my father was alive . . .' Ivo broke off as if in pain.

Cora was bewildered. 'Did your father know?'

'Of course he knew,' Ivo said bitterly. 'Everybody knew. My mother made sure of that. She even had that snake tattooed on her wrist to show she was part of "the club", as she called it.'

Cora was struggling to understand. 'But couldn't your father stop her? He could have threatened to divorce her.'

Ivo shook his head. 'Catholics don't get divorced and, besides, you can't name the Prince of Wales as co-respondent. No, my mother knew exactly what she was doing. My poor father, all he could do was stand by and let it happen. The worst thing was that he really loved her. Plenty of women would have consoled him but he wasn't interested. And all the time my mother was acting as if she was doing him a favour by becoming a royal favourite. I didn't understand what was happening at first, but now I can hardly believe how callous she was. She would open her love letters from the Prince in front of him, and he would sit there and watch.' Ivo bowed his head in an unconscious imitation of his father's acquiescence. 'In the end, of course, the Prince got bored, which she accepted gracefully enough – I don't think she ever cared for him deeply – and simply replaced him with Buckingham. When my father realised what had happened, he just gave up. He died a year later.' He shook his head, as if trying to shake off the memories.

Cora felt a surge of pity. She saw the naked hollow at the base of his skull – when he turned his head there was a vulnerability in Ivo she had never noticed before.

'And the worst of it was that Mother never understood what she had done. If anything, she was proud of herself. She was the reason that Guy was so devout. I think he was trying to atone for her sins. God knows there are enough of them. It wasn't just the Prince, although he was the most public. She always had admirers – I think she even amused herself with the servants.' His voice was bitter.

Cora put her hand on his arm. 'But don't you like being Duke now?' she said.

'It is not about liking. I am a link in a chain that stretches from the past through me into the future. Even though I never wanted it, I don't have a choice.' He looked down at her and his face softened. 'But thanks to you I don't have to watch Lulworth falling down, or part with its contents piece by piece. Our son will not have to grow up watching land being sold and farms crumbling because there is no money to repair them.' He put his arm around her and pulled her to him.

Cora was relieved that Ivo's mood appeared to have lightened. She was encouraged by the reference to their child and to the healing power of money. She liked the idea that thanks to her this ancient institution would get up off its knees and walk again. It gave her particular pleasure to think that she would be able to reverse the depredations wrought by the Double Duchess. She smiled to think how her mother-in-law would react when she saw the water terraces she was planning for the south front, or the Canova statues she had bought for the summerhouse. (After the contretemps with the Rubens, she had made sure that the statues of Eros and Psyche and Venus bathing came free of unwelcome associations.)

There was a tap at the door and Bertha entered carrying a tray.

'I brought your hot milk, Miss Cora. The doctor said you should drink it before going to bed.'

'Thank you, Bertha. I had quite forgotten.'

Bertha turned to go, when she heard the Duke's voice.

'Bertha!'

The maid wheeled round to face him.

The Duke said quietly, 'Bertha, I would prefer it if you could address my wife by her proper title. I appreciate that you have grown up in a country without such niceties, but here we set much store by them. Please remember in future.'

Bertha stood motionless, her head bowed.

Cora leapt in. 'It's not her fault, Ivo. I encourage her to call me Miss Cora because it reminds me of home. What does it matter what my maid calls me in the privacy of my bedroom?'

'Bertha, you may go.' Ivo waited for the door to close behind her before he turned to his wife. 'Cora, please remember that everything you say to me in front of Bertha is repeated word for word in the servants' hall.' He turned his back to her. Cora flew at him; the words she could forgive, but not this physical snub. She put her hands on his shoulders and pulled him round to face her.

'What is the matter with you! One minute you say you never wanted to be Duke, and now you are scolding my maid for not calling me Your Grace. I don't understand you.'

Ivo looked down at her tear-stained face. His face had an expression she could not read. He took her hands from his shoulders and clasped them in his own.

'I have been thoughtless, Cora. You are tired. Women in your condition need a great deal of rest. We will talk about this tomorrow.'

Cora tried to respond but he led her to the bed and as she lay down she realised that sleep was all she wanted. She took his hand.

'Stay here with me, Ivo.'

He lay down beside her and she put her head on his chest. She knew there was something she had to tell him but sleep overcame her before she could remember what it was.

In the attic Bertha turned up the gas so that she could get a better look at the seam she was unpicking. All Miss Cora's bodices needed taking out now that she was beginning to show. Cora refused to accept her thickening body and simply ordered her maid to pull the laces harder, but Bertha worried that the tight lacing would harm the baby. By surreptitiously letting out the seams at night, Bertha was able to convince her mistress that she was still able to fit into her wardrobe. These secret tailoring sessions could not go on indefinitely, of course; Bertha hoped that Cora would soon accept the realities of her condition.

Bertha got to the end of the seam, pricking her finger in the process; a bead of red dropped on to the pink silk, soaking into the weave of the fabric, following the threads so that it looked like one of the tiny scarlet money spiders of Bertha's childhood. She spat on the stain and rubbed it with her thumb, turning the spider into a rusty bruise. It was on the wrong side of the cloth, she would be the only witness to what lay beneath the Duchess of Wareham's pink silk. She put the dress down and got ready for bed. Her mind was still turning over the Duke's rebuke and she wondered how long Miss Cora would defend her. She had around three hundred dollars in the chest under her bed, the product of various gifts from Cora, the profits from the sale of used gloves and what she put away from her salary, and she also had the 'boulder'. She had intended to send some of the money to her mother, but now she wondered whether her need might be greater. If only she could be sure of Jim, that he would have the courage to follow her into a new life.

CHAPTER 19

'The Faint Half-Flush'

LOUVAIN'S STUDIO WAS IN CHELSEA, A PART OF London that Cora had only heard of. The coachman had looked astonished when she gave him the address and was forced to consult his fellows before setting off. The fog grew thicker as the carriage got closer to the river, so Cora could barely see the outline of the house through the yellow mist. All she could make out was a red painted door set in a Gothic stone arch. The coachman made to go and ring the bell but Cora stopped him.

'I'll go myself. Come back in an hour.'

She rang the bell and heard it tinkling far off in the distance. After a few minutes the door was opened by a manservant who Cora thought might be Japanese. He bowed to her and gestured for her to follow him down a long corridor lit from above by a skylight. Hanging from the picture rail on either side were black and white prints that looked oriental; Cora stopped to look at one as she went past and saw that it was an exquisitely detailed drawing of a man and woman embracing. Cora felt a quiver of shock mixed with curiosity. She would have liked to have examined the picture more closely but she couldn't risk the servant turning and seeing her. She felt the blood pounding at her temple, she almost turned round and walked away, but she could see the servant holding back the heavy damask portière and she felt herself move forward. Charlotte had said a chaperone was quite unnecessary but now Cora wished she had brought Bertha with her.

The studio was a double-height room with a north-facing window that ran from the ceiling almost to the floor. At the base of the window was a window seat covered in a paisley shawl and velvet cushions. To the right of the window was Louvain's easel and a table covered in brushes, rags and paints. At the other end of the room was a Japanese screen, a chaise longue and a fern in a brass pot. The parquet floor was covered in Persian carpets. Stacked against the walls were canvases and portfolios. Skylights bathed the room in rippling grey light. Cora felt as if she was walking underwater. The impression was reinforced when she heard Louvain's voice echoing through the room. He was wearing a velvet smoking jacket that was flecked with paint.

'Good morning, Duchess, you are late but not unforgivably so. Please give Itaro your things. Good. You have dressed simply.' Louvain stood about four feet away, looking at her through half-narrowed eyes. Cora felt his gaze sweep up and down her body.

'I'm sorry for my unpunctuality, but the fog, you know, slows everything down. We nearly had to give up and go home. My coachman was quite worried about bringing me to Chelsea, he thinks that it is not a respectable neighbourhood.' Cora was talking nervously, aware that Louvain's eyes had not left her for a moment.

'Don't worry, you will be quite safe. There is no one here to molest you apart from a few impoverished artists looking for patronage.' He took her arm. 'Why don't you come and sit down here.' He led her to the chaise longue upholstered in green velvet.

She sat down on the edge, her back as upright as if she was wearing the spine stiffener.

Louvain stood back from her. 'No, no, you look as though you were at a missionary tea. Can't you lie back a little? Here, let me give you some cushions.' He went over to the window seat and picked up some cushions which he placed behind her. 'Now lean back. That's right.' He paced up and down in front of her, looking at her so closely that Cora felt hot with the scrutiny. She sat rather stiffly against the cushions, trying to arrange her arms gracefully.

'Would you like me to fold my hands? I've heard that hands are the hardest thing to paint.'

'Who told you that?' Louvain asked.

'An American friend, who was studying art. He said that the hands always defeated him.'

'Did he paint you? This friend?'

'No, he said he wasn't ready.' Cora thought of Teddy and smiled.

'Not ready for you! He must have been scared.' Louvain shrugged.

'Perhaps.' Cora wished she had said nothing. Louvain had a way of turning every conversation into an intimacy.

He came closer to her and picked up one of her hands which he draped along the back of the chaise longue.

'Yes, that looks better. But it's not enough.'

Cora looked at him nervously. 'I want you – no, I need you, to take down your hair,' Louvain said.

'My hair? I can't possibly.' Cora was firm.

'But why not? You are so young, what could be more natural? I want to paint you as a goddess from the New World, beautiful and unbound. I don't want you trussed up like a society goose. Please take down your hair, I don't think I have ever seen hair quite your colour before.' He reached out a hand to touch one of the tendrils that hung by her cheek.

Cora was alarmed at how close he was to her.

'I think it would look . . . odd.' She could feel his breath against her cheek.

'Then, Duchess, I think you have had a wasted journey.' He turned away from her and started to walk towards the door.

Cora twisted with indecision. She thought of what her mother would say about her taking down her hair and then she remembered Charlotte's cool recklessness. She was not going to be dismissed as a provincial American.

'Wait!' she said. Slowly, Louvain turned round.

She stood up and started to take the pins out of her hair. There were so many of them that she could not hold them all.

'Here, let me take them.' Louvain stretched out his hand.

At last they were all out, Cora shook her head and felt her hair fall heavy and luxurious on to her shoulders. Louvain had been right, she did feel unbound. She looked at him shyly, meeting that ever-present gaze. Although her body was completely covered, she felt naked. She had to stop herself from putting her arms across her breasts.

Louvain said nothing but walked round her slowly. Cora stood still as if pinned to the spot but at last she forced herself to speak.

'Is that what you wanted?'

Louvain still did not speak. Then he moved towards her and quickly and firmly kissed her on the mouth.

'No, Duchess, that's what I wanted. Now, perhaps you would like to resume your pose?'

Cora blinked. Had he really kissed her? Yes, she knew he had because she could still feel the scrape from the bristles of his moustache. And now he was behaving as if nothing had happened. She knew that she was losing control of the situation. She should have slapped him at least.

'I must go. Your conduct is disgraceful.' But Cora did not move.

Louvain, who had walked over to his easel and paints, laughed.

'Oh, don't be in a huff, it was only a kiss. You looked so promising with your hair down. I had to satisfy my curiosity. Anyway it serves you right for teasing me with your American friend and coming here unchaperoned. But I apologise for taking such a liberty and I promise not to do it again.' He made a solemn sign of the cross in the air, and continued, 'If it will help your conscience, I only did it for the sake of the painting. I could see that you were wondering if I was going to pounce and now that I have, you can relax. You know I find you attractive which means you can be sure that the portrait will flatter you.'

Cora was aware that she should leave immediately but she knew that she would stay. She sat down on the chaise longue and lay back against the cushions.

'You see, that's much better, stay just like that.' Louvain had a sketch pad and was rapidly drawing with a pencil.

'Is this the way you behave with all your sitters?' Cora tried to sound nonchalant.

'I don't kiss the men!'

'What about Lady Beauchamp? Did you kiss her?'

'What do you think?' Louvain's tone was dismissive.

Cora fell into her pose. Louvain was right. She did feel more relaxed. She wondered if he would try again and what she would do if he did.

He stopped sketching and looked at her directly. 'Do you want to undo your jacket? You're expecting, aren't you? You might feel more comfortable.'

'How did you know? About the baby? I'm not showing yet, am I?' Cora looked down at her still defined waist.

'My job, Duchess, is to see you and I can see that you are full of expectation. Women in your condition have a certain milky quality. Medieval painters believed that you can see babies in the eyes of pregnant women.'

'And what else do you see, Mr Louvain?' she asked.

'Oh, I'm not going to tell you that, it will all be there in the painting. Which, before you ask, I am not going to show you until it is quite finished. Now, I want you to stop talking so I can concentrate on your mouth.'

As soon as he said this, Cora felt her lips tingle. She looked up at the grey clouds through the skylight.

'No, don't look up there, keep your eyes on me.'

Cora nodded dumbly, there was evidently no escape. The rest of the session was virtually silent, apart from the scratching of Louvain's pencil and the smacking noises he made with his mouth as he rubbed out a line that was less than satisfactory. Every so often there was the muffled sound of a foghorn from a boat on the river and the faint mewings of distant gulls. After a while, despite the kiss, Cora found herself subsiding into a kind of torpor. She found the effort of being looked at exhausting. After about an hour the silence was broken by the crash of a gong being struck. Cora started and Louvain put down his pencil.

'Lunch! Will you stay, Duchess? Itaro is quite a talented cook.'

'No, thank you. I must go home.' Cora rose to her feet.

'I'll see you tomorrow at the same time. And don't be late again, we have a lot of work to do.'

As Cora left, she ran her eyes over some of the other black and white Japanese prints that lined the hallway. She did not dare to linger as Louvain was following her to the door, but he noticed the turn of her head.

'Do you like them? They are called *shunga*. These ones are by Utamaro – they are of the courtesans of the Yoshiwara district where he lived. They apparently thought it was a great honour to pose for him. His pictures are such an exotic mixture of the real and the imagined. Look at this one.' He pointed to one of the prints. Cora came over to look at it. It was a woman embracing a squid. Cora stood back quickly, her face pink with embarrassment.

Louvain laughed. 'That one is called the fisherman's wife. Lovely, isn't it?'

'Unexpected, certainly,' said Cora faintly.

'Till tomorrow then, Duchess.' Itaro opened the door, bowing, She looked round to tell Louvain that in no circumstances would she be coming back tomorrow, but he had gone.

But the next day Cora found herself in the carriage heading towards Chelsea. This time she had brought Bertha with her.

She had decided to make the portrait a surprise gift for Ivo. Something to remind him of the way she looked now, before she was all swollen with the baby. She sensed that his attitude to her had changed since she had started to show; she wanted to remind him that she would not always look like this.

Her mind wandered. Perhaps there would be a party for Ivo's birthday. It was not the season, of course, but there would be enough people in town to have a reception. She would ask Mrs Wyndham.

She tried not to look at the *shunga* as she walked down the corridor towards the studio. Louvain started towards her as she came in but stopped and smiled when he saw Bertha.

'So you have come prepared,' he said.

'Well, I felt awkward yesterday going home with my hair down. If Bertha is here she can make me look respectable first.' Cora smiled.

'Respectability must be preserved at all costs, Duchess. Perhaps your maid would like to sit here.'

He pulled out a chair from behind a screen and placed it so that Bertha would have no view of the painting. Cora went over to the chaise longue and turned her back to him as she began to take the pins out of her hair; she found she did not want to look at him as she did so, it was too intimate somehow. But she spoke to him over her shoulder.

'How long do you think the portrait will take, Mr Louvain? I want to surprise my husband with it for his birthday.'

'It will take as long as it takes. If you sit still and don't fidget, it might be faster,' Louvian said tetchily.

'I will be as still as a graven image, I promise, but would a month be unreasonable?' Cora put a pleading edge to her voice.

'I never give guarantees. But if you are an obedient model, there is a chance the picture might be finished in a month. But you will have to do exactly as I say, mind. Now, unbutton your jacket like you did yesterday. And try to remember how you felt yesterday, the expression on your face was just as it should be.' He winked at Cora who blushed.

'I'm not sure if I can remember how I felt yesterday. I think I was trying not to fall asleep. It is hard keeping still for so long,' she said.

'Would you like me to remind you, Duchess?' Louvain made a step towards her. Cora moved back alarmed.

'Oh no, that won't be necessary. I am sure I can remember enough. Bertha, come here and help me with my hair.'

Bertha started the long process of unpinning hair that she had put up only an hour or two ago. Now she understood why Miss Cora had rushed off yesterday wearing the simplest navy-blue tailor-made and had come back with her hair knotted under her hat. She had scurried into her room and insisted on Bertha fixing her hair properly before going downstairs, but she had not offered a word of explanation. Bertha had been surprised, to say the least. Miss Cora never made morning calls, and as for the hair, that was completely unprecedented. The speculation in the servants' hall had been rife. The coachman, who had seen an oriental servant opening the door, had hinted that Her Grace had been visiting an opium den. He knew all about them as his last employer Lord Mandeville had been that way. Bertha had laughed this off but she had been curious and a little apprehensive.

So she was relieved to find out that Miss Cora was sitting for a portrait, although there was something going on between the painter and her mistress that made her uncomfortable. Miss Cora had always been a flirt, but now she was married she should be more careful. Bertha wondered what had happened yesterday. She looked at her mistress who lay on the chaise longue with her chestnut hair falling over her shoulders to her waist and her jacket unbuttoned to reveal her chemise, her mouth parted in a half smile. She looked as she had on her honeymoon in Venice, her sharp edges blurred. Bertha sat awkwardly between Cora and the painter; every so often she would look up from the mending she had brought with her and feel the heat of their mutual gaze.

On the way home, Cora told Bertha to get in beside her instead of sitting on the box with the coachman.

'What did you think of the studio and Mr Louvain, Bertha?'

'Does he make money from his painting, Miss Cora?' Bertha asked.

'I'm sure.' Cora spoke with the unconcern of a girl for whom money had never been anything but abundant. 'I would imagine he can charge what he likes. We haven't discussed a fee for this painting but I've no doubt it will be exorbitant. Father says that being American adds fifty per cent to everything.' She leaned over to Bertha's side of the carriage conspiratorially. 'This must be kept a secret from the Duke. I want to hold a reception before I get too big and give it to him then. I'd like to do something while I am still respectable.'

Bertha could see some pitfalls to this scheme.

'But suppose you don't like the picture, Miss Cora? Won't it be awkward asking folks to see a picture you ain't fond of?'

'Well, that's not going to happen! Louvain is a genius. This is going to be his last portrait,' Cora said.

'And what if the Duke don't like it? I ain't sure he cares for surprises,' Bertha said carefully. There was something about Louvain that worried her.

Cora remembered the scene in the chapel. Perhaps Bertha had a point. And yet she felt reluctant to tell her husband what she was doing. The thought of him in the studio made her feel quite uncomfortable. And surely this picture was quite different from the Rubens.

'I think he will be delighted to have a portrait of the woman he fell in love with,' Cora said firmly. 'Louvain says he can't work with other people's opinions hanging over him. He says if you want something completely faithful, take a photograph.'

Bertha thought that Louvain had found a way of spending unlimited time with beautiful women without their husbands, and getting paid for it.

Cora was delighted when Charlotte sent up her card that afternoon. She wanted to talk to her about the party. She was determined it should be smart and she needed Charlotte's advice. Mrs Wyndham was always reliable but Charlotte had style.

To her relief, Charlotte approved of all her plans.

'You're so wise not to make it too serious, Cora. London really doesn't need any more high-mindedness.'

'I want to give Ivo the portrait. I thought it should be an occasion.'

Charlotte smiled slyly. 'And there is no harm in reminding the world that Louvain has chosen you as the subject of his last portrait.'

Cora blushed. 'Well, I suppose you could look at it that way. But don't tell anyone, please.'

Charlotte leant forward. 'And how do you like Louvain? Is he being frightfully strict with you?'

Cora busied herself with the tea things. 'He certainly knows what he wants. It's very hard to argue with him.' To her relief Sybil arrived at that moment, gleeful because she had managed to evade her stepmother. Sybil had come to rely on Cora for sympathy when she found life under Duchess Fanny particularly trying.

Charlotte was less warm to Sybil than she had been to Cora. She listened to her complaints for a few minutes and then said a touch impatiently, 'But if Aunt Fanny is making your life so irksome, why don't you get married? You must have had plenty of offers.'

Sybil looked stricken and Cora, seeing her expression, jumped in. 'You must come and stay with me, Sybil. I would love some company at Lulworth and who knows, we might be able to get up a party.' She looked meaningfully at Sybil, who found her smile again. She knew that by 'party' Cora meant Reggie Greatorex, who so far had failed to make her an offer. Charlotte, who had no interest in matchmaking, made her excuses and left.

After she had gone, Sybil sighed. 'Charlotte is so magnificent, isn't she, but don't you think she's just a tiny bit frightening?'

Cora thought for a moment. 'You know, I thought that at first, but she has been quite charming to me. Apart from you, dear Sybil, I would say that she is my only friend here in England.'

Sybil made no reply.

When Cora told Ivo that she wanted to give a reception before, as she put it, she became indecent, he was, rather to her surprise, enthusiastic.

'So you are going to be a hostess, are you? I am delighted. There are some people I would like you to invite.'

The list, when Ivo handed it to her at breakfast, surprised Cora. It was full of politicians, many of them titled, it was true, but politicians none the less. At home, politicians were in the same league as actresses, an unavoidable fact of life but not suitable for the drawing room.

'Ivo, do you really want me to invite all these politicians? I don't want my first party to be dreary.' Cora's tone was light but Ivo replied in his quietest voice.

'So you think politicians are dreary, do you, Cora?'

Cora bridled. 'I don't think they are the ideal guests.'

Ivo turned on her. 'Doesn't it occur to you that I might have a reason?'

Cora looked at him resentfully. She hated the way that Ivo, who made fun of everything, would suddenly become serious without warning.

'I'm sorry, Ivo, I had no idea that you had political ambition. You've always laughed at me when I've asked you about the House of Lords. Forgive me for my ignorance, but in my country, we don't have aristocrats, we have men like my father who go to work.'

There was a pause before Ivo spoke.

'Oh yes, your father, the Golden Miller's son, who came into his first million when he was twenty-one years old. What work, exactly, does your father do? Apart from auditioning promising chorus girls, that is. I thought his only employment was avoiding your mother.'

Cora threw the cup she was holding at her husband. He ducked, and the cup landed on the floor in a mess of china and milk.

'How dare you sneer at my father? What did you ever do before you became Duke except have "friendships" with the likes of Mrs Stanley? My father, on the other hand, runs the biggest mill in North America. Sure, he inherited his fortune, but he has made it grow. Don't forget that his money paid for this house and every-thing in it.' She stopped, panting with rage.

'Even the china that you just you hurled at my head, I believe. And what exactly is your point, Cora? If you had such a yearning for men who do things, why didn't you stay in America and marry one of them? I am sure a girl like you must have had plenty of suitors. And yet you chose to come to England and marry a duke. What could you have been thinking?'

Ivo stopped as a footman came in with a silver chafing dish.

'Robert, I have been very clumsy.' He pointed at the mess on the floor. 'Can you ask one of the maids to clear it up? And I will have some more coffee while you're about it. Oh, and I believe Her Grace needs a new cup.'

Ivo's tone to the footman was completely neutral, without any of the heat he had displayed a few moments earlier. His self-possession enraged Cora even more than his jibes about her father.

'That won't be necessary, Robert, I am finished.' Cora left the room without looking back.

In her bedroom she picked up one of her silver-backed hair-brushes and hurled it against the wall. Then she kicked the bedpost so hard that she hurt her foot and only after that did she sit down on the bed and cry fat tears of anger and frustration.

Five minutes later, the door opened and she heard Ivo's light tread.

'Go away, I don't want to speak to you.'

'You don't have to say a word. In fact, I would rather you didn't. I just came to tell you that the reason I wanted you to ask Rosebery is that he has been looking for my support in the Lords. I think he may even want me to join his ministry. I don't know if you understand what that means; my family have been beyond the political pale for three hundred years because we are Catholic. You asked me if I had any ambitions, well, I don't for myself but I do for my family. The Maltravers have a chance to be some-thing again and it is my duty to make that happen.'

He paused. Cora knew without looking that he was stroking his chin, which he always did when he was serious.

'Your fortune has made that possible, Cora. None of this would have happened if I hadn't found you that day in Paradise Wood. So let's not quarrel any more.'

She felt his hand touch her shoulder; she rolled over slowly, reluctant to show him her tear-stained face.

'I like you when you've been crying.' He snaked a finger across her wet cheeks. She tried to bat his hand away but he was determined, stroking her face and hair now as if she were a frightened animal that needed soothing. And then his breathing began to quicken.

Cora tried not to look at him but he was already pulling at the buttons on her dress. She was still angry with him, but he had hardly touched her since she had told him about the baby and she could not help but arch towards him as he began to kiss her throat and chest. She was relieved that there was still that same sense of urgency. He began to push her skirts up.

'Oh, Ivo, do you think we should? What about . . .'

But Ivo was kissing her and there was no more resistance she could offer. He pulled away the layers of petticoats and pushed himself inside her there and then. She was surprised at how little difference there was between the rage she had felt earlier and what she felt now; both passions were equally consuming. As she felt her body begin to contract with desire, she opened her eyes and looked at Ivo. His face was stern, concentrating; was he still angry with her? But the thought was lost as she felt the snap of fulfilment and her body went quiet.

The following day she was in Louvain's studio, stretched out on the chaise longue, Bertha sitting in her usual corner. Louvain had barely spoken to her when she came in but when he looked at her, she noticed that his pale eyes were alight with excitement. He was working very fast, almost quivering as he attacked the canvas with his brush.

'Good news, Duchess, this will be our last session. The picture will be ready next week.'

Cora felt a tiny stab of disappointment. She had come to enjoy her hours in the studio, she liked watching Louvain's concentration. She knew there were moments when she ceased to exist for him as anything more than a collection of planes and colours. But she didn't mind, she found his detachment appealing.

'Will you let me have a look, Mr Louvain?'

'Not yet, not yet. But I can tell you I am very happy with it.'

As she left the studio for the last time, Cora dropped her handkerchief in the corridor. As she stooped to retrieve it, she saw the face of one of Utamaro's courtesans, contorted in a spiral of desire.

CHAPTER 20

'That Pictured Countenance'

CORA HAD SENT ONLY A HUNDRED CARDS FOR THE reception but by the day of the event, she had made so many new 'friends' that the likely number of guests had at least tripled. Mrs Wyndham, who had made much of her connection with the new American Duchess, suddenly found herself taken up by the very same people who had vanished so completely from her life after the death of her husband. Some women might have seized this opportunity to exact revenge on those who had slighted them, but Mrs Wyndham was far too pragmatic for that. She knew that people generally behaved only as well as they had to, so she was admirably even-handed in the recommendations she made to her friend the Duchess, only proposing those whom she thought might genuinely add to the evening's entertainment.

To every would-be invitee she said the same thing. 'The Duchess wants this to be an intimate affair, where she can really get a chance to talk to people. I am sure the Duchess would love to meet you. She said to me, "Dear Mrs Wyndham, help me to make a short cut through London society and bring me its best and brightest." I know she is longing to make real friends here in London. She really is a lovely girl, so unaffected and devoted to the Duke. And generous, my goodness. When she saw how shabby my stole had become she insisted on giving me this gorgeous sable. Of course, money means nothing to her, you know, she is the richest heiress of her generation. In the New York papers they call her an American princess and I must say her manners would not be out of place at Windsor. Even Duchess Fanny can't find fault with her.'

Mrs Wyndham thought that Cora was looking suitably princess-like tonight. She was wearing a pink and white striped silk dress with huge bows at the shoulders and at the waist. In her hair she wore a tiara of diamond stars and round her neck the black pearls. The enormous width at the shoulder led the eye away from the thickening waist. Only those women, and it would be women, who looked carefully would guess that she was expecting. Cora and the Duke were standing at the top of the marble staircase greeting their guests. Mrs Wyndham had thought she would be early but there was already a crush of people on the stairs. She could smell that unique mixture of powder, lily of the valley and sweat that always heralded a society event. Just ahead of her was an unusual-looking man with artistic hair that fell almost to his shoulders. She had hinted to Cora that it might be unwise to be too experimental in her guest list, but Cora had been firm that she did not want a stuffy party. As a result there was a greater mixture of guests than Mrs Wyndham was used to seeing: artistic young men, a few members of the Cabinet, idle aristocrats like Ivo's friend Reggie Greatorex and busy ones like Lord Curzon, old money like the Atholls who owned most of Scotland's land and new money like the Tennants who owned most of Scotland's breweries: and the women ranged from the Double Duchess right through to Mrs Stanley. Such a mix would not have happened when Mrs Wyndham had first arrived in London, but these days society was no longer a closed circle. The thing was to have 'tin', lots of it, and then your place in the social firmament was assured.

Mrs Wyndham's small blue eyes criss-crossed the room looking for young men with titles and no tin who might be interested in Adelaide Schiller, from Ohio, who had three million dollars and an accent that could only improve. Mrs Wyndham had hoped to bring Miss Schiller with her tonight, but Cora had been firm. 'No Miss Schiller. I don't care how long she studied at the conservatory, I'm not being unkind but I don't want to give anyone the chance to make scathing remarks about American heiresses. And I don't want anyone who might flirt with Reggie Greatorex. Sybil would never forgive me.' Mrs Wyndham had wheedled but Cora would not budge. 'Ivo's already been through my list twice, I daren't add anyone else. But bring Miss Schiller for tea one day and I will look her over.' It didn't take long, thought Mrs Wyndham, for a girl from New York to turn into a grande dame. She had no doubt that Miss Schiller herself would be equally fastidious when she had landed her title.

Cora and Ivo were standing close to each other, closer than you might expect a married couple to stand. They looked in accord; Ivo was just behind his wife and every so often he would whisper into her ear and make her laugh.

Sir Odo and Lady Beauchamp were next in the procession to be announced. Charlotte was wearing gold satin which made her look literally radiant, everyone around her seemed lacklustre by comparison. Only her husband with his blond curls, red shiny cheeks and elaborately embroidered brocade waistcoat could stand the juxtaposition. Most of the people on the staircase had an air of eagerness, there was a sense of anticipation – a new hostess, a new way of doing things – but the Beauchamps did not hurry up the staircase, they sauntered, creating a pocket of space around them as they stopped to exchange greetings with people in the hall below. They contrived to create a hiatus on the crowded steps, so that it was the Duke and Duchess who stood waiting, while the Beauchamps greeted those around them. And when, eventually, the Beauchamps glided towards their hosts, they had an air of slight fatigue as if the party had already begun to pall.

Cora, who had no choice but to observe these manoeuvres, did not let her smile of welcome falter even as Ivo was muttering in her ear, 'What is that buffoon Odo wearing? The man's absurd.'

'How lovely to see you.' She leant forward to kiss Charlotte on the cheek. 'You must both stand by me tonight. You are, after all, my oldest English friends.'

'Indeed, Duchess,' sniggered Odo. 'Charlotte and I like to claim we invented you!'

'No one could invent Cora, Odo,' said the Duke. 'Not even a man possessed of your imagination. My wife is part of a new and wonderful species that has evolved independently in the Americas. Nothing scares her, except perhaps her mother.'

'Ivo, stop talking nonsense,' said Cora, pleased nevertheless that Ivo had resisted Odo's attempt to patronise her. 'Perhaps you could tell the orchestra to play something else. I must have heard that waltz ten times already. I can see Mr Stebbings wincing at the predictability of it all. Please, Ivo.'

'Is it really that bad? I thought it was rather charming myself, but if you insist. We can't have a party with wincing poets.' Ivo walked off in the direction of the musicians.

Charlotte leant forward so that her husband could not hear. 'Is Louvain here?'

'Not yet,' Cora whispered back. 'I still haven't seen the picture.'

Charlotte touched her on the arm with her fan. 'Don't worry, I'm sure he'll have done you justice.'

The Beauchamps moved into the drawing room and Cora let her smile slip just a little and felt the ache in her cheeks. She could see the line of guests stretching down the stairs almost into the street itself. She wondered when Louvain would arrive. Every time she thought about the picture, she felt her pulse quicken. It had only been one kiss after all, but she could still feel it sometimes – the scrape of his moustache against her lips.

Duchess Fanny was in front of her, her blond head a little on one side as if she was trying to remember who her hostess was.

'My dear Cora, what a charming occasion. I had no idea there were so many people in London in November. You look a little peaky though, dear, I do hope you are not overdoing it. Really, you don't have to stand here any longer, I think half an hour is quite long enough to be in the receiving line.' She gave Cora a gracious smile.

'But I don't know everybody. I would feel discourteous if I wasn't here to greet my guests,' said Cora.

'I suppose you are still young enough to think that you should set a good example. By all means, do the right thing, dear, but don't expect anyone to thank you for it.' Duchess Fanny moved off into the drawing room, the light catching the diamond drops hanging from her ears so that Cora fancied for one moment that her mother-in-law's head had caught fire.

'Don't take any notice of her, Cora.' Sybil was beside her. 'She is furious that you are having a party without asking for her advice. I think everything looks lovely. There can hardly be an orchid left in London. Very forward of you to invite Mrs Stanley, I know there are all sorts of stories about her but I have been dying to meet her since I saw her in *Lady Windermere's Fan.*' Cora could see that Sybil's eyes were searching the room.

'Would you like me to introduce you? I am sure she would like to meet an admirer.'

'No need, I can see she is talking to Reggie.' Sybil sped off, her bright red hair clearly visible in the crowd. Judging by the reddening of an inch of skin between Reggie's collar and his hair, he too was an admirer of Mrs Stanley.

'Your Grace.' The butler was standing beside her. 'Mr Louvain is in the library and everything has been arranged as you asked.'

'Tell him I will be down directly the guests have stopped arriving.'

She wanted to go down at once, but she knew that Duchess Fanny would think she was following her advice, and that she was determined *not* to do.

Downstairs in the library, Bertha was looking at the portrait of her mistress. She had been right, she thought, to suspect Louvain's intentions. Louvain had painted her lying back on the green chaise longue, one arm draped invitingly along its buttoned back, the other demurely in her lap. The abundant chestnut hair fell down over her shoulders as if she had just released it, the jacket of her dress was open with a suggestion of white lace beneath. It was a provocative pose with a hint that Cora had been surprised in the act of undressing, but the most striking feature of the painting was the expression on her face as she looked directly out of the canvas. The only word Bertha could think of to describe it was a word she had heard used time and again in her Carolina childhood: wanton. Louvain had made Cora look wanton. Her eyelids appeared weighed down by the long eyelashes, her mouth was slightly open and on each cheek was a splash of colour. Bertha, who had seen her mistress look like this often in Venice and occasionally since, was amazed at how accurate the painting was. You could almost feel the heat coming from the canvas, from the golden browns and umber tones that Louvain had used for the hair. Cora's grey-green eyes looked unfocused, the pupils dilated. Bertha could almost taste Cora's soft red lips again; Cora had changed so much since she had asked her maid for kissing lessons, but this painting managed to get across something of the innocence of those days as well as the woman she was now. But there was nothing yielding about the picture, it was the image of a woman who wanted satisfaction.

Louvain was watching her with a smile, showing his teeth.

'So, what do you think?'

'It's very like her, sir. I reckon Miss Cora will be pleased.' She could say that in truth; her mistress would like it, she was sure, but she wondered whether the Duke would feel the same way.

'And you? Do you like the picture?' he pressed her.

'That ain't the point, is it, sir?' Bertha looked at him directly.

'Why not?'

'Because you didn't paint it for me. You did it for her and I reckon she will like what you've done.'

Louvain was staring at her with narrowed eyes.

'You know, I would like to paint you, Bertha. You have such beautiful skin, it would be a challenge.'

'I don't think that would be right, sir, and besides, my young man wouldn't like it.' She knew the kind of picture Louvain had in mind, and she had no intention of taking her clothes off.

'Are you sure, Bertha? There are plenty of women upstairs who are longing to pose for me. Wouldn't you like to hang alongside a duchess?' He moved towards her to stroke her cheek, but Bertha saw him coming and took a step aside to look at the picture more closely.

'I don't think the ladies who want you to paint them would be too happy if you start painting their maids,' she said.

'Perhaps not, but no one tells me what to paint,' Louvain said without hesitation.

She looked at him as blankly as she could, thinking that no one could tell her to be painted either. He caught the sense of her silence and smiled.

'Do you realise, you are the first woman ever to turn me down.'

'We all of us need practice in being disappointed, sir.' Bertha made a perfunctory little curtsy. She had to find Miss Cora at once. 'If you'll excuse me, sir.'

'Run away then. You'll regret this one day.' Louvain dismissed her with a wave.

Bertha went out into the black and white checkered hall. There was still a stream of guests coming in from the cold, surrendering their coats and furs to the maids at the door and making their way up the wide curving stairway to where Cora stood. Bertha wondered how she could reach her mistress discreetly. It would have been simpler if she had been in uniform, but as a lady's maid she did not wear a cap and apron. But to her surprise, no one so much as glanced at her as she went up the stairs. Back home it would have been unthinkable for a coloured maid to make her way through a crowd of white folks without leaving a trail of disapproving stares in her wake. Most people in this country didn't realise that she was coloured. The English cared more about class, and here the society people simply did not see those who were not in their world. Bertha wondered what she disliked most: to be noticed for her colour or to be ignored for her class. But right now it suited her to be invisible. She waited until Cora had greeted an older lady wearing some threadbare ostrich plumes in her hair and her two gawky daughters whose kid gloves, Bertha couldn't help noticing, were soiled. That family was sorely in need of a new lady's maid, she thought – or perhaps they did not care. English ladies, she had observed, were a lot less particular than the Americans. Miss Cora would rather stay at home than wear dirty gloves. But at last the grubby family moved on and Bertha sidled up to her mistress.

'Miss Cora,' she said quietly, but Cora was in what Bertha thought of as her 'Duchess' mode.

'Bertha, you must remember to call me Your Grace in public, you know how the Duke feels about it.'

'Your Grace, I think you should come and look at your portrait,' Bertha said.

Cora said impatiently, 'I will be down as soon as all the guests are here. I am going to present it to Ivo.'

'But don't you think you ought to see it first?' Bertha persisted.

'Why, what's wrong with it?' She seized Bertha's arm. 'Does it make me look ugly? Or fat?'

'No, Miss Cora, I mean, Your Grace, you look fine in the picture. I just think you should see the picture, is all.' Bertha was beginning to regret her mission. Perhaps she had imagined things.

'Well, in that case, I have nothing to worry about.' Cora turned away. 'Dear Father Oliver, I am so pleased you could come to my little soirée.'

Bertha left her there. She felt full of foreboding about the portrait, but there was no more she could do. She went downstairs to the servants' hall. Jim was in the pantry eating a piece of cold pie. He looked up guiltily as she walked in.

'Oh crikey, I thought you was Mr Clewes.' He smiled at her. 'But I'm so glad you're not.' He brushed the crumbs away from his mouth and gave her a kiss. She pushed him away.

'Jim, don't. It's not worth it.'

He kissed her again, his lips still greasy from the pie. 'I'll be the judge of that.'

She wriggled away and stood in front of him, her arms folded. 'I'm worried, Jim.'

'Don't worry about Clewes and the others. They're all busy upstairs. I'm meant to be helping but luckily the spare livery didn't fit.'

'No, it's not that. It's about Miss Cora's picture. It ain't respectful, and she don't know it.' Bertha shook her head.

'Why, is she naked?' Jim rolled his eyes.

'No, of course not! Thing is, she looks like she could be, if you know what I mean,' Bertha said.

'Nothing wrong with that. There are lots of pictures of naked women at Lulworth.'

'But not of ladies, Jim. Those goddesses and such ain't ladies.' Bertha looked at him.

'Ladies look the same underneath, don't they, or is there some secret you aren't telling me?'

Jim was whispering in her ear now. Bertha felt his breath tickling her neck. She wanted to fold herself into him, to press her heart against his heart and feel the warmth between them, but she could not contain her worry. There were times when she didn't much care for Miss Cora but she was her mistress and she could not be indifferent. She knew Jim did not understand the connection she felt. He felt loyalty to the Duke but he did not feel responsible for him; the Duke was his employer not his charge. But for Bertha it was different.

'Come upstairs with me, Jim, come and look at the picture. Maybe I'm fancying things that ain't there.'

'Not likely, Bertha! If I go up there, I'll be workin' all night. Ain't a man entitled to a spot of leisure once in a while, with his best girl?' Jim put his arm round her waist and drew her to him. She let her head rest on his chest for a moment but then she remembered the look in the painted Cora's eyes and pulled back.

'I must go, Jim.'

He released her reluctantly, saying, 'Remember, Bertha, all we do is wait on them.'

But she was gone, her dark bombazine skirts rustling against the stone stairs.

Upstairs, the drawing room was now full to bursting. Women were having to turn sideways to pass each other on account of the enormous width of their leg-of-mutton sleeves. Heads crowned with ostrich plumes and diamond aigrettes twisted and craned to get the best view of the new Duchess. There was general agreement that she was pretty, in an American way, 'vivacious rather than soulful', but more interesting was the speculation as to the extent of her wealth. A viscount who had visited the United States on an unsuccessful gold prospecting expedition assured his listeners that every slice of bread that passed American lips was made from Cash's finest flour. Another man said that the Cash family ate all their meals from gold plate, and that in their house in Newport even the servants had bathrooms. There was much talk about the Duchess's settlement. One countess had it on very good authority that she had half a million a year. A silence followed this remark as her listeners tried to estimate how many noughts there were in a million. It was agreed that reviving houses like Lulworth was the very best use for American money, and there was generally expressed relief that the new Duchess appeared to be a woman of some taste. Her gown was much admired, after it had been identified as a Worth, and there was satisfaction that her jewels, though fine, were not overwhelming. There was surprise at the presence of Mrs Stanley, given her previous friendship with the Duke, but the feeling was that inviting her had been a stylish gesture on the part of the Duchess. There was some confusion among the more frivolous-minded guests at the presence of the Prime Minister and the Foreign Secretary – did the new Duchess intend to be a political hostess? It was really too tiresome if that was the case as there were far too many serious-minded hostesses and not nearly enough fun. Mr Stebbings, who had come hoping for a tête-à-tête with the Duchess about his work, was disappointed to see her so firmly hemmed in by philistines, but he had been rewarded by the sight of *The Yellow Book* on one of the occasional tables. He had picked it up and been gratified to find that the volume fell open at the page on which his poem 'Stella Maris' appeared, and as he read it through, he felt the usual prickle of surprise at the felicity of his own expression.

The prevailing mood of satisfaction was rendered all the more piquant by the fact that there were a significant number of people who had not been invited. This was a satisfyingly select gathering. Even those who had previously condemned American forays into English society as impertinent could find nothing to criticise. Only Charlotte Beauchamp looked restless, her eyes constantly straying to the door to see who was arriving. Some of the less generous members of the party put her lack of composure down to being in the house of a rival to her status as the most fashionable woman in London. Charlotte Beauchamp was possibly the more beautiful, that Grecian profile was without parallel, but the new Duchess had such a scintillating smile.

Sir Odo, however, did not think his wife was restless because she was in the presence of a rival. He knew that Charlotte would never allow herself to show weakness. 'You are the most beautiful woman in the room tonight, my dear.'

She turned to him in surprise. 'A compliment, Odo?'

'No, merely a statement of fact. Why do you keep looking at the door?' he asked.

'I was hoping to catch Louvain before he gets mobbed by all his would-be sitters.'

'Are you sure he's coming?' Odo asked.

'Oh yes, he told me he'd be here.' Charlotte stopped, realising too late that she had made an admission.

'Do you have something in mind then, Charlotte?' Odo looked at her closely. 'It really is too bad of you to work alone. You know how I enjoy our little games.'

Charlotte adjusted her glove, pulling the kid leather taut over her knuckles. 'But I wanted to surprise you,' she said, stretching out her fingers. 'I wanted the satisfaction of seeing your face when you realised how clever I'd been.'

'Really?' Odo took one of her hands in his own, folding his fingers around her kid-gloved fist. 'I hope we understand each other, Charlotte, that we are on the same side.'

She pulled away from him, but he held on. 'Don't do that, you'll wrinkle my gloves. Lady Tavistock is looking at us, you don't want her to think that we are having a scene, do you?'

Odo released the hand and she shook it out. And then as if by mutual consent they moved in opposite directions, greeting the people on either side of them with enthusiasm.

Cora had moved from her station at the top of the stairs. The line of guests had dwindled to a few latecomers who had come on from the theatre. She was talking to Mrs Wyndham and Lady Tavistock, telling them how parties in Newport were conducted.

'The balls there never start till at least midnight. It gets so hot during the day there.'

'It sounds too, too exhausting,' sighed Lady Tavistock. 'I can barely stay awake past midnight these days.'

'Oh, I think you might manage to stay awake for one of Mrs Vanderbilt's fancy dress affairs.' Cora said brightly. 'Last year she brought the whole cast of *The Gaiety Revue* from New York to perform after dinner. And the favours were all replicas of jewels worn by the court of Louis the Fourteenth. It was quite spectacular.'

'I still think it sounds exhausting, dear Duchess. You Americans are so energetic.'

'Well, we are still a young nation, we haven't had time to get bored.' And then Cora saw the unmistakable figure of Louvain with his pelt of silvery blond hair, his pale blue eyes assessing the company. He saw her and raised one hand in greeting, but before he could move towards her he was accosted by a trio of ladies, their shoulders raised like hackles.

'Can that be Louvain over there?' said Lady Tavistock, without a trace of her former languor.

'Yes, he has come to show me my portrait. It is so exciting, I haven't seen so much as a drawing yet.' Cora was anxious to get to the painter but Lady Tavistock was still talking.

'Well, that's quite a coup. To be painted by Louvain already. Lady Sale and her daughters have been waiting for years to sit for him. I suppose you must have offered him a fortune.'

'Oh, we never discussed money. He asked me, as a matter of fact. He was really quite insistent.' She caught Louvain's eye again. 'He is impossible to refuse.'

'So I've heard,' said Lady Tavistock, her eyes glittering with malice. 'Louvain always gets what he wants.'

Mrs Wyndham, alarmed at the edge the conversation was developing, looked about her for a distraction. 'I think the Duke might be looking for you, my dear. He is over there with Duchess Fanny.'

'Thank you, Mrs Wyndham. Will you excuse me?' And with a grateful glance to Mrs Wyndham, Cora sailed off towards her husband.

'You've done well with that one, Madeleine,' said Lady Tavistock. 'Quite the Duchess already. You would hardly know she was an American, apart from the voice of course.'

'Do you know, I really can't take the credit for her,' said Mrs Wyndham. 'Some of these American heiresses now are as regal as any of our own princesses. She's certainly better educated than most English girls of her age. But what is so interesting is her fearlessness, she doesn't seem to be afraid of anything.'

'That's just as well, considering that she has Fanny Buckingham as her mother-in-law,' Lady Tavistock said. 'I haven't seen those emeralds in years. I wonder why Fanny decided to wear them tonight? Do you think she might be trying to make a point?'

Ivo met Cora half way across the room. He nodded his head at Louvain.

'Who is that man over there with the peculiar hair surrounded by women? I've seen him before.'

'You mean Louvain,' Cora said.

'The one who painted Charlotte? What on earth is he doing here?'

Cora was puzzled by the sharp tone in his voice. 'I asked him, of course,' she said. She went on quickly before Ivo could protest further. 'In fact, he has brought something with him I want you to see. It's in the library. Come with me now, quickly, before we get caught by Lady Tavistock.'

But Ivo did not move. 'Cora! We can't simply disappear. Not even for Mr Louvain.' Cora caught the edge again in his voice. 'Whatever it is can surely wait.'

Cora could have stamped her foot with impatience. But here was Lady Tavistock bearing down on them.

'My dear Duke, I can't wait to see the portrait, what a coup!' And then, seeing the Duke's face, she tittered and turned to Cora. 'Oh my dear, was it to be a surprise? What an idiot I am.' She looked at the couple curiously.

Cora stood frozen for a moment and then she recovered. 'Not at all, Lady Tavistock. I was just about to show him the picture.' And then to demonstrate she was not intimidated, she made a sign to the butler. 'Clewes, could you arrange to have the picture brought up here.'

Lady Tavistock said, 'To see the unveiling of a Louvain. How exciting! Your wife is so original, Duke.'

Ivo nodded. His eyes were on the object being carried into the room by two footmen, who at Cora's signal set it down in front of him. The picture, which stood on an easel, was covered by a heavy red velvet cloth.

Cora found herself trembling with excitement. She had to stop herself from tearing the cloth down. Instead she beckoned to Louvain who was standing to her left, next to Charlotte Beauchamp. The painter approached the picture, and then hesitated with his hand on the drape. Cora turned to her husband.

'Shall we ask Mr Louvain to do the honours, Ivo? Or would you like to be the first?' She put a hand on his arm and looked at him in appeal.

Ivo did not answer but simply gestured to the painter to carry on. The room went quiet around them.

Louvain pulled the crimson velvet away with a flourish, letting it pool on the floor like blood.

There was a sound as the whole room breathed out. From where she stood, short-sighted Cora could only see a golden blur. She narrowed her eyes to sharpen her vision but all she could identify was the brown sweep of her hair. She needed to get much closer. Bertha had been right, she should have gone to see the picture first so she could prepare herself. Now she would look ridiculous if she started to peer at it. She had forgotten Ivo in her anxiety to see the picture better, but then she heard his voice, quiet but clear. It broke the silence that had frozen the room since the unveiling of the picture.

'May I congratulate you, Mr Louvain, on the likeness. And such a refreshing pose. There will be time for formal pictures later, but you have caught the woman not the title.' Cora tried desperately to see what Ivo meant without screwing up her eyes.

'The Duchess was a pleasure to paint.' Louvain nodded towards Cora. The room which had been so quiet began to hum with conversation again as the guests surged forward to see the picture properly. Cora relaxed a little. The picture was a success. She began to edge forward to have a proper look, but she felt Ivo's hand on her arm, restraining her. He spoke very quietly.

'We will talk about this later.'

Cora looked at him in surprise. 'Talk about it? Why, is there something wrong?' She felt salty bile rise into her mouth as she saw the tension in his face. He was about to reply when Charlotte Beauchamp appeared in front of them.

'I'm really quite jealous, Cora, your portrait is causing a sensation. I think Louvain has excelled himself. It's amazing what a painter sees.' She smiled warmly at Cora and looked up at Ivo. 'And what do you think of your surprise?' She raised an eyebrow. Cora held her breath.

'It is a remarkable picture. I believe you were responsible for the introduction, Lady Beauchamp?' There was an unmistakable edge to Ivo's question, but Charlotte did not flinch.

'All I did was to put your wife and Louvain in the same room. What happened next was between them.' She gestured to the portrait and smiled.

Cora said brightly, 'Charlotte has been so helpful, Ivo. I don't know what I would have done without her.' She put her hand on Charlotte's arm to emphasise the point. Ivo looked at them both, his face expressionless. Cora thought for a moment he was going to quarrel with Charlotte. But then he smiled, not warmly, but enough to make her anxiety subside. Now he was drawing her away. She wondered what he was so anxious to avoid and then she understood. Duchess Fanny was inspecting the picture.

But they were not quick enough. Duchess Fanny turned to Cora and said loudly, 'And what character are you representing, dear? Rapunzel? Or Guinevere? Such abundant hair, and such a charming rustic costume. Really, we shall all have to be painted in character now.' Her blue eyes were very round. Cora heard the malice in her words and felt Ivo stiffen beside her, but it was Louvain who spoke.

He made a little bow. 'Well, I would be happy to paint you as Cleopatra, Your Grace.'

The Duchess inclined her head graciously as if the compliment was only her due, and gave Louvain one of her creamy smiles. Perhaps, Cora thought, it was not the picture that her mother-in-law was objecting to but the lack of focus on herself. She moved a bit closer to the canvas and looked at it properly. Really, it was most flattering; perhaps not very Duchess-like but surely Ivo would rather have this — she saw the warm tones of her painted skin and the attractive curve of her mouth — than some full-length stately thing. She couldn't help smiling. But at the same time she was aware that she was being watched by the guests milling around her. There was something about the atmosphere that reminded her of the night her mother had burst into flames. There was a crackling to the conversations across the room that made her uneasy. But before she could decide whether there was triumph or disaster in the air, Charlotte was beside her, her voice soothing.

'You look so natural. It is almost as if you weren't being painted at all. I can't imagine how you managed to look so relaxed. Louvain was always barking at me if I lost my pose for an instant. But I suppose you were lying down . . .' Her voice trailed off.

Cora said without thinking, 'Well, in my condition, it can be tiring to stand for too long.' Then she blushed, realising what she had done, and put her hand to her mouth. She looked around, hoping that no one had noticed, she did not want to tell the world yet. Once her condition became known she would be expected to retire to Lulworth until the birth, and she very much wanted to stay in London.

She noticed that Charlotte did not look at her but at Ivo, who stood very still, staring intently at his champagne glass. Perhaps he had not heard. But she had forgotten her mother-in-law who said loudly and unmistakably, 'Cora, does this mean there is to be a happy event?' Cora's blush was answer enough. Duchess Fanny looked reproachfully at her son. 'You might have told me, Ivo.'

Ivo looked at her coldly. 'I believe it is usual to wait until the sixth month before making an announcement. And besides, it was really for Cora to tell you.'

Cora broke in, 'Why, I haven't told anybody apart from Ivo. Back home we like to keep these things private. I only wrote Mother last week.'

'But in your country, dear Cora, you are not giving birth to dukes!' The Double Duchess looked at her in astonishment.

Charlotte had remained quite still during this exchange. Cora wondered if it was because she was still childless, and felt a pang of sympathy; Charlotte was clasping her hands together as if frightened they might do some damage. In the end it was Odo who spoke.

'Allow me to congratulate you on behalf of Charlotte and myself. Such a relief to know that there will be a new generation of Maltravers. And such a treat to see your portrait, Duchess, especially as it is such an intimate work.' Odo took Charlotte by the elbow and shepherded her away. But Charlotte stopped and looked back at the group beside the portrait.

'How clever of you, Mr Louvain, to paint the Duchess as a Madonna in waiting. You miss nothing, do you?'

The Duke signalled to the butler to remove the painting. 'Cora, I believe we are neglecting our guests. Mother, Mr Louvain, will you excuse us?' Ivo did not look at Cora directly but put his hand on her elbow to urge her on. She stood for a moment trying to understand what had been said and what had been omitted.

'Cora!' Ivo's voice was soft but urgent. She began to move but as she passed Louvain she stopped.

'Thank you, Mr Louvain. The picture is everything you promised.' She extended her hand to him, intending to shake his, but the painter forestalled her by bringing her hand to his lips.

'No one could do you justice, Duchess, but I have done my best.'

Ivo was pinching her elbow now. Cora disengaged her hand from Louvain and walked on.

Ivo muttered in her ear, 'Please try and remember who you are.'

Cora could not mistake the fury in his voice now. She looked at him but he had already turned away. To follow him now would be too public. She forced herself to smile, as if he had just been murmuring an endearment to her, and then drew her shoulders back and assumed her Duchess pose.

'Did you tell him that I kissed you?' It was Louvain standing behind her, whispering into her ear so closely that she could feel the bristles of his moustache.

'Of course not! There would be no point. You yourself said that it was only to improve the painting.' She kept her smile fixed.

'And you believed me? Do they not have red-blooded men in

your country then, that you believe the excuses of scoundrels like myself?'

'I don't want to talk about it, Mr Louvain. I wonder if sitting for you was a mistake.'

'How can anything that results in a work of art be a mistake? It's a great painting.' Louvain grasped her arm. 'Honestly, what did you think when you first saw it?' He looked directly into her eyes. She lowered her gaze. 'You liked it. You recognised yourself, didn't you?'

She was moved by the urgency of his voice. She realised that he was right.

'Yes, there was . . . something in the picture that I recognised. But perhaps it is something that should not have been painted.'

Louvain laughed. 'There are no secrets in a painting, not a good one anyway. And there is nothing you should keep hidden, Cora.'

The use of her Christian name brought her up short. This conversation should not be happening, not now, not here. He was presuming upon an intimacy between them that should not exist. She tried to compose herself, and said in a bright social voice, 'You know, Mr Louvain, this is my first big party. If I spend the evening talking to you, all of London society will go home saying that I am just another uncouth American. You must excuse me, Mr Louvain, you really must.' And with that she walked away from him. She looked around for Mrs Wyndham. She caught her eye and Mrs Wyndham hurried across the room towards her.

'Are you feeling quite well, Duchess? Do you need some air?' Mrs Wyndham was all concern.

'Yes, perhaps some air might be good.'

At a sign from Mrs Wyndham, a footman opened the long window on to the balcony and Cora leant out, feeling the cold

November air on her face with relief. She longed for a cigarette. At last she asked the question.

'Please, Mrs Wyndham, be honest with me. Is it a disaster?'

There was a pause as Mrs Wyndham composed her answer.

'Oh no, my dear, not a disaster. I think there may be a few people who are surprised by the portrait – it's a very unusual pose for a duchess to adopt. If you had told me that you were sitting for Louvain,' her voice took on a reproachful tinge, 'I would have warned you that he is not a man of unblemished reputation. There have been rumours . . . ' Her voice trailed off. 'But I hardly think that anyone could possibly attach any scandal to you.' She looked keenly at Cora for any sign of guilt. But the girl looked too bewildered. If there had been something between her and Louvain she would hardly have engineered such a very public denouement.

She went on briskly, 'If you behave as if nothing has happened, then nothing will have happened. This is your party, it is for you to set the tone. And if there is a little gossip, that is nothing to be afraid of – at least no one can say you are insipid. But now you must take charge. The real crime is to show weakness.'

Cora whispered, 'My husband is angry. I don't understand.'

Mrs Wyndham looked at her, surprised; could Cora really be so naive?

'Well, Louvain has an unsavoury reputation, and your picture, though charming in every way, has a certain intimate quality that might be open to misinterpretation. But only if you let it, my dear.' She saw with alarm that Cora's shoulders were sagging. It was imperative that the girl kept her head. She must take charge of the situation now or take years to recover her position. Mrs Wyndham shuddered. If Cora failed now then Miss Schiller and her compatriots would find their matrimonial prospects in England much reduced. So she said with a certain sharpness in her tone, 'Come, Duchess, your guests are waiting.'

And to her great relief she saw the young woman pull herself upright, and with her head tilted at an angle calculated to charm, she rejoined the party.

From her post by the door Bertha watched her mistress advance towards her guests. She could see all was not well. Bertha had seen the looks that had been exchanged when the picture had been unveiled and knew her misgivings about the picture had been well-founded. If only Miss Cora had listened to her – but Bertha felt no comfort in being right, she only felt pity for her mistress. She did not want to go back to the servants' hall, she knew they would all be revelling in the scandal. She wanted to be on hand in case Cora needed her. Her mistress had moved out of sight now. Bertha moved along the wall and found a niche where there had once been a statue now covered by a velvet drape. She slipped behind the curtain, pleased that she had found a spot where she could observe her mistress without being overlooked herself.

A couple stood in front of her, Bertha could not see their faces but she recognised the Duke's back.

'. . . Such an intimate pose, what a pleasant change from the grand manner. I suppose that was your idea, Duke – you wanted a boudoir portrait of your new wife.' The woman's voice was probing.

'You make it sound as if I had a whole cupboard of wives stashed away in the west wing.' The Duke's voice was doggedly light.

'And how did you find Mr Louvain to deal with? You hear such stories. But I suppose if you had any doubts you would not have allowed the Duchess to sit for him.'

Bertha stood very still waiting for his reply

'Like most artists he seems more interested in money than anything else.'

Bertha heard the woman laugh. The Duke was hiding his feelings about the portrait in public at least but she doubted whether he had relinquished his anger. Jim had told her that when the Duke was furious he liked to tear a sheet of paper into as many pieces as he could. It was hard to shave his master in the morning, he had told her, because the Duke's jaw muscles were so tight from grinding his teeth all night. No, Bertha did not think that her mistress's husband was a forgiving man.

And then she heard his voice again.

'You did this.' This time his voice was low and private.

'All I did was open the door. She chose to walk through.' A different woman's voice, almost whispering, one Bertha knew but could not place.

'But why?'

'You know why.' There was a silence. Bertha wanted to look through the curtains but she knew that if the Duke was looking that way, he would see her at once.

She heard a sigh and the sound of rustling silk.

'I . . . can't . . . bear . . . this.' The Duke spoke as if the words were being carved out of him.

'There is no choice.' The woman's voice was flat.

Bertha could hear murmuring but was unable to make out the words. And then the music started again and she could hear nothing. After a minute she dared to look through the curtain, but the Duke and his companion were gone.

Cora's head was aching now from the strain of smiling as if she had not a care in the world. She had faced down all the curious stares with her sparkling American smile. She found that brightness acted like an acid on the web of evasion and unspoken thoughts that characterised so much English conversation. If she stood there smiling and looking people in the eye, they were forced to meet her gaze. She began to feel better. Mrs Wyndham had been right, she could set the tone.

She could see Ivo talking to the Prime Minister. She would join him. Ivo was being unreasonable; Louvain was right, she had nothing to hide.

As she walked across the room, she heard Odo's high-pitched voice shrieking, 'A picture of abandonment, my dear, you should have seen his face.' She tried to pass by without noticing, but Odo had seen her and was elaborating. 'So naive, but then I suppose we must make allowances for Americans.'

Cora moved on, her eyes on Ivo, trying not to be distracted. There was nothing she could do about Odo.

At last she reached her husband. He was talking to Lord Rosebery and a younger man she recognised from the party at Conyers, the Prince's equerry, Colonel Ferrers.

Cora put her hand on Ivo's arm. She saw with dismay the expression on his face as he turned to her.

'Cora, may I present the Prime Minister? Rosebery, my wife.' They shook hands.

'And Colonel Ferrers I believe you already know.'

The equerry made her a little bow.

The Prime Minister spoke. 'I was just telling the Duke how delighted I am that he has agreed to accompany Prince Eddy. We need more peers with your husband's sense of public duty.'

Cora smiled blankly. She had no idea what he was talking about but clearly she could not admit that. She glanced at Ivo but could only see his profile.

'It is quite true, Lord Rosebery, Ivo has a strong sense of what is right in his position. But surely he is not alone in that?'

'I wish your husband's selflessness was more common, Duchess. Public service should be the companion of privilege, but so often these days it is not.' The Prime Minister's tone was sombre. He did not, Cora thought, look like a man who enjoyed his role in life. Ivo had told her that the only thing he really liked talking about was his horses.

'I have heard so much about your stable, Lord Rosebery. Have you ever been to America? My father won the triple crown over there last year with his horse Adelaide.'

Ivo broke in. 'I think perhaps the Prime Minister may be too busy to follow foreign horseflesh, Cora.'

But Rosebery was smiling. 'Oh no, Wareham, I am never too busy for racing. Too busy for parliament perhaps but never for horses. Tell me about your father's stable, Duchess. Are the blood lines Arabian?'

Cora began an intricate conversation about the breeding of thoroughbreds which involved a good deal of listening on her part. But at the edge of her vision she could see Ivo fidgeting. Finally Rosebery released her and turned to her husband.

'I must say, Wareham, now that I have met your charming Duchess, I appreciate your sense of duty all the more.' Rosebery smiled at Cora, who managed to smile back.

The crowd was at last beginning to thin out. At midnight two footmen had brought out flowered baskets full of party favours, gold cigarette cases with the Maltravers crest engraved on the front for the men, and mother-of-pearl opera glasses for the women, with the crest in gold filigree on each barrel. This had immediately shifted the party's centre of gravity – like iron filings unable to resist a magnetic field, the guests had clustered around the source of the attraction. Some people, of course, had muttered that this munificence was a vulgar American practice but the baskets had emptied nonetheless. Cora was relieved that she had insisted on importing this Newport custom even though Ivo had laughed when she suggested it; the glittering trinkets had distracted her guests from the affair of the portrait. She was hoarse now from saying goodbye. 'Oh, I am so glad you came – no, thank *you* for coming – I just wanted everyone to have something to remember my first party.' She guessed that the Beauchamps had spread the news of her pregnancy, as many of the women had urged her to get some rest as they pressed her hand in saying goodbye.

Duchess Fanny had been crisp. 'You must go to Lulworth, Cora, at once. You are lucky that everyone is leaving town so the talk will blow over very quickly. You can't afford to have a reputation, at least not until after your son is born.'

'But I have done nothing to deserve one!' Cora was indignant.

The Duchess smiled from a great height. 'Most people who have reputations don't deserve them. I, on the other hand, don't have the reputation I deserve. Just follow my advice, Cora, and there will be no lasting damage. And don't look so martyred, my dear. It's not me who minds these things but my son. He has always worried about the way things look.'

Cora retreated. 'Oh dear, I can see some kind of problem over there with the favours. I had better go and intervene. Goodnight, Duchess.'

'Remember my advice, Cora.'

At last everyone had gone and Cora was able to go to her room. She had not seen Ivo for the last hour, but she was too weary to look for him. So many things had happened that night that she simply could not fit them all in her thoughts. She dragged herself up the stairs to her bedroom. Ivo was not there. She sent Bertha away – she didn't want her presence to annoy Ivo even more. As she started to undress she felt a fluttering in her stomach as if there was a butterfly trapped in her belly. She put her hand there, but she could feel nothing through the layers of petticoats. Impatiently she tugged at her skirts, pulling at the ties which fastened them, but Bertha's knots would not be undone. In a frenzy she found some nail scissors and began to cut at her bonds. By twisting and wriggling she even managed to cut the laces of her corset. At last everything was off. It was still there, that strange light feeling deep inside her. She lay down on her bed and looked up at the ceiling. She put her hands on her stomach just above her groin and waited. Would the flicker come again? Suddenly nothing else, not the picture, not Ivo, mattered. She lay there watching the glow from the dying fire until miraculously she felt it again. She had not quite believed in the baby until now, the soreness in her breasts and the fatigue had simply been unwelcome. But this, this quickening was something else – new life, new hope. This was the bond between her and Ivo. Surely he would be kinder to her now that the line was assured.

The door opened.

'Ivo?'

Ivo said nothing.

Cora tried to stay bright. 'Oh Ivo, the most amazing thing. I felt the baby move, such a queer feeling like a fish darting about. It's doing it now. Put your hand here, perhaps you can feel it too.'

But her husband did not move towards her. He stood in the half-open doorway, his face silhouetted against the light from the corridor.

'Cora, Lord Rosebery has asked me to accompany Prince Eddy on his Indian tour. The Queen and the Prince of Wales are anxious that he takes some part in public life, but Prince Eddy is not, in Rosebery's view, "capable". There have been incidents that . . . He wants me to make sure that the Prince does not cause the government any embarrassment. It is a position of trust and I have agreed to go. I think that after tonight's debacle, it is the best thing.' He paused and rubbed the bridge of his nose with his hand. 'I must go to Lulworth first thing tomorrow to make arrangements with Father Oliver and then straight to Southampton. I suggest that you go to Lulworth as soon you can. I would feel happier if you were there. I am sure that Sybil or Mrs Wyndham would come with you, if you feel you need the company. As you have your own resources, I have not made any financial arrangements for you, but all the wages and estate upkeep will be taken care of.'

Cora sat up and turned on the light, her sleepiness forgotten.

'You're going to India? Now? I don't understand.' She looked up at him. He was still standing in the doorway, his dark face set.

'Really?' He looked at her intently, as if searching for something in her face. 'You sit in secret for a man like Louvain and you don't understand? You may not mind being talked about, Cora, but I do. I don't want people looking at me and wondering about my wife.' His face softened a little. 'I have done my best to contain the scandal by pretending, although it pained me, to like the picture. I don't know if anyone believed me but at least they won't have the satisfaction of knowing that we have quarrelled. By the time I return, it will be forgotten.'

Cora walked towards him and took his hands. He did not resist, but simply let her hold them, inert and unfeeling.

She began to plead, 'I didn't know about Louvain's "reputation". I met him at the Beauchamps, after all. Charlotte almost insisted that I should sit for him. Don't be like this, Ivo, please.' Ivo remained motionless. Cora put her hand to her throat and whispered, 'Look at these pearls you gave me – don't you remember that afternoon?'

'Of course I remember. I thought then that we had a chance of happiness.' His voice was full of sadness.

'But we do.' She put his hand on her stomach.

'Cora, please,' but he did not take his hand away. She put her other hand to his cheek.

He moved away from her and she thought she had lost him, but then with a jerky movement he put his arms round her and held her to him. They stood in silence for a long moment.

Finally she summoned the courage to speak. She could feel his heart beating. 'Do you really have to go?'

'Yes.'

'Because of me?'

'Because of many things. I have agreed to go now.'

'And when are you coming back?'

'In the spring.'

'Before . . . ?'

'Yes, before.' Ivo pulled away from her.

'And are you still angry?'

He looked at her, his face dark. 'I don't know any more what I feel. Sometimes I feel nothing at all.' He turned his face away.

'But I need you to stay. I can't manage all this,' she gestured at her stomach, at the room, at this strange English world that surrounded her.

Ivo's face flickered with amusement. 'Oh, I think you under-estimate yourself, Cora,' and then he kissed her on the cheek and closed the door behind him.

She sat after he left her for a long time, feeling the touch of his lips on her cheek; and then just as she thought she would never move again, she felt the slow beating of the life in her womb and she lay down, cradling her belly with her hands, and within seconds she was asleep.

Part Three

The English married ladies . . . are the brightest and most venomous politicians in English society.

Titled Americans, 1890

CHAPTER 21

At Sea

*B*ERTHA FELT A TRICKLE OF SWEAT RUN FROM her neck down her back. It had been unseasonably warm for April all week, and the maid wished she had worn something lighter. There was no shade here on the beach apart from her parasol but that could not shelter her from the glare from the sea. She hoped that Cora would get out soon. Bertha did not want her complexion to be darkened by the sun. It was tiring squinting into the glare, following the dark head bobbing through the waves. It was pointless really, her vigil: if her mistress were to get into difficulties, what could she do? Bertha had never learnt to swim. Keeping a watch on Cora was her way of expressing her disapproval. A woman in her ninth month had no business to be swimming in the icy sea. It was undignified, not to mention dangerous, but Cora had ignored all her sighs and tuttings.

Bertha wished that Mrs Cash was here already. The Cashes were due any day now; Mrs Cash had seen no reason to cut short the New York season to be with Cora while she was cooped up at Lulworth, but she had no intention of missing the birth of her grandson, the future Duke (Mrs Cash had not even entertained the possibility that the child might be a girl). But Bertha thought that Mrs Cash should have been here months before. Miss Cora needed some of her own folks at this time. They had been at Lulworth for five months now, time enough to feel homesick. Miss Cora would never admit it but Bertha had seen the piles of letters to the States which went into the wooden post box in the shape of a castle that stood in the great hall. Every day at eleven, two and five, the butler opened the box with a special brass key and gave the letters to the postman. Some days Bertha would see letters to America leaving by every post. There was also the daily letter to India. Occasionally Bertha would send one of her own, but she had told Jim not to reply – a letter from India would cause too much talk in the servants' hall. She knew that every letter was thoroughly scrutinised by the butler and Mrs Softley and she was pretty sure that a letter addressed to her from India would be steamed open before she received it. One of the parlour-maids had been dismissed after Christmas because she had received a love letter from a groom at Sutton Veney. Strictly speaking, it was for the Duchess to dismiss the maid, but Mrs Softley had not found it necessary to consult the mistress. Bertha was not sure now that even the Duchess would be able to protect her if her relationship with Jim was discovered.

Bertha wondered whether her mistress realised how little control she had over the household at Lulworth, how the servants that treated her with such deference in public laughed at her in the servants' hall. Miss Cora had not taken command of Lulworth in the way that Mrs Cash had run Sans Souci. Miss Cora had been full of schemes for 'improving' the house: some things like the bathrooms had been achieved, but her attempts to change the way the house was run – she had been astonished to discover that there was one man who was employed simply to wind all the clocks in the house – had mostly come to nothing. She gave orders but could not enforce them. One of her first orders had been to remove the photographs of the Double Duchess, usually in the company of the Prince of Wales, that were in every guest bedroom. Last time Bertha had looked, the photographs were still there, the silver frames gleaming from constant polishing. Miss Cora had not yet noticed; Bertha wondered what she might do when she did. Probably nothing, Cora's spirit seemed to be waning as the baby grew bigger and there was still no sign of the Duke's return. He should have been back in early February but he had written at the beginning of the month to say that he would be delayed. Bertha had seen her mistress's face crumple after reading that letter and impulsively she had taken her hand. She could see that Cora needed someone to hold on to. These months of seclusion and waiting had made Bertha acutely aware of her mistress's isolation. A few nights ago Cora had asked her to sleep in her bed. She said that it was in case the baby came but Bertha knew that her mistress just wanted a body beside her. Sometimes she felt the same way herself. When she had heard Cora calling Ivo's name in her sleep, Bertha had found herself, rather to her surprise, feeling sorry for her.

Since they had come to Lulworth, Cora had seen almost no one. Father Oliver had been there for a month working on the History. Mrs Wyndham had come to stay for a week, as had Sybil Lytchett, but otherwise Cora had been alone at Lulworth, in as much as you could ever be alone in a house with eighty-one servants. Bertha had been surprised that there had not been more callers from the neighbourhood but when she remarked on this to Mrs Softley, the housekeeper had been astonished at her ignorance. 'No one is going to be calling on the Duchess when she is expecting, not when the Duke's away. It wouldn't be right.' So Cora ate alone most nights, her diamonds sparkling unseen as she picked her way through the six courses that constituted a 'light dinner'.

The sea was much colder than the warm weather would suggest but Cora hardly noticed, she was lit from within by an internal furnace. Her daily swim was the only time she felt relieved of her burden. To float on her back weightless and cool was all she craved. She found the walk down to the beach harder with each passing day but it was worth it to take off all her clothes and step inch by inch into the water, shivering with pleasure and pain as it lapped her ankles, then her calves, her thighs until it reached her swollen belly. When the water was shoulder height she would take a deep breath and plunge her head underwater, blowing out so that a stream of bubbles pierced the surface of the water. Then she would float on her back, kicking her legs sporadically and watching the odd fugitive cloud as it floated over the cove. Sometimes she would turn on her front and on a clear day she would look at the small brown fish that darted beneath the seaweed. She noticed that when she swam, the creature inside her would stop kicking. It was the only time that she could be sure that it would be quiet. Now as she swam across the cove she could imagine that she was the girl she had been two summers before in Newport; although there she had been weighed down with an elaborate bathing costume whereas here she was naked. She had tried swimming with a costume here, but the combination of her pregnant belly and the sodden serge skirts of her bathing dress made her wish that she could swim unencumbered. She had confided this desire to Sybil Lytchett, who had been visiting. Sybil had laughed and said, 'But Cora, nothing could be easier. Tell the servants that the swimming cove is out of bounds and you can swim in what-ever you want!' Cora had found it awkward to explain to Bugler that she wanted to be private during her daily swim, she had felt as if she was asking permission instead of giving orders. But in the event, the butler had been quite accommodating and had taken to running up a red flag on the flagpole when Cora set off to the cove, which told everyone on the estate that the beach was out of bounds.

So far, this rule had been observed absolutely; no one from the house would go near the beach while the red flag was flying, but this morning as she surfaced from one of her seal-like plunges underwater, Cora saw a figure coming down the path to the beach. Her poor eyesight meant that she could not see the figure clearly, but from the black and white of his clothes it could only be Bugler. He stood at the edge of the beach hovering, to step on to the beach would be heresy, but whatever it was must have been urgent for the man to have come this far. In compromise he called to Bertha to come over to him. Cora, treading water just out of her depth so that the water concealed everything except her head, watched as the maid picked her way gingerly across the shingle. The butler bent down to speak to her and Cora saw the maid start and then run back down the beach, waving and shouting. The butler retreated up the hill. Cora could not make out what Bertha was saying but she understood that she wanted her to get out. She swam slowly to the shore and started to pick her way across the sharp stones, feeling the wind dry the salt on her skin. She reached gratefully for the linen sheet that Bertha held out to her.

'What's happened, Bertha? Is it Ivo?'

'No, Miss Cora, it is the Double Duchess. She is arriving by the morning train.' Bertha's voice was neutral. She knew that her news would not be welcome.

Cora gasped. 'But I haven't invited her! She can't just arrive like this, without notice. Does she think that she is still mistress of Lulworth?' Bertha said nothing, but held out Cora's wrapper. Cora struggled to get it on over her damp skin.

'I haven't seen her since Ivo went to India and now she is here. She knows he's on his way back, of course.' Bertha knelt down and helped Cora into her slippers. Cora leant on her as they walked slowly back across the shingle beach. Duchess Fanny had written to her several times since she had been at Lulworth, letters full of detail about her visits to Sandringham and Chatsworth and plenty of exhortations to Cora to take care of her unborn child. Cora had long ago stopped reading the letters with attention: she really had no desire to know how many birds the Prince of Wales had bagged or that the Duchess of Rutland, whom she had never met, had quite lost her figure. She had been unpleasantly surprised by how well informed Duchess Fanny was about her life at Lulworth; her last letter had been a lecture on the follies of swimming in her condition. The letter had been so irritating that she had thrown it into the fire. But the arrival of the Duchess in person was far worse. Cora knew that the Duchess had enjoyed the debacle over the Louvain portrait, and she suspected from what Mrs Wyndham and Sybil had hinted that the Duchess lost no opportunity to mock her American daugher-in-law.

At the top of the cliff was the little donkey cart that Cora used to get around the estate now that she could no longer ride or even walk very far in comfort. Cora picked up the reins and gave them an irritable shake as they headed back to the house. She shook her head impatiently as Bertha tried to spread her wet hair out to dry.

'Oh, leave it alone, Bertha.'

'But Miss Cora, supposing the Duchess has already arrived?' Bertha sounded worried.

'Well, what if she has? This is my house now. If I choose to go about with wet hair, it is really none of her concern.' But as they approached the house and Cora saw the carriage already drawn up outside the house, she tried to shape her damp locks into a more seemly braid. She thought for a moment of going into the house through the servants' wing and avoiding the Double Duchess until she had had a chance to change, but she could not face the idea of walking past the servants, who would know, of course, exactly why she was coming in the back way.

As she hesitated at the door, she heard the Duchess's voice already taking possession.

'The Stuart room, I think, Bugler. The Prince was always very happy there, despite its Jacobite associations. So strange to be here and not to sleep in my bedroom.' There was a trace of huskiness in the Duchess's voice and Cora imagined Bugler's sympathetic bow. But the Duchess recovered herself and said, 'Sybil can have her usual room.'

Cora's spirits lifted at the mention of Sybil, and she made herself walk into the room. Duchess Fanny was sitting in one of the carved chairs by the fireplace, flanked by Bugler and her step-daughter. She did not get up when she saw Cora but simply beck-oned to her with one long white hand. Cora could see the flash of diamonds as her mother-in-law tilted her wrist.

'Cora, my dear girl.' Duchess Fanny's voice trailed away in reproach. 'When Bugler told me you had gone swimming I was simply amazed. Surely you must understand the risks to someone in your condition. Didn't you get my letter?' As she waved her hands the diamonds flashed again.

Cora felt the baby turn and kick her under the ribs. She gave a little gasp of discomfort, but the prod dissipated the irritation the Duchess had provoked. She nodded to the Duchess and smiled at Sybil.

'Welcome to Lulworth. I apologise for not being here to meet you but then I had no idea you were coming today.' She said this as affably as she could. 'You must excuse me while I change. Bugler will look after you, of course.' She looked over at the butler who, she noticed, did not look at all surprised by the arrival of the Double Duchess.

She turned towards the staircase and started the heavy climb to her room. That was why she swam, to remember what it was to feel light again. She heard a step behind her and felt Sybil's hand at her elbow.

'Let me help you, Cora.'

As they got to the landing, Sybil burst out, 'I am so sorry. I thought you knew we were coming. Mama said she had written to you.'

Cora remembered the letter she had thrown on the fire.

'Don't worry, Sybil, I am always glad to see *you*. How is Reggie?'

Sybil blushed, her skin clashing with her red-gold hair. 'I think he was about to make an offer but then Mama insisted that we come down here.' She realised what she had said and reddened even more. 'I wanted to see you, of course, but I had arranged to go riding in the park with Reggie tomorrow.'

Cora began to feel better. She felt sorry for Sybil, of course, but she was happy to be reminded that as a married woman she was no longer subject to the whims of mothers. She suspected that Duchess Fanny knew all about Sybil's hopes and was determined to thwart them. Reggie Greatorex was a perfectly suitable husband for Sybil but the Double Duchess did not want to lose her companion, particularly one whose youthful charms did nothing to eclipse her own. If Sybil had looked like Charlotte Beauchamp, the Duchess would have married her off without a moment's hesitation, but gawky Sybil was a foil, not a rival.

She smiled. 'Well, perhaps we can prevail on Reggie to come and ride with you here. When Ivo comes back.' Cora paused. 'It can't be long now. His last letter was from Port Said.' She put her hand on her belly and sighed. 'He really should be here. Still, I am delighted you have come, Sybil, even if the circumstances are not ideal. Do you know how long the Duchess intends to stay? It's not a question I can very well ask.'

Sybil looked surprised. 'Well, I think she wants to be here for the . . .' She trailed off and colour mottled her cheeks. Sybil could not bring herself to say the word birth.

Cora looked at her in dismay. 'She plans to stay here until the baby comes? But what on earth for? Is it some kind of custom that she should be present? Another Maltravers tradition that I don't know about?' Cora's voice came out high and strained, she could feel tears gathering behind her eyelids.

Sybil shook her head miserably, 'I don't think it's a tradition, I think it's just what Mama thought was right. She said she wanted to be sure that everything was done properly.'

Cora tipped her head back to hold back the tears. She did not want to cry in front of Sybil. But she felt as if she had been invaded. She had spent the last few months trying to feel at home at Lulworth and now the precarious balance she had achieved was about to be upset. She had spent so much time in these last lonely months imagining the reunion with Ivo. There had been nights when she had cried because she could not quite remember his face. She did not know exactly who Ivo would be when he came home, but she was certain that he would not welcome the presence of his mother.

'Cora, don't you think there should be somebody here? It's not right that you should be on your own at this time.' Sybil put her hand timidly on Cora's arm. 'I know Mama can be overbearing but she is at least experienced.'

Cora forced herself to smile. 'Indeed she is! But I shan't be on my own. My parents will be here next week and I expect Ivo any day now. Your stepmother would have known this if she had asked me.' She put her hand on Sybil's. 'You always call her Mama even though she is only your stepmother. Don't you mind?'

Sybil looked confused by the change of subject. 'She asked me to when she married Father, and actually, Cora, I don't mind. My mother died when I was little. I can hardly remember her now. You can't imagine what it's like to grow up in a family of men, with no one there to tell you what to wear or how to behave. I remember once coming down to tea when Father had guests, wearing a red dress of my mother's. I thought it looked lovely but I knew the moment I walked into the room that it was all wrong. All the women in the room were trying not to laugh. It was Mama – well, she wasn't Mama then, but still Duchess of Wareham – who took me aside and told me that the dress was too grown-up for me, and she actually spoke to Father and told him that I needed some "suitable" clothes. Father didn't see the point of spending money on things that couldn't be ridden or shot, but he couldn't refuse when Mama asked him.'

Cora's surprise must have shown on her face, because Sybil said, 'I know you think she's interfering, Cora, but that's because you have a mother already. You don't need guidance.'

Cora was about to say that she didn't think that Sybil really needed the kind of guidance that stopped her from marrying the man she had set her heart on, but then she thought better of it. She did, indeed, have a mother and while she found little to rejoice about in that relation, when she looked at Sybil with her rounded back and awkward stride, it occurred to her that perhaps her mother had been useful after all.

Feeling sorry for Sybil cheered Cora up and she said briskly, 'Well, I must get changed if I am to have any chance of sitting down to lunch with you all. Not to be late for meals was something my mother did teach me.' She gestured towards her dressing room. 'And afterwards, Sybil, we must see what is in there that will do for you. It will be a season out of date, of course, but I dare say nobody in London will notice.' She smiled at Sybil.

'Reggie certainly won't,' she said.

As there were only ladies present, Cora asked for lunch to be served in the long gallery to take advantage of the afternoon sunshine. She had the satisfaction of seeing her mother-in-law give a theatrical gasp of surprise as she walked in.

'How charming this is! I never thought to eat in here. But for a cold lunch, what could be nicer.' Duchess Fanny swept down the gallery and waited for the footman to pull out her chair. 'Of course, I would have hesitated before giving the servants any extra trouble. Poor Wareham used to say that I was much too soft-hearted to run a house like Lulworth. But I believe that a sympathetic mistress is always rewarded with loyalty.' Cora watched as Duchess Fanny lifted her heavy blue eyes to look at Bugler who was handing round the crayfish soufflé. Bugler did not actually reply but the reverential tilt of his body as he leant in towards the Duchess with the soufflé was assent enough.

Cora ignored this taunt, looking up instead at the vaulted stone roof. Every time she sat in this room she was reminded that everything around her was older than anything in her native country. Whatever was said and done in here would fade away but the room itself would endure.

The soothing nature of this thought was dispelled when she heard Duchess Fanny say, 'But you have changed things around in here, Cora. I remember my wedding bouquet always used to stand here,' she gestured, 'next to the fireplace. I had it cast in wax after I married Wareham. Such a lovely memento. I remember feeling sad about leaving it here but then it would hardly have done to take it to Conyers.' She looked at Sybil. 'You know I would never do anything that would upset your dear father. But Cora, I hope my bouquet is safe and sound?' She raised an eyebrow at her daughter-in-law.

Before Cora could reply, Bugler coughed softly and said, 'I think Your Grace will find that the bouquet is at the other end of the gallery. It was moved at the request of Her Grace.' His tone made it quite clear which Duchess could better lay claim to the title. Cora did not notice the implied insult at first, she was just relieved that the wretched object had not been removed to the attics as she had asked a month ago. How was she to know that it was a wedding bouquet? Then it struck her that the wax bouquet was still in the gallery because her orders had been ignored. She might be the Duchess of Wareham now, but it was clear that, unlike her predecessor, she did not command the loyalty of her servants.

Duchess Fanny smiled serenely. 'It is sentimental of me, I know, but as one gets older, these things become so precious.' She gave a charming sigh and raised a glittering hand to dab her eyes with a tiny handkerchief. There were perhaps not quite enough tears to warrant this gesture.

'But enough of my nonsense.' Duchess Fanny tilted her chin bravely at Cora. 'Tell me, my dear, when does Wilson expect your confinement?'

'But I am not using Wilson. Sir Julius Sercombe will be attending. He thinks it will be another two weeks.' Cora laid a hand across her belly.

Duchess Fanny's wistfulness evaporated. 'Julius Sercombe! But he's in Harley Street. Surely you don't intend to travel to London?'

Cora shook her head, 'Oh no. As I have been told often enough that the Maltravers heirs are born at Lulworth, Sir Julius has kindly agreed to come here. I expect him at the end of next week.' Cora took a mouthful of the soufflé, she felt ravenous.

'Sir Julius is prepared to leave his practice and all his London engagements to await your confinement? How . . . accommodating of him. But if you had asked me I would have told you to use Wilson. He is an excellent doctor and has looked after the Maltravers for years. Why, he was there when Ivo came into the world.' The Duchess's hand began to reach for the handkerchief.

Cora smiled. 'Dr Wilson is most amiable but as this is my first child I wanted to be sure that I had the best and Sir Julius delivers all the royal babies, you know. He was reluctant to leave London to begin with, but he was so pleased with the Maltravers Wing for his new hospital that he changed his mind.' She gestured to

Bugler to bring her a second helping of the soufflé, it really was quite delicious.

'The Maltravers Wing! How magnificent that sounds,' said Sybil who had been following the conversation warily.

'Indeed,' said Duchess Fanny, widening her eyes. 'What kind of hospital is it, dear?'

'For women and children, in Whitechapel. Sir Julius believes that there is a great deal to be done in that part of London. There are women there who are forced to wrap their newborn babies in flour sacks because they have no money for baby clothes. When he told me of his plans and the difficulties he was having raising the money, I was determined to help him.'

A footman passed round the table, taking away the empty plates. When he had finished, Duchess Fanny asked, 'And tell me, Cora, whose idea was it to call it the Maltravers Wing? Yours or Ivo's?'

Cora was shifting in her chair, trying to relieve the pressure on her diaphragm from her belly, so she did not see the alert expression on her mother-in-law's face, or the blush that was beginning to threaten Sybil's freckles.

'Actually, it was my mother's idea. She and Father made the endowment as all my money here is tied up in the estate, and I wanted to do something more substantial than my allowance permitted.' Cora sat up straight, having at last shifted the pressure from her chest. She saw that Duchess Fanny was smiling at her a little too warmly.

'Well, I think it might be wise to let Ivo know before you commit to a name,' said the Double Duchess. 'Donate to good causes by all means, but I think there is something rather ... unnecessary about putting your name on things.'

Cora took a sip of water and struggled to swallow. She realised, to her horror, that Ivo might react to this use of the Maltravers name as the Duchess had done. He might have another attack of the 'scruples' that made him so peculiar about the Rubens. At last the water slipped past the lump in her throat. But she would not give her mother-in-law the satisfaction of knowing this. She took a deep breath.

'At home there are three hospitals, a college and a library named after my family. My father often says that anyone can acquire wealth, the real art is giving it away.' Cora took a generous helping of the sole veronique. The food seemed especially appetising today; clearly the Double Duchess's arrival was having its effect in the kitchen.

'Your father is such a charming man.' Duchess Fanny's emphasis on the word 'father' implied that such charm did not extend to his wife or daughter. 'But we do things rather differently here. I suppose you are familiar with the phrase, "charity begins at home". Of course, hospitals and libraries are fine things, but I always think it is the simple personal touch that makes such a difference to people's lives.'

The Duchess turned to Sybil for support but her stepdaughter was staring intently at the plate in front of her, cutting her food into smaller and smaller pieces, desperate not to be involved in the duel in front of her. With a little shake of her head, the Duchess continued, 'Why, only last week I spent the afternoon reading to old Mrs Patchett, one of the Conyers pensioners, who is blind. She always says that when I read to her it brings the words to life and she can see all the characters. It's really quite embarrassing how grateful she is, but I feel it is the least I can do – I only wish it were possible for me to visit her more often. Bricks and mortar have their own value, of course, but nothing can take the place of simple human contact, of personal kindness given and bestowed.' Duchess Fanny leant back in her chair, quite pink with the memory of her own benevolence.

Cora put down her fork with a clatter; the other woman's self-satisfaction was intolerable to her, she would not be lectured by this univited guest, family or not.

'Well, that explains why there is no school in the village and why the Maltravers almshouses are permanently damp. As soon as Ivo returns, I intend to set up a proper schoolhouse and to make the almshouses habitable. I think that would be a true kindness to the villagers of Lulworth.' She took a bite of the boneless quail stuffed with sausage meat and noticed that the Duchess had left hers untouched. Sybil was doing her best to look fully absorbed in the process of eating.

Duchess Fanny sighed in mock defeat. 'You Americans are always so practical – no room in your brave new world for our faded notions of honour and duty.' She half closed her eyes as if focusing on a target and sat up a little straighter, readying herself to deliver the *coup de grâce*. 'And when is Ivo coming back, dear? I rather thought he might be here already.'

Cora looked up, surprised by the certainty in her mother-in-law's tone. 'His last letter was from Port Said. So I expect him next week.'

The Double Duchess's mouth curved triumphantly. 'But dear Cora, Ivo is already back in England. I saw the Prince of Wales last night and he said that Prince Eddy and the whole party had docked yesterday at Southampton.'

Cora put down the fork that was halfway to her mouth and forced herself to smile. She would not give her mother-in-law the satisfaction of seeing her consternation.

'Oh, that is wonderful news. I expect he is on his way here now. He must have been hoping to surprise me.' She looked at Sybil, wondering why she, at least, had not told her that Ivo was back, but Sybil was looking at her stepmother in astonishment. The Double Duchess had clearly been hoarding this information.

The Double Duchess put her hand to her mouth in a pantomime of apology. 'Oh no, how thoughtless of me! I will have spoilt his scheme. But after all, in your condition, perhaps that is not such a bad thing. How unfortunate if anything were to happen before the arrival of Sir Julius.' Her voice was sympathetic, but Cora could see the glint of malice in her eyes. She had to get away, so taking a deep breath, she said as calmly as she could, 'I am sorry but I must ask you to excuse me. I am tired and if Ivo is to arrive at any moment I would like to rest now. Perhaps, Duchess, you would be kind enough to tell Bugler that the Duke is to be expected. I am sure all the servants will want to be there to greet him.' She stood up painfully, her body heavy with the shock. She bit her lip, desperate to stop the tears that were threatening to overwhelm her. Ivo was back, this was the moment she had been waiting for all these months, but now it had all been spoilt. She stumbled away down the gallery, the Duchess's voice in her ears.

'Oh, I am sure Bugler knows already. It's uncanny how servants always sense these things.' Duchess Fanny looked up, with a complicit smile, at the footman who was serving the crème brulée. The footman's face did not flicker but his hand shook slightly as the Duchess struck the caramel with a swift sharp blow, plunging the spoon into the yielding custard beneath.

CHAPTER 22

The Homecoming

TOM, THE TELEGRAPH BOY, WONDERED WHAT would happen if he removed his cap. It was expressly forbidden under post office rules but it was a warm day and there was no one to see him here in the Lulworth woods. On the other hand, if Mr Veale was to hear that he had been improperly dressed, he would be sent back to his mother in Langton Maltravers. Mr Veale had fined Tom sixpence the week before for allowing the silver buttons on his tunic to become tarnished; another boy had been dismissed for delivering a telegram with his stiff collar unfastened. Tom decided that the immediate relief of removing his cap, which was too small and rubbed painfully against his temples, was not worth the risk of being discovered. Mr Veale had a way of knowing when rules had been broken. He was fond of saying that he could 'smell an infringement'. Tom had not been clear what an infringement was, until the incident with the buttons, and even now he wondered how they could be smelt. All five remaining telegraph boys reeked of the same things: inky serge, sweat and the bicarbonate of soda they used to shine their buttons. In winter they smelt a bit less and in summer a bit more.

It was three miles from the post office in Lulworth to the house.

Mr Veale always sent Tom because he could walk the fastest. Twenty-one minutes on the way there and seventeen on the return journey, which was downhill. Mr Veale had told him to do it today in twenty minutes because the telegram was from the Duke. Tom was doing his best, bowling along at a loping pace midway between a walk and a run. He had set off at nine exactly and although he did not carry a pocket watch, he knew that he was making good time because he had heard the single chime from the Lulworth church bell which marked the quarter hour. He was at the part of the drive that curved behind a clump of beech trees before emerging into the open and revealing the house itself. There was no longer any question of removing his cap, Tom knew that he could be seen from any one of the glittering windows ahead of him. He loosened the strap under his chin a notch so that there would not be a red welt there, and thought of the glass of lemonade he would be given in the cool kitchen, as he pressed on towards the house.

Bertha spotted him from the window of Miss Cora's room. Her mistress was still in bed, not sleeping but staring up at the canopy as if it was a map. Bertha was unnerved by this, as she was by Cora's silence. She had heard the rumours last night at supper about the Duke's return. Mr Bugler thought he would be home today and had all the footmen put on their dress livery. Bertha herself had put on her best cream silk tussore blouse. It had been Miss Cora's, of course, but she had never worn it. As a rule Bertha avoided light colours because they made her appear darker but after an English winter her skin needed the glow of the pearly silk. She had laid out the pale green tea gown with the swans-down trim for her mistress, which to her mind was the most becoming of Miss Cora's current ensembles. But Cora had refused to entertain the notion of getting dressed, shaking her head when Bertha tried to coax her out of bed. She had even refused Bertha's attempts to do her hair, which lay in limp hanks on her pillow. Bertha was used to her mistress's moods but she had never known them to interfere with dressing her hair before. Miss Cora could be tiresome but she didn't give up on things. Bertha didn't understand why her mistress was moping like this. All she had been doing for the last five months was wait for the Duke to come home, and now he was most likely on his way she was lying there like a corpse.

She turned from the window. 'I can see the telegraph boy, Miss Cora.'

There was no reply.

'I expect it'll be from the Duke. Maybe he is coming on the afternoon train.'

The silence continued. Bertha watched as the telegraph boy started to climb the steps up to the house.

'I reckon Mr Bugler will be bringing the telegram up here in a minute, Miss Cora. Maybe you want to get ready?'

Cora's eyes did not flicker from her scrutiny of the canopy.

Bertha began to feel irritated. If Cora couldn't see the truth of things, she would have to tell her. There were times of late when she felt more like Cora's mother than her maid. She began to speak briskly.

'If I was coming home after five months in India, I would like to see my wife dressed up and looking pleased to see me, not lying in her bed staring at the ceiling. Come on, Miss Cora, you don't want Mr Bugler to see you like this.'

Cora gave a sigh and rolled over on to her side before pushing herself upright. She rubbed her eyes with the heel of her hands.

'All right, all right, you can stop scolding me. You're right, of course, Bertha. Bugler will go straight to Duchess Fanny, and then she will come up here and start interfering. Lord knows I thought my mother was bad enough, but the Duchess really is the end.' She stretched out her hands and then let them drop in her lap. 'I just don't understand why Ivo didn't come straight home.'

Bertha had almost finished pinning Cora's hair in place when Bugler came in with the telegram on a silver salver. Cora opened it without haste and dropped the telegram on to the polished tray when she had finished.

'The Duke will be here for dinner tonight, Bugler. If you could let Cook know, I am sure she will want to prepare something special.'

Bugler bent his head in the shallowest possible bow. 'I believe the Duchess of Buckingham has already spoken to Mrs Whitchurch, Your Grace.'

Bertha was impressed by the way that Cora did not react to this. Instead, she smiled without showing her teeth, and said, 'Indeed! How thoughtful of her.' She put her hand to her hair and brought down one ringlet that she proceeded to curl round her fingers. Bugler hovered, clearly impatient to be gone but unable to move until he had been formally dismissed.

'Will that be all, Your Grace?'

'Yes, I think so, Bugler. No, actually, I do have one request.' She spoke to Bugler in the mirror. 'Duchess Fanny's bouquet, the one from her first wedding. I thought I had asked for it to be removed from the long gallery. Kindly see to it before the Duke arrives.'

Cora caught Bertha's eye in the mirror and tilted her chin. Bertha saw that her mistress's face had lost its sulky heaviness and that there were spots of colour in her cheeks. When she had finished pinning Cora's hair she stood back and said, 'You look quite fine today, Miss Cora.'

Cora looked back at Bertha. 'Do you really think so? I've changed so much though. When Ivo left, I was still in corsets. If he had been here, he would have had time to get used to me . . . swelling.' She put her hands over her stomach. 'When he is confronted with this, I'm afraid he will get quite a shock.' She picked up the black pearl necklace from its green velvet home and handed it to Bertha to fasten.

Bertha slid the gold hook through the eye and pushed it into the diamond clasp. She wondered if the Duke would indeed be taken aback by Cora's appearance. When he left she had been hardly showing; now her whole body had altered; as well as the round globe of her stomach, there were blue veins crossing her décolletage and her face was softer and rounder. Even Cora's voice had changed; as her pregnancy progressed, it had become deeper and huskier, she had quite lost her pert American twang. But at least, thought Bertha, she no longer looks so like the girl in the portrait which had been left leaning unwanted against the wall of the gallery at Bridgewater House. Bugler was fond of describing the picture as shocking, even though to Bertha's knowledge he had never actually seen it. She was the only servant at Lulworth who had set eyes upon the portrait, but when asked her opinion she had pretended ignorance. She knew that Bugler, for one, had not believed her, but she did not want to join them in condemning it. She understood that to do so was really a way of running down Cora herself; Bugler could not allow disrespectful talk of the

Duchess herself in the servants' hall, but the portrait was another matter. There had been times over the last few months when Bertha had wondered whether her decision to hold herself aloof from the gossip in the servants' hall had been the right one, but some loyalty to Cora and a feeling that no concession to her fellow servants would ever make her belong stopped her.

She caught Cora's eye in the mirror and said with more firmness than she felt, 'I think the Duke will be happy enough to see you carrying his child.'

Cora nodded her head. 'Perhaps. It is, after all, the thing only *I* can give him. An heir.'

The Duke's telegram had simply said, 'Arriving this evening. Wareham.' Even allowing for the essentially public nature of the communication which would be read by the postmasters in London and Lulworth, not to mention the telegraph boy, Cora felt the economy of those four words keenly. There was nothing for her there, no hint that he was looking forward to coming home, to seeing her again. Even his letters to her from India had been signed, 'Your affectionate husband, Wareham.' At the time she had found 'affectionate' less than adequate as a term of endearment, but now she would have welcomed anything more conciliatory than this stark statement of facts. She still could not believe that Ivo had been in the country for two whole days without letting her know.

She had been anticipating the moment of his return for so long, rehearsing the conversations she would have with him in her head, planning the food, the company, the flowers. She had ordered the head gardener, Mr Jackson, to force hundreds of jasmine plants so they would be ready for his arrival, as he had once told her that it was his favourite flower. She had been practising the Schubert duets they had played together so that she could play her part from memory. She had spent many hours with Father Oliver trying to piece together the complicated narrative of the Maltravers family so that she could refer casually to the Fourth Duke's stammer or the bloodlines of the Lulworth lurchers. She had done everything she could think of to be a convincing Duchess. An English Duchess, who knew the rules, who knew how to do more than spend money. But it had not occurred to her that Ivo might not be as eager to play his part in the reunion as she was. She had imagined him arriving post-haste from Southampton, salty and fervent. And yet here she was with the sort of telegram he might have sent to his butler. Surely she had done her penance for the portrait affair, sequestered here at Lulworth with nothing to do for months.

She decided that she would not go down to lunch. She had no desire for another skirmish with the Double Duchess. Perhaps she would send for Sybil and sort out some dresses for her.

There was a knock at the door and a footman brought in the second post of the day. There were two letters, one from London, the other from Paris. On one she recognised Mrs Wyndham's handwriting; the other hand also looked familiar but it took her a moment to remember where she had seen it before. Those backward-leaning strokes that betrayed the author's left-handedness she recalled from the ivory tablets that were used as dance cards at the Newport balls. She reached for the paper knife and opened the letter impatiently.

Dear Cora,

I hope I may still call you Cora. I am afraid I still think of you as Cora Cash even though I know that you are now that very august creation, an English duchess. I write to you because I am coming to London for the summer – I have been invited to share a studio in Chelsea and I have been furnished with an introduction to Louvain, whose work, as you know, I admire greatly. But of course the greatest attraction of England is that it is now the country where you live. I imagine that your days and nights are filled with your new duties but may I claim the privilege of an old friend and visit with you? If, in view of our last encounter, this prospect seems painful to you then I can only apologise in advance; but if you can think of me now as a friend whose affection is nothing but disinterested, then please send me word. We have known each other since childhood after all and I hope that our friendship may continue.

Your affectionate friend,

Teddy Van Der Leyden

Cora felt a dull ache at the base of her spine as she read the letter. She started when she saw the name Louvain and wondered if Teddy had heard about the portrait. But as she read on, she realised that Teddy would not have written with such candour if he had known about her contretemps last summer. He was, she reflected, still in Paris and so it was quite possible that the little scandal surrounding the portrait had not reached him. He would learn of it, she was sure, but at least she would have the chance to talk to him first. She thought sadly that the tone of Teddy's letter was more affectionate than anything she had received from her husband. Teddy had written to *her*. Ivo's letters had been well written, full of wry observations about the Indian princes and their courts and the difficulties of anticipating Prince Eddy's erratic behaviour. But though they were letters worth reading, they were not the letters she wanted to read. She had longed for a letter that was for her and her alone, a letter which would give her some glimpse into his heart. But apart from some of the less circumspect remarks about the Prince, there was nothing in Ivo's letters that could not have been published in *The Times*. It was if they had been sent merely as a record of his visit; nowhere did she find a sentence or even a phrase – and she had looked with considerable thoroughness – which suggested that he was writing to a woman he still loved. She had hoped that perhaps this lack of epistolary emotion was one of those English habits that had to be understood and tolerated, like the strange reluctance to shake hands or their pride in speaking in such an exaggerated drawl as to be almost incomprehensible. She knew she was still learning the customs of the country, but Teddy's letter with its open plea for her friendship could only make her wonder if her husband's reserve was not so much a product of his upbringing as a sign that he no longer cared for her.

She wrote a short note to Teddy, inviting him to stay in the summer at his convenience. She extolled the beauties of Lulworth, 'Indeed the light here is softer and more luminous in the late afternoons than anything we have at home,' and hinted at the forthcoming birth, 'When I see you I hope I will be able to introduce you to a new member of my family.' They were, she thought, the words of an English duchess. But at the end she tried to match his candour with her own. 'I look forward to seeing you again very much. My life has changed greatly but not so much that I can discard the friends of my youth. I may be called Duchess now but I am still an American girl who sometimes misses the country of her birth. Please come to Lulworth, it would give me great pleasure to see you again. Sincerely yours, Cora Wareham.' She read the note through and then added as a postscript, 'And I look forward to introducing you to my husband.'

She directed the letter to Teddy care of the Traveller's Club and rang for the footman. When her note had been safely dispatched, she turned to the other letter. This turned out to be a gossipy dissection of the London season so far; Mrs Wyndham was acting as sponsor to the Tempest twins from San Francisco, who were as rich as they were pert and had already acquired a number of aristocratic suitors, 'But my dear Cora,' Mrs Wyndham wrote, 'they are well aware of your magnificent marriage, and have declared themselves indifferent to anyone below the rank of duke. Indeed they frequently speculate whether they should spend the rest of the summer in Europe where it would be considerably easier for them to become princesses. I have pointed out, in vain, that a marquis or an earl of an early creation here in England is quite the equal of any continental prince but now that you have become a duchess they can think of nothing else but outranking you!'

Cora smiled at this. She knew Mrs Wyndham was concerned that she was losing some of her most promising protégées to Paris or Italy where princes and dukes were plentiful. Winaretta Singer, the sewing machine heiress, had gone straight to Paris for her debut and had married the Prince de Polignac eight weeks after her arrival. The only princes in England were of royal blood and they were still beyond the reach of American money. But Cora did not envy the new Princess de Polignac. She had found Parisian society to be even less welcoming than London. Thanks to a succession of French governesses, Cora spoke the language with some fluency but even so she had difficulty in following the brittle chatter of the Parisian *bon ton*. Besides, it was rumoured that all Frenchmen kept mistresses whether they were married or not. She remembered seeing a ravishing woman in the Bois de Boulogne. She had been wearing a striped lilac silk gown trimmed with black lace, but it had been the sinuous quality of her walk that had arrested Cora. She moved so fluidly that Cora found herself staring at her just for the pleasure of seeing her glide along the gravel paths of the Bois. When she had asked Madame St Jacques, their companion in Paris, who the woman was, she had said quite matter-of-factly that she was Liane de Rougement, and that she was currently under the protection of the Baron Gallimard. 'Although there has been talk that she may transfer her favours to the Duc de Ligne.' Cora had tried to conceal her astonishment. She knew that such women existed, of course, but she had not expected to find one so immaculately dressed walking unconcerned through the cream of Parisian high society. No, she did not envy the Princess de Polignac.

She scanned the rest of Mrs Wyndham's letter. Although she understood why the other woman felt she had to include the genealogy of all the people she mentioned – 'I went to the Londonderrys last night, the Marchioness is of course a Percy and is related to the Beauchamps through her mother': knowledge that Madeline Wyndham felt was essential if the American Duchess was ever to blend into her new background – Cora found the skein of connections tedious. But the penultimate paragraph did pique her interest. Mrs Wyndham was describing the *tableaux vivants* given by Lady Salisbury in aid of the Red Cross the day before. The *tableaux* had been of great women of history. The

Duchess of Manchester had appeared as Queen Elizabeth, Lady Elcho had been Boadicea, in a chariot drawn by real ponies, but the *pièce de résistance* was to be Charlotte Beauchamp as Joan of Arc – 'in rehearsal she was quite magnificent dressed as a boy soldier'. But in the interval between the dress rehearsal in the morning and the performance itself, Charlotte Beauchamp had simply disappeared. 'In the end Violet Paget had to take her place but she was no substitute for Lady Beauchamp. I could see that Sir Odo, who was in the audience, had no idea what had happened to his wife although he did say that she had complained of a headache that morning. Personally, I thought she looked the picture of health at the dress rehearsal. Their Royal Highnesses went so far as to express their concern.'

Cora was surprised by this story. She found it hard to imagine what would prevent Charlotte from taking centre stage in front of the Prince and Princess of Wales. She thought it unlikely that anything as trivial as a headache would deter Charlotte from performing at such an event. Parts in Lady Salisbury's *tableaux vivants* were keenly sought after. Leading roles were reserved for the acknowledged beauties of the age. Something, Cora thought, quite momentous must have happened to stop Charlotte from stepping on to the stage in her Joan of Arc costume, her long slim legs clad only in hose.

At the end of her letter, after a gentle hint that Cora might like to entertain her twin heiresses – 'you would find them quite in awe of you' – Mrs Wyndham wrote, 'I have just heard that the Duke is back in the country. You must be so happy to have him home. I trust that that unfortunate business with Louvain is now quite forgotten and you can take up the position in society that is rightfully yours.'

Cora put the letter down and leant back in her chair – the ache in her back was now more pronounced. She was clearly the last person in the country to know that her husband was back. Even Mrs Wyndham knew more about her husband's movements than she did. It was humiliating. She stood up painfully and started to move slowly around the room. When she stopped to gaze out of the window overlooking the lawns down to the sea, she could just make out a pink shape and a green shape moving towards the summer house. It could only be her mother-in-law and Sybil. Her eyesight was too bad to make out their faces, but she felt cheered, imagining the older woman's discovery of the statue of Eros and Psyche by Canova in the pavilion. It was a beautiful piece, but Cora thought it unlikely that her mother-in-law would share that view.

Her train of thought was interrupted by a sudden acceleration of the grumbling pain in her back, as if iron fingers were squeezing her innards. She put her hand on the window frame to steady herself and the pain subsided. Sir Julius had said that if the pain came regularly it was a sign that the baby was coming. She put her forehead against the glass and breathed out slowly, trying to still her bubbling thoughts. She did not want the baby to come today, she wanted to be ready, fragrant and charming, her black pearl necklace round her neck, when her husband returned. Even if he did not care for her any more, she still wanted to look her best. But as the pink and green shapes disappeared into the summer house, she felt another spasm and she understood that this was beyond her control. She rang the bell and was relieved to see Bertha come into the room moments later.

'Bertha, you need to send for Sir Julius. I think it is time.' Cora winced. 'Go down to the post office and send a cable telling him to come at once.'

Bertha looked at her in concern. 'Of course, Miss Cora, but do you think you should be here on your own? Would you like me to fetch the Duchess or Lady Sybil?'

Cora grimaced. 'No, absolutely not. I don't want to see anyone, particularly not the Duchess. I don't want her to start interfering. No, you must take the donkey cart and go down to Lulworth as quick as you can. Send the cable and wait for the answer. With any luck Sir Julius will catch the afternoon train.'

Bertha hesitated. She could see that Miss Cora's face had turned pale and there were beads of moisture along her hairline. But Bertha knew better than to argue with her.

On her way down to the stables, she wondered if she should tell any of the servants, Mabel perhaps; but then she reflected that nobody could be relied on. Bugler would hear of it, and then it was only a matter of time before the Double Duchess knew everything. Nothing that happened at Lulworth could be concealed from the Double Duchess for long. She had Mrs Cash's relentless eye for detail.

There was a flyblown mirror set in the hatstand that stood in the corridor between the servants' staircase and the back door leading out into the stable yard. Bertha caught her reflection and adjusted her hat so that it perched at the most becoming angle, the brim casting a slight shadow over her eyes.

Mr Veale the postmaster was surprised to see Bertha. Normally any telegrams from the house were brought down by the stable boy. He was alert, naturally, to the implications of the maid's arrival: the contents of this telegram were to be kept private. He looked curiously at the Duchess's maid as she handed him the form. He had heard about her from his niece who worked up at the house in the still room. 'The Duchess gives her dresses that are hardly worn, you wouldn't know from looking at her that she was in service.' Mr Veale, as he looked up at Bertha – she was a little taller than he was – thought that this was almost true, only the tinge of her skin meant that she could never be mistaken for a lady.

He tapped out the message – 'Please come at once, Cora Wareham.' When he had finished and had received an acknowledgement from the post office in Cavendish Square, he looked up again at the maid.

'That's gone through then, Miss . . .'

'Jackson.' The maid's voice was deep and her accent was strong.

'I'll send one of the boys up with the reply, Miss Jackson.'

Bertha shook her head. 'The Duchess wants me to wait.'

Mr Veale felt an itch underneath the hard collar of his uniform. He bristled at the implication that his boys were not to be trusted with a message of a confidential nature. He wanted to remonstrate but he reflected that the Duchess and her maid were both foreigners. They did not know how things were done here.

'Well, if you would care to take a seat, Miss Jackson.' He spoke clearly to be sure that she understood and gestured to the wooden bench that stood against one wall of the post office.

'Thank you, but I would prefer the fresh air. I will go for a walk in the village.'

Mr Veale watched as she stood in the doorway, unfurling her parasol. At this angle, with her back to him, she did indeed look like a lady.

344

Bertha strolled slowly down the village street. She had not been to Lulworth more than once or twice since they had come to the house. On her rare days off she preferred to walk in the park or stay in her room and read illustrated magazines. It was a pretty enough street, the houses all built from the same grey stone, their roofs mostly thatched although some of the larger ones had slate roofs. Bertha had been amazed when she first saw the thatched cottages. Miss Cora had called them quaint but Bertha thought they looked shabby. She thought that the overhanging eaves looked like the hairy eyebrows of old men. She twirled her parasol. Its colour exactly matched the cream of her blouse. Miss Cora had ordered them at the same time; she would only carry a parasol that matched her dress.

Bertha was aware that she was being watched as she walked down the street. There were a few women hanging up washing, as it was a fine day, and the bench in front of the Square and Compass was, as usual, filled with old men. She had been surprised when she had first come to Dorset by how small the villagers were. At home she was tall, but not excessively so, but here in the village she felt like a giant. She regularly saw men, working in the fields, who only came up to her shoulder. Bertha looked at the cottages with their frowning roofs and low doors and wondered whether their inhabitants simply had no room to grow. As she walked past a line of washing, she saw how patched and worn the smocks and petticoats were, they reminded her of the washing lines back in South Carolina. She smoothed her skirts, the silky material reminding her that she had escaped that threadbare existence. If it hadn't been for the Reverend and Mrs Cash, she would have been like those women hanging out rags. She wondered if her mother had got the last letter she had sent her and the money.

She had sent her twenty-five pounds, that was a hundred and twenty-five dollars. How many mothers had daughters who could send them that kind of money? That thought, along with the swish of her silk skirt, distracted her from the knowledge that she had not heard from her mother since she had come to England and the realisation that, no matter how hard she screwed up her eyes, she could no longer visualise her mother's face.

She turned and walked back to the post office. Mr Veale was standing in the doorway waving at her.

'The answer has come through, Miss Jackson.' He handed her the cable. 'Will be on the 5 o'clock train, Julius Sercombe.' Bertha felt her shoulders fall in relief and she put the paper in her pocket.

'Will that be all, Miss Jackson?' Mr Veale hovered curiously.

'Yes, thank you.'

'I trust everything is well at the house. There must be great excitement about the Duke's return.'

Bertha nodded and took up the reins of the donkey cart, aware that Cora would be counting the minutes till she came back. The postmaster cleared his throat nervously.

'Please convey my respects to Her Grace and tell her that we would be honoured if she were to visit the post office. I would be most happy to show her the telegraph machine at her convenience. It is the latest model, quite the equal of anything in the metropolis.'

Bertha said, 'I will do that, and now if you'll excuse me,' and she flicked her switch across the donkey's broad back. Why on earth did that man imagine that Miss Cora would want to poke around his post office? Perhaps he thought there would be money in it.

She set off along the road that ran up from the station to the gates of the house. She heard the church bells strike quarter to – she had been gone for an hour and a half. She hoped Miss Cora was managing. She gave the donkey another flick. She could see a man a few hundred yards ahead of her, walking along the side of the road. He was moving energetically, his arms and legs pumping, his head held high, so different from the old men shuffling outside the pub. He was smartly dressed too, wearing a dark jacket and a bowler hat. A delicious suspicion ran through her as she shook the reins and urged the donkey to move faster. As the distance between them narrowed, she felt a lurching in her stomach and blood rushing to her cheeks.

'Jim,' she called, her voice cracking with excitement. The man stopped and turned round. For a moment she thought perhaps she had been mistaken, he was so brown and his face was much thinner than she remembered. But then he took off his hat and ran towards her.

'I was just thinking about you,' he said and he smiled. There were new creases around his eyes and mouth, but she remembered the look he was giving her now. She smiled back and put out her arms.

After a few minutes he said, 'What a stroke of luck meeting you on the road like this. I'd been thinking all the way down here how I could get you to myself.' He had climbed up on to the cart and was sitting next to Bertha, leg to leg, their hands touching as she moved the reins.

He breathed into her ear, 'Why don't we pull up in the woods for a bit before we go up to the house? Oh Bertha, it's so good to see you again.' He put his hand over hers and she felt his touch flood through her. She leant against him and allowed him to take the reins. He steered them into woods at the edge of the park.

She watched as he jumped down lightly and tied the reins to a tree. His skin was much darker than she remembered, and his hair was fairer, but his expression was still the same, his blue eyes eager and shining. He held out his hand and she hesitated for a second, thinking of Cora's white face, but he was pulling her down now and there was no space in her mind for anything else but the fact of him.

She pulled away from him at last. 'We can't, not . . . not now.' She tried to push him away as he leant forward to kiss her neck.

'I've waited so long for this . . .' Jim's voice was muffled in her hair.

'I know, but Miss Cora's baby is starting and there is no one with her. I must go back.'

But Jim did not release his hold on her. 'Stay with me, Bertha. She's got a husband and a houseful of servants. I only have you. You don't know how much I've wanted you.' She could feel his fingers fumbling with the buttons at her collar.

She arched away from him and looked at him full on. 'But the Duke's not there and she doesn't want anyone else to know until the doctor comes.'

Jim's fingers stopped trying to tease the tiny mother-of-pearl buttons through the tight little loops.

'The Duke's not at Lulworth?' he said reluctantly.

'He sent a cable to say he would be here this evening. You mean you thought he'd be here?' Bertha felt nervous. Had Jim quarrelled with the Duke, lost his position even?

'I thought he must be. When he didn't come back this morning, I thought he must have come down here and forgotten to send for me.' He frowned. 'His Grace won't be pleased if he goes back to the club and finds I've packed up and brought everything down here. Still, it can't be helped.' He smiled at Bertha. 'I'll just tell him that I couldn't stay away from you a moment longer. He'll understand.'

Bertha felt warmed by the smile, but she could not suppress the twinge of pity she felt for Cora. She shook her head. 'I have to go back, Jim. It's her time and she needs me.'

But Jim pulled her to him and held her fast. 'Oh, she doesn't need you like I do.'

She could hear his breath coming fast and strong. She could smell the starch from his stiff collar melting. She let herself relax against him for a moment, remembering how well they fitted together, but then she twisted away from him and jumped up on to the donkey cart. She did not trust him to let her go willingly, and she knew it would take so very little to make her stay.

CHAPTER 23

'A Bough of Cherries'

*B*ERTHA DID NOT KNOCK. SHE WALKED STRAIGHT in and found Cora leaning against the fireplace with her hands outstretched, her face contorted with the effort of not screaming. Sybil was standing next to her with a handkerchief soaked in eau de cologne.

She was saying to Cora, 'Please, Cora, let me fetch Mama.'

Cora gasped, 'No – I – do – not – want – her – to interfere.' And then the spasm passed and she stood up and saw Bertha.

'Sir Julius is coming, Miss Cora. He'll be here soon.' Bertha would have liked to touch her mistress's arm, to reassure her, but she felt constrained by Sybil's presence.

'Oh, thank God. I don't how much more of this I can bear.' She winced as another contraction began.

Bertha said, 'Excuse me a moment, Miss Cora, I think I know what will help with the pain.' She rushed down the corridor to the servants' staircase where she clattered down the uncarpeted stairs to the warren of offices behind the servants' hall. She knocked on the pantry door where she knew Bugler would be. He was in his shirt sleeves polishing a silver candlestick.

'Mr Bugler, the Duchess needs the key to the poisons cupboard.'

She held out her hand. As soon as she did so she realised that this was a mistake. Bugler did not like the presumption: the poisons cupboard was his responsibility.

'Indeed. May I ask why the Duchess did not ring for me herself?'

Bertha swallowed. 'She is indisposed, Mr Bugler. She does not wish to see anyone just at the present.'

Slowly, Bugler put down the candlestick and motioned Bertha to leave the room with him. She hoped that he would not fully understand the significance of her errand. When he opened the poisons cupboard, which was underneath the cabinet where all the most valuable plate was kept, she walked towards it, hoping to see the bottle straight away, but Bugler was too quick for her. He positioned himself in front of the cabinet, forcing her to ask him for the bottle of Hallston's patent cough medicine.

He handed it over grudgingly. 'You will bring it straight back when Her Grace has finished with it, Miss Jackson. I don't like to leave these preparations lying around. Some of the maids can be very foolish.' He looked directly at Bertha. But she kept her eyes lowered and took the bottle as respectfully as she could; she found herself even giving a little placatory bend of the knees. It worked, evidently, as Bugler said nothing more, and turned his back to her, making a great show of locking up the cupboard again.

Bertha walked as quickly as she could without actually running along the corridor to the servants' staircase. As she passed the door to the kitchen, she could hear a clamour of welcome surrounding Jim. He was very popular with the other servants – a local boy who had achieved great things. They would not be so welcoming, Bertha thought, if they knew that she was his sweetheart.

As she scurried crab-like up the stairs – her petticoats wouldn't let her take them two at a time – she misjudged a step and tripped, the bottle falling out of her hand. For a frozen second she thought it would shatter on the wooden boards but the sturdy brown glass was clearly designed to be proof against trembling fingers and had landed unharmed. The cough medicine was famous for containing large quantities of ether which, according to the legend on the front, dulled all pain and blunted all aches. Bertha had taken some for a toothache when she first arrived in England and had been amazed at the way the sharpness of the pain had been reduced. She had not been tempted to go back for more after the initial pain had faded away but she knew that there were many girls who kept a bottle under their mattress. One of the housemaids had taken so much that, before Christmas, her eyes glassy and her hands wet with sweat, she had dropped a whole tea service on to the scullery floor. The girl's wages for a year were a fraction of the tea service's worth so she had been dismissed. When her room was turned out they had found ten empty bottles of Hallston's patent cough medicine under the mattress. Since then all patent medicines were kept in the poisons cupboard.

Cora was pacing up and down holding on to Sybil when Bertha got back. She wrinkled her nose as she drank the medicine but within a few moments Bertha could see her mistress's eyes begin to lose their focus. Sybil led her to the chaise longue and once she was lying down, Bertha began to loosen the ribbons and laces of her tea gown and to undo the buttons on the patent kid boots.

When the ether began to wear off, Cora noticed what her maid was doing.

'Bertha! I want to look nice for my husband when he comes. You will make sure, won't you?'

Bertha smiled. 'Don't worry about that, Miss Cora.'

Cora held out her hand for some more of the medicine.

The arrival of Sir Julius from London some four hours later confirmed the rumours flying around the village that the Duchess had gone into labour. Outside the Square and Compass the long view taken by the clay-pipe smokers was that a healthy boy could only be good news, as money would have to be spent on improving the estate if the heir was to have anything to inherit. They had all heard of the fabulous wealth of the new Duchess but so far they had seen no evidence of it in repairs to their houses, the draining of ditches or the replanting of hedgerows. In the general store, the talk was more short term, concentrating on the new dresses to be worn at the tenants' dinner traditionally held to celebrate the birth of an heir to the Dukedom. There were mothers who wondered if their daughter might be chosen to work in the nursery and fathers of large families who hoped that their wife might gain employment as a wet nurse. Weld, the stationmaster, anticipated a royal presence at the christening and thought about floral displays, and the churchwarden considered which of his team of bell ringers deserved the honour of ringing in the news.

In the house itself, the servants were being pulled between the activity necessary for the imminent arrival of the Duke and the natural desire to congregate in the kitchen and interpret every call for hot water or clean linen from the Duchess's bedroom. Much of this discussion was theoretical as neither the cook nor Mrs Softley had ever given birth – the title of Mrs was an honorific bestowed with the office, and the maids were, of course, unmarried. Mr Bugler had had to come in more than once to remind his staff that their master was expected any moment and there was still no fire lit in the music room.

Upstairs in the Duchess's apartments there were periods of quiet punctuated by screams that became progressively closer together as the evening drew in. The screams might have been louder if Sir Julius had not been a keen supporter of anaesthesia in childbirth. He held no brief for the argument that physical suffering was a necessary part of labour – a punishment visited on women since Eve's tasting of the forbidden fruit – and neither, in his experience, did his aristocratic clients. He had never attended a birth where a woman had refused the blessed relief of chloroform.

The Duchess's labour was progressing slowly, but that was to be expected in a first delivery. He was a little uneasy that the Duke was not present. In case of difficulty it was imperative to have the husband's consent to any procedures that might be necessary. The Duchess of Buckingham, the famous Double Duchess, had already hinted to him that the Duke wanted an heir 'above all else' but Sir Julius had attended enough noble births to know that the mother-in-law's wishes might not always be that of the husband. He sincerely hoped that there would be no choice to make. He liked the American Duchess. When he had told her about the hospital he was building so that poor women could give birth safely, she had listened carefully and had pledged a sum that had made all the difference to his plans. He had other patients, ladies with money and position who had organised whist drives, bazaars and even concerts in aid of the hospital, but he suspected that they did so as much for their own social ends as out of any great devotion to philanthropy. Certainly the sums raised bore no relation to the effort expended or the numbers of frocks that were ordered. So he had appreciated the Duchess's straightforwardness when it came to money, very much.

The evening was drawing in, and there was still no sign of the baby or of its father. Cora was lost in a twilight world punctuated by pain. She would swim towards consciousness on a contraction and then the sweet smell of the chloroform would knock her back into blankness. Finally she woke to a pain so intense that she imagined for a moment that she was being cut open, and then she heard Bertha telling her that it was going to be all right, and then nothing.

As she came round again, snatches of conversation sank into her emerging consciousness.

'. . . the Maltravers nose, definitely.'

'. . . difficult delivery, I had to use the forceps . . .'

'He's dark, just like his father.'

And then a different sound, one that jerked her into full wakefulness, the thin, clear cry of her baby.

She opened her eyes and saw her mother-in-law, like a great blue crow, holding a white bundle. Cora struggled to sit up and there was Bertha on her other side putting a pillow behind her back.

She tried to speak but her voice was scratched and hoarse.

'My baby . . .' and she put out her arms. The Double Duchess looked across the room at Sir Julius and lowered the baby so that Cora could see him.

'Here he is, the Marquis of Salcombe.' Cora tried to take the baby from her but the Duchess drew back a fraction.

'Don't you want to recover a little, Cora?' she said tightly.

Cora shook her head, 'Give him to me,' she whispered.

The Duchess again looked across at Sir Julius and he said, 'I am delighted to tell you, Duchess, that you have a healthy baby boy.' And then he gestured to Duchess Fanny so that she had no choice but to put the child into Cora's arms.

Cora looked at the tiny wrinkled face, the milky unfocused eyes, the surprisingly abundant hair and she folded him to her.

The light had gone and Cora was in a half sleep, the baby lying in the crook of her elbow. The Double Duchess had left and now there was only the nurse Sir Julius had brought with him, busying herself over the carved and gilded bassinet that Mrs Cash had sent the week before. Cora could hardly resist the downward droop of her eyelids when she heard the first bells. The noise carried so clearly over the valley that Cora did not hear the door open; she brought the baby closer to swaddle him against the clamour and then she felt a hand on her cheek, and there was Ivo kneeling beside her, his lips brushing their son's head.

'You have a son,' she said.

He took her free hand and kissed it. She saw at once that his face was soft with tenderness. There was no trace of anger or constraint there. He had come back to her. He would be the husband she had known on her honeymoon, and now the father to her son. All the waiting was over. She forgot everything, all the worry and anxiety, as she recognised the tenderness in his face. She wanted to give him something in return.

'I thought that the baby should be called Guy, after your brother.'

He said nothing and then he stood up and turned his face away from her towards the window. For an awful moment she thought she had blundered. Ivo hardly talked about his brother but she sensed that he was always somewhere in his thoughts. She had wanted to show him that she understood his loss, but all she had done was to remind him of his grief. She was about to call his name when he turned round. His face was in shadow and she couldn't quite make out the cast of his countenance, but there was no mistaking the tone of his voice.

'Thank you, Cora, now I have everything I want.'

And he lay down beside her and at last she could breathe him in.

CHAPTER 24

Protocols

ORA LOOKED AT THE PLACEMENT ONCE MORE. THE red morocco leather blotter with slots for each place round the dining table had been a wedding present from Mrs Wyndham. It was the first time she had used it and she wished that Mrs Wyndham herself was here – she would know whether Lady Tavistock as the wife of a peer ranked higher than Sybil who was the daughter of a duke. Of course Sybil would not mind where she sat, as long as it was near Reggie, but any breach of etiquette on Cora's part would be pounced upon by her detractors, the Double Duchess in particular.

The Prince of Wales was only staying for two nights and he came without the Princess, but he travelled with two equerries, a private secretary and eight servants. Cora had received minute and irritating instructions from her mother-in-law about how to entertain the royal visitor. Lobster thermidor was his favourite dish, he liked to drink brandy after dinner, not port, and he would not tolerate a delay between courses. He would want to play baccarat after dinner, so Cora must ensure that there were enough seasoned players who understood that the Prince should always think that he had won on account of his skill. There were the bath salts he preferred, the cold roast chicken he liked by his bed in case of night-time hunger and the royal standard that must fly from the roof as long as he was in residence.

Cora had been delighted when the letter had come from the Double Duchess saying that the Prince wanted to act as sponsor to her son. Such a sign of royal favour suggested that the Louvain affair had not permanently damaged her social worth. After nearly a year in the seclusion of Lulworth, she was longing to return to London. But Ivo had shrugged when he heard the news. 'More trouble than it's worth, but we can hardly refuse.' As a result Cora tried to conceal her pleasure about the royal visit from her husband but her mother had no reason to. The Cashes, who had arrived a few days after Cora had given birth, had been due to go back to Newport for the end of the season, as Mrs Cash found staying in a house of which she was not the mistress trying; but the prospect of standing next to the Prince of Wales changed everything. Mrs Cash had cabled M. Worth in Paris for new gowns and she had sent her pearls to be restrung.

Cora picked up the card that read 'Teddy Van Der Leyden'. He was to be a godfather to little Guy. When she had suggested this to Ivo he had, rather to her surprise, smiled and said, 'Of course he needs an American godfather. What's this one like? I hope he has a railway, at the very least.' Cora had protested that Teddy came from an old Knickerbocker family that was not the railway-owning kind at all, not that there was anything wrong with railroads, and that he was actually an artist. Ivo had looked at her a touch more closely but then he laughed. 'An American painter, my mother will be *delighted*.' They had agreed that Sybil and Reggie should both be godparents; Cora hoped that it might precipitate a proposal and Ivo saw another opportunity to irritate the Double Duchess. But when Cora had suggested Charlotte Beauchamp, Ivo had hesitated. 'Do you really think Charlotte is a suitable moral guardian? Wouldn't you rather have someone more solid? And what about Odo?' But Cora had insisted.

'I like Charlotte, at least she's not boring.'

Ivo had turned his head away and, looking out of the window, he had said, 'If that's what you want, Cora, I won't stop you.'

Cora decided to put Teddy next to Charlotte tonight. She, of course, would have to sit next to the Prince but she thought that Teddy would find Charlotte intriguing; after all, she had been painted by his hero, Louvain. Her greatest difficulty was where to place her mother. Reggie Greatorex was safe enough but she knew that her mother would be mortified if she was not close to the Prince, but for protocol's sake she would have to put Duchess Fanny next to His Royal Highness. She decided to put her mother opposite but one, so that the Prince would be able to see her good side. And she would place her father next to the Double Duchess, so she could see for herself if there was a flirtation there.

At last the seating plan was finished. She really ought to have a secretary to write out all the cards, some nice girl who would deal with her correspondence and remember the right way to address a baronet. Her mother and her mother-in-law had both suggested it, but Cora did not want to have an English girl with a long nose and droopy clothes pointing out all the things she didn't know. She was tired of being made to feel like a hick by the people who worked for her. She was sick of Bugler's little pauses, by which he indicated that she had crossed an unwritten Rubicon of correct behaviour. When she had asked for all the ladies staying at the house to be brought breakfast in their rooms, he had paused and then said, 'At Lulworth, Your Grace, it is customary for the ladies to come down to breakfast.'

Cora had stared him down. 'Well, it is time that Lulworth had some new customs. I have no intention of coming down to breakfast and I think it unfair to expect my guests to do so.' She turned away in dismissal, but Bugler did not move. 'Thank you, Bugler, that will be all.'

He was looking at a spot somewhere around her knees. She could see a wiry tendril of hair snaking out of his nostril.

'Excuse me, Your Grace, but I wondered if the Duchess of Buckingham was aware of the change?' Bugler kept his gaze lowered and his voice neutral but there was no mistaking the meaning of his words.

'I am not in the habit of consulting the Duchess about my domestic arrangements, Bugler, not that it is any business of yours. You may go.'

Bugler had withdrawn, leaving Cora feeling foolish for allowing herself to be provoked. She comforted herself with the thought that she would dismiss him after the christening. She had wanted to do this for ages but she had not dared to make such a move while Ivo was away. Now he was back she felt that it was time for her to take charge.

Cora looked up at the portrait of Eleanor Maltravers that hung on the wall opposite her desk. She was still getting used to having the picture in her room. It used to hang in the corridor leading to the north tower in a dark alcove. Cora had found her there one day during one of her long perambulations around the house during her pregnancy, and had been intrigued. From the orange satin of her dress and the deep décolleté this likeness had been made before the Grey Lady had earned her soubriquet. Cora thought that Eleanor must have been about her own age when the picture was painted. But it was hard to tell as it was submerged under layers of dust and dirt. After some hesitation she sent the portrait to Duveen's in London to be cleaned, deciding that Ivo could hardly object to her restoring a picture that no one had noticed for centuries. She had forgotten about the picture in the excitement of the birth and Ivo's return, and she had been surprised when the crate was delivered. Ivo had raised an eyebrow when he saw the Duveen stencil on the crate.

'Have you been shopping again, Cora?' he said.

Cora shook her head. She signalled to the footman to open the crate, biting her lip as he prised the nails out of the wood. Ivo lingered at the doorway scratching his dog's head and whistling. Cora held her breath as the footman started to take off the wrappings; Ivo's presence was making her nervous. Then the piece of canvas came off and Eleanor was revealed. Her skin was white now and her dress glowed, the cleaning had revealed the background to be full of details, there was even a lurcher curled up on a green tasselled cushion. Ivo stopped whistling and stepped forward to take a better look.

'Is it really Eleanor?' he said, peering at the picture. 'She's quite something.' Cora listened for a note of disapproval, but then he turned to her and smiled.

'You're a clever girl, Cora. I've walked past that picture all my life but I don't think I have ever really seen it before. Thank you for making me look.' He put his hand on her shoulder and she felt her body sag with relief. She didn't want him to know how nervous she had been, so she said as brightly as she could, 'Mr Fox says he believes this is by Van Dyck. The face certainly, even if the rest of the picture was finished off in the studio.' She took his hand. 'I would like to hang it in my bedroom, you don't mind do you?'

'Of course I don't mind. Lucky Eleanor, you've turned her from a ghost into a beauty. I think we should have all the pictures cleaned, it's time we saw things differently here.' He swung her hand. 'My new broom, that's what you are. I want you to sweep away all the shadows, all the dust. You're the only one brave enough to do it.'

'Brave?' said Cora, 'It's not so very frightening to have a few pictures cleaned.' She put her face close to his, basking in his approval. He touched her cheek.

'Not for you darling, which is why I am so glad that you are my wife.'

She remembered this scene every time she saw a raised eyebrow, or heard a sharp intake of breath from the servants when she suggested changes to the way the house was run. They might not like her ideas but none of that mattered if Ivo approved. If he wanted to make a break with the past then nothing would stop her. She was not going to be a grey lady languishing in corners. She would be the mistress of Lulworth.

She rang the bell for Mrs Softley. She wanted to make an inspection of the guest bedrooms to ensure that they were all as they should be, and that those awful photographs of the Duke and Duchess had been put away. But at that moment Ivo walked in. He had been riding and he was pulling off his jacket as he came towards her. He kissed her lightly on the mouth.

'Good morning, Duchess. How are the battle plans?' He looked over her shoulder at the placement. 'And who am I sitting next to?'

'Between my mother and Lady Tavistock.'

'Scylla and Charybdis, eh? Well, at least my ordeal will be swift. His Highness doesn't like to linger over dinner. Just promise I don't have to play cards with him. He is such a lamentable player, it can be quite tricky sometimes to let him win.' He stroked the inch of Cora's neck that was visible above the high collar of her blouse with his finger. She took his other hand and kissed it.

'I promise to spare you the cards. I am going to take the ladies to the long gallery.'

She could feel his finger tracing the knobs of her spine under the thin silk. He was always touching her now when he was with her. These last few weeks at Lulworth with Ivo and the baby had been the happiest in her marriage since their honeymoon. When she remembered how worried she had been before his return, she almost laughed. Ever since he had come back he had been everything she had hoped for. Even the presence of her parents and the Double Duchess had not spoilt things. The Double Duchess had shown unusual tact in inviting Mr and Mrs Cash to Conyers before the christening. Cora could not have been more surprised by the invitation, but Ivo had said, 'The Double Duchess has clearly got over her aversion to Americans, or American men, I should say. I almost feel sorry for your mother.'

It had taken Cora a moment to catch his meaning, and then she had shaken her head in disbelief.

Ivo had laughed at her. 'I'm sorry, Cora, have I offended your Puritan sensibilities?' And then more seriously, 'It's the way she operates, I'm afraid.'

'Do you think I should tell Mother?'

'Lord, no. Let the situation develop. Besides, I want to be here alone with you.'

Cora could not refuse.

Now Ivo was pulling a strand of her hair out of its chignon. She put up her hand to stop him.

There was so much still to be done. She turned to him and said, 'Come with me to the nursery. I want to show you something.'

He put his hands down in a show of mock surrender. 'As you wish, my dear, as you wish.'

He followed her down the corridor to the nursery. This was not the room where he had stayed as a child, that was on the north side of the house on a higher floor. Cora had chosen to put little Guy and his attendants in the rooms adjacent to hers; she could not bear to think of him being so far away. The nanny had grumbled at first about losing her sanctum which had its own staircase down to the servants' hall, but Cora had raised her wages by ten pounds a year and her objections had vanished.

The baby was lying in the great gilded bassinet that Mrs Cash had bought from Venice. Ivo had laughed when he saw it and said it must have been made from pieces of the True Cross at the very least. Ignoring the flusterings of the nurse, Cora went straight to the cradle and picked up her baby. His body was heavy against her shoulder and his fingers went straight to her hair, just as his father's had done a few minutes before.

'He smiled me this morning, Ivo! Open your eyes wide and see if he'll smile at you too.'

Ivo put out his arms to take his son.

'Were you smiling at your beautiful mother, young man? I see you have taste.' Cora felt herself beaming with pride and happiness. When Ivo was with the baby, she could see that his eyes, usually so dark, were in fact tawny, flecked through with gold. She knew that Ivo had wanted an heir but she had not imagined that he would be so delighted to be a father. Nanny Snowden had said to her, with disapproval in her voice, that she had never known a man to spend so much time in the nursery.

She stood beside him and smiled at the baby lying in his arms. She was rewarded with a flash of gums and sparkling eyes. 'There it is, Ivo, he smiled at us.' And she looked up at her husband's face and saw that it was taut with emotion, his mouth set in a code she could not decipher.

Cora said, 'I think he is going to be a happy boy.'

'Happiness is a talent,' Ivo said slowly and then he kissed the top of the baby's head and gave him to Nanny Snowden who was hovering in the doorway, only just concealing her irritation at their presence.

'Thank you, Nanny,' said Ivo. 'Guy must have his rest for tomorrow.'

'Don't worry, Your Grace, His Lordship will be quite prepared.' Cora felt the same wriggle of surprise every time she heard her baby called 'His Lordship'. Ivo might laugh at her mother's idea of a cradle but surely there was something equally absurd about giving a tiny scrap of a baby a title? She stopped to look at the christening gown which was laid out on a table. The gown had been in the family for generations, Ivo and his father before him had worn it. The silk was yellowed with age and the lace was covered with brown spots, like an old lady's hands. But Cora knew better now than to suggest a replacement.

Ivo was waiting for her in the passage. He took her hand and pulled her into his bedroom. This room had remained untouched during Cora's renovations of Lulworth. The magnificent blue brocade on the tester was dusty and tattered and the curtains hung in limp folds, faded where the sun had touched them.

'Now I have something to show *you*, darling.' He made her sit down in one of the heavily carved wooden chairs. Ivo walked over to the bureau and unlocked a drawer from which he took a velvet pouch. He came over to her and, kneeling in front of her, he emptied it on to her lap. The sun falling in through the window hit the gems as they lay across her skirt, dazzling them both. It took her a moment to realise that she was looking at a necklace that had at its centre an emerald the size of a quail's egg.

'I bought it in Hyderabad. I think it might just be magnificent enough for you.' Cora put her hands to her neck, she was as usual wearing her pearls. 'Take them off and try this on.'

Obediently Cora unclasped the pearls and he put the necklace round her neck. It felt heavy and spiky after the smooth weight of the pearls. He took her hand and stood her in front of the cheval glass. The mirror was foxed with age and her reflection rippled slightly but there was no disguising the splendour of the necklace. The emerald fell just above her breasts; the teardrop facets allowed it to glow like a mossy pool with limitless depths, and the diamond sprays above it looked like a waterfall. It was quite the most spectacular thing she had ever seen, nothing even in her mother's glittering collection could match this.

'It is quite unbelievable, Ivo.' She turned her head from side to side admiring the green rays from the gem. He stood behind her and put his arms on her shoulders. 'Even the Nizam was impressed. He offered to buy it from me for twice what I paid for it. But I said that it could only belong to you, as you were the only woman in the world who wouldn't be outshone by it.'

'I think my mother will be jealous,' said Cora.

'And mine,' said Ivo with a smile. 'It's the perfect present.'

That evening Cora wore a dress of gold brocade overlaid with silver lace. The glowing material brought out the bronze lights in her hair and the emerald hanging round her neck nudged her eyes from grey to green. She was standing by the window in the long gallery talking to her father, and every so often she would move so that the low rays of the setting sun would catch the gems round her neck and scatter their reflections over the vaulted roof. She was standing under this, her own constellation, when Teddy walked into the room. He stood still for a moment, dazzled. The restless girl he remembered had turned into a magnificent force. She seemed taller than he had pictured her. There was a definiteness about her that was new. He sensed that she had taken on her final shape. He was relieved that she had changed so much. This new, grand personage would finally shake the memory of the girl asking him to kiss her that night in Newport.

The footman announced his name and Cora swept up to him, her arms outstretched.

'Dearest Teddy, I can't believe you're actually here.' She leant forward to kiss his cheek and he smelt the foxy scent of her hair that he remembered from the terrace at Sans Souci. He knew then that nothing had changed – Cora could be as grand and as duchessy as she liked but she was still the woman he wanted to hold in his arms.

Still clasping his hands, she smiled at him conspiratorially. 'I guess we are kissing cousins now, us both being Americans abroad.'

'Indeed, Duchess.' Teddy gave her title its full weight.

'Oh please, you of all people have to call me Cora. I am still the same girl.' She was laughing but Teddy thought he heard a shard of anxiety in her voice.

'If you're sure that's allowed.'

He was smiling as he said this but it was a real question. He was not sure what he wanted the answer to be. He noticed the small scar on the underside of her wrist that he had once kissed and wondered, not by any means for the first time, what she had done with the letter he had written her before her wedding. Had she kept it as a memento – folded carefully in the secret compartment of a jewellery box or tucked away into a volume of poetry? Or had she torn it up, or thrown it into the fire? She had not replied, of course, he had not really expected her to, but he wondered about the expression on her face as she had read his letter. Cora met his eyes for a moment and Teddy wanted to kiss her so much that he had to clasp his hands behind his back so that he would not reach out and take hold of her. Perhaps Cora sensed this because she pulled back a fraction and said firmly, 'Come and meet my husband before the Prince comes down.'

Teddy followed her to the fireplace where the Duke was talking to another man and the red-haired girl he remembered from the boat. He wondered for a moment if the Duke would remember his face, but as he came closer he thought that dukes were probably not in the habit of noticing strangers.

Cora fluttered between them, making the introduction. Teddy

could see that she was nervous, which pleased him. He wanted some acknowledgement of their past, to see a hairline crack in her aristocratic composure.

'Welcome to Lulworth, Mr Van Der Leyden. Is this your first visit to England?' The Duke's face was politely curious, Teddy saw no flicker of recognition. The Duke looked somehow different to the man he had seen pacing the deck of the SS *Berengaria*. He looked looser now, as the French said: he looked happy in his skin.

'No, I was here about eighteen months ago, on my way back to America. I believe we may have travelled on the same boat. I remember your name from the manifest.'

Ivo tilted his head to observe Teddy properly. 'What a pity we were not introduced, you could have told me all Cora's secrets. I know remarkably little about her American life.' His gaze met Teddy's and Teddy forced himself not to blink. The Duke was looking at him closely as if he knew just how Teddy felt about his wife. Teddy found himself squaring off against his rival; the Duke was perhaps an inch taller but Teddy felt that he was the stronger.

Cora, who had been following this exchange closely, broke in, her hand closing round Teddy's wrist.

'If I had any secrets, I know that Teddy would never have told! We Americans are the soul of discretion.'

'I don't know about every American, Cora, but this one certainly is,' said Teddy.

Cora's grip on his arm tightened. 'Now, Teddy, you must come and talk to Mother. You can't put it off any longer.'

Teddy nodded to the Duke and said, 'It's no secret that American girls must be obeyed, I think.'

The Duke showed his teeth in amusement. 'In my experience all women expect obedience.'

Teddy allowed himself to be shepherded in front of Mrs Cash, who looked at him without enthusiasm. She hated to be reminded of her accident. She had told Cora that she thought Teddy's presence at Lulworth was in very poor taste.

'And how is your mother, Mr Van Der Leyden, and your sister?' She shifted slightly so that Teddy was facing her good side.

'Both well, thank you, ma'am, though I suspect you may have seen them more recently than I. I have been in Europe for over a year now.'

'Oh yes, I believe I heard you were in Paris – painting.' Mrs Cash let her voice fall on the last word. But Teddy did not waver.

'That's correct. I was studying with Menasche.'

'And do you ever intend to return to New York, Mr Van Der Leyden? It must be hard for your mother to have her only son so far away.'

'Well, I have received a commission from the New York Public Library for a mural, so I am coming home in the fall.'

Cora clapped her hands at this. 'Oh Teddy, that's splendid. I am so pleased. I know you will do something wonderful. What is your subject?'

Teddy saw that she was genuinely pleased and that her mother disliked this.

'I haven't decided yet. There was a thought of doing the Persephone myth. I only wish I could use you as a model, Cora, you would be exactly right.'

Teddy had meant this as a compliment so he was surprised to see the alarm on Cora's face.

'What a pity that I am here then. To be immortalised in a public library, that would be quite something.'

Teddy was about to say that he could work from sketches when there was an intake of breath and a rustling of skirts as the footman announced, 'His Royal Highness, the Prince of Wales.'

Teddy took a step back. He did not want to appear eager to meet the Prince. He hoped that he was immune to the lure of royalty although he could not help looking at the Prince closely. He was smaller than Teddy had imagined and much rounder. Even the dinner jacket which the Prince wore in preference to the more revealing tails could not disguise his girth. His mouth and chin were covered by a pointed Vandyke beard and he surveyed the room through a pair of chilly blue eyes under heavy lids.

The first person he spoke to was a blonde lady, whose curtsy was so abject that her forehead practically touched the ground at the Prince's feet. The Prince smiled at this and kissed the woman's hand when she surfaced. 'Duchess Fanny, such a pleasure to see you here in your old setting.' Teddy noticed that Cora's smile was losing its warmth, her curtsy was stiff, almost jerky – an italic comma in contrast to the other woman's flowing cursive signature. But the Prince appeared not to notice and said, 'Yes, I am verrry pleased to be back here, and in such charming company.' Now Cora was guiding the Prince through the guests to where her mother stood. Mrs Cash's curtsy was a model of dignity, she did not bow her head but kept her back erect throughout and her eyes fixed on the Prince's face. Despite the depth of her curtsy, there was no mistaking, in the regal tilt of Mrs Cash's head, the sense that she was meeting someone of her own rank at last. The Prince was complimenting her on her daughter. 'I don't know where we would be without you Amerrricans.' Mrs Cash half closed her eyes as if to agree.

Cora looked at Teddy and he stepped forward reluctantly.

'Sir, may I present Mr Van Der Leyden, who is one of my childhood friends and is also a godfather to my son.'

Teddy thought for a moment that he might stand his ground but as the Prince stood in front of him, he felt himself bowing as if pulled forward by the inexorable force of royal gravity.

'Whereabouts in Amerrrica are you from, Mr Van Der Leyden?'

'New York . . . sir.' Teddy could not bring himself to say Your Highness.

'Such an enerrrgetic city. I would like very much to go back but it is impossible these days for me to go so far away, I have too many responsibilities. Duty before pleasure, eh.'

Teddy looked at the Prince's rounded form and heavy-lidded eyes and wondered how much pleasure exactly the Prince had sacrificed for duty. It was not, he thought, a face that he wanted to paint.

As the Prince moved sedately on, Teddy looked up and saw that the Duke was looking at him, and to Teddy's surprise he gave him an imperceptible nod as if to say that he had read his thoughts and was in agreement.

The Prince was being offered a glass of champagne but he waved it away and turned to Cora. 'But my dear Amerrrican Duchess, may we not have a cocktail? I met a charming gentleman from Louisiana who showed me how to make a most splendid drink with whisky, marrraschino and champagne. I would so like to taste it again.' The Prince looked wistful although fully aware that his every whim would of course be indulged.

Cora signalled to Bugler. A few moments later two footmen entered carrying a tray with bottles, decanters and a large silver punchbowl.

The Prince busied himself mixing the drink. 'One part whisky to a measure of marrraschino and two parts of champagne. Now, Duchess Fanny, I want you to try this, and you too, Mrs Cash. You can tell me whether it tastes the way it should.' Both women approached, the Double Duchess eagerly, Mrs Cash with due republican reticence. The Prince poured a bottle of Pol Roger into the mixture and then he dipped two glasses into the bowl and offered one to each lady. Duchess Fanny sipped hers and pronounced it, 'Quite delicious, sir, although of course a little stronger than I am used to.'

'Splendid,' cried the Prince, his pendulous lower lip glistening. 'And what do you think, Mrs Cash?'

'I think it would benefit from the addition of some fresh mint.' The Prince looked at her for a moment in surprise; he frequently asked for honest opinions but he was not in the habit of receiving them. There was a tiny pause while he wondered whether there had been any affront to his dignity and then he laughed and said, 'Well now, I know why Amerrrican women make such good hostesses, Mrs Cash. Attention to detail. By all means, let us add mint.'

Teddy tried not to smile. He was used to seeing Mrs Cash prevailing but the assembled company were not. He noticed the blonde woman, whom he now knew to be Duchess Fanny, looking at Mrs Cash warily, as if re-evaluating an opponent.

The Prince was offering a glass to Cora when the footman announced, 'Sir Odo and Lady Beauchamp.' Teddy saw the Prince stiffen; and he remembered Cora's instructions in her letter to him:

'The Prince of Wales breaks all the rules, but he expects perfect behaviour from everyone else. He hates it if people are late, even though the Princess is notorious for her tardiness. So please hurry down to dinner the moment you are dressed. We Americans have to have the best manners of all, of course, as we can get away with nothing.'

The couple that came in, however, did not look at all abashed. The man was flushed, his protruding blue eyes glittering, his lips slightly parted, showing his small white teeth. He bowed gracefully before the Prince, displaying his extravagant profusion of yellow curls.

'You must forgive me, sir, but my wife could not decide between the chartreuse and the mauve. She would not budge until I had advised her, and do you know I just could not make a decision. She looked simply ravishing in both, so in the end she had to wear red, as you see.' He gestured towards his wife who sank into a curtsy that did much to display her décolletage.

'Highness,' she murmured and she raised her shining blond head to look at the Prince with a smile that was quite unrepentant.

'It is your hostess who must forgive you, of course, though I am inclined to agree with you, Sir Odo, that the result was worth the wait.' The Prince gestured towards Lady Beauchamp. Her dress was crimson satin embroidered in black in a repeating motif of bees, ants and scorpions. The neckline and hem were edged with jet beads that shook slightly as she moved. It was a theatrical dress, preposterous even, but Lady Beauchamp was equal to it, Teddy thought. She held her head high, and Teddy could see the strong lines of her neck as it met the collarbone below. She looked beautiful and terrible in equal measure. Teddy thought of Salome holding up the head of John the Baptist. But it wasn't just her perfect, implacable profile that made him stare at her, transfixed. He had seen this woman before, a year ago, standing on the platform of Euston Station with the Duke. He had never forgotten the way she had pulled the Duke's hand into her muff – such ferocious intimacy in that public place. He could still remember the gorgeous curve of her cheek, and the way her eyes were fixed on the Duke's face. It was an image that had never left him, because he knew he had seen the face of a woman saying farewell to the man she loved.

CHAPTER 25

Eros and Psyche

THE DINING ROOM AT LULWORTH WAS IN THE oldest part of the house. The entrance to the room was down a shallow flight of steps and even on a summer's evening the stone walls and floors meant that the room felt a few degrees colder than the rest of the house. Tonight, however, the faintly crypt-like atmosphere was dispelled by the heat from the twelve silver gilt candelabra on the table and the sweet smell coming from banks of jasmine in the window bays. The room glittered as the candlelight hit the crystal glasses, the brilliants dangling from the chandeliers and the diamonds around the women's necks. But the warmth and light were only on the surface, every so often there would be a chill current of air that brushed a bare shoulder or a naked neck and made its owner shiver. Comfort was not the natural order of things here, this room had been built to contain the violent carousing of medieval barons fighting for the favours of the King, not the powdered politenesses of *fin de siècle* aristocrats. The floor was mainly covered by an Aubusson carpet but underneath lay cold hard stone. The footmen who lined the room knew this, they stood on the cold perimeter waiting to pull out chairs, fill glasses and serve food to guests who gave no more thought to their existence than they did to the larks whose tongues lay in aspic before them.

Teddy emptied his glass. He knew that he was drinking too fast. The reappearance of the woman he had seen on the station platform had shaken him. It had taken every scrap of his Knickerbocker composure not to flinch when Cora had beckoned to him to take Lady Beauchamp in to dinner. Charlotte had sensed his confusion but had misattributed the cause, saying, 'Don't worry, Mr Van Der Leyden, the dress is just for show. I won't bite,' and had placed one black-gloved hand on his arm with a great play of docility. At the table, he won a temporary respite as she turned away to talk to the man on her right. Teddy busied himself making agreeable conversation to Lady Tavistock who sat on his left, but he knew that when the mock turtle soup was finished, there would be no escape from Charlotte Beauchamp.

Lady Tavistock was not much interested in him once she had ascertained that Teddy was not a rich American. When he told her that he was an artist, she put on the brightly curious expression that she might have worn on visiting an institute for the blind.

'Oh, how fascinating. You know I have never actually met an artist before, not socially, I mean. Of course dear Duchess Cora has such a fondness for painters. I was at Bridgewater House when Louvain showed the portrait. Such a sensation.' She glanced to the end of the table where Cora was listening to the Prince of Wales and nodded. 'I am so glad to see her back again.'

Teddy did not fully understand the substance of her remarks but he guessed he did not need to. Lady Tavistock was much like one of his mother's cronies: women trained from birth to calibrate social standing. They would follow success like sunflowers tracing the arc of the day, but once the light and heat had gone, they were merciless. He felt a kind of guilty relief. In Paris he had imagined Cora to be invincible, and yet here she was subject to the scrutiny of women like Lady Tavistock.

He was still trying to make sense of the presence of Lady Beauchamp here at Lulworth. Did Cora know about her connection with her husband? He knew that liaisons with married women were commonplace in Paris and he supposed here too, but he could not imagine Cora complacently entertaining her husband's mistress. The idea of a rival would be quite foreign to her – she had been raised to be the prize, not the woman who pretended not to see.

He noticed that Odo Beauchamp, sitting opposite him, was drinking even faster than he was. Teddy wondered how much he knew about his wife and the Duke. From the way his eyes kept flicking between them, Teddy thought that he definitely had suspicions.

A footman came in carrying a silver contraption with a large screw at the side – Teddy thought it looked like a cider press – but from the excited murmurs around him he gathered that this was a meat press and that they were to be given *caneton à la Rouennaise*, a great delicacy much appreciated by the Prince. Teddy watched as the butler turned the screw of the device and collected the blood in a silver jug.

He heard Odo Beauchamp saying, 'The ducks are smothered, you know, so that none of the blood is lost.'

Teddy wondered if Cora, who had always mocked her mother's elaborate dinners, enjoyed all this pomp and spectacle. He remembered the phrase in her letter, 'I am still an American girl who sometimes misses the country of her birth.' He wondered again how much she knew about the currents of deception coursing around the table. She looked so radiant sitting there next to the Prince, yet Teddy felt a certain low satisfaction in knowing that Cora's life was not as perfect as the fabulous jewel that hung around her neck.

The footman was offering him a dish of the pressed duck in its bloody sauce. Teddy looked at the red liquid pooling on his plate and realised that Charlotte Beauchamp was speaking to him.

'So, Mr Van Der Leyden, Cora tells me you have known each other since childhood.' Her voice was low and she turned to look at him as if her entire future depended on his answer.

'New York is a great city but it can be quite small all the same. Cora and I have attended the same parties, picnics and dancing lessons since we were very young. I taught Cora how to ride a bicycle, she stopped me embarrassing myself at the Governor's Cotillion. We were partners in crime.'

'Indeed? Then I am surprised that you let her go so easily. It can be hard to give up your first accomplice.' She half lowered her eyelids and Teddy felt for a moment the intensity of the woman he had seen saying goodbye to her lover.

'Oh, Cora was always destined for greater things,' he said as lightly as he could. 'We always knew that her time with us mere mortals would be limited.' He let his eyes flicker towards the gauzy profile of Mrs Cash.

Charlotte understood him at once and leant over to murmur, 'She is quite regal, isn't she? I think the poor Prince feels quite upstaged.'

'Believe me, in New York Mrs Cash is considered a lightweight.' Charlotte laughed at this and the moment of intensity was gone.

Teddy had no doubt about the intimacy that had existed

between this woman and the Duke. The question in his mind now was whether it still continued. He was used to interpreting people through their body and the mass they displaced around them; there was a certain deliberateness to Charlotte's movements, from the way she picked up her wine glass to the graceful swerve of her shoulder that brought her round to face him, that made him think that she was not a woman who wavered in her feelings.

'I hope you are not tantalising my wife with an ocean-going steam yacht, Mr Van Der Leyden.' Teddy looked across the table at Odo Beauchamp whose shining rosy cheeks were at odds with the set of his narrow lips. 'You Americans with your extravagant toys make it very difficult for humdrum Englishmen like myself.' He lifted his glass and drained it, and Teddy noticed that his hand shook slightly as he put it down.

Teddy laughed. 'I am sorry to disappoint you, sir, but I have no steam yacht, railway line or even a motor car. I have nothing to tantalise your wife with beyond my limited powers of conversation.'

Odo subsided into his seat and Charlotte said, 'Besides, Odo, no one could describe you as humdrum.'

This remark evidently pleased her husband who shook his yellow curls as if to acknowledge the truth of her remark. But Teddy had seen the flash of jealousy and again he wondered about the woman sitting next to him. He could make out a scorpion embroidered on the red puff of her sleeve. He could not decide whether it was a warning or a mark of how often she herself had been stung.

Exactly one hour and fifteen minutes after they had sat down to dinner, Cora was preparing herself to catch her mother's good eye and give the signal that it was time for the ladies to withdraw, when she saw the Double Duchess rising in her seat, her eyes sweeping the room. Cora clenched her teeth; she could hardly believe that even her mother-in-law would make such a brazen play for power. But she knew that she must not let herself be provoked, so she said as sweetly as she could, 'Oh, Duchess Fanny, thank you so much for taking the lead. I was enjoying my conversation with His Royal Highness so much that I declare I would have sat here all night.' She stood up and was grateful for the good two inches she had over her mother-in-law. 'Ladies, shall we?'

The footmen stepped forward and the women got to their feet in a murmur of silk. The men stood. It fell to the Prince to escort Cora to the door as he was sitting on her right hand. As she went past he murmured, 'Are you waging another Amerrrican war of independence, Duchess?'

Cora looked at the fat old man whose eyes were lit up with malice.

'That depends, sir, on whether I have royal approval.'

The Prince swept his eyes over Cora and nodded imperceptibly. 'I have always thought that the New World would one day prevail.'

The men did not linger in the dining room but soon joined the ladies in the long gallery. Ivo came in last and Cora could tell from the stiff set of his shoulders and the lines around his mouth that her husband was not happy. She wondered what had happened when the ladies had retired.

After she had settled the Prince with a game of baccarat, she sought him out.

'I thought you might like to play the piano, Ivo,' and then lowering her voice she said, 'that way you won't have to talk to anyone.'

He nodded. 'Is it that obvious? I'm not sure I can stand Odo Beauchamp a moment longer. I don't care for him when he's sober, but when he's drunk, he's unspeakable. You're right, I shall play for a while until I can bring myself to look at him again.' He walked through the door into the music room.

Cora surveyed the room like a scout on a reconnaissance patrol, looking for signs of trouble. The Prince was happily playing baccarat with Mr Cash, his equerry Ferrers and the Double Duchess. Cora hoped that her father would realise that the point of the game was to put up a gallant fight before losing to the Prince. Teddy was looking at a portrait of the Fourth Duke with Father Oliver; her mother was sitting in another group with Charlotte, Odo and Lady Tavistock, and Reggie and Sybil were sitting in a corner pretending to play chess.

Cora went over to where her mother was sitting. Odo was talking about a play he had seen in London. With his bright red cheeks and round blue eyes, Cora thought that he looked rather like a doll she had once been fond of. He paused for a second and at that moment the piano started in the music room – a Chopin nocturne, Cora thought.

Odo turned towards the music, listening with his head to one side. 'Really, I had no idea that Maltravers was such a romantic, did you, Charlotte?' As he turned to his wife, Cora saw that he was swaying slightly and she realised that he was as drunk as her husband had said.

'He plays with expression, certainly.' Charlotte's tone was neutral.

'Oh, it's more than just expression, Charlotte. To hear him you would think he was a soul in torment.'

There was something in Odo's tone that Cora found unsettling.

'Oh, I hope not, Sir Odo,' she said. 'What kind of wife would that make me?' She laughed and turned to Charlotte. 'Charlotte, I am trying to get a bicycling party together for tomorrow. If it's fine I thought we might have lunch by the folly and those who were so minded could cycle there. What do you think?'

Charlotte shook her head. 'I must be the only woman in England who hasn't yet learnt how to ride a bicycle. Besides, I don't have suitable clothes.'

Cora was about to offer to lend her something when Odo said, 'But what about that charming costume you had as Joan of Arc? Just the thing for cycling. Such a shame that it was never revealed at Lady Salisbury's pageant. Everyone was so disappointed. Remind me again, Charlotte, why you didn't appear that day. What was it now – a headache? It was so bad you wouldn't even let me see you. And yet look at you now, radiant with health.' He took his wife's hand and raised it to his lips. 'There must be something in the Lulworth air that agrees with you.'

Cora saw Charlotte pull her hand away and brush it on her skirt to remove the imprint of his lips. She turned to Cora as if her husband had not spoken.

'If you can lend me something to wear, I will certainly try to conquer the bicycle. What about you, Lady Tavistock, Mrs Cash? Will you join me in my humiliation?'

Mrs Cash said, 'Oh, I learnt to ride a few years ago, but I think I shall leave it to you young people. There are too many hills around here for my liking.' Lady Tavistock nodded in agreement.

Odo leant forward. 'If you are riding, my dear, then I shall certainly be of the party.' Cora felt a damp spray of spittle on her cheek. 'I don't want you to disappear again. It's really quite a struggle,' he leant back to address the assembled company, 'to keep up with my wife.'

He had raised his voice and the challenge in it rang out across the room. Cora saw Teddy turn round and the card players look up. She knew that she must do something to contain the situation – her mother was glaring at her as if to say that it was her duty to take this in hand. Odo was swaying more obviously now, and he was clearly working up to another outburst. She glanced over at Charlotte but she was looking at the floor. This was a test of her mettle as a hostess, she was being watched to see how she would handle this.

She stepped forward and put her hand on Odo's arm, and said with all the charm she could muster, 'Well, there I have to agree with you, we all struggle to keep up with your wife. She is the standard we aspire to. Why, I am sure that in a matter of weeks we will all be wearing dresses that are crawling with insects, because where Charlotte Beauchamp leads, we can but follow. But now I want you to come with me, Sir Odo. We have a new statue in the summer house that I would love your opinion of, and yours too, Teddy. I would very much like to know what you two connoisseurs think of the Canova by moonlight.'

Odo looked reluctant but allowed himself to be led out of the room, Teddy following behind. Charlotte's eyes had not moved from the floor during this exchange. Now she raised her head and looked at Mrs Cash.

'Your daughter has so many accomplishments, Mrs Cash.'

Mrs Cash gave a regal nod. 'I like to think that I raised her so that she could handle any situation.'

The evening air was still warm, Cora could smell roses and the slight whiff of salt coming in from the sea. The moon was a day or two away from being full and lit up the white stone of the summer house. Cora waved away the footman holding a lantern.

'No, I think we should see this by moonlight.'

They walked down the gravel path, the stones scraping beneath their feet, loud in the still garden. Odo had subsided, he was silent until they stopped in front of the pavilion, which had a bell-shaped roof supported on six columns. Behind the dull stone of the pillars, Pysche was being revived by Eros's kiss, her naked torso stretching upwards to meet his lips. Cora had bought the statue from Duveen's sight unseen (after checking its provenance, of course). She had once heard Ivo admire a Canova statue in Venice and she thought it might please him. When it had emerged from the packing case, she had been surprised and faintly disturbed by Eros's muscular arms and the ecstatic arch of Psyche's back as she sought her lover's mouth. By day the statue was arresting but now in the silvery half-light it was unbearably intimate. The flickers of light on the sinuous marble curves made Cora feel as if she was trespassing on a moment of private rapture.

Odo stepped forward and ran his hand down Psyche's naked flank.

'Such a glorious finish, don't you agree, Mr Van Der Leyden? Almost as good as the real thing.'

'The technique, certainly, is faultless,' said Teddy carefully. He felt almost nervous standing in front of the statue with Cora. He knew that she had brought him down here as ballast against Odo but it was hard not to think of that other moonlit night in Newport when she had twisted her face up to his, Psyche to his Eros.

'I'm glad you approve, Sir Odo. I feel it works quite well here in the summer house,' Cora said, wishing that Odo would stop caressing the statue.

'I daresay Ivo likes it,' Odo said. 'There's a man who appreciates the female form.'

Teddy felt for his cigarette case. As he struck the match he saw the yellow flare in Odo's eyes.

'Oh Teddy, may I?' Cora looked at his cigarette.

'Of course, forgive me.' He offered her his case.

'My mother would be horrified if she could see this.' She leant forward into the flame and the emerald around her neck flickered. Teddy watched her put the cigarette to her lips.

'We won't tell her then, will we?' Teddy appealed to Odo. 'We can be depended on to keep a secret.' But Odo wouldn't look at him. He was resting his flushed cheek against the cool marble of Eros's wing.

Cora inhaled gratefully. 'Do you remember, Teddy, the Goelet party where the cigarettes were made out of hundred-dollar bills? Do you think many people actually smoked them?'

Teddy laughed. 'I certainly didn't. In fact, I don't think anyone did. All those Newport millionaires take money much too seriously to see it go up in smoke.'

'It seems vulgar now, doesn't it?' Cora said hesitantly. 'Although at the time I remember thinking it was rather smart.' She blew out a thin stream of smoke.

Teddy said, '*Autre temps, autre moeurs*. I find lots of things feel different over here.' He looked her straight in the eye. 'But there are a few things that feel just the same.'

Cora felt the meaning in his glance and frowned as if he had brought something difficult into her garden of delightful reminiscence. She tossed her cigarette on to the grass and ground it down with her foot.

'I must go in and check on the Prince,' she said.

Teddy watched her disappear into the house and he found that he was holding his breath.

'What a touching little scene.' Odo's voice startled him, and Teddy coughed on his cigarette. 'Sadly for you, the Duchess must be the only woman in England who is in love with her husband. Beautiful, rich and faithful, how foolish of you to let her get away.'

Teddy clenched his fist in his pocket. He knew he should not rise to the bait but he could not help himself saying, 'Funnily enough, I didn't want to be the husband of a fortune.'

'How very honourable of you.' Odo's tone was bitter. His hand was still stroking the Psyche's cool flank. 'I wish I could say the same of my wife. She was beautiful and I was rich. I thought it was a fair exchange, but Lady Beauchamp hasn't kept her side of the bargain. All she had to do was play the wife in public. I guessed, of course, that she had a *tendresse* for the Duke – but then everybody has a weakness, even me,' and he giggled. 'But she had to flaunt her feelings in public. I could have forgiven her everything but not that.'

Teddy lit another cigarette. He didn't offer one to Odo.

'So why have you come here?' he said. 'I would have thought this was the last place you wanted to be.'

'Too good an opportunity to resist, old boy. I knew it would come and here it is. My dear wife is not the only one who can behave badly in public. I intend to cause a nice little scene.' He giggled again and started to move towards the house.

Teddy, catching his meaning, put his hand out to grab the other man's arm but Odo was too quick for him. He darted behind the statue, and said, 'Don't try and stop me, it's really not in your interests to do so. Surely you must see that the sooner your old friend the Duchess knows what's going on under her nose, the sooner she will need the comfort of an "old friend".' Teddy tried to make another grab for him but Odo saw him coming and stepped behind a pillar. They were both very drunk but Teddy had been made clumsy by alcohol while Odo seemed to be quite surefooted. Teddy reached out again to catch his arm but Odo made a sudden movement away and Teddy fell to the ground, hitting his head. He lay on the ground stunned, his mouth tasting the granite. His thoughts and feelings were swirling around his head like quicksilver, unpredictable and reluctant to coalesce. He knew that he must act, that he should stop what was about to happen, but he found himself quite passive, his limbs relaxing into their stone bed, because somewhere he also knew, and hated himself for it, that Odo was right.

Cora surveyed the long gallery from the door. The Prince was still playing cards, Father Oliver was with her mother and Lady Tavistock, Sybil and Reggie had not moved – nor, it seemed, had their chess pieces – and Ivo was still playing in the music room. She wondered where Charlotte was – she wouldn't blame her for retiring to bed so that she could escape from Odo. She tried to imagine what their marriage could be like. Anyone could see they were not happy and yet when they were together they seemed so glittering and powerful that you could not bear to look away. She wondered what they talked about when they were alone. Clearly there must be something that bound them together, some affinity or more likely weakness that they shared. Cora had been shocked when Charlotte had confessed her contempt for her husband, but there was something even more disturbing about the way she was acting up to him tonight, as if they were playing a game, the rules of which only they knew. She shivered with unease as she walked down the gallery towards the music room. She wanted to see Ivo, to remind herself of her own good fortune.

He was playing something she didn't recognise, something fast and showy with cascades of notes. She walked into the music room and saw, rather to her surprise, that Charlotte was standing beside the piano. They were both facing away from Cora. As Ivo came to the end of a passage, Cora saw Charlotte lean across and turn the page of the music. She did this deftly, without fuss, and as far as Cora could see no look passed between her and Ivo, yet there was something in the intimacy of the movement, the antici- pation and answering of need without any apparent communica- tion, that troubled Cora more than any look could have done. She stood there in the doorway, trying not to put the dread she felt into words, trying to summon up the bright smile and the outstretched hand, trying to go back to the way she had felt a moment ago – when she felt a gust of hot breath on the back of her neck, and Odo's voice in her ear.

'They make such a lovely couple, don't they? It's as if they understand each other perfectly.'

Cora felt herself go rigid at this revelation of her own unspoken thought. She was about to move away when he went on, 'Such a pity really that you and I are here. So inconvenient.' Odo's voice was hardly louder than a whisper, but he was so close to her that it was impossible to pretend she had not heard.

She turned her head a little and said, 'Oh, but I'm not jealous, Sir Odo. Charlotte and Ivo are old friends. I could hardly expect him to discard all his acquaintances on my account. And besides, I like your wife too. Shouldn't a husband and wife share the same tastes?'

Odo said nothing and Cora waited. Waited for him to advance or retreat – she would not give him the opening, she would do nothing to invite the revelation that she sensed burning up those bright, fleshy cheeks. If he turned away now she would go on as if nothing had happened, pretend that she had never seen Charlotte lean over Ivo as if she owned him, or that Ivo had played on without looking up because he knew that Charlotte would turn the page at exactly the right moment. Cora fingered the emerald on her breast. She could do it, she thought. She would touch her husband on the shoulder and suggest that he played something from *La Belle Hélène* as the Prince was so partial of Offenbach; she would smile at them both without disturbing the surface, and the Prince would compliment her on a lovely evening and they would all go peacefully to bed. That is what she would do and she would not look back.

But then Charlotte leant over to turn another page and her lips half parted. Odo was breathing hard now, and Cora knew even as she saw herself sliding gracefully along the long gallery, a hostess in command of her troops, that he was about to shatter her elegant campaign and that she was glad of it.

He stepped back from her and turned his body so that his next remark could be heard by everyone in the long gallery.

'I don't think you would like my wife so much, Duchess, if you knew where she went on the day of Lady Salisbury's pageant. Slipping away like a bitch on heat to meet your husband at the docks. She didn't even bother to make up a credible excuse. Not that anyone would have believed it, as everybody knew where she'd gone. Perhaps I'm being unreasonable but I really think she could have waited till after the show.' Odo started quietly enough but as his rage overtook him, his voice became higher and louder. The music stopped and Cora felt the silence around her sting. She stared at the floor, she could not bear to look up and see the confirmation in their faces – that everyone knew about Charlotte Beauchamp and her husband, everyone, that was, except her.

And then, at last, the silence was broken.

'It's time you went to bed, Sir Odo. You can apologise in the morrrning, when you've sobered up.' The Prince's voice was thick with contempt. 'Now, Duchess Corrra, perrrhaps you would like to show me your Canova. I feel the need for some fresh air.'

Cora felt a hand on her arm and she looked up and saw that the Prince's pale blue eyes had lost their heavy-lidded indolence and were filled with something approaching concern. She swallowed and managed to say, 'Yes, it is a lovely evening, sir.'

The Prince smiled his approval and steered her down the gallery. She looked straight ahead, trying not to let her American smile falter. As they reached the door she heard the noise behind her swell.

On the steps they passed Teddy, who noticed the angry welts on Cora's chest, flaming red against the dark green gem. He realised that Odo must have made his 'nice little scene'. Cora's face was set, her mouth drawn back into a horrible imitation of a smile; she looked straight through him and she walked down the steps with the Prince as if she was made of glass. Teddy felt his palms go sweaty with guilt. He could have stopped Odo going back inside, he had had the chance and yet he had done nothing. He walked up the stairs into the gallery, trying not to think of Cora's brittle shoulders and that terrible smile. No one looked at him as he walked in, the company had formed into little clumps around the room; only Odo stood alone, bent over with his hands on his knees as if he had just been running. No one was speaking to him or even looking at him, he was like a prizefighter collapsed after losing a bout, his audience indifferent. Teddy hesitated for a moment. Then he caught sight of the Duke at the piano with Charlotte Beauchamp standing beside him. They were not looking at each other, it was as if they were enchanted, as if they were trapped there forever, waiting for the spell to break.

Teddy walked over to Odo and tapped him on the shoulder. Odo looked up at him, his cheeks scarlet, his blue eyes bloodshot, and when he saw Teddy he smiled.

'Too late, Mr Van Der Leyden, you've missed all the fun.'

The force of Teddy's punch sent Odo sprawling on the floor. When he picked himself up his nose was bloody but his smile was still there.

'I'm not sure what I did to deserve that. You should be grateful to me, old boy.'

Teddy reached back to hit him again, but he felt a hand on his arm. He saw it was the Duke's friend, Greatorex.

'Leave him, he's not worth it,' Reggie said. 'Besides, he's drunk. Wait till he's sober.'

Teddy allowed himself to be led away. He heard a woman say

in a low, commanding voice, 'Bugler, help Sir Odo to his room. He is feeling unwell.'

Bugler clicked his fingers and two footmen took Odo by the elbows and marched him the length of the gallery. Odo's smile did not falter for a second.

Teddy said, 'I tried to stop him, coming in, you know. Was it very bad?'

Reggie looked at him and said, 'Bad enough. Beauchamp is a cad.'

Teddy groaned. 'I should have punched him in the garden.'

'Perhaps, but it's not your quarrel, is it?' and Reggie glanced over at the Duke. Teddy followed his gaze and saw the Duke stand up and close the piano lid with a click. Ignoring Charlotte, who still stood with her back to the long gallery, he walked towards the company and looked across them with a mirthless smile.

'Well, I think that's enough entertainment for the evening, so if you will excuse me.' He made a half bow in the direction of Mrs Cash and the Double Duchess and walked down the gallery, his long strides striking the stone flags with metronomic precision.

Teddy looked at Charlotte Beauchamp's profile. How would she react, he wondered, to what had happened? In a moment, she turned and he had his answer – she was smiling and, unlike the Duke's, her smile appeared to be one of genuine delight.

She glided towards him. 'I confess I'm in your debt, Mr Van Der Leyden. I know I am being disloyal, but Odo deserved that. He has a shocking head for drink. I wouldn't mind if it made him maudlin, but he just gets nasty. Poor Cora. I shall make Odo grovel tomorrow, if he dares show his face, that is.' And she put her hand lightly on Teddy's arm to show that they were all connected whether they liked it or not.

Despite himself, Teddy was impressed by her bravura. He glanced over at Mrs Cash and the Double Duchess to see if they would challenge her, but both women looked relieved to see that order had been restored.

Teddy made a little bow to acknowledge his appreciation of her performance and signalled to the footman to bring him a drink. The man brought him a schooner of brandy. He was downing it when Mr Cash walked over to him.

'Well done, Teddy. That son-of-a-bitch got what was coming to him. Would have hit him myself, but my wife would never have forgiven me.' He shrugged to indicate his helplessness.

Teddy finished his brandy.

'It was my pleasure.' He looked at the older man's handsome, acquiescent face and he felt a wave of rage and scorn flood through him. They were all going to pretend that nothing had happened, they would leave the unpleasantness behind and go on serenely like swans sailing over filthy water. And Cora would have no choice but to swim with them, never looking down. He put down his glass but it missed the table and fell to the ground, shattering as it hit the stone floor.

He looked around at the faces that had turned to the source of the noise.

'I think I've had enough,' he said.

CHAPTER 26

'Never to Stoop'

THE NEWS OF ODO'S OUTBURST REACHED THE servants' hall before Cora and the Prince had got halfway to the summer house. The footman was so full of his news that he forgot to put down the heavy silver tray he was carrying and stood there holding it, laden with glasses, as he told them what had happened upstairs. The upper servants were taking their pudding in Mrs Softley's room so they missed the first telling but word soon reached them via the maid when she brought in the Madeira and sponge cake.

'. . . And the new Duchess was standing there the whole time until His Highness came and took her away into the garden. What do you think will happen, Mrs Softley?' the girl said breathlessly.

The housekeeper finished pouring the Madeira into small cutwork glasses.

'That's enough, Mabel. You know I won't tolerate gossip in the servants' hall. Get back to your work.' But when Mabel disappeared, she said, 'Well, I have always said that Sir Odo Beauchamp was a bad lot. She should never have married him. Men like that never get any better.' She looked across at Bertha who was sitting next to Lady Beauchamp's maid.

'You had better go upstairs, Miss Jackson, and you too, Miss Beauchamp. I have some sal volatile in my cupboard if you need it.'

Bertha got up reluctantly, she knew she was being dismissed so that the Lulworth servants could talk about this freely. She tried to catch Jim's eye. But he was looking at his hands, his jaw set. She walked out as slowly as she could but still he did not look up. She lingered in the corridor, telling the other maid that she needed to fetch a new nightgown from the laundry room. She could see the long panel of bells above the door; when Miss Cora rang she would go up, but she wanted to talk to Jim first.

At last he came walking along the corridor with Bugler. Cora thought that the butler was bound to see her but he stopped at the pantry and went inside. As Jim came past the laundry, Bertha caught him by the arm, and he pulled her to him and kissed her. She tried to push him away, but as always she felt the urge to hold him closer.

'Not now, Jim. Not here.'

Jim said, 'So when then, Miss Bertha Jackson? We live in the same house and yet for all I see of you, I could still be in India.' He spoke lightly, but she could hear the frustration in his voice. It had been exciting to begin with: the stolen kisses and hurried embraces in empty corridors, but it could not go on much longer. Jim had not talked of marriage since he had come home, and though Bertha wanted him, she was not prepared to risk her job without at least the prospect of a ring.

'You didn't look at me in there, Jim. Does that mean you knew about the Duke and Lady Beauchamp?'

Jim said nothing and Bertha knew she had her answer. 'But why didn't you tell me? I should have known. I could have . . .' She stopped.

'You could have done nothing, Bertha, and that's the truth. That's why I didn't tell you. What they do upstairs is their business. You don't want to interfere. Anyway, there was nothing to stop you figuring it out for yourself. The only reason you didn't is that you take Miss Cora's side on everything. She's a foreigner, Bertha, and the Duke likes things that are home-grown.'

Bertha began to feel angry. 'What, and that makes carrying on behind Miss Cora's back with that woman all right?' She pushed at him with her hand. 'I'm a foreigner too, remember.'

Jim took her hand. 'Don't take it that way, Bertha. You will never be foreign to me.'

Mollified, she left her hand in his.

'Poor Miss Cora, this is going to be mighty hard on her. She thought she had it all figured out.'

Jim said, 'I don't know that anyone could figure out the Duke. One minute he's throwing shaving water at me because it's cold, next thing he's giving me twenty guineas to get some new clothes. Some days he treats me like dirt, won't say a civil word, and then he'll be as charming as you like, wants to know if I have a sweetheart, if I intend to see out my days in service. There were days on the boat going out when I would have gladly jumped off and swum home – if I'd known how to swim, that is,' he laughed. 'Coming back wasn't so bad, I think he was looking forward to getting home. One thing I do know, he wasn't expecting to see Lady Beauchamp right away. We'd only just got to the club when she sent a note up for him. He looked pretty put out, and threw it on the floor.'

'How did you know the note was from Lady Beauchamp? Did he tell you?'

'Not likely! No, I picked it up after he'd gone and then I saw it was from her. It just said, "I'm waiting for you," signed with a C.'

'But how did you know it was Lady Beauchamp? C could have stood for Cora,' Bertha said.

'It was on plain writing paper, no crest, nothing. And why would the Duchess not sign her name? Anyway, I knew it was from *her*. She came to say goodbye to him before we left for the wedding in America. Rode in the carriage with him all the way to the station. Looked like she was going to a funeral.' A bell began to ring. Bertha looked up from Jim's shoulder and saw that it was the bell for the Duchess's room.

'It's Miss Cora, I must go.' She started to move away from him but Jim held her hand.

'We should leave soon, Bertha. Take our chances. Before it's too late.'

Bertha met his eyes, but then the bell rang again, and she heard footsteps coming down the hall.

She wondered if that had been a proposal. 'I'll need to get my trousseau together first,' she said smiling.

His eyes widened in understanding and he was about to speak when the bell rang and they heard Bugler's door open. 'Later,' Bertha said.

In her bedroom Cora was pacing round the furniture, tearing at the necklace round her neck. The clasp had got caught in her hair and she was desperate to get it off. She gave it one last tug and the necklace exploded, scattering diamonds across the room. Bertha opened the door, and Cora shouted at her, 'Where've you been?

Look what's happened, I couldn't get it off by myself.' Cora knew she was being unreasonable but she was so angry that she had to yell at someone.

Bertha started to pick up the sparkling debris. 'Don't worry, Miss Cora, it shouldn't be too difficult to mend.'

'Oh, just leave it, get me out of this infernal dress.' Cora twitched furiously in the golden brocade. Bertha got up slowly, her movements a reproach. She set down the gems on the dressing table with a clatter, taking a moment to shape them into a neat pile.

Cora screamed with impatience. She felt as if there were ants crawling all over her body. But when, at last, Bertha untied the strings of her corset, her skin felt cold and clammy. She looked at herself in the glass. There were two red smudges on her cheekbones but her lips were pale. She felt herself shivering, all the heat and irritation that had possessed her a few minutes ago had left her and now she felt cold and so weary. She wanted to lie down, close her eyes and obliterate everything that had just passed. She thought of the Prince carefully guiding her round the garden, telling her again about the time he had seen Blondin walk across the Niagara Falls on a tightrope. 'Such a little man, I thought he might be blown away by the sprrray. I confess I had to close my eyes several times.' The Prince had stopped to admire the Canova. 'He was prrresented to me afterwards. He was very composed, as if he had been for a walk in the park. I asked him what his trrrick was, and he said the most important thing was always to look forward and concentrate on the next step and never look down. He was so earnest when he spoke, as if he was passing on a secret. I meet so many people who tell me things but I have never forgotten him.' He paused. 'A fine statue, Duchess, you Amerrricans have such style.' He did not mention Odo's outburst in the gallery but

Cora understood that he had, nonetheless, been giving her advice.

Cora heard the door open. She knew it was Ivo, anyone else would have knocked. She looked up and saw to her amazement that he was smiling. He looked completely at ease as if this was the end to a perfect evening

'So this is where you are hiding. I was beginning to wonder if the Prince had carried you off.' His tone was bantering. 'You really are quite the hostess, darling. No one could complain of boredom at one of your parties.'

Their eyes met. He smiled at her equably; his eyes too dark for her to read. She had the satisfaction of seeing him take in the sparkling rubble of her necklace lying on the dressing table and flinch.

'I don't want to talk to you,' she said quietly. 'Not now, at any rate, not until after the christening.'

Ivo stepped towards her and bent down to put his face at her level, as if he was addressing a child. His smile did not falter.

'Don't tell me you're sulking, Cora. So unlike you. Surely you're not taking Odo's outburst seriously. Everybody knows he lives to make trouble. Most people won't have him in the house, but I seem to remember that it was *you* who insisted on having the Beauchamps to stay.' He shrugged.

Cora took a step back. 'What happened tonight was hardly my fault,' she said angrily.

'Did you know that your American friend knocked Odo down, after you left? Quite a lot of spectres at this particular feast, I'd say.' He was still smiling, but Cora could see that a muscle in his jaw was twitching.

Bertha, who had been standing behind the wardrobe, unseen by Ivo, decided she must make her presence known before the conversation went any further. She coughed and came out with Cora's nightdress and wrapper and laid them on the bed. She tried to keep her expression blank as if she had heard nothing.

'Will that be all, Your Grace?' she said meekly to Cora as she made for the door.

Cora put out her hand to stop her.

'No, I'd like you to stay.' She turned to Ivo. 'The Duke was just leaving.' She wondered if he would protest but he continued to smile, as if nothing was wrong.

'Of course, you will need all your strength for tomorrow. Sleep well, Cora,' and he turned and left them, closing the door behind him softly.

Cora sank back on to the bed. She could not understand what was happening. Ivo was behaving as if nothing had taken place, that if anyone was at fault, it was her. This made her angry but also hopeful. Would Ivo dare to be angry with her if Odo's accusations were true? But then she remembered, almost against her will, Ivo and Charlotte at the piano and the space between them, thick with intimacy. She started to feel cold again and she pulled the wrapper around her. Ivo and she had been so close since his return. All the misunderstandings that had flawed the first days of their marriage seemed to have disappeared. Did Odo's outburst mean that all that closeness had been a lie? Who was she to believe?

Bertha saw Cora huddled on the bed, her hands twisting themselves into a lattice of anxiety. She could see the bewilderment on her mistress's face and she wondered if she should tell her what she knew about the Duke and Lady Beauchamp. But she heard Jim's voice saying, 'It's not our business, Bertha,' and she hesitated.

'You look cold, Miss Cora. Would you like some hot milk?'

Cora looked up gratefully. 'Yes, thank you, Bertha, that would be nice,' and she lay back among the drifts of pillows and closed her eyes.

When Bertha went into the servants' hall, the room fell silent.

'Some hot milk for the Duchess, please,' Bertha asked one of the kitchen maids who was looking at her with round guilty eyes. As the girl scuttled off to get the milk from the dairy, Bertha looked up at a silver cup that stood on a high shelf. Every year there was a cricket match between the house and the village. This year the house had won. Bertha had found the game quite baffling but she had enjoyed watching Jim running down the pitch, his sleeves rolled up, his long arms strong, and she had felt warm with pride when something he did provoked applause. She could not imagine such a scene at home, the masters and the servants on the same team. Then she looked down at the faces surveying her curiously, hungry for scraps about the American Duchess; this was her home now, she thought, but she belonged here as little as she had in Newport. She was always the outsider, the stranger who stopped the flow of conversation, who made people feel uncomfortable. She remembered the cabin where she had grown up but there, too, she knew she would be a stranger with her silk dress and her fancy accent.

She deliberately kept her eyes fixed on the cup until the milk was brought to her by the kitchen maid. She took the tray up the back stairs to the Duchess's bedroom, hoping to see Jim, but no one was about. As she walked along the passage that led to Miss Cora's room, she heard a door shut and a flash of red at the other end. Bertha started. Had Lady Beauchamp really been to see Miss Cora? After all that had happened? She hurried towards the bedroom as fast as the hot milk would allow her and opened the door. But her alarm had been unnecessary, Cora was fast asleep, her face slack, her arms outstretched. Bertha thought she looked hardly a day older than the girl who had asked her for kissing lessons. She put the milk down and pulled the covers around her mistress, tucking her into a linen cocoon. She pushed a strand of hair out of Cora's face.

The room was dark but there was a sliver of moonlight coming in through the gap in the curtains. Cora opened her eyes reluctantly, she did not want to be awake now when everything was still and quiet. She had wanted to sleep through till morning when the bustle and urgency of the day would drive all her thoughts into a small manageable corner of her brain. But she was fully conscious now, her head humming with all the images of the evening before – Charlotte leaning over to turn the page of music, Odo whispering in her ear, the Prince's touch on her arm, Ivo's defiant smile and his opaque eyes. She got up and lit the lamp by her bedside. She pulled on her wrapper – she would go to the nursery. She wanted to feel Guy's small warm body and smell his soft downy head. Her son, at least, was certain.

The nursery smelt of eucalyptus and baby. Cora walked in and put down her lamp. She could hear Guy snuffling in his golden crib. Through the nursery door she could make out the deeper rumbling snores of the nanny. She went over to Guy and picked him up, cradling him against her chest. She tried to think of nothing but the sweet smell of his scalp and the tiny arpeggios of his breathing. But she could not obliterate the image of Charlotte reaching over to turn the page of music. She remembered the way the Double Duchess had looked after Odo's outburst, not shocked or surprised but assessing, as if she were calculating the damage.

Cora held the baby a little closer as she thought how everyone must have known except her. She found the thought of her ignorance almost as distressing as the thought of Ivo's treachery. She felt like a sapling that had begun to put down roots, pushing into the soil for stability and nurture, only to meet with emptiness. She thought of the servants, Sybil, even Mrs Wyndham – had they all known that her husband loved another woman? Had they all smiled and smoothed things over so that Ivo could marry the fortune that had fallen so conveniently at his feet that day in Paradise Wood?

And then she thought of Charlotte, her 'friend', the only woman in London whose wardrobe she envied. She had thought that they were equals – in looks, clothes and position. They had caught each other's eye over the drabness. Had Charlotte been pretending all along? She remembered standing in another room in darkness the night before her wedding, and the note she had found in the dressing case. 'May your marriage be as happy as mine has been.' Even then, she had known the note to be malign and she had destroyed it. She thought back for other signs that she had ignored. Was her ignorance her own fault?

The baby made a shuddering squeak and Cora realised that she was holding him too tightly. She tried to relax her grip and walked over to the window and pulled back the curtain. The moon was over the sea now. She could see the bell-shaped shadow of the summer house stretched out across the silvery lawn. The metal spire sent a long thin stripe like a tightrope over the grass. But could she go forward like Blondin, never looking down?

And then she felt a hand on her shoulder, a breath in her ear. She turned round. Ivo's face was in shadow but she heard him say, 'I told you, Cora, I have everything I want.' And even though she could not see his eyes, she heard the plea in his voice and she could not resist it. She let him put his arms round her and Guy and leant into him as he kissed her hair and her forehead. This was all she wanted too.

CHAPTER 27

'Then all Smiles Stopped'

THE FIRST THING TEDDY FELT WHEN HE WOKE that morning was the throbbing in his right hand, from where his knuckles had met Odo Beauchamp's nose. But the warm pulse of pain was followed by a blush of shame. He did not regret hitting Odo, the man had deserved it, but he knew now that what had seemed noble the night before was, on reflection, quite selfish. He had failed to stop Odo from making his horrible revelation and had assuaged his guilt with violence. He thought of what his mother would say if she knew that he was knocking English baronets about. She would be embarrassed by his lack of self-control but she would be horrified by the emotions behind it. As Teddy tried to stretch out his bruised fingers, he knew that the man he had wanted to hit was not his actual victim but the Duke himself.

The door opened and a footman came in with hot water and towels. He set Teddy's shaving things out in front of the mirror. When Teddy walked over, the footman saw his hand and winced sympathetically.

'Would you like me to get some ointment for that, sir? It looks nasty.'

Teddy understood from the man's knowing look that he had been in the gallery last night.

'Yes,' he said ruefully, 'it is surprisingly painful.'

The footman took this admission as an invitation and continued, 'Never mind, sir, you should see the other fellow! His valet was up and down all night with beefsteak and ice. And then this morning he had to get him all packed up as Sir Odo is leaving on the morning train. He has to go and see a doctor in London, thinks his nose is broken.' From the smile on the footman's face, Sir Odo's injury was clearly a popular one.

Teddy said, 'I didn't realise I'd hit him that hard.'

'Not sure you did, sir. But maybe he thought he wouldn't be welcome any longer.' The footman glanced at Teddy to see if he would be reproved for gossiping, and then he handed him the razor. 'It's Lady Beauchamp I feel sorry for. Whatever she's done, it would be purgatory to be married to a man like that. My cousin was a housemaid there and the stories she told were shocking and I've been in service fifteen years.'

Teddy would have liked to ask what Sir Odo was guilty of, but he was in the middle of shaving and could not speak.

'She said it was a terrible place. Even though the pay was good, she gave in her notice after six months.'

The footman handed Teddy a towel.

'Are you joining the cycling party, sir? Will you be wearing the blazer?'

Teddy nodded.

The footman laid out his clothes and said, 'Is that all, sir?'

Teddy felt in his pockets for a coin and held it out to him.

'That's very kind of you, sir, but I couldn't take it. Reckon you did us all a favour there, punching Sir Odious.'

Teddy took his time getting dressed. Odo Beauchamp might have left but he had no desire to see the Duke at breakfast. He now regretted the impulse which had made him write to Cora and to accept her invitation. He would have done better leaving her alone. He had had his chance in Newport and he had not taken it. She had not replied to the letter he had written to her before her wedding, but it had been too late to tell her then that he loved her. If only he hadn't been so squeamish about the encounter he had witnessed at Euston Station, that would have been useful information for Cora, not some redundant declaration of love. But he had not wanted to get his hands dirty, he had half hoped that Cora would renounce her Duke and confound her mother because he, Teddy, had finally made up his mind that he loved her. And now he was faced with the consequences of his own delicacy: Cora had married a man whose real nature she did not know and, worse still, she had married for love. Teddy remembered the way her face had changed when he went to see her in New York, how she had lost her glorious selfish certainty. And he had seen in the brittle set of her shoulders last night just how much Odo's revelations must have hurt her. He could have warned her. But he had not been interested in protecting Cora then, he had just wanted her to choose him.

He looked out of the window at the water garden on the terrace below, with its statues and fountains. The evening before he had heard Lady Tavistock say to the Double Duchess as she surveyed the glittering parterre, 'So glorious now. Say what you like, Fanny, there are uses for American heiresses and their money after all.'

Had Cora realised, he wondered, exactly what sort of bargain she had made? He was sure not.

And now? Now that she knew what kind of man she had married, how would she proceed? Would she carry on, happy enough with the title her money had bought? Through the window, Teddy saw a man scrubbing one of the fountains, scraping off the slimy legacy of the spring rains. Teddy felt angry on Cora's behalf; she had been deceived so that the marble fountains of Lulworth could be scrubbed clean. She was, he thought, worth a great deal more than that. He could not offer her all this, this panoply of fountains and balustrades and princes, but his feelings for her were at least straightforward: he loved the woman, not the heiress. He could give her a way out. The scandal would be immense for both of them. He would surely have to abandon his commission from the New York Public Library but that was proof of his love. He had given her up before because of his art, now he told himself that he would put Cora first.

Yes, he thought, he would act. The world might be shocked that he would offer his love to a married woman but he did not care for that. He dismissed the thought of his mother's hooded blue eyes and the pious rectitude of her Washington Square friends. He was not an opportunist or an adulterer but a man who would sacrifice everything to rescue the woman he loved.

He caught sight of himself in the mirror and smiled at his own look of resolution. Then he set off down the stairs to join the cycling party.

The Prince of Wales was the first to cycle down the gravel path. His balance was unsteady but he managed to round the first corner without incident. No one dared smile at the portly figure as he wobbled off, he was so sensitive about his weight that anyone who hoped to remain in his favour had to pretend to see the slim young man that the Prince still imagined himself to be. The Prince's equerry Colonel Ferrers rode off next at a pace calculated not to challenge his royal master. Sybil and Reggie followed, Reggie riding close to Sybil, ostensibly in case of accidents. Cora and Teddy were the last in the party as the older ladies had declined to risk their dignity, Charlotte Beauchamp had not yet appeared and Ivo claimed that he had business on the estate.

Cora pushed off quickly. She could see that Teddy wanted to talk to her about last night and she was reluctant to do so. She could still feel Ivo's arm round her when she had greeted her guests that morning, which had allowed her to keep her smile radiant when confronted by so many curious faces. She had ignored all their unspoken questions and had outlined the day's plans as if nothing had happened. Her mother had nodded at her approvingly and even the Double Duchess had given her a gracious incline of the head. But Cora knew that her self-command was fragile, she could not afford to look down. She saw that Teddy was struggling to contain his emotions and she tried to head him off with her best Duchess manner.

'It is such a treat to see you again, Teddy. I am so glad that you are going to be Guy's godfather, I don't want him to be completely British. Don't worry about the ceremony, it will be very simple. The Catholic ritual is pretty much the same as the Episcopalian one.'

Teddy did not reply for a moment and then he said, 'It's not the ceremony I am worried about.'

Cora speeded up a little and pebbles flew out from under her wheels.

Teddy kept pace with her.

At last she said in irritation, the Duchess manner abandoned, 'You only made it worse last night, hitting Odo Beauchamp. I know you meant well, but can't you see that it makes things . . . awkward?' Teddy noticed that Cora was beginning to pick up a British accent. 'I know that inviting Odo was a mistake but I did want Charlotte to be here. She is my particular friend, you see.' Cora slowed down a little, she did not want to get too close to the others.

'Really? What if I were to tell you that she is the last person who deserves your friendship?'

Cora pumped her brakes and stopped with a skid of gravel. She looked at him seriously. 'I would ignore you. Charlotte has not been fortunate in her choice of husband but that doesn't mean that she shouldn't have friends.'

Teddy was annoyed by Cora's composure. This was not the scene he had imagined. He had thought that Cora would be heartbroken by last night's revelations, distraught over her husband's betrayal, but instead she seemed to be blaming *him* for causing a scene. Had she really become part of this British world which seemed to him like a smooth sea on an unlit night, the calm surface concealing the strong currents beneath. He decided to plunge, and putting one hand on Cora's wrist he said, 'Are you just going to ignore the fact that your husband is Charlotte Beauchamp's lover?'

Cora took her hand away and replied boldly, 'And how would you know that, Teddy? You have known my husband and Charlotte Beauchamp for less than a day. If I choose to believe there is nothing between them, how can you possibly say otherwise?'

The sun came out from behind a cloud and Cora had to squint to see him properly. Teddy had never seen her look so plain, her eyes screwed up and her face mottled with anger, her figure hidden in those ridiculous cycling bloomers; but he found this sudden ugliness more endearing than the perfectly dressed woman he had seen last night.

'I have no *right* to say anything. Except for the fact that I care for you and I cannot bear to see you deceived.'

They were both silent for a moment. Cora took a deep breath and resumed her Duchess manner. 'The Prince will be at the picnic tent by now, we should catch up with him, otherwise Mother will be arranging a royal visit to Newport.' She made a show of getting on her bicycle. But Teddy pulled her round to face him. Cora tried to evade him but he held on to her so that she had to listen to him.

'No, Cora, I can't let you pretend that nothing has happened. You are not a girl who can live in the shadows. You deserve to be surrounded by truth and light. Your husband and Lady Beauchamp have lied to you all along. I *saw* them together at Euston Station before he came over for your wedding. I didn't know who they were then, of course, but it made such an impression on me that when I saw Lady Beauchamp last night, I recognised her at once.'

Cora was shaking her hands in front of her in a gesture he remembered. It was as if she was trying to bat away unpleasantness. 'I don't understand you. Why are you doing this?' And he could see that she was blinking fast.

'Because I love you, Cora.' He said it quietly and for a moment he thought she hadn't heard him. 'I *know* you and I love you. I came here ready to be your friend and nothing more but now I see your true situation, the way you have been deceived – all these . . . these vultures hovering around you wanting your money – I have to speak out. This isn't the life you should have, Cora, pandering to princes and worrying whether one raddled old duchess should walk in front of another. None of them *do* anything, except shoot things and gossip. Of course the houses are beautiful and everyone has perfect manners, but how can you live like this in a world built on lies?'

Cora had turned her head away from him but he knew she was listening. He thought briefly of his mother and how disappointed she would be by this squandering of emotion, he felt a flicker of regret for the respectable career he might have as a painter in New York, but with Cora in front of him he had no choice but to press on.

'Cora, come away with me. I love *you*, not your money or anything else. We could have a life with no lies, no subterfuge, where we could be open and honest with each other. We could live in France or Italy among people who don't care about duchesses and rules. You used to care for me once, Cora; I can't believe all that feeling has gone.'

At last she turned her head to look at him. 'Feeling? I wanted to marry you, Teddy, but you were scared. And now it's too late.'

He began to protest but her face was fierce.

'No more, please!' But he was pleased to see that there was a tear escaping from the corner of one eye. She had heard him, he thought.

Then she shook her head and said, 'We must catch up with the Prince. He does not like to be kept waiting.'

And she pedalled away from him, her front wheel jerking from side to side as if she were not quite able to balance. Teddy followed behind her.

Lunch had been laid out in the shade of two beech trees. The white tablecloth was overlaid with the lacy shadows of the leaves. The meal was to be served in a tented pavilion which Cora had ordered from London. She knew that the Prince would not consider dining al fresco, an excuse for inferior food. In the tent there was a barrel of oysters in ice, lobsters, caviar, tureens of vichyssoise, lark tongues in aspic, game pies, salmagundi, a variety of ice creams and a spirit stove for making soufflé omelettes; and to drink there was champagne, hock, claret, sauternes and brandy as well as iced tea and lemon barley water. Cora hoped that there was sufficient ice; in Newport the sun had been so strong in the summer that meals like these would always end up lukewarm in a pool of water. At least the weather here was more temperate. She found that if she concentrated very hard on the details of the meal, trying to remember exactly what she had ordered, she could keep out the other thoughts that were trying to push in. Teddy might dismiss this life as trivial but right now all she wanted was to get through this day, she wanted there to be enough ice and no silences. This lunch, after all, was under her control.

The Prince was already sitting down with Lady Tavistock. Her mother, to Cora's relief, was being expertly charmed by the Prince's equerry. Duchess Fanny was flirting with her father, although the odd flick of her eyes suggested that she was keeping the Prince under surveillance. Reggie was giving Sybil some cycling 'tuition' which involved running alongside while she pedalled, his arm firmly round her waist. Father Oliver was sitting back in his chair, his eyes half closed, although Cora suspected that he was listening intently to the conversations around him. She saw Teddy pull up a chair close to him.

Ivo must be on his way. She tried to make out the tiny jewelled hands of her wrist watch: it was nearly one o'clock. When he had left her this morning he had promised he would be here in good time. 'Don't worry, Duchess Cora, I will be present and correct.' She didn't like it usually when he called her Duchess Cora with that ironic glint in his eye, she suspected that he was comparing her to his mother, but that morning she had not minded the connection so much. She peered across the green swell of the park for him; she hoped no one could see her screwing up her nose so that her short-sighted eyes could focus. She thought she could see something moving in the middle distance but she didn't dare stand there for much longer with her face twisted up like a gargoyle. Bugler was standing a few feet away and she waved him over.

'Is that the Duke coming down from the house?'

Bugler nodded and then said, 'He has a lady with him, Your Grace. I can't be certain at this distance but I would say it was Lady Beauchamp.' He permitted himself a flicker of a smile. 'I will make sure there is another place set.'

Cora stared at the figures approaching across the green turf. As they came into focus she could see that Charlotte was wearing white and was carrying a pink parasol in one hand, the other was resting on Ivo's arm. Cora could not see their faces but she fancied they were not talking. She knew she should move but she found their progress towards her mesmerising. It was so deliberate, so steady.

She heard a cough behind her. It was Colonel Ferrers.

'I believe, Duchess, that the Prince is getting hungry.'

Cora started. 'Of course, how thoughtless of me.' She signalled to Bugler to start serving and approached the Prince.

'Forgive me, sir, for keeping you waiting. I would curtsy in apology but I think I would look very comical doing so in this costume. As you can see, the Duke and Lady Beauchamp are on their way over here, but we shall punish them for their tardiness by starting immediately.' She started to direct the company around the table, placing her mother next to the Prince and Teddy next to Sybil. She sat at the head of the table with the Prince on one side and Reggie on the other. Reggie needed no attention and the Prince would be in thrall to her mother; Cora wanted to be able to observe the table without having to talk. She felt numb. This morning she had felt quite sure of Ivo and now he was testing her faith again.

Ivo made a little bow to the table when he arrived. 'What a wonderful sight. I feel as if I have stumbled upon an oasis in the desert. As I have had nothing to do with this, I can say that this is quite magnificent. I always thought that eating outside involved sand and midges. Cora, it never ceases to amaze me how comfortable you Americans insist life should be.'

Cora tilted her head towards her mother. She did not quite trust herself to speak.

'Well, it's true that in my country we see no reason to suffer,' Mrs Cash said, delighted to have a conversational opening. 'In my view there is no excuse for inconvenience if a little thought and planning is exercised ahead of time. At home I ensure that all the picnics and bicycle parties are as well appointed as if they were taking place at Sans Souci. There really is no reason for anyone to be too cold or too hot or uncomfortable in any way. I am quite a martinet in these matters, I daresay, but my guests are always grateful.' She smiled warmly at the Prince. 'I hope we can tempt you back to the United States before too long, Your Highness. We have entertained quite a few members of European royalty. The Grand Duke Alexander of Russia, and the Crown Prince of Prussia among them. I think if Your Highness were to come we could guarantee your comfort.'

The Prince took a large helping of caviar before replying. 'I have no doubt of that, Mrs Cash. I have always thought that Amerrricans were the most hospitable people, at home and abroad. Indeed I think that Amerrrican hostesses like your daughter have done so much to lift the spirits of society. I know when I go to a party given by an Amerrrican hostess that the food will be delicious, the atmosphere warm, the women will be the last word in fashion and the caviar plentiful.' He smiled greedily, his small blue eyes taking in both Mrs Cash's pleasure and the Double Duchess's rage at this speech. 'But sadly, I won't be able to visit Amerrrica in the foreseeable future. The Queen is, thank God, in good health, but I am aware that I may be called upon at any time.' The Prince looked solemn and Ferrers, sensing a change in the royal mood, asked Mrs Cash if she knew anything of the new electric motor cars.

Cora had gathered herself after the shock of seeing Ivo arrive with Charlotte. She tried to dismiss Odo's outburst and Teddy's revelation from her mind. Ivo must, she reasoned, have brought Charlotte deliberately. It was his riposte to last night. There could be no gossip if he was willing to escort Charlotte in public in front of his wife. Accordingly, she smiled at Charlotte, who said, 'I'm afraid I have lost Odo. He had urgent business to attend to in town. He was full of apologies and he insisted that I stay on for the christening. I hope that doesn't throw out your numbers too much.'

Cora hardly heard Charlotte's words, she was struck by how well the other woman looked. Her customary sullen languor had been replaced by a new vigour. She was, again, the woman that Louvain had painted as a beautiful predator.

'I think we can manage. I am sure that Duchess Fanny will happily go in to dinner with Lady Tavistock.' They both laughed and Cora felt that she had done well until she saw Teddy looking at her. She felt a dull ache beginning at the base of her skull.

After lunch Cora decided to go back to the house in the donkey trap. She did not want another tête-à-tête with Teddy and she needed time to prepare herself for the christening. Rather to her surprise she found her mother-in-law being helped on to the seat beside her. Ivo had sent round the barouche landau for the other ladies and Cora had hoped to ride back alone. But the Double Duchess had insisted on Mr Cash riding with his wife and had protested that a ride in the donkey trap would remind her of 'the old days' when she had spent many happy hours wandering around the grounds.

Cora set off in silence. Her head was too full to make conversation with Duchess Fanny.

'This takes me back to my years at Lulworth,' said the Duchess. 'I was so happy here.' She sighed wistfully and Cora responded by giving the donkey a hard tap from her switch. Duchess Fanny continued in her most soothing tones, 'When I first met you, Cora, I have to confess I wondered if you understood what it meant to be mistress of Lulworth. I thought you were too head-strong, too used to your own way to appreciate the sacrifices that would be demanded of you. Ivo is not an easy man and I suspected you wouldn't have the patience to deal with him. I thought that an English girl would understand better what would be required. But it seems that I was wrong. Not many women would have dealt with Charlotte Beauchamp so calmly. You didn't let your own feelings get in the way.'

Cora looked at the flies hovering around the donkey's head and the steady rhythm of its flanks moving in the harness.

'But if I may give you some advice, it is time for you to speak to Charlotte. You must make it clear to her that you will not tolerate such flagrant behaviour. Tell her that you have the Prince's support and mine and that if she and her awful husband cannot be discreet, she will find herself friendless. I think she will understand.' Duchess Fanny put her hand on Cora's arm. 'And don't worry, Ivo won't interfere. He seems quite uxorious now that you have given him a son. After all, women like Charlotte are so exhausting.'

Cora tugged on the reins and pulled the donkey to a grumbling stop.

'Thank you for the advice, Duchess Fanny, but I prefer to handle things in my own way.' She handed the reins to the Duchess. 'I believe I am going to get out and walk now. I am sure you will remember how to manage the donkey.'

She jumped down from the cart and walked away as fast as she could until she could no longer see the cart or the Double Duchess's look of surprise. She sat down on the grass for a moment and put her head between her knees.

When at last, raising her head, she caught a glimpse of the sea filling the gap in the hills, she felt a sudden longing to throw herself into the water and swim free of all the weight that was being piled upon her. But when she looked in the other direction she could see the royal standard flying above the house and hear the chapel clock striking the half hour. The nurse would be dressing Guy in his christening robe now, swathing his wriggling body in the yellowing lace. Guy was part of this too. Soon they would all be gathering round the font in the chapel; the only thing she could do now was to go back, get dressed and smile while they christened her son. She would not look down, not yet.

CHAPTER 28

'The Dropping of the Daylight'

CORA HAD CONSIDERED EVERY DETAIL OF THE christening, from the flowers in the chapel to the white and silver bonbonnières, but she had not given much thought to the ceremony itself. Normally she found herself becoming slightly impatient in church, wishing the repetition and the ritual would go more quickly so that she could be somewhere else. But today, as she stood by the font, she was grateful for the ceremony that demanded nothing from her but a silent nod of the head. She heard the baby's baptismal name read out, 'Albert Edward Guy Winthrop Maltravers'. She had protested about the Albert, but the Double Duchess had told her, 'If you want the Prince of Wales to act as sponsor you will have to name the baby after him. You don't have to call him that; even the Prince doesn't care for the name Albert, but it is a mark of respect.' Cora looked over at the line of godparents: the Prince of Wales very loud with his amens, Sybil and Reggie exchanging complicit glances as they made their vows, Teddy staring at her as he promised to bring up the child in the ways of God – his eyes telling her that he would look after them both. Cora dropped her gaze, she couldn't bear to think about what Teddy was offering her, now. When she looked up again, she saw Charlotte staring at the baby with an intentness that shocked her. It wasn't just the empty gaze of a childless woman looking at somebody else's baby; there was something watchful and predatory about her, as if she was waiting to spring.

Cora felt light-headed, her legs were shaking and she put her hand on Ivo's arm to steady herself. He glanced down at her and put his hand over hers. Cora felt her mouth filling with saliva; she swallowed desperately and looked up at the sky through the glass cupola. She willed her body not to panic, she must keep moving forward.

She saw Father Oliver look at her and she realised that he wanted her to take Guy. For a second she wondered whether she would be able to hold the baby, she felt so weak, but she caught another glimpse of Charlotte's face and put out her arms to take her son.

She kept her eyes fixed on the baby as everyone gathered around her to admire him. He was unmistakably Ivo's child, the tiny face dominated by his father's Roman nose. She heard the Double Duchess saying, 'He has the Maltravers profile of course,' and Father Oliver agreeing that he had 'something about him of the Fourth Duke'.

Deliberately, as if she was conferring an enormous honour, the Double Duchess held out her arms to take her grandson, and reluctantly Cora handed him over. To her secret delight Guy started to howl the moment the Duchess took him in her arms, and she could not soothe him. Cora saw the look of annoyance on the Duchess's face and was about to take Guy back when Ivo intervened, saying lightly to his mother, 'I see you haven't lost your touch,' as he took little Guy and rested him against his shoulder, the long lace skirts of the christening gown flowing like a waterfall over his frock coat.

Guy's sobs faded to hiccups. Cora wanted to laugh and to put her arms round her husband and her son. But she could sense Teddy and Charlotte on either side of her and she could not move.

It was a relief to be outside as the christening party walked back to the house for tea. All the outdoor servants and the villagers were lined up along the path between the chapel and the house and as the Prince walked past talking with Ivo, who was still holding the baby, shouts rang out from the crowd of 'God save the Prince of Wales' and 'God save the Duke of Wareham', and then some wit said, 'It's the Duchess who needs saving.' The Prince and Ivo were too far ahead to hear this last remark but Cora, who was next to Mrs Cash, was not. Cora looked over to her mother to see if she had heard too, but she was on Mrs Cash's bad side so she could not read her mother's expression. Cora's cheeks burned. The thought that her life was being picked over by the villagers was intolerable. She wanted to look round and find out who had been responsible but she could not show them that she minded.

She heard her mother saying, 'I have to congratulate you, Cora, you have arranged this very nicely. Lulworth is improved beyond recognition. Of course the servants here are so good, you don't have to train them the way I do at home. Still, you have made things so much more comfortable. When I think what it used to be like.' She shuddered. 'As the Prince himself said, we Americans have such a talent for hospitality and you can understand when you go about here just why he appreciates it so much. Perhaps Mr Cash and I should take a house in London for the season next year.'

Cora felt the stares of the villagers lining the route like blows. She turned to her mother and said, 'Actually, Mother, I was thinking of coming home for a few months. It would be so nice to see all my old friends again, and I long to show off little Guy. I thought perhaps I could sail back with you when you go.'

Mrs Cash did not reply for a moment and Cora wished she was walking on her mother's other side so she could see what she was thinking.

'Well, of course I would love to have you visit with us. You know I just adore my grandson, the Marquis.' Mrs Cash paused reverently over the title. 'But are you sure that my son-in-law is ready for a trip? He has just come back from one, after all.'

Cora said quickly, 'I was thinking of coming alone, Mother, just me and the baby. Ivo has so much to do here . . .' She tailed off.

'But a wife's place is with her husband, Cora. Whatever your own inclinations are, your duty is to stay by his side. Surely I have raised you to understand that there is more to life than your own pleasure.' Mrs Cash stopped and turned to face her. Cora could see her good eye glittering.

'I don't know, Mother, that Ivo would mind,' she said.

'Nonsense, Cora. It's not a question of minding. You are man and wife and that is all there is to it.'

'But it's so hard, Mother. Everyone here has known each other all their lives, so I am always the outsider. You don't know how much I long to be somewhere where people aren't gossiping about my accent or my latest faux pas.' And her marriage, Cora thought but didn't say.

Mrs Cash took Cora's hand and squeezed it, hard. It was not a gesture of affection.

'And do you think that if you came home after one year of marriage without your husband that you wouldn't be gossiped about? I assure you, Cora, people would talk of little else. There is nothing New York society would enjoy more than the sight of my daughter the Duchess failing in her marriage. I can't have you ruining everything I have worked for because you can't manage your husband. I'm sorry, Cora, but this is your affair, not mine.' Mrs Cash dropped Cora's hand and turned to talk to the Double Duchess and Mr Cash, who had just caught up with them.

Cora stopped so that she could put up her parasol. She would rather be stared at by the crowd than spend one more minute with her mother. She almost broke the parasol's ivory handle in her urgency to get the shade up; her hands were trembling so much that she could not slide the spokes over the catch. There was a moment's respite as the glare of the afternoon sun was filtered by the cream silk. Cora took a deep breath, and tried to compose her face. She should have known that her mother would react this way and yet it was shocking nonetheless that she would put her social supremacy so far ahead of her daughter's happiness. She tested the corners of her mouth, seeing if she could stretch them into a smile. Then she felt a hand on her elbow, and heard a squeak of excitement.

'You are going to hate me for doing this today but I can't help myself.' Sybil took Cora's hand and swung it enthusiastically. 'Dearest Cora, he's proposed and I've accepted!' Sybil was bobbing with delight. 'We're going to announce our engagement at the tea. Please don't be cross with me for stealing Guy's thunder, but if the Prince is there then Mama can't have a conniption fit. Oh, I am so happy, I could burst.'

Cora felt her face soften. 'Dear Sybil, I am glad. I am sure you will be very happy. You two were meant to be together. Where is Reggie? I want to be the first to congratulate him.' Reggie was produced, and the three of them entered the house together. As they walked up the steps to the terrace, Sybil went ahead so that she could fetch a handkerchief. 'I know I'm going to cry.'

As Sybil ran up the steps, Cora said to Reggie, 'I have always hoped this would happen. But what took you so long?'

Reggie laughed. 'Now, I have no idea. I suppose I had some notion that a man should make something of himself before he marries. But then I realised that all I was doing was making Sybil unhappy and really there was no point in waiting. We shall have no money, of course, but I don't think she really cares about that. And last night, well, I realised what could happen if I didn't act. I didn't want Sybil to be thwarted.' Reggie's eyes flickered over to where Charlotte Beauchamp was standing with Lady Tavistock.

Cora followed his gaze. 'No, that would never do,' she said as lightly as she could. 'And now you must tell Ivo. He will want the satisfaction of observing his mother's face when she realises that she is about to lose her lady-in-waiting.'

The news of the engagement gave Cora the lift she needed to preside over the christening tea. The cake was cut and Guy's health was drunk in tea and champagne. After the toast had been drunk, Reggie got to his feet and made a deft little speech announcing his engagement to Sybil. Ivo called for more champagne and the company then drank to the couple – everyone, that is, except for Duchess Fanny who collapsed in a graceful swoon instead. Sybil was about to rush to her side, but Ivo stopped her and called for some smelling salts. He propped his mother against the love seat where she had fallen and waved the sal volatile under her nose. When she started to show signs of consciousness he said, 'Now, now, Mother, you mustn't worry about losing Sybil. With her gone, you will be able to knock a good ten years off your age, so that no one will dare to believe that you are a day over thirty-five.'

The Duchess glared at her son but the Prince of Wales laughed so much that she was forced to join in and her smile did not waver when the Prince said, 'Hard to believe that you are a grandmother now, Fanny. You will always be a slender young thing to me.'

The Duchess put her hands to her tightly corseted waist and said, 'I hope so, sir,' and sighed theatrically. But there was no way back to her previous position and she was obliged to look on nobly while Sybil chattered to Cora about bridesmaids and veils.

The Prince took his leave after the tea; he was taking the overnight train to Balmoral. As Cora walked him to his carriage, he paused to look across the hills to the horizon softening in the evening light. 'It's a glorious spot, Duchess. It has always been a favourite of mine and now that you are here, I find I apprrreciate its charms all the more. I look forward to coming back.'

Cora smiled and curtsied, but when the carriage had at last driven out of sight, she felt herself go limp and if Ivo had not been standing behind her she would have fallen to the ground.

'What was the Prince whispering to you just now, Cora, that made you go weak at the knees? I hope he knows that this Duchess of Wareham, at least, is not his to command. Or were you tempted by Tum Tum? Although judging by his performance on the bicycle today, I doubt that he has much to offer.' Cora knew that Ivo was teasing her but there was a bitterness to his tone that jangled. Surely he could not be jealous of the Prince?

She pulled away from him and said, 'I have a headache, Ivo, I am going to lie down. I am sorry, but you will have to manage without me this evening.'

'Don't worry, I am sure my mother will be only too happy to resume the role of chatelaine. Or shall I ask your mother? What a prospect.' Ivo put his hand against her cheek. 'Shall I send for the doctor, I don't think I can manage without you for long.'

'No, I'm sure I will feel better once I have rested. It has been a long day.'

'The longest,' said Ivo and took her arm as they walked up the steps to the house.

Bertha was just about to join the upper servants who were gathering for their own version of the christening tea when the hall boy stopped her in the corridor, holding out a parcel.

'Miss Jackson, Miss Jackson, this came for you.' He shook it. 'I think it's from America.'

Bertha took the parcel from him. The parcel had been redirected many times. It had gone to New York, to London and now here to Dorset. The return address was the Rev. Caleb Spragge, South Carolina. She felt her mouth go dry. She took the parcel into the pressing room and put it down on the table. She found a pair of scissors and cut the thick twine that held it together. She pulled away the brown paper to reveal a cardboard box about two feet long and one foot wide. Bertha could hear the bustle and clatter of the housemaids in the corridor, she wanted very much to walk out and join them, she did not want to open the box. But then she saw the pile of string and the elaborately tied knots and she knew she could not ignore what lay inside.

She lifted the lid. Inside was a letter and something that looked like clothing wrapped in tissue paper. She opened the letter – the date was 12 March, four months ago.

My dear Bertha,

It is with great regret that I write to tell you that your mother passed away yesterday. She had been sickly for some time and I think she was happy to go to her Maker in the end. She spoke of you often and she often said how proud she was that you were making your way in the world. In the last few months she started to make this quilt for you. She finished it a day or two before she passed. It was evidently a labour of love.

I am sorry to be the bearer of such bad news but be comforted by the thought that your mother is in a better place.

Your affectionate friend,
Caleb Spragge

Bertha leant against the table for a moment. She had known, of course, when she came to England that she would never see her mother again, but the fact of it still made her faint with loss. She folded back the shroud of tissue paper and took out the quilt.

It was not so big, perhaps the size of the table in the cabin, twelve squares, four by three, of interlocking strips of material around a central motif. With a lurch of her heart she saw a strip of blue and white striped cotton from her mother's skirt, and opposite, a scrap of paisley from the shawl that Bertha had sent her. In every square she found some memento of the life she could only dimly remember, a faded strip from some overalls, a scrap of material from a flour sack with the letters *ash's finest flo*. Bertha recognised in the centre of one square a piece of the red and white bandanna that her mother had used to tie back her unruly hair. The stitching was fine and even in some parts of the quilt, but in others the sewing was erratic, rushed as if her mother was desperate to get to the end. She was sending her daughter a message and she would not go until she had finished it. She could not read or write, so this quilt was her last will and testament, her parting gift to her only child. Bertha held it up to her face, feeling her mother's hands on the warm soft fabric. For the first time since she had left South Carolina ten years before, she allowed herself to cry.

A bell rang and Mabel came in.

'The Duchess is down, Miss Jackson. You're wanted upstairs.' She saw Bertha's face and stopped. 'Are you all right? Was it bad news?' She seemed eager for details

Bertha nodded. 'Yes, it was bad news, but it was a long time ago.'

She folded the quilt carefully and wrapped it up in the tissue paper. She went upstairs to her bedroom and laid it out. Only then did she go down to Miss Cora.

Cora was sitting in the window seat when Bertha came in, her face pressed against the glass. She had taken her hair down and the russet weight of it fell over her shoulders like an animal pelt. She had lost her Duchess look, Bertha thought.

'Oh, there you are. I have got such a headache, Bertha.' Her voice sounded weak and uncertain.

Bertha poured some eau de cologne on to a flannel and pressed it to Cora's temples.

'Thank you.' Cora looked up at her for a moment, as if deciding something, and then said, 'Bertha, have you ever been in love?'

Bertha stiffened, she wondered where this was leading. 'I couldn't say, Miss Cora.'

Cora shook her head. 'Well, have you ever known someone who

is nice *and* nasty, who makes you love them one minute and hate them the next? Who makes you feel wonderful and terrible and you never know which one it is going to be?'

Cora's hands were twisting through her hair, rolling it around her fingers so tightly that they went white from lack of circulation. Bertha thought that the only person in her life who fitted Miss Cora's description was Miss Cora herself, who did an excellent job in being nice and nasty. But that was not a thought she could utter. She knew that her mistress was talking about the Duke, so she kept her answer as non-committal as possible.

'I guess the world is full of contrary folks, Miss Cora.'

'Oh, but he's not just contrary, Bertha, it's as if he wants to unbalance me.' Cora stopped. 'I shouldn't be talking to you about this, you're my maid and he's my husband but I don't know what to think any more.' Bertha saw that one of Cora's fingers was turning blue and she gently disengaged it from the hair.

'Why don't you talk to Mrs Cash? She knows a lot more about married life than I do, Miss Cora.'

'Oh, I tried that. All Mother wants is a duchess for a daughter. She doesn't care how I feel.' Cora knocked her head against the glass.

Bertha could say nothing to this as she knew it was true.

'I just don't know who Ivo *is* any more. Sometimes I think – no, I *know* – he loves me but then the next moment he is someone else entirely. Last night, just before Odo made that scene, I saw something between Ivo and Charlotte. I know there is something there, some feeling that I can't be part of. Yet when Ivo says he loves me, I believe him, but he can't love us both, can he?' She looked at Bertha in entreaty as if the maid's answer had the power to decide her fate.

Bertha wanted to wipe Cora's face clean of worry, but she could not lie to her. She knew that Jim would be angry with her for what she was about to do, but she could not stand by while Miss Cora tortured herself.

'Miss Cora, if I tell you something, do you promise not to be angry with me?'

Bertha sat down on the window seat opposite her mistress so that she could look directly into her eyes.

'Of course, why would I be angry with you?'

'Because you won't like what I have to say. Do you want me to go on?'

'Yes, yes, I promise that nothing you say can be worse than I have imagined.' A tear slid out of Cora's eye, but she did not appear to notice.

Bertha fumbled in her bodice and drew out Jim's pearl from its resting place next to her heart.

'Do you recognise this, Miss Cora?'

Cora picked up the pearl and rolled it around her palm. 'This looks as if it could be from my necklace, but it can't be, unless someone has broken it . . .' She looked over at her dressing table in alarm.

'No, *your* necklace is quite safe. This pearl came from another necklace, just like yours.'

Cora tested the pearl against her front teeth. 'It's real enough, but what's it got to do with me?' She held the pearl in one hand and with the other she rubbed her neck where the necklace would have sat. She thought of Ivo fastening it for her that afternoon in Venice.

'All I can tell you, Miss Cora, and I am sorry to be the one to do so, is that Lady Beauchamp had a necklace of black pearls just like yours. It broke one night when we were staying over at Sutton Veney and I . . .' Bertha paused; she did not want Cora to know that it had been Jim who had stolen the pearl. 'It was the night you didn't come back from the hunt. She was wearing it at dinner and it snapped. I guess she picked them all up except this one.'

Cora spoke slowly as if she was trying to add things up in her head. 'Are you saying that Ivo gave Charlotte a necklace like mine?' She frowned.

'Yes, he did.'

Cora stood up and went to the dressing table. She took her necklace out of its green morocco leather box. She compared her pearls to the one in her hand.

'Identical.' She turned and looked at Bertha.

Bertha stood up to face her. She could not tell from Cora's expression whether she was to be blamed for what she had said. She had broken through the invisible wall of deference that lay between them by speaking out. But then she thought of all the things she had never said to her mother and she decided that she could not stop now. She had gone against Jim's advice, her own self-interest even, to tell Miss Cora something that she might very well decide not to hear. But then she remembered how certain and bright Cora had once been and how dim she seemed now. She was only her maid, but Cora mattered to her. She would not just be a bystander.

'There's something else as well,' she said. 'Just before your wedding, you got a letter from Mr Van Der Leyden. Your mother didn't want you to read anything that might upset you so I kept the letter. I didn't read it, and I didn't give it to the Madam, but I thought you should know.' Bertha hoped that Miss Cora would not ask her for the letter, but her mistress did not seem to have heard what she had said. She was rolling the pearls between her fingers.

'Why didn't you tell me about this before?' She gestured with the pearls.

Bertha hesitated. 'It wasn't my place to, Miss Cora. So long as you were happy, what good would it have done?'

'So why are you telling me now?'

'Because now I think you need to know the truth, Miss Cora.'

The pearls clattered against the wood as Cora dropped them on the table.

'Yes, I suppose I do.' She closed her eyes for a moment and then opened them wide, pulling back her shoulders as if she was rising from a long sleep. She looked at herself in the pier glass and made a face. 'I need you to put my hair up again.' She sat down at the dressing table and handed Cora the brush. Her eyes met Bertha's in the mirror. 'And then I want you to find out whether Lady Beauchamp has gone to bed. I think it's time I paid her a visit.'

Bertha nodded and began to brush the conker-coloured hair, which crackled to life with every stroke. When her hair was fully alive like a crown of flames, Cora put her hand on Bertha's.

'Thank you,' she said.

CHAPTER 29

'Taming a Sea Horse'

CHARLOTTE BEAUCHAMP'S ROOM WAS IN THE MEDIEVAL part of the house in one of the towers above the long gallery. Cora had not wanted to put her there, as this part of the house had not yet been modernised, but when she had been discussing the accommodations for the house party with Bugler, the butler had said that Lady Beauchamp preferred the tower room. And when Charlotte had written to her accepting her invitation to the christening, she had said, 'Please can I sleep in my old tower bedroom, Cora? It was my room when I lived at Lulworth and it always reminds me of those happy days.' At the time Cora had thought nothing much of it, besides surprise that anyone would choose to sleep in the coldest part of the house, but now as she walked up the worn stone steps to the tower, she realised that Charlotte had been claiming her territory. It was also true that the tower bedroom's isolation meant that Sir Odo had been housed some distance away.

Cora rubbed the black pearl Bertha had given her between her fingers. She had wanted to pulverise it into dust, but now she held on to it and welcomed the anger it aroused in her. The idea that Ivo had given her and Charlotte the exact same necklace made her kick the stone flags as she walked. She had been deceived, not just about his relationship with Charlotte, but also in his feelings for her. She had held on to that necklace as if to a talisman, she had treasured the memory of that afternoon in Venice through all the long dark months of her exile in Lulworth; at that moment, she had told herself, they had been quite married. But now as she felt her way along the stone corridor, she had no such comfort. Nothing was hers alone. He may have loved her in his way but there was nothing special about it; all he had given her was her allotted ration of love, nothing more, nothing less. He had not cared enough to think of a different present.

She stopped outside Charlotte's door. Next to it was a brass bracket with 'Lady Beauchamp' written in her own best hand-writing on the card. Cora took the paper out and ripped it into as many pieces as she could. She knocked on the door and walked in without waiting for an answer.

The room was dark but Cora could see Charlotte silhouetted against the moonlit window. She was clearly waiting for someone, for she turned round expectantly when Cora entered, her arms stretched out in welcome. As she stepped into a patch of moonlight, Cora could see that she was wearing a peignoir made of some silvery material trimmed with swansdown. With her pale hair shining down her back, she looked like some ethereal water nymph.

Cora lit the gas lamp on the table with her candle and adjusted the wick so that the golden flame obliterated Charlotte's shimmering aura. She wanted to look at Charlotte properly. When they had been friends, Cora had enjoyed Charlotte's elegance and beauty, rather as she appreciated her thoroughbred, Lincoln, or the statues of Eros and Psyche in the summer house. Cora liked the best and Charlotte was undoubtedly the most attractive woman in her circle. Too many English women looked weathered, but Lady Beauchamp had skin as smooth and waxy as an orchid. It had never occurred to Cora before to feel jealous of Charlotte's poise or perfect clothes but now she was looking at her not as a friend but as a rival. Charlotte was only four years older than her, but the years had given her face more character. They were about the same height, but despite all the afternoons strapped into the spine stiffener, Cora knew that Charlotte was the more graceful. When Charlotte walked across a room, her movements were so fluid that she appeared to glide. She looks more like a duchess than I do, thought Cora angrily.

Charlotte tried to hide her surprise at seeing Cora instead of the visitor she had been expecting.

'I am so glad you are feeling better, Cora. I heard that you had gone down with a migraine. I was going to bring you a *cachet fièvre* – I have them sent over from Paris as I find they are the only things that work, but I thought you would be asleep.' She spoke in her usual breathy drawl, but her hands were picking at the swansdown trimming of her gown.

Cora held out her hand where the pearl lay in the oyster of her palm.

'I believe this belongs to you.'

Charlotte looked at Cora for a moment. Then she took the black pearl from Cora's hand.

'I thought there was one missing. But I never knew for sure. After they broke I never had the heart to have them restrung.' She tilted her head to one side. 'But you're not wearing your necklace, Cora. I hope finding this didn't put you off,' and she smiled, a fulsome smile that showed her dimples.

Cora wanted to speak but the sight of Charlotte's dimples made her mute with rage.

Charlotte gestured towards her. 'So now you know how it feels, Cora. To be a duplicate.' She gave a little laugh. 'Do you know how rare pearls this size and colour are? God knows where Ivo managed to get a second necklace.'

Cora said almost to herself, 'I can't believe I didn't see this. I have been so stupid.'

Charlotte ignored her; she was pacing up and down the room, her body sinuous even in its agitation. 'I was to wear it when we were apart to remind me of him. I have never understood why he gave you pearls too. Was he trying to torment me? He knows how to be cruel. He never forgave me for marrying Odo, even when he knew I had no choice, even though he knew what kind of man he is.' Charlotte took a deep breath. 'And then you came out of nowhere. An American, who knew nothing and understood nothing. I thought he had done it for your money at first but when I saw you at Conyers wearing your black pearls, I realised that he was punishing me too. But I had my revenge, I introduced you to Louvain. I knew you were exactly the kind of pretty spoilt creature who would find Louvain irresistible. I knew that once Ivo saw you for what you were, he would come back to me.' She turned to Cora and smiled again, showing her small white teeth.

Cora felt that she knew about the kiss in Louvain's studio. She felt ashamed that this woman had known how she would behave. But one kiss was all it had been.

'He's my husband, Charlotte,' she said, 'whether you like it or not. He married me, we have a son. And I believe that Ivo loves me.' Cora thought of the way he had embraced her last night in the nursery.

'Really.' Charlotte's dimples were in evidence again. 'Just because you have bought yourself a title and all this,' she gestured around the tower room, 'doesn't mean that you have bought his love. He's grateful to you, of course, for saving Lulworth and giving him a son. In many ways you have made his life easier, but Ivo's not the sort of man who settles. Yes, you are his wife but I am the woman he loves. Sadly it's not a position you can buy.'

Cora could not bear to hear any more. She picked up the lamp on the table and threw it as hard as she could at Charlotte. But the other woman dodged and the lamp hit the cheval glass behind her, causing the mirror to shatter. The paraffin poured out over the floor and rivulets of fire spread out across the carpet. Cora watched as flames began to lick the bottom of the curtains. Charlotte wrapped the silvery peignoir round herself and walked to the door.

'I see I will have to find somewhere else to sleep', she said as she left the room. 'Perhaps you should ring the bell. Of course, you can afford to rebuild the house from scratch but I know that your husband is rather attached to the place as it is.'

Cora tugged the bell pull as hard as she could, but no one came. Realising that Charlotte could not be trusted to raise the alarm, she picked up the pitcher of water and threw it over the burning material. Only some of the flames were extinguished. Cora snatched up the velvet counterpane from the bed and threw it over what was left of the blaze. The brocade sizzled faintly under the counterpane. The singed material smelt like her hair did when the curling irons were too hot. She remembered the smell of her mother's hair burning, and she stamped on the heaped velvet until she was sure that all the flames were out.

The room was dark now but as she turned to leave, the moon

came out from behind a cloud and the silvery light revealed something small and dark lying on the exposed bed sheet. Cora thought it might be the pearl from the necklace but as she bent to pick it up, she realised that although it was a black pearl, it was a small one. This pearl was framed in gold, with a shank that went through the buttonhole of a shirt to fasten it. Cora dropped it in disgust and ran out of the room. She blundered down the dark corridor without a candle and ran into someone coming the other way.

'Cora?' It was Teddy's voice. 'Is it really you?'

Cora said nothing for a moment, she just put her head against the wool of Teddy's jacket. He smelt of cigar smoke. She leant against his warm solidity, and felt safe.

'You're trembling, Cora, what's going on? I was just going to bed when I heard an almighty crash. But this isn't your room. What have you been doing?' Teddy sounded worried but he was holding Cora in his arms, one hand was stroking her hair and the other was pressing her closer to him. They stood there for a minute in silence and then Cora said, her voice muffled in his jacket, 'I am so glad you are here.'

Then she pulled back and looked at him. Her face was shadowed, her eyes dark sockets.

She said, 'You wrote me a letter before my wedding. But I never got it, Teddy. My mother didn't want me to read it. But now I would like to know what it said.'

Teddy took one of her hands and kissed it. 'It said that my biggest regret was leaving you that night in Newport. It said that I left you out of fear, because I thought that I would always be in the shadow of your money, but when I got to Paris I realised that I had been a coward. Yes, I was following what I believed to be my vocation but the cost of losing you had been too great. And then I offered you my love, Cora, even though I knew it was too late.'

She nodded and put her hand to his cheek. 'I wouldn't have listened to you then. But it's different now. I can't bear it any more. I've been such a fool, Teddy. I thought it was me he wanted. But it could have been anybody, so long as they were rich.'

Teddy squeezed her hands. 'Leave him behind, Cora, leave all of it behind. I want you, only you, and I will take care of you.'

She looked at him. 'But you have to understand that I am not the girl you left in Newport. I have changed. I have a child, and I can't leave him behind. I don't want Guy to grow up like this. Helping me means helping him too.'

He took her hands. 'If that's what you want, Cora. I won't let you down again.'

In the darkness they heard the chapel clock strike one.

Bertha was waiting up when Cora got back to her room. She gasped when she saw that Cora's dress and hands were covered in soot. She looked at her mistress for an explanation but Cora waved away her unspoken inquiry.

'I want you to pack a case for me, just a change of clothes and my nightdress, and leave some space for Guy's things. I am going to London with the baby. But it's a secret, Bertha. I don't want anyone to know I am going.'

Bertha swallowed. 'And do you want me to come with you, Miss Cora?'

'Of course. You will have to help me look after Guy. I can't leave him behind and I am not taking that old trout of a nurse.'

'Will we be gone long?' Bertha put her hand on the table for support.

'For ever.'

Bertha began to shake, but Cora did not notice her agitation and she went on, urgently, 'I will take Guy for a walk in the park after breakfast. I want you to take the donkey cart and meet me in that bend in the drive just before the lodge. From there we can take the cart to the station and get the train to London. Mr Van Der Leyden is going to engage some rooms for me at an hotel. I don't want anyone to be able to find me.'

Bertha sagged. She had set this in motion, but she had not foreseen the consequences. Whatever happened now, she would have to leave someone she loved behind. She had no real family any more, only Miss Cora and Jim. For a long time she had thought she could have them both, but not any more. Now she would have to choose.

Cora, she could see, was too agitated to sleep. Bertha poured some water into a basin and washed her face and hands and brought her a clean nightdress.

'You should get some rest now, Miss Cora. You will need your strength for tomorrow.'

She helped Cora get into bed and said good night.

As she reached the door, she heard Cora say, 'Do you think I am doing the right thing?'

Bertha wondered if she could pretend she hadn't heard but Cora said, 'Bertha?' her voice quavering slightly.

Bertha looked back at her. 'I don't know as I could say it was the right thing, but I know you won't be happy until you do something and I reckon this is your way forward.' She turned the doorknob and walked out. She had no more time for Cora tonight.

Bertha had never visited Jim's bedroom before. The male servants all slept in rooms in the basement, as far as possible from the female servants, who slept in the attics. Bertha was not even sure which was his room. She knew that if she bumped into Bugler down in the male quarters at this time of night, she would be dismissed on the spot, but that was the least of her worries.

The male servants' corridor was lit by one pilot light. She crept along it, listening to the snores and muttering that came from behind the closed doors to see if she could recognise Jim's. But all the snores and muttering sounded the same. She only found his door through his boots which he had put outside his door for the hall boy to collect and clean. Only Jim and Mr Bugler had the privilege of having their shoes cleaned and Jim's feet were much larger than the butler's.

She took one more look along the corridor and pushed Jim's door open and slipped inside. It was a warm night and he was lying face down with only a sheet covering the lower half of his body. She could not resist running her hand down his back towards the swell of his buttocks. He woke with a start and grabbed her wrist.

'Bertha! What are you doing here?' Jim turned to face her. She saw that he was naked under the sheet.

'I wanted to talk to you,' she said. He pulled her down on the bed and started kissing her.

After a moment he said, 'So talk then,' but his hands were fumbling with the buttons of her blouse. Bertha tried to summon the words but she found that she could not say anything. She did not want to think of anything but Jim's hands on her body, and the feel of his skin next to hers. In answer she undid the last button and began to unlace the strings of her corset.

When she had shed all her clothes, Jim whispered in her ear, 'Are you sure, my dearest?'

And she put her arms round him in reply.

But later she would not allow herself the warm comfort of Jim's arms. She started to hunt around in the dark for her clothes. When she was dressed, she shook Jim awake.

'Jim, there is something I must tell you.'

Jim rolled away from her sleepily. 'Not now, Bertha.'

'No, you must listen to me. I came to tell you that the Duchess is going to London today and taking me with her.' She tried to keep her voice a whisper but it was hard not to let the emotion break through. 'She isn't coming back, Jim. She's leaving him. I think she means to run away with Mr Van Der Leyden.'

Jim roused himself at this and grabbed her hand. 'You can't go with her, Bertha. What if she decides to go back to America? Let your Miss Cora ruin her life if she wants to. Your place is with me.' He was whispering, but the anger in his voice was unmistakable.

Bertha twisted away from him. 'I can't just leave her. You see, I made it worse. I showed her the black pearl you gave me from Lady Beauchamp's necklace. I felt sorry for her – everyone was lying to her. I wanted to give her the truth.'

Jim let his hand drop. 'She's got a family, Bertha. You are just her maid.'

'But she needs me. I know she does. She really doesn't have anyone else.'

'So what was this?' He pointed to the bed. 'Some kind of consolation prize?'

She looked away. 'I . . . I wanted you, Jim.' She put out a hand to caress him, but he threw it off.

'And I want you, all the time. But now you are leaving. If you want to go with her I can't stop you, but I don't know if I'll ever see you again.' He turned away from her and buried his face in the pillow.

Bertha put her hand on his shoulder and said, 'I love you, Jim.'

He hit the pillow with his fist. 'Then don't leave.' He sat up and grabbed her by the shoulders. 'Marry me, Bertha. We can go to London. I can get work as a valet in one of those hotels. We can have a new life. Don't leave me because that spoilt mistress of yours can't live without her maid.'

Bertha stood up. 'Miss Cora ain't always easy or pleasant but I can't give up on her now.' She thought of the quilt lying on her bed. Miss Cora was the closest thing she had to family now – they were stitched together by time and circumstance. Miss Cora was part of the fabric of her life. Bertha knew everything about her mistress, from the mole on her right shoulder blade to the way she would blow the hair away from her eyes when she was angry. She could tell Cora's mood from the set of her shoulders, she knew what she was going to say by the curve of her lips. It did not much matter to her that Cora did not observe her in return. Cora was her territory; her home was where Cora was.

She knew she could not explain this to Jim. He would laugh at her; tell her again that they were just there to clean up the mess. She had thought that perhaps she would feel differently after lying down with Jim, but she knew now that desire was not enough. Even his offer of marriage didn't change the way she felt.

There were so many things she wanted to say, but she heard a noise in the passage outside and she could do no more than press her lips against his sullen flesh before scuttling away.

446

In the corridor she saw the hall boy stooping over Bugler's shoes. She put her fingers to her lips and he nodded. She felt in her pocket and found a sixpence. Silently she put it into the little boy's hands and crept away down the corridor as fast as she could.

CHAPTER 30

'A Nine-Hundred-Year-Old Name'

THE BABY WAS SLEEPING, CORA COULD HEAR his tiny whinnying snores as she pushed the perambulator down the gravel path as gently as she could. She did not want him to start crying now. Nanny Snowden had bristled with disapproval when Cora announced she was taking the baby for a walk. 'But Your Grace, the Marquis is sleeping. He always sleeps in the morning at this time.' But Cora had simply lifted Guy out of his cradle and told the nurse to get the baby carriage ready.

She had passed the summer house now and was about to turn on to the drive itself. She looked up and saw the chapel on its mound. The sight of it made her realise how much she would be leaving behind, this cool grey stone building had housed so much of her joy and her disappointment. She wanted to have one last look but then she heard Guy give a little snuffling roar and she knew that she must press on before he woke up in earnest.

Carefully she pushed the perambulator on to the drive and proceeded as casually as she could. This was the most exposed part of her journey; anyone looking down from the house would be astonished to see the Duchess venturing so far from the house with the baby carriage. The servants might put it down to another example of her American eccentricity but if Ivo saw her he would know something was up. She reassured herself that Ivo always went riding at this time, but she speeded up as she pushed the carriage up the hill; once she got over the crest she would be out of sight of the house. From the top she could see the clover-leaf-shaped lodges of the North Gate on the next ridge; in the dip between lay Conger Wood where Bertha would be waiting for her.

Cora knew that Bertha was not altogether happy about this clandestine escape but there was no other way. She could not bear to see Ivo; she knew that if she did, all her certainty would be clouded by his presence. She would never be able to reconcile what she knew about him now with the overwhelming attraction she still felt for him, and she did not want to soften. She had been used, deceived, humiliated. Every time she thought of the necklaces and Charlotte's dimples, she wanted to smash something. How could she have forgotten that it was always about the money? He had married her because she was rich and he had used her to punish the woman he really loved.

She pushed the baby carriage so hard that Guy woke up and started to whimper. She put her hand to his cheek and tried to soothe him. Reassured by the sound of her voice, he closed his eyes again. She gripped the handle as the road went downhill. She was almost at the track that led through the woods where Bertha would be waiting. She could feel beads of perspiration running down her back; her hair was beginning to stick to her face. And then at last she stepped under the canopy of the trees and smelt the mossy coolness of the ancient forest. She pushed on down the grassy track until she heard the donkey snorting . . .

'Bertha?' she called.

Bertha came down the track towards her on foot. Her steps were slow and her face was swollen and heavy. Cora felt a flicker of annoyance. Why should Bertha take on so? She wasn't leaving her marriage behind.

'I will hold Guy and you can drive, Bertha. Did you get some clothes for him?'

'I had to take them from the laundry. I couldn't get into the nursery.' Bertha's voice was flat. 'They aren't all clean.'

'Never mind, we can get fresh ones in London.' Cora tried to sound bright. She took the still sleeping baby out of the perambulator and climbed on to the back seat of the donkey cart. Bertha got up in front of her and took the reins. The donkey began to amble along the path, but then it stopped. Cora heard Bertha gasp. She turned round and saw Ivo standing in the path, his hand absently patting the donkey's muzzle.

'Going somewhere, Cora? I don't think this fellow here has the stamina to get you very far. But you have a bag, I see. Perhaps you are going to the station.' He stood aside, to let them pass. Cora wondered how he had known where to find them. She looked at Bertha, but her maid's face was set hard.

'Well, I won't stop you if you have a train to catch. But Cora, I am not Bluebeard. If you want to leave Lulworth you are perfectly at liberty to do so. Surely you know that.' He walked round to where Cora was sitting and looked at her, his brown eyes unreadable in the forest gloom.

She shook her head. 'I'm not sure of anything about you, Ivo.'

Guy gave a little cry and she started to rock him in her arms.

Ivo reached over and put his hand on the baby's head. The noise stopped.

'I am not here to stop you. But I would like to talk to you.' He swallowed. 'Come for a drive with me. I have something to tell you.'

Cora had never heard Ivo ask for anything so nakedly. She tried to think about Charlotte's dimples, about the black pearl stud on the white sheet, about Teddy and the letter she had never read. But all she could see was her husband's large brown hand stroking her son's head.

She could feel Bertha's gaze burning into the back of her head and she could hear the donkey snorting and stomping.

'Please, Cora?' Ivo was almost whispering.

'It's too late, Ivo. Whatever it is you have to tell me, it's too late.' She looked down at the baby as she said this, trying to control her face.

Ivo spoke louder now. 'Right from the very first moment we met, I thought you had courage, Cora, but here you are running away from me. Aren't you brave enough to hear what I have to say?'

Cora stood up.

'Bertha, take the baby back to the house in the perambulator for now. I will let you know when I want to leave.'

Bertha got out of the cart and Cora put Guy in her arms. Then she turned to her husband.

Ivo hesitated for moment and then climbed up into the cart and took the reins.

They drove along in silence, sitting side by side, following the road that led to the sea. When they reached the cliffs, Ivo turned the cart to the left.

Cora wondered if Ivo was ever going to speak. The donkey laboured up a steep hill and only when they reached the top did Ivo turn to her.

'I wanted to bring you here, Cora, to explain.'

Cora looked down at the coast spread before her. There was a cove just below them where a spur of rock curved out defiantly into the sea. The waves had responded by tearing into the grey stone, eating away two holes, so that the cliff looked like a coiled sea serpent. The water squeezed in and out of the openings, creating concentric rings which rippled out over the leathery sea.

'That's Durdle Door. Guy and I used to swim here when we were boys. There's a trick to swimming through the holes. You have to go with the wave or you can get smashed on the rocks. We could manage the bigger hole all right but one day when I was eleven or so I dared Guy to go through the smaller one. It's much harder because there are only a few inches for error either way. I could see that Guy didn't really want to do it but I kept on at him, teasing him until he had to go. I remember he went right down under the water so that he would not get smashed by the waves, but the gap was so narrow that I couldn't see him come up on the other side. I waited for a minute, and then another, and I began to worry. Maybe the undertow had pulled Guy against a rock and knocked him unconscious. I shouted for him and got no answer. I remember even now how terrified I was.' He pushed back his sleeve and Cora could see that the black hairs on his arm were standing on end. 'I shouted a bit more but I realised that I would have to go and look for him. I didn't want to, one bit, but I remember feeling that as I had sent Guy in there, I had to go in after him. And if we both died, that was only fair.' He paused and they both looked down at the sea churning through the rocky channels.

'I dived in as deep as I could, my eyes wide open so that I

could see Guy if he was trapped, but the water was murky and I could hardly see a thing. But I stayed down there looking for a fraction too long and I got caught by the undertow which started dragging me along the rocks. My leg got wedged and I couldn't move, my lungs were bursting and I thought I was going to drown. But then I felt an arm under my shoulders pulling me free. Guy had swum back through the bigger hole and when he saw that I wasn't there waiting for him, he guessed what had happened and came to rescue me. If he'd hesitated I wouldn't be here.' Ivo turned to look at Cora. 'He saved my life, but I killed him.'

Cora looked at him in astonishment. 'But I thought he died in a riding accident.'

'Yes, he did, but Guy was a wonderful rider. He wanted to break his neck.'

'You can't know that, Ivo.' Cora was alarmed by the darkness in his voice. Ivo was standing on the cliff now and she thought how close he was to the edge.

'But I do know. It was because of Charlotte.' Cora stiffened. 'You see she was the first, the only thing, to come between us. When she came to Lulworth, she was just sixteen and so lovely.' He caught the expression on Cora's face. 'She was different then. I suppose she still had . . . hope.' He stopped for a moment. 'I was enchanted by her, and she liked me. But then Guy, who took no interest in women, noticed her and he was quite smitten. He didn't flirt with her or even talk to her; he just worshipped her as if she was one of his saints. She didn't realise at first how he felt, but I could see it. I did everything I could that summer to make her mine. I wanted to marry her before Guy ruined it all. I knew, you see, that Charlotte wouldn't hesitate. She loved me, I think, but not enough to give up a chance of being a duchess.'

'My mother noticed what was going on and she took Charlotte to London for the season. She didn't want Charlotte to be the next Duchess any more than she wanted you, Cora.' He almost smiled, and took a step closer to the edge.

Cora said, 'I would much rather hear this story sitting over there.' She pointed to a small chalk outcrop a good ten yards back.

Ivo looked startled. 'Do you really think I would . . . Oh no, Cora, you have that quite wrong.'

But Cora took the reins of the donkey cart and pulled the animal over to the rock. When she looked round she saw that Ivo was following.

'Then my father died and we came back to Lulworth for the funeral. We were all in mourning, there was nothing to do, no one to see. All we could do was look at each other.'

Ivo sat down next to Cora on the rock and started to throw the pebbles at his feet towards the cliff.

'My mother went off to Conyers to secure her next husband. She left Charlotte behind – she didn't want anyone to cloud the Duke's vision, I suppose. And with my mother gone, there was nothing to prevent Guy following Charlotte around like a pilgrim. She noticed and encouraged him. But she didn't drop me – we had gone too far for that. Charlotte would listen to Guy telling her about the Maltravers and their glorious Catholic past and then she would come and meet me, somewhere we wouldn't be found.'

Ivo pitched a larger stone so that it hit the edge of the cliff and curved upwards before disappearing.

'We both knew that Guy was going to propose and that Charlotte would accept and it made us reckless. We couldn't meet in the house because of the servants, so we used the chapel. I should have known better, but I have always wondered whether really deep down I wanted to be caught.'

Cora glanced at his face but he was looking straight out to sea.

'Guy discovered us one afternoon in the organ loft. There could be no mistake. He didn't say anything, he just went away. I should have run after him but I was glad he had found us. He would never marry Charlotte now. Then his horse came back without him that evening and I knew what had happened, what I had done.'

Cora laid her hand on his arm for a moment.

'The day after Guy's funeral, Charlotte asked me when we were getting married. "After all," she said, "there is nothing to stop us now." She couldn't hide her satisfaction and I hated her for it. I told her that we had killed my brother. When she realised that I would never marry her, she went off and married Odo because he was the richest man she could find. I should have stopped her, I knew that Odo was vicious, always has been – his only talent is for making trouble – but I never wanted to see her again. As far as I was concerned they deserved each other. But then a year later I met Charlotte when I was out with the Myddleton. She told me how bad things were and I liked her more because she was suffering. We started again, it was a terrible mistake – we were both trying to find a way out of our misery, but it wasn't a happy thing.' He shaded his eyes with the back of his hand. 'Ironically it was Charlotte that brought us together. If I hadn't been with her that day in Paradise Wood, I would never have found you lying there.'

Cora put her face in her hands; she realised for the first time how hot her face was, she simply had not noticed the sun.

'You had been with her, in the wood.' She started to get up but Ivo pulled her back.

'You can't go yet, Cora. Please let me finish my story.'

She subsided.

'When I met you I felt as if there might be a chance for me. You were so bright and free and . . .'

'Rich?' said Cora.

'Yes, rich, but dearest Cora, you were not the only heiress looking for a title, although you were,' he made a little flourish with his hands and laughed, 'by far the richest. Of course I had to marry a woman with money but it wasn't your fortune I wanted, Cora, it was you. You were never going to be like my mother or even Charlotte. You can't keep secrets and you are a terrible liar. You have no idea how to hide your emotions.'

Cora closed her eyes; she could feel the sun beating through her eyelids.

'Then you will know how I am feeling now.'

'You are angry and humiliated and I can't blame you for that. I should have told you about my past with Charlotte but to do so would mean admitting what I had done to Guy.'

'Your past with Charlotte, or your present?' Cora was surprised at how angry she sounded.

Ivo stood up in front of her, so that the sun was behind him. Cora wondered whether he had done it deliberately because it meant that she could not see his face.

'Don't you understand, Cora? I would give anything, everything, never to see Charlotte again. Do you remember the pearls I gave you in Venice?'

Cora nodded her head a fraction.

'I once gave a necklace like that to Charlotte. I gave you the same necklace as a sign to Charlotte that I loved *you* now. I wanted her to realise that our marriage was not some financial arrangement but a real thing.'

Cora said, almost involuntarily, 'But how *cruel.*'

'Maybe, but I wanted to drive her away. She got her revenge, though, by befriending you and introducing you to that painter.'

'But nothing happened, Ivo.' She stopped. 'Louvain tried to kiss me once, but that was all.'

Ivo shook his head, batting her comment away. 'I was so angry with you that night. That vulgar party, the portrait, everything. I thought the whole evening was about your vanity and that you didn't mind humiliating me in the process. It was as if you were turning into my mother.' Ivo laughed bitterly. 'Charlotte knew that, of course. I should have realised that while you were perhaps a bit vain and certainly a little foolish, you were an innocent in all this mess. It took months for me to understand what had happened. Charlotte wrote to me every day when I was in India, and I began to see what she was about. It was the baby, you see, that made her so desperate.'

Cora remembered the look of hunger on Charlotte's face at the christening.

'When I came back to England, she found me. She begged me to start again. I told her that I could never be with her. There was a terrible scene. And then I came home and found you with the baby.'

Ivo picked a daisy from the bank and started to shred it with his fingers.

'She must have been delighted when you asked her to

Lulworth. I should have stopped you but I didn't know how. And, well, you know the rest. She wanted Odo to make his revelation. I think she would sacrifice everything now if it would guarantee my unhappiness. They have that in common, those two, they both enjoy inflicting pain on other people. If you leave me, then she has won.'

Cora got to her feet. She could see the coast stretching away in both directions and she wondered which way was home. She stood in front of Ivo so that she could see his eyes.

'I went to see Charlotte last night. I found one of your dress studs in her bed.'

'In her bed?' Ivo blinked. 'Are you sure it was mine? Cora, I promise you I have never been near Charlotte's bed. Not since we married. You must believe me. I know that I haven't told you things in the past, but I have never lied to you.'

'I am certain it was yours, Ivo.' Cora pronounced her words slowly and sadly. She got up on to the seat of the donkey cart. 'I am going back. I have a train to catch.' She hit the donkey's rump with her switch and it started to plod in the direction of home.

'Cora, please! Wait.'

She did not look round but gave the donkey another switch. Now Ivo was running beside her.

'It must have been an accident. I never went to her room, but she came to mine, Cora. Just before dinner. I said I had nothing to say to her but she threw herself at me. She – well, she knelt in front of me. I pushed her away but her hair got caught in my shirt. We were struggling. The stud must have caught in her hair.'

Cora looked down at him. She could see a bead of sweat

forming on his forehead. She realised that she had never seen him sweat before.

But she did not stop.

Ivo ran in front of the cart and held the donkey's head.

'That's all there is. All of it. I have no more secrets. If you want to leave and be with your American then I won't stop you.' He saw her surprise. 'I know everything, Cora. Your maid told Harness, who came to me. He's in love with Bertha and doesn't want to lose her.' He shrugged ruefully, acknowledging the similarity between master and man. 'Maybe you can be happy with Van Der Leyden, he looks decent enough. But Cora, he doesn't need you. He is free to go where he likes, do what he pleases, but I can only be the Duke of Wareham. You alone can blow away all the shadows, Cora. Before you came I lived in a world of secrets and lies, but you aren't like that, you live in the light.' He paused as if amazed at his own words. 'I can't imagine life without you now, Cora, I can't go back. If you go now, I am lost.'

He stopped. Cora saw that he was close to the edge. His words had been underscored by the crash and churn of the sea below. His eyes were quite black, the pupils wide open. There was a muscle trembling in his jaw. She put out her hand and pulled him to her.

As soon as the cart had disappeared, Jim found Bertha. He put his hand on her arm but she shook him off and carried on pushing the baby carriage.

'I had to do it, Bertha.'

Bertha did not reply but kept walking, her eyes fixed on the sleeping baby.

Jim walked alongside her, his blue eyes pleading with her. 'I thought she would take you away, Bertha, and then there would be an end to us. I told the Duke that I want to marry you and that if he would give me a reference I would tell him what his wife was planning.'

Bertha looked at him for the first time. 'You had no right to do that, Jim.'

Jim looked at her levelly. 'I want you to be my wife, Bertha. I couldn't just let you leave.'

Bertha stopped pushing the pram and turned to face him. 'But that's my decision, not yours.'

He put his hand on hers where it held the handle of the baby carriage. 'But you were going to do the wrong thing, Bertha. You were going to give me up just because you feel sorry for a woman who doesn't need your sympathy.' Bertha took her hand away. 'Do you think she would do the same for you, Bertha? Do you think that your precious Miss Cora would lift one finger on your behalf?' Jim put his face close to hers. 'You haven't told her about me, have you? Because you know that she won't like it. She doesn't care how you feel, so long as you are there to do what she wants.'

Bertha knew that he was, to some extent, right. Cora would not be pleased to hear that she had a beau.

'Maybe it's not about Miss Cora, maybe it's about me, Jim.' She took a breath. 'I got word yesterday that my mother is dead. She was all the family I had and now she's gone. I have been with Miss Cora every day for the last ten years. Yes, I am only her maid but if I leave her, I leave everything behind. You say you want to marry me but remember I'm a foreigner; things won't be easy for us. Maybe I just want a future I can understand.'

Jim put his hand under her chin to make her look at him. 'Remember in New York, Bertha, you were too scared to hold my hand in public? Do you really want to go back to that? Nobody's going to look at us in London. Everyone's foreign there. I'm scared too, Bertha. I've been in service all my life, but I reckon that together we have a chance.'

She couldn't speak; she started to push the pram up across the gravel towards the house. He didn't move and when she turned her head to look at him he was standing there on the path, holding his hat in his hands, turning it over and over. She stopped. He had been wearing that bowler the day he had come back from India. Only then he had been jaunty, his hair blonder, his skin dark. She realised that she was beginning to fashion her own patchwork of memories, with him at the centre. She called to him, her voice loud and definite.

'Walk with me, Jim, I need to take the baby back to the nursery. And then, maybe, we'll see.'

He threw the bowler up in the air so that it landed on his head, and ran towards her.

There had been three trains that day from Lulworth and Teddy had met every one. Cora had told him that she would send a telegram to his club, but after he had engaged rooms for her at the hotel he decided to go straight to the station. He wanted to welcome her to her new life, he wanted to pluck her out of the steam and confusion of the station and take her straight to the future shining in front of her.

He looked up at the station clock – the next train was due in five minutes. He took out his cigarette case. He thought of Cora smoking in the dark by the summer house at Lulworth, the way she had touched the cigarette with her lips. He remembered holding her in his arms last night, her bony shoulders, her small, delicate ears.

A porter was walking along the platform whistling a tune that Teddy thought was 'Onward Christian Soldiers'. A woman in a straw boater rubbed at a smut on her face with a handkerchief. There was a small square of sunlight on the platform corresponding to a hole in the glass roof. Teddy looked up and saw that there were starlings flying in out and out of the iron beams. In front of him was a poster advertising the delights of Weymouth with 'its health-giving sea air and salubrious surroundings'. He threw his cigarette end on to the platform and ground it out with his heel. He could not stand the waiting much longer. When she arrived, when he actually saw her, he thought he would lose the sick feeling in his stomach warning him that his life was about to be tinted a different colour, telling him that from the moment the train pulled in to the platform, he would always be known as the man who had run away with Cora Cash.

He heard the hoot of the locomotive and the platform began to fill with steam as the Weymouth train pulled in. Teddy stood back as the passengers swarmed towards him, families returning from a holiday by the sea, two men wearing black hats with crepe streamers on their way back from a funeral, an old lady carrying a pug. The crowd began to thin. The doors to the first-class carriages were, Teddy could now make out, all open. He thought he saw a perambulator being taken out on to the platform but as the steam evaporated he saw that the wheels belonged to a bath chair. He held his breath for a moment. If Cora wasn't on this train, it meant that she wasn't coming. His mouth was dry, all his doubts from a moment before now replaced by a lurching hollowness in his heart. And then he saw two women coming down the platform towards him, both of them wearing hats with travelling veils; one of them was Cora's height, the other walked slightly behind with a porter who was pushing a pile of cases on his trolley. Teddy began to walk towards them, his step quickening until he was almost running. Then he stopped, his heart thudding in his chest. It must be Cora, he thought; she was stopping to speak to him and yet he had never seen Cora move so gracefully. The woman lifted her veil and then he saw with shattering vividness the sweep of blond hair.

'Mr Van Der Leyden. What a pleasant surprise this is.' Charlotte Beauchamp gave him a crooked little smile, acknowledging the fact that they were both the losers in this particular game. 'But I am afraid you were not looking for me,' she continued. He looked at her as she said this and she shrank a little from the full force of his disappointment.

'No,' he said, 'I wasn't.' She put a gloved hand on his arm. As she looked up at him, he could see that the whites of her eyes were touched with red. He could see his own pain and loss mirrored in her wide blue gaze. How strange, he thought, that this woman that he had disliked so much should be the only person who could understand him now.

She tilted her head to one side and blinked rapidly as if there were something in her eye.

'I understand your despair, Mr Van Der Leyden. I know what

it is to lose the thing you most desire. But you must be strong and wait. All you have to do is wait.' With that, Charlotte Beauchamp nodded to him and walked off into the station, her maid following behind. Teddy looked after her, wondering how he could ever have mistaken her slippery grace for Cora's urgent stride.

The platform was empty now, but he could not bring himself to move away from the spot where for a few hours he had had the future that he wanted. A pigeon flew down from its perch under the glass roof and began to circle his feet, mistaking him perhaps for a statue. With a great effort he started to move, feeling each step as a betrayal. Charlotte Beauchamp had told him to wait, but what, he wondered, was he waiting for? A quick stride on a platform somewhere one day or the morning when he would wake up without the band of misery that was already beginning to tighten around his chest.

In the nursery, Cora pulled her finger out of her baby's fist. He was sleeping now. The sky was beginning to darken and soon she would go and dress for dinner. In her room, Ivo was also sleeping. She lay down on the bed beside him, putting her face next to his so that she would be the first thing he saw when he woke up. His features were soft now and although his eyes were shut, his countenance was quite open. Cora wondered if at last she had the measure of her husband. Whatever happened, she knew now, and the thought filled her with warmth, that he needed her. Then he stirred, a dream chasing behind his eyelids, and he stiffened as if he had been dealt some unseen blow.

Perhaps she would never really know him. A year and a half ago that thought would have been unbearable to her, but now she had learnt to live with uncertainty, even to love it. Since she had come to England she had learnt to prize the rare bright and beautiful days which broke through the mist and murk, loving them all the more for their randomness. You could buy a more agreeable climate, she thought, but not that feeling of unexpected joy when a shaft of sunlight fell through the curtains, promising a sparkling new day.

Acknowledgements

The characters in this book are by and large fictional, but the circumstances they find themselves in are not. When it comes to the Gilded Age, the more fantastical the circumstance, the more likely it is to be true. There really was a magazine called *The Titled American Lady* and the gossip rags of 1890s New York were every bit as obsessed with celebrity as magazines like *Heat* are today. Here are a few of the books that give a flavour of that overheated era: *The Glitter and the Gold* by Consuelo Vanderbilt Balsam; *The Mrs Vanderbilt* by Cornelius Vanderbilt Jr; *The Memoirs of Lady Randolph Churchill*; *The Decline of the English Aristocracy* by David Cannadine; *The Duke's Children* by Anthony Trollope; *The Shuttle* by Frances Hodgson Burnett; *The Buccaneers* by Edith Wharton; *Consuelo and Alva* by Amanda Mackenzie Stuart.

Anyone familiar with the Dorset coast will know there is a Lulworth Castle, which I have supersized, but the Duke of Wareham and his family are, of course, entirely fictional. Readers who know their nineteenth-century royalty will realise that I have taken one liberty with chronology – Prince Eddy was sent away to India in 1888 rather than 1894 – but I couldn't quite resist borrowing this for my plot.

This book has taken me an age to finish, and I must thank the London Library and the South West Railway London to Crewkerne line for giving me some quiet space to write. Along the way I was encouraged by my faithful and perceptive readers, Tanya Shaw, Emma Fearnhamm, Ottilie Wilford, Richard Goodwin, Jocasta Innes, Caroline Michel, Sam Lawrence, and Kristie Morris. I am eternally grateful to Tabitha Potts for her plot suggestions, and to Paul Benney for his thoughts on portraits. Thanks to Ivor Schlosberg for the pre-orders, among other things. Georgina Moore is a heroine among publicists. Derek Johns is everything you could want in an agent and it was a joy to work with Harriet Evans, albeit briefly. But the real thanks must go to Mary-Anne Harrington who is as brilliant as she is patient and to Hope Dellon whose emails were like getting gold stars for homework. And my thanks to Marcus and Lydia for sending me away right at the end. It made all the difference.

Reading
Group
Gold

THE AMERICAN HEIRESS

by Daisy Goodwin

*A
Reading
Group Gold
Selection*

About the Author

- Biography and Conversation

Behind the Novel

- "Why English Noblemen Seek American Brides"
  An excerpt from *Titled Americans* © 1890

Keep on Reading

- Recommended Reading
- Reading Group Questions

For more reading group suggestions,
visit www.readinggroupgold.com.

ST. MARTIN'S GRIFFIN

Biography and Conversation

MIKE HOGAN

Daisy Goodwin is the daughter of film producer Richard B. Goodwin (*A Passage to India, Seven Years in Tibet*) and writer/interior designer Jocasta Innes (*Paint Magic*), and the sister of the Edgar—winning writer Jason Goodwin (*The Janissary Tree*). She earned a B.A. with honors in history from Trinity College, Cambridge, followed by a Harkness Fellowship to Columbia University Film School; and now runs her own independent television company in the UK.

In addition to publishing eight poetry anthologies, she has presented award-winning television series on poetry and on the enduring appeal of romantic fiction, and is a commentator and columnist for the London *Sunday Times*. In 2010, she served as chair of the judging panel for the Orange Prize for the best novel written in English by a woman. Daisy lives in London with two daughters, three dogs, and a husband who is an executive for ABC News. *The American Heiress* is her first novel.

What was the inspiration for *The American Heiress*?

I was visiting Blenheim Palace and saw the portrait of Consuelo Vanderbilt, the American heiress who married the Duke of Marlborough. She was very beautiful, but she also looked spectacularly unhappy. When I read that she was basically blackmailed into marrying the Duke by her social-climbing mother, I thought about what a great setup this would be for a novel. American girls basically propped up the English aristocracy for a generation. In modern terms, Consuelo's dowry was about $100 million.

"American girls basically propped up the English aristocracy for a generation."

No wonder a quarter of the British nobility made transatlantic marriages!

I started writing this book at the height of the boom (remember the boom?), when I was fascinated by the parallels between all these new billionaires and the plutocrats of the Gilded Age. How does getting rich that fast affect you? It has to be said, though, that the rich today are small fry compared to the Vanderbilts and their ilk, whose idea of a party favor was a jewel-encrusted Fabergé egg, and who would offer their guests cigarettes rolled from hundred-dollar bills.

Was there anything you found especially surprising while researching *The American Heiress*?

While certain details in *The American Heiress* might seem unbelievable, like the solid gold on the corset that Cora Cash wears on her wedding day, her trousseau is a replica of Consuelo Vanderbilt's. At her wedding to the Duke, Consuelo carried orchids that had been grown in the greenhouses of Blenheim and then shipped to New York in a specially refrigerated chamber because Marlborough brides always carried flowers from Blenheim. When I borrowed the detail about Cora's bouquet being brought over from England for my novel, my editor produced her red pencil and said, "This can't possibly be true." But in fact, you would have to have a very vivid imagination indeed to match the real extravagance and excess of the Gilded Age. Just as contemporary starlets are written about in the media today, every detail of Consuelo's wedding was chronicled in *Vogue*.

How typical was Cora Cash's experience for an American marrying an English nobleman?

Girls like Consuelo Vanderbilt came to England thinking it would be the height of sophistication.

But for many of these American brides, a title really didn't make up for the horrors of English country life. A dollar princess frequently found herself isolated and miserable in a great pile of a house that, however exquisite, was miles away from anywhere, with no heating apart from open fires and—horror of horror—no bathrooms. One titled American bride wrote home to her mother that she hadn't taken her furs off all winter even when she went to bed. Another heiress gave up going to dinner at people's country houses because she couldn't bear the arctic temperatures in an evening dress. And English society was not exactly welcoming to these rich newcomers: Imagine Kim Kardashian marrying Prince Harry today and you get the general idea of the suspicion and disdain that the Americans encountered.

Those of you who enjoyed the Masterpiece Theatre series *Downton Abbey* will remember that the Earl of Grantham married an American heiress (also called Cora) whose dowry saved the family estate from ruin. But *Downton Abbey* is set twenty years after *The American Heiress.* By that time even the stuffiest English aristocrats had realized that American money had stopped the roof leaking. In *Downton Abbey*, when Cora, Countess of Grantham, wonders whether a potential suitor for her daughter comes from an old family, her mother-in-law, played by Maggie Smith, retorts, "Older than yours, I imagine." And even the Countess's own daughter, Lady Mary, dismisses her mother by saying, "You wouldn't understand. You're American."

The traces of these American girls are everywhere in Britain today; most people know that Winston Churchill's mother was American, but the great-grandmother of Princess Diana was also an American heiress.

"[F]or many... American brides, a title didn't really make up for the horrors of English country life."

What kind of experience was writing this book for you?

People are always asking me, how do you find time to write a book—when you run a company, write for the newspapers, have a family (and three dogs), etc.? My answer to this is noise-cancelling headphones. Once I plug these in, I can write anytime, anywhere. A great deal of this novel was written on trains, planes, and in between meetings.

I absolutely loved writing *The American Heiress*. To be able to escape into a world full of beautiful frocks and perfectly trained servants was a joy.

Who are some of your favorite writers? What authors have influenced your work?

I love Edith Wharton and Henry James, and anyone familiar with their work will see echoes in *The American Heiress*. I also admire Daphne du Maurier for the way she handles suspense and Sarah Waters for her utter command of historical period. I really enjoyed Julian Fellowes's books for the way they dissect snobbery, and Hilary Mantel is an extraordinary writer both for her present-day and period novels.

When Daisy Goodwin was researching *The American Heiress,* she discovered that rich American girls (and their mothers) who were seeking a match with an English lord would typically start by consulting the quarterly publication, *Titled Americans,* which listed all the eligible titled bachelors still on the market, with a handy description of their age, accomplishments, and prospects.

The following is an excerpt from *Titled Americans* © 1890

WHY ENGLISH NOBLEMEN SEEK AMERICAN BRIDES

CHAUNCEY M. DEPEW'S VIEWS ON THE SUBJECT

"Why do Englishmen select American wives?" was asked the silver-tongued orator, Mr. Chauncey M. Depew, who submitted himself graciously to a reporter's inquisition on the subject of paramount interest and continuous discussion since the Endicott-Chamberlain wedding.

"Do you think I can answer that question without getting up another war with England? If I may express my opinion, without shattering the international treaty, I should say that the American girl has the advantage of her English sister in that she possesses all that the other lacks. This is due to the different methods in which the two girls are brought up. An English girl is, as a rule, brought up very strictly, kept under rigid discipline, sees nothing of society until formally brought out, is not permitted to think or act for herself, or allowed to display any individuality.

As a result, she is shy, self-conscious, easily embarrassed, has little or no conversation, and needs to be helped, lifted. The English young man has not the helpful qualities that characterize the typical American masher, and, in consequence, the two present, as I have often seen them, a very helpless combination. Then the American girl comes along, prettier than her English sister, full of dash, and snap, and go, sprightly, dazzling, and audacious, and she is a revelation to the Englishman. She gives him more pleasure in one hour, at a dinner or ball, than he thought the universe could produce in a whole life-time. Speedily he comes to the conclusion that he must marry her or die. As a rule he belongs to an old and historic family, is well educated, traveled, and polished, but poor. He knows nothing of business, and to support his estate requires an increased income. The American girl whom he gets acquainted with has that income, so in marrying her he goes to heaven and gets—the earth."

A Carefully Compiled List of Peers

Who Are Supposed to Be Eager to Lay Their Coronets, and Incidentally Their Hearts, at the Feet of the All-Conquering American Girl.

LORD ASHTOWN.

Is third Baron.

The entailed estates are at Woodlawn, County Galway, and at Kilfinane, County Limerick, Ireland. They yield but a small income, in consequence of the agricultural distress in Ireland.

Lord Ashtown is twenty-two years old, and was educated at Eton.

Family seat: Lotherton Hall, Milford Junction, Ireland.

THE EARL OF AVA.

Eldest son and heir of the first Marquis of Dufferin.

The entailed estates amount to 18,200 acres, but owing to mortgages do not yield their nominal value of $100,000 income.

Lord Ava, who is twenty-six years of age, is a lieutenant in the 17th Lancers.

Family seat: Clandeboye, County Down, Ireland.

LORD BENNET.

Eldest son and heir of the sixth Earl of Tankerville.

The entailed estates amount to 31,000 acres, yielding an income of $150,000.

The Earl owns the only herd of wild cattle to be found in Great Britain.

Lord Bennet, who has at present nothing but a very small allowance, has served in the navy and in the army, and is thirty-six years of age.

Family seat: Chillingham Castle, Northumberland.

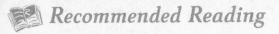 ## *Recommended Reading*

The Shuttle by Frances Hodgson Burnett
A gloriously over-the-top story of a wicked English
aristocrat and an American bride.

The Buccaneers by Edith Wharton
Wharton's last novel, which she left unfinished,
but is wonderful nonetheless. The Buccaneers
are four American girls who take English society
by storm in the 1880s.

The Duke's Children by Anthony Trollope
The last in the Palliser series; it has an
American heroine.

*Consuelo and Alva Vanderbilt: The Story of a
Daughter and a Mother in the Gilded Age*
by Amanda Mackenzie Stuart
Great double biography of Consuelo Vanderbilt,
who married the 9th duke of Marlborough in
1895, and her formidable mother, Alva. I found
this book very helpful when I was writing
The American Heiress.

The Glitter and the Gold by Consuelo Vanderbilt
Balsan Consuelo's memoirs. She doesn't tell the
whole story, of course, but it is full of fabulous
*Downton
Abbey*–type detail.

The Pursuit of Love by Nancy Mitford
The English aristocracy from the inside.

The Go-Between by L. P. Hartley
A brilliant novel of the Edwardian summer of 1910.

 *Reading Group Questions*

1. What is your initial impression of Cora Cash? How does she develop as a person in the course of the novel?

2. In America, Cora is clearly at the top of society, while Bertha is very near the bottom. In what ways do their circumstances change when they move to England?

3. What role do the mothers in the story—Mrs. Cash, Mrs. Van Der Leyden, and the Double Duchess— play in the central characters' lives?

4. Cora is always aware that "no one was unaffected by the money." How does the money affect Cora herself? What are the pleasures and perils of great wealth?

5. What is your opinion of Teddy and the Duke? What about Charlotte?

6. What do you think about Cora's decision at the end of the book? Would you have made the same choice? (The author has said she was of two minds up until the last chapter.)

7. What are the differences between the Old World and the New in the novel? Do both worlds seem remote in the twenty-first century, or do you see parallels to contemporary society?

8. Why do modern readers enjoy reading novels about the past? Take a moment to discuss your experiences as a reader of historical fiction, in general, and of *The American Heiress* in particular.

9. When she was chair of the Orange Prize for Fiction in 2010, Daisy Goodwin wrote a controversial essay lamenting the "unrelenting grimness" of so many of the novels and pointing out that "generally great fiction contains light and shade"—not only misery but joy and humor. What do you think about Daisy's argument that "it is time for publishers to stop treating literary fiction as the novelistic equivalent of cod-liver oil: if it's nasty it must be good for you"?

10. *Kirkus Reviews* called *The American Heiress* a "shrewd, spirited historical romance with flavors of Edith Wharton, Daphne du Maurier, and Jane Austen." Other critics have also seen echoes of Henry James. If you have read any of these earlier novelists, what parallels and differences do you see in Daisy's work?

Discussion Questions

Turn the page for a sneak peek at
Daisy Goodwin's next novel

The Fortune Hunter

AVAILABLE AUGUST 2014

A Night at the Opera

THE OPERA HOUSE WAS FULL. IT WAS ADELINA PATTI'S last performance of *La Sonnambula* before she returned to New York. Every box was full, every seat from the stalls to the gods was taken. Bay Middleton sat in the second row, so close to the stage that he could see the lattice of blue veins that snaked across La Patti's décolletage, the rivulets of sweat that ran down her painted cheeks.

But though he had his eyes on the stage, Bay Middleton's senses were concentrated on a box in the Grand Tier. He felt Blanche's presence as vividly as if she were sitting next to him; he knew without looking round that her shoulders were bare and that two blond wisps of hair would tremble on the back of her neck. He could almost smell the cologne she used to bathe her temples. Still, he would not look up. He had been aware that he was making a mistake in coming tonight even as he fastened the dress studs in his shirt and adjusted the points of his white tie. But tomorrow Blanche would be gone and he wanted to be near her even if he could not bear to look at her.

The music fed his melancholy. He was not, like most of the audience, here merely to be seen. Bay felt the music; sometimes he would find the hairs on his arm standing on end, just as they did when he knew he was about to win a race, or when a woman looked at him in a certain way. It had happened the first time he had seen Blanche. She had pressed her foot against his at dinner and he had known, at once, that it was no accident. She had looked at him with her heavy-lidded eyes and had smiled, showing small white teeth and a glimpse of pink tongue. It had been the first of many such moments. She had been looking at him across dinner tables and ballrooms for the last year. There had been other women before her, of course, but Blanche Hozier was the first woman he had ever missed a day's hunting for.

She had not been smiling earlier that afternoon as she stood in front of the mirror, tucking away the curls that had come loose a few minutes before. He had been marvelling, as usual, at how quickly Blanche could change back from the woman who had led him by the hand to the chaise longue to the one who stood there now checking that every hair was in place. She was still flushed, but she was once again the mistress of the house and the Colonel's wife. She had caught his eyes in the mirror and had said without expression, 'I am going to Combe tomorrow.'

He had said nothing, sensing that this was a declaration.

'The Colonel is there all the time working on his drainage schemes, and as there is no chance of him coming to London, I must go to him.' She turned to face Bay, tilting her head a little to one side as she looked at him, one of her diamond ear drops catching the light and dazzling him.

He considered this for a moment. There could be only one reason why Blanche would leave London before the end of the Season. His eyes dropped to her waist.

He blinked. 'Are you sure?'

Blanche lifted her chin. 'Sure enough.'

He stood up and walked towards her. She crossed her hands in front of her like a gate. He stood still. 'A child? Oh Blanche, I am so . . .' But she cut him off, as if she couldn't bear the emotion in his voice.

'Combe is lovely at this time of year. Isobel has a cough and I believe the country air will do her good.'

The slight huskiness that he found so beguiling had gone and she had resumed the commanding tones of Lady Blanche Hozier, the daughter of an earl and the mistress of Combe. He looked in vain for some trace of her former softness, but she was as hard as the looking glass behind her. He felt both desolation at the thought of losing her and irritation that he should be so summarily dismissed.

'You will write to me.' It was not a question, but Blanche had shaken her head.

'No letters, not until afterwards. I have to be careful. If the child is a boy . . .' He had seen her twist the wedding ring around her finger.

'I will miss you, Blanche,' he had said, putting his hand out to take hers. But she had shrunk away from him, as if he had become red hot. He had punched his fist into his other hand in frustration.

'I wonder that you didn't tell me, earlier?' His eyes flickered over to the chaise longue.

Blanche looked at him, her drooping eyelids belying the fierceness of her tone.

'I think you should leave now before the servants come back. They have seen too much already.'

He had wanted, very much, to tear her hair down and to shake her porcelain composure, but he had let his arms drop and said, 'Are you sure the child is mine?'

This time she had turned her whole body away from him and had just pointed to the door. He had picked up his hat and gloves from the chair and left without another word.

Now, as he listened to Adelina Patti as Amina singing of her love for Elvino, he felt the blood creeping to his ears as he thought of that last remark. He wanted to look up and show Blanche that he had not meant to wound her, but he could not turn his head. He knew that her retreat to the country was the only prudent course, but he had been hurt by the manner of his sending off. If only there had been some expression of regret, some tenderness. But their liaison had ended as abruptly as it had started. He suspected that he was not Blanche's first lover, but she had always been discreet. Bay knew that her marriage with Hozier was not a happy one. Indeed, there had been a moment when he thought that Blanche had wanted more than their afternoons in the blue drawing room and he had been terrified and excited in equal measure. But that moment had passed and he had felt nothing but relief. To elope with Blanche would have meant leaving the regiment, the country, probably. So he knew he had no right to feel aggrieved, but still – a child. He remembered the way that Blanche had refused to look at him as he left that afternoon, as if she had already erased him from her life.

La Patti hung her head at the end of her aria to receive her applause. The stage was soon covered with flowers thrown by her admirers. Bay looked up at the other side of the theatre from Blanche's box and saw his friends Fred Baird and Chicken Hartopp in a box with two ladies. One he recognised as Fred's aunt and the young girl he thought must be Fred's sister. He supposed that Lady Lisle must be bringing the girl out as the mother had died years ago. He picked up his opera glasses to get a better look at the girl, conscious as he did so that Blanche might be watching him. It would do her no harm, he thought, to see that he had other interests.

But the Baird girl had drawn back, her face was in shadow, and all Bay could see of her was a kid-gloved hand tapping a fan on the side of the box. He held his glasses up for a minute longer, waiting for a glimpse of her face, but she did not reappear. It was almost as if she were hiding from his gaze.

At the interval he decided to leave; he thought he would go to his club and have a brandy. He thought of Blanche looking down at his empty seat. But as he reached the corridor he felt a hand on his shoulder.

'Middleton, what are you doing down here?' Chicken Hartopp looked down at him, beaming. His dundreary whiskers covered almost his entire face, but what skin there was visible was flushed with the heat. 'Thought you would be in a box, old man, not down here with the plebs. Couldn't help noticing a certain lady sitting opposite.' Chicken squeezed one eye in a clumsy wink.

Bay said quickly, 'I thought I'd listen to the music for a change. This is La Patti's last performance before she goes back to America.'

'An opera lover too, eh?' Chicken started to laugh at his own joke. Bay was about to leave him to his mirth when he saw Fred Baird coming towards them.

'Middleton, my dear chap, I thought I saw you down in the stalls. Will you come up to the box and meet my sister?'

Bay was about to refuse, but then he remembered the Baird box was in full view of where Blanche and her companions were sitting. He followed Bay and Hartopp through the crimson corridors to the box.

'Aunt Adelaide, you know Captain Middleton, of course, and may I present my sister Charlotte.'

Bay bowed to Lady Lisle and turned to Charlotte Baird, who was small and dun-coloured, quite unlike her brother, who was large and vivid. She stretched out her hand to him and as he brushed his lips against the knuckles of her glove, he felt her hand tremble slightly.

'How are you enjoying the Opera, Miss Baird? La Patti will be a sad loss to the company here, when she returns to New York.' Bay was standing with his back to the auditorium. He turned slightly to the left so that an observer might notice that he was talking to a young lady. Charlotte Baird looked up at him. Bay was not as tall as Hartopp or Baird, but Charlotte still had to tilt her head up to address him.

'I haven't had much chance to form an opinion about the music, Captain Middleton. I don't think my brother or Captain Hartopp have drawn breath since we arrived.' She gave a crooked little smile. 'Perhaps you can persuade them to be quiet. I should so like to hear the opera as well as see it.' Bay noticed that she had a trace of freckles across the bridge of her nose.

'I will do my best, Miss Baird, but I doubt that even the Archbishop of Canterbury himself could silence Chicken Hartopp.'

She looked at him and he saw that her eyes were the most definite thing about her face: large, with very long black lashes. He could not quite make out the colour in the gloom of the box. She held his gaze.

'But you, Captain Middleton, you like to listen. Is that why you sit down there in the stalls?'

The crooked smile reappeared. He realised she had noticed him earlier. He thought again, how different she was from her brother. Fred was an amiable bully who was happy as long as he was in front. But this girl came up on the inside, in the blind spot.

'I like to look up at the singers, Miss Baird; I want to feel in the middle of things.'

'But that's what I want, and yet here I am, surrounded by distractions.' She waved her hands at the young men who were standing with her aunt and shrugged. The bell rang to signal the end of the interval.

'Delighted to have met you, Miss Baird.' Bay looked over at Fred Baird and Chicken Hartopp and said, 'I hope you are allowed to enjoy the rest of the opera in peace.'

'I hope so too. But Captain Middleton, you aren't thinking of returning to your seat already? There is a lady in blue who has been staring at you these last few minutes while we have been talking; she looks as though she wants to tell you something. Won't you look round and see what it is she has to say?' Charlotte Baird's voice was soft but there was something sharp in there as well. Bay did not look round, but made his way to the door at the back of the box.

'I don't believe anything can be more important than the Second Act, Miss Baird.' He nodded to the others and left. Rather to his own surprise, he found himself making his way back to his seat in the stalls, aware now that he was being observed from two sides. He thought with some satisfaction of Blanche watching his conversation with Charlotte Baird from the other side of the House.